PENGUIN BOOKS

EIGHT MONTHS ON GHAZZAH STREET

Hilary Mantel was born in Derbyshire in 1952. She has been a
teacher and a social worker and lived in Botswana and Saudi
Arabia. In 1987 she was awarded the Shiva Naipaul Memorial Prize
for travel writing. Her other books – all published by Penguin – are
Every Day is Mother's Day, *Vacant Possession* and *Fludd*, which won the
1989 Winifred Holtby Memorial Prize and was shortlisted for the
1989 *Sunday Express* Book of the Year Award. Hilary Mantel is the
film critic of *The Spectator*.

Eight Months on Ghazzah Street was shortlisted for the 1988 *Sunday
Express* Book of the Year Award.

HILARY MANTEL

*Eight Months
on
Ghazzah Street*

PENGUIN BOOKS

PENGUIN BOOKS

Published by the Penguin Group
Penguin Books Ltd, 27 Wrights Lane, London W8 5TZ, England
Penguin Books USA Inc., 375 Hudson Street, New York, New York 10014, USA
Penguin Books Australia Ltd, Ringwood, Victoria, Australia
Penguin Books Canada Ltd, 10 Alcorn Avenue, Toronto, Ontario, Canada M4V 3B2
Penguin Books (NZ) Ltd, 182–190 Wairau Road, Auckland 10, New Zealand

Penguin Books Ltd, Registered Offices: Harmondsworth, Middlesex, England

First published by Viking 1988
Published in Penguin Books 1989
7 9 10 8 6

Copyright © Hilary Mantel, 1988
All rights reserved

Printed in England by Clays Ltd, St Ives plc

Except in the United States of America, this book is sold subject
to the condition that it shall not, by way of trade or otherwise, be lent,
re-sold, hired out, or otherwise circulated without the publisher's
prior consent in any form of binding or cover other than that in
which it is published and without a similar condition including this
condition being imposed on the subsequent purchaser

FOR VIC AND JEANIE CAMP

Note

Saudi Arabia employs the Hijra calendar, which starts from the year AD 622, when Muhammed left Mecca for Medina. It is a lunar calendar, and the Hijra year is eleven days shorter than the Gregorian year. The months (with many variations in transliteration) are as follows: Muharram, Safar, Rabi al-awal, Rabi al-thani, Jamadi al-awal, Jamadi al-thani, Rajab, Shaban, Ramadhan, Shawal, Dhu-al-qudah, Dhu-al-hijjah. By a recent Royal Decree, a 365-day year has been instituted for fiscal purposes, and 22 December 1986 became 1 Capricorn. The recalculations involved make the fiscal year some forty years behind the Hijra year. So, not the least surprising aspect of life in the Kingdom is that time can appear to run backwards.

Part One

Part One

CONFIDENTIAL MEMORANDUM
FROM: Director, Turadup, William and Schaper,
Kingdom of Saudi Arabia
TO: All expatriate staff
DATED: 15 Shawal/3 July 1985
I need not remind anyone of this week's tragic events
involving Turadup employees. In order to safeguard
the company's position in these very difficult times, I
must request all staff and families about to depart on
leave to behave as follows:
A. Refrain from talking to the press – whatever your
holiday destination.
B: Refrain from public speculation about the recent
deaths – remember that the matter is still under
investigation by the Saudi police and Her Majesty's
representatives.
C. Exercise the utmost caution in personal conduct
between now and your departure – dispose (carefully)
of all items or substances which could attract the interest
of the police, and do not leave your compound without
your documents.

I feel sure that if these precautions are observed, we
may expect a continuance of good relations with the
Saudi authorities, and a smooth passage into the next
Five-Year Plan.

May I take this opportunity to wish you, on behalf
of Daphne and myself, a pleasant vacation and a safe
return to the Kingdom after Haj. Sincerely –

ERIC PARSONS

September 1984

IN FLIGHT

'Would you like champagne?'

This was the beginning; an hour or so out from Heathrow. Already it felt further; watches moved on, a day in a life condensed to a scramble at a check-in desk, a walk to a departure gate; a day cut short and eclipsed, hurtling on into advancing night. And now the steward leaned over her, putting this question.

'I don't think so.' They had already eaten; dinner, she supposed. So much smoked salmon is consumed on aircraft that it is a wonder there is any left to eat at ground level. The steward had just now whisked her tray from under her nose. 'You could give me some brandy,' she said.

'Two to get you started?' Hand hovering over the trolley, he seemed to approve her choice; as if what lay ahead were something to brace yourself for, not to celebrate.

'And one of those nice plastic glasses,' Frances Shore said. 'Please.'

Across the aisle grown men were getting drunk on Cointreau. One of them cocked an eyebrow at the steward. He leaned over them; his face, pale and seamy under the late-night lights, showed a kind of patient disgust. Drinks were free of course, but on the Saudi run this standard airline ploy had the status of charity work. His fingers, dispensing the miniature bottles, were as clean and careful as a bishop's.

The businessmen had done their talking earlier; passed sales charts to each other. 'I wonder how Fairfax is doing in Kowloon?' one of them asked.

His companion dug his plastic fork into a millefeuille, and made no reply. 'How long now?' he asked after a while.

'Three hours.'

'Keep the drinks going then.'

'Enjoy it, gentlemen,' the steward said. The woman held up her coffee cup. He swayed towards her with the pot. 'Non-dairy creamer, Madam?'

'I always wonder about this stuff,' she said, accepting the foil packet. 'It says what it isn't, but not what it is.'

'That's life,' the steward said. He moved away again. Dull clunk of ice cubes against plastic. Flimsy cushions flatten under head and back. Onwards. The man with the tough millefeuille stares at the dial of his watch, as if he could make the time go faster. Or hold it back.

Left alone, she closed her eyes. She was apprehensive, yes. She turned over the steward's comment in her mind, because she was not one to let flippancies go unexamined; it paid to examine them, as there was so little, she always thought, in what people said when they were trying to be serious. You could only describe the future by exclusion; say what will not occur. Say what you will not be: an ice dancer, a cosmonaut, a mother of twelve. Much less easy to make a single positive prediction even for the coming week; much less easy to say what, in a month's time, you will have become.

Andrew's letters had been short, practical. They told her to bring flat sandals, British postage stamps, a bottle of Bovril. His voice on the phone had been hesitant. There had been the odd, expensive silence. He didn't know how to describe Jeddah. She must, he said, see for herself.

She picked up the half-cup of coffee: black, and almost cold now. When she moved her legs, newsprint rustled, a paperback slid from her lap on to the seat. She felt stiff, uncomfortable. She began to think of lurching along to the lavatory, braving the bleary stares.

When the steward came back she said to him, 'There aren't many women on this flight.'

14

'It's not the time of year. Christmas and Easter, the wives fly out.'

'Why don't they stay?'

'They can't stick it. More coffee?' She shook her head. 'It must be your first trip. Got a husband out there?'

She nodded.

'Visa all in order?'

'I hope so. But I don't read Arabic.'

'Be waiting for you, will he?'

Again: 'I hope so.'

'Been out there long?'

'Six weeks.'

'Quick work,' the steward said. 'To get you out so soon.'

'It's the company who organized it. He says it's not that easy, but they've been in Saudi for a while and they know how things are done.'

'We all know how things are done,' the steward said; he rubbed finger and thumb together, rustling an imaginary wad of notes. 'What's his line of country?'

'He's a civil engineer. They're putting up a big new building for one of the Ministries.'

'Likes it all right, does he?'

'I don't really know.' During those phone calls (direct dial, good clear line) she'd not inquired of Andrew, are you happy? It would have meant another expensive silence, because he did not deal in that sort of question. He'd have found it strange from three paces, never mind three thousand miles. Could the man be right, she wondered, had someone been bribed on her behalf? It seemed such a small thing, obtaining a visa for one unimportant woman to join her unimportant husband, but she had once been assured, by a man called Jeff Pollard, who understood these things, that when corruption took root in a country it spread in no time at all from monarchs to tea boys, from ministers to filing clerks. She believed him; but did not feel herself a better person for the belief. She had been round and about southern

Africa for five years, in regions where, by and large, the possibilities of corruption had not been fully explored. Andrew thought that, once, someone might have offered him a bribe; but through the other party's ineptitude and poor English, and Andrew's naïvety, the occasion had passed without profit.

As this occasion will pass, she thought; and in time, this flight. 'More brandy?' the steward inquired.

'No thanks.'

'Lived abroad before?'

'Yes.' He had a boring job, she supposed, and a right to people's life-stories. 'Zambia for a bit, then Botswana.'

'Oh, sweet Jesus,' said the steward, animated now, but not impressed. 'I've been to Botswana, the Holiday Inn, Gaborone. It's a hole, Botswana. I went in the coffee shop and asked them for a toasted cheese sandwich, and do you know what they said?'

'Cheese it is finished?'

'Right on. You must have been there.'

'Of course I've been there.'

'But no cheese in the whole place? I ask you. They could have sent out for some.'

'Look,' Frances said, 'there are two kinds of cheese in Botswana, Cheddar and Sweetmilk. They are imported from South Africa, which makes any number of kinds of cheese, but they only import two; they realize that people must have cheese, but to have too much of it might seem to condone apartheid. You're with me?'

'Not exactly.'

'Never mind. So what kind of sandwich did you have?'

'I had ham.'

'Lucky you.'

'Where would the ham be from?'

'Zimbabwe,' she said. 'Was it called that when you were there?'

'I think it was still Rhodesia. They had sanctions.'

'But the ham got through.'

'Well, I take your word for it. But still, what a hole it is,

Gaborone. Bunch of tarts sitting in the dust outside selling woolly hats. Sit by the pool, play the fruit machines, bugger all else to do.' He paused, the tirade halted by a scruple of politeness. 'Was that where you lived?'

'Well no, actually, we lived in a much smaller place. We used to go up to Gaborone for a bit of excitement.'

'You poor things, that's all I can say. And you were in Zambia too? I've been to Lusaka, done a couple of stop-overs. They're thieves in Lusaka. They'll take the wheels off your hire-car as soon as look at you. This friend of mine went into a pharmacy for a drop of penicillin, he was planning, you know, on being a bit naughty that night, and he believed in dosing himself first; and he came out, and no bloody wheels.'

She smiled. 'My friend wasn't amused,' the steward said.

'No, I'm sure. It was very trying when they took your wheels off. It was quite common though. You could never plan on being anywhere by a set time.'

'And there was never any sugar. I take sugar, in coffee.'

'It's true, there were a lot of shortages.'

'I've not been out that way for a while. They tell me it's worse now.'

'Oh, Africa's always worse.'

'Quite the cynic.'

'No, not really,' she said. 'I think I was just there for too long. I liked it, in a way. At least, I'm glad I went there. I wouldn't have missed it.'

'I expect you'll find your Saudi lifestyle very different.'

'Yes, I expect I will.'

He was hovering, waiting to tell her some horror stories. There were always stories out of the Middle East, and no doubt Jeff Pollard would have told her some, if he had not been so anxious to recruit Andrew for his building project. But her tone wrapped up the conversation. 'Sure on that brandy?' the steward said; and moved away. The slightest encouragement, and he would have asked, 'Do you remember that Helen Smith case?'

A dozen people had raised the question, in her two-month stay in England. It was strange how it had stuck in people's minds, considering how little they usually remembered of what they read in the newspapers: young north-country girl, a nurse, found dead after an all-night party; nurse's father, dogged ex-policeman, off out there to get at the truth. And then the inquests, and the coroner's reports, and the hints of diplomatic cover-ups and skulduggery in high places; the pleasures of moral censure, the *frisson* of violent death in faraway places. The press reports had left an image in people's minds, of lazy, glitzy, transient lives, of hard liquor and easy money, of amoral people turned scared and sour; so now when you were off to Jeddah, people said, 'Don't fall off any balconies, will you?' It became monotonous. And their talk had left an image in her mind, which she did not like but could not now eradicate; the image of the broken body, still in its mortuary drawer.

A part of her, now, thought the persistence of the image sinister; a part of her said, things happen everywhere, and after all, she said, comforting herself, there's only the world. Travel ends and routine begins and old habits which you thought you had left behind in one country catch up with you in the next, and old problems resurface, but if you are lucky you carry as part of your baggage the means of solving those problems and accommodating those habits, and you take with you an open mind, and discretion, and common sense; if you have those with you, you can manage anywhere. I make large claims for myself, she thought. She pushed up the window shade and looked out, into featureless darkness. There was no sensation of movement, no intimation that they were in flight. She closed her eyes. Sleep now, she coaxed herself. Tomorrow I will have people to meet and there will be a good deal to do. How pleased I will be, to do it; and to be there, at last.

It was at the Holiday Inn, Gaborone – but in the bar, not in the coffee shop – that Andrew had met Jeff Pollard. They had run into him once before, in Lusaka, and not liked him particularly; but now Pollard was offering a job, and Andrew needed one. His contract in Botswana was a month away from its termination date, and they were already packing and selling things off. The U K building trade had slumped into what seemed chronic recession; they didn't know what they were going to do. They didn't want to stay in Botswana, even if there had been the option. With the advent of the black-top road across the South African border, life had changed for the worse, their severe small-town isolation ended, the single street full of new faces. It was true that you could go as far as Johannesburg now without steeling yourself for the journey over dirt roads; it ought to have been an advantage, but in fact it made life too easy. They were a direct connection on the string of dorps that ran across the Transvaal and over the frontier; the day would come soon when they would feel like a suburb.

At this point – one morning over breakfast – Andrew had said, 'What about the Middle East?'

'Oh no,' she'd said. 'I'd have to go around with a head-scarf on all day. I couldn't put up with that.'

'Fran,' he said, 'we have to make some money. We haven't made any here. I thought we would, but it's not worked out. We have to get something behind us.'

'Yes. I suppose so.'

She had known he was serious; because he addressed her by her name. It had not escaped her notice that women were always using men's christian names, but that men only did it when there was something in the offing: a rebuke, a plea. Andrew had never been communicative, so it had been necessary to notice these things. He was a silent man, who never asked for anything, or set arrangements in train, or egged life on; instead he waited for what he wanted, with a powerful, active patience which seemed to surround him, like an aura: an aura of forbearance, of self-control. His patience was not like other people's, a rather feeble virtue, which had, by its nature, to be its own reward; it was a virtue like a strong magnet, which drew solutions to problems. And now drew Jeff Pollard.

Jeff Pollard was a sometime employee of Turadup, William and Schaper, a firm known throughout the construction business as Throw'em Up, Bill'em, and Scarper. Since the European Development Fund had decided to finance the building of the black-top road, he had been in and out of southern Africa, weighing up prospects and buying people drinks. He was a man of thirty-five, unmarried, with a loose and dusty appearance and shifting eyes; he had a grey-white skin, but the back of his neck was at all times mysteriously and painfully sunburned. He had an unsparing fund of anecdote, a knowing, dirty laugh; a British passport, and a vaguely Australian accent. He wore his shirt open, and around his neck on a chain a small block of gold incised with the legend CREDIT SUISSE. When the Shores were leaving Africa there had been a lot of people like Jeff around, doing their recruiting in golf-club bars. They were cowboys, headhunters, entrepreneurs; anywhere they hung their hat was their domicile, for fiscal purposes.

Turadup had got a toe-hold in Zambia before the bottom dropped out of copper, putting up expatriate housing in Kabwe, the mining town that had once been known as Broken Hill; then when Zambia went down the drain they moved south a bit, putting in an unsuccessful tender for work on the new international airport at Gaborone; then picking up work around that city, piping water and building a clinic for a shanty town that had become permanent *faute de mieux*. They operated over the South African border too, putting up a much-needed casino in a bantustan. But since the early 1970s the Middle East had been what they called their major theatre of operations. It happened that at the time when Andrew Shore was ready to move on, Turadup's Saudi Arabian manager, a man called Eric Parsons, was in Johannesburg trawling for expertise; and on that day – always described by Andrew as 'the day I ran slap-bang into Pollard' – the relevant phone number was handed over, and their future was set in train. 'Give old Eric a call,' Jeff said. 'You can't lose by it.'

Andrew first poured himself a brandy; then he sat for some time, and regarded the phone in their bungalow, like a man in a trance, or a man praying. Then he picked up the receiver; the lines were not down that day, and it was a mere ten minutes before he got an answer from the operator in Gaborone. He told her what he wanted: Johannesburg. There seemed to be a party going on in the background. He could hear women laughing, and what was perhaps crockery being smashed. The operator came back once or twice. bellowing in his ear, but she didn't forget him entirely; in time she came up with what might be her best offer, a line to Mafeking. He took it. A guttural voice answered him in Afrikaans. Seconds later he was speaking to Eric Parsons, at his hotel. It was the Carlton, he noted; Turadup did not penny-pinch.

He did not suggest making the drive to Johannesburg, but waited until Parsons said, 'I'll come to you then, shall I?' He knew how he would employ the time, as he drove to Gaborone to meet Parsons; he pictured himself at the wheel of his truck, the empty road and the low brown hills unwinding before him, while his practised eye was half-alert for cattle and children, and his inner will concentrated, mile after mile, upon making Parsons offer him more money than he had ever dreamed of earning in his life. This, in due course, Parsons did.

The details were fixed up, at the President Hotel this time (there being, in Gaborone, a choice of two) over a tough T-bone steak and a glass of Lion lager. Andrew Shore shook hands with Eric Parsons, the Saudi man; Jeff Pollard, talking, conducted him down from the terrace and out into the street. Across the road, the nation's only cinema was showing a double bill: a kung fu drama, and *Mary Poppins*. Andrew stood in the dusty thoroughfare known as the Mall, gazing into the window of the President Hotel's gift shop;

crocodile handbags, skin rugs, complete bushmen kits with arrows and ostrich shells, direct from the small factory in Palapye which had recently started turning them out. 'I can hardly believe I'm finished in Africa,' he said.

When he arrived home late that afternoon, Frances was on the stoep packing a tea-chest, wrapping up their dinner service in pieces of the *Mafeking Mail*. 'Well, did you do it?' she said. She straightened up and kissed his cheek.

'Yes, I did it, it's all fixed. But we can't go together – I have to be in the Kingdom before they'll grant you a visa. When we finish up here I'm to fly to Nairobi, and pick up a businessman's entry permit – then once I'm in, Turadup will fix it for me to stay. They're in a hurry.'

'Why? Has someone quit without notice?'

'I didn't ask.'

'I would have asked.'

'I didn't think of it.'

'So you won't even be coming to England first?'

'And stay with your mother?'

'It looks as if I'll have to.'

'Well listen, Fran, we won't be apart for long. And by the time you get out to Jeddah, we'll be fixed up with a house, and everything will be ready for you.'

'I'd rather go with you. But I suppose they have their rules. Oh, look, am I to pack these?' She held out a candlestick, one of a pair from a local pottery, rough, heavy, unglazed.

'Sure,' he said. 'Souvenir. Take those funny baskets as well, the ones that fall over.'

She began to wrap the candlestick, rolling it in her hands. 'Are you sure that this is the right thing to do?' she said. 'Is this what you want?'

'They're doubling my salary,' he said flatly.

'What?'

'You heard.'

She turned away and bent over the tea-chest again, cleanly stabbed by avarice, like a peach with a silver knife.

'We could be in and out within three years,' he said.

'Your salary is paid in riyals, tax-free. All you need out of it is your day-to-day living expenses and you can bank the rest where you like, in any currency you like. Turadup are offering free housing, a car allowance, paid utilities, yearly leave ticket, school fees – though of course –'

'That would be plain greedy,' she said, 'having children so that you could get their school fees paid.'

'Pollard did say –' He looked at her in slight anxiety. 'He said that his only reservation was how you'd settle in. As you've been a working woman.'

'I won't be able to work?'

'Unlikely, he thinks.'

'Well, if you're going to earn all that money, I'm sure I can occupy myself. After all, it's not for ever, is it?'

'No, it's not for ever. We should think of it as a chance for us, to build up some security –'

'Will you pass me those salad bowls?'

Andrew was silent. He passed them, one by one. Why, really, should she share his vision of their future? She had come to Africa at her own behest, a single woman, one of the few recruited for her line of work. She had lived alone before they met; for three nights in succession, he had sat by himself, seemingly disconsolate, on a corner stool in the bar of an expatriate club, not even looking her way, but concentrating hard; until she had asked him to go home with her. She had fed her dog, and then cooked eggs for them, and asked him what he wanted out of life. Later, in the sagging double bed with which her government bungalow was furnished, he had lain awake while she slept, wishing furiously for her to act and understand; and although it had taken a little time to work, within a matter of weeks she had turned to him and said, 'We could get married if that's what you want.'

So perhaps, too, he should have wished her into suggesting Saudi Arabia; then she would have known it was her own decision. But from what he had heard it was a part of the world in which women's decisions did not operate. He made

23

a leap of faith: it will be all right, I know it will. 'Frances,' he said, 'we won't go unless you want to.'

She slotted a wrapped teacup into place. 'I want to.'

It had been raining, earlier that day, and there was a heavy, animal scent of drenched earth and crushed flowers. In the kitchen their housemaid, Elizabeth, was washing glasses – pointless really as they would soon be crated up – and they could hear the separate clink that each one made as she put it down on the draining-board. The dogs and cats were coming in to be fed, wandering to the back door to wait around, like the Victorian poor. 'I really think we ought,' Andrew said.

'In point of fact, I don't think we've anywhere else to go.' She picked up a broad felt marker and daubed their name on the side of the tea-chest. SHORE. FRAGILE. GABORONE – LONDON.

'No,' Andrew said. 'No point.'

She crossed out LONDON, wrote JEDDAH. Another pang stabbed her, as sharp as the first. She imagined herself already in Saudi, a discreet teetotal housewife, homesick for this place that was not home in another place that was not home. It was almost dark now; the air was cooling, the sun dipping behind the hill. 'What was Jeff Pollard doing, recruiting you? I thought he was trying to persuade everybody what a grand life it was as a freelance consultant?'

'Well, it can't be such a grand life, because he's just signed up with Turadup himself. He's going to manage their Jeddah business; he's had experience out there, of course.'

'So you mean you'll be working with him?'

'There is that tiny drawback.'

'I hope we don't end up living near him as well.'

'They do pay for your housing, so it's probably a case of taking what you're given.'

'That's fine,' she said, 'but just try to ensure that what we're given doesn't include Pollard. Do you think they'll all be like him?'

'He's a type. You get them everywhere. But Parsons isn't like that.'

'I suppose he's another type.'

'Yes, you'd know the one. Genial old duffer. Safari suit, doing the African bit. Two sons at medical school, showed me their photographs. His wife's called Daphne.'

'And did he show you a photograph of her?'

'He didn't, come to think of it.'

'Perhaps he thought it would over-excite you.'

'When he asks you what you want to drink, he says, "Name your poison."'

'I see. Weybridge abroad.'

'Melbourne, I think. He keeps a place in the Cotswolds though. He's been with Turadup for twenty years. He's a shareholder. Pollard says he's a millionaire. Anyway, he seems very enthusiastic about this building. About the whole scene in Jeddah. He says it's a very stimulating place to work if you're in the construction business.' He paused. 'I'll tell you what he said exactly.'

'Go on.'

Andrew bit his lip. 'He said, "I have witnessed the biggest transportation of ready-mixed concrete in the history of the human race."'

'I'd like to witness a large gin. Let's celebrate.'

'We're late,' said the man across the aisle. She jerked out of her doze; she'd not realized, at first, that he was speaking to her.

'Are we?' She consulted her watch.

'It's always late,' the man said tetchily. 'Of course, if you fly Saudia, they're always late as well.'

'Do you go often to Jeddah?'

'Too often. The Saudia flight's supposed to take off at twelve-thirty, but it never does. Not in my experience. I suppose the staff are having prayers. Bowing to Mecca, and so forth.'

'How long do prayers last?'

25

'As long as it takes to inconvenience you totally,' the man said. 'I can tell you've never been in the Kingdom. Noon is movable, you see. Noon can very well be at twelve-thirty. Nothing's what it says it is.'

Oh dear, a philosopher, she thought. She might as well put on her Walkman. She leaned down to inch out her bag from under the seat in front, and as she groped for it she felt his eyes on the back of her neck. 'Nurse, are you?' he inquired.

'No.'

'What are you doing out there then?'

'I'm going to join my husband.' She filled in the details again, aware that she was more polite in the air than she was on the ground: the six years in Africa, and now Turadup, and the new ministry building; aware too that as soon as she had said 'husband', the slight interest he had taken in her had faded completely.

'Pity,' he said. 'We,' he indicated his cohorts, 'are stopping at the Marriot. I thought if you'd been a nurse we could have had dinner. Of course, I'm not sure if they let them out nowadays. I think they've got rules now that they all have to be locked in their own quarters by nine at night. It's after that Helen Smith business.'

'Oh, that.'

'It was a damn funny business, if you ask me. That Dr Arnott, the chap that lived in the flat she fell out of . . . and that wife of his, Penny wasn't it . . . and the British Embassy? You can't tell me it wasn't a cover-up.'

'I wouldn't try, I'm sure.'

'It stinks.'

'I'm sure you're right.'

'You find a young girl dead outside a high-rise block, after a wild party – you ask yourself, did she fall or was she pushed? Take it from me, it's a funny place, Jeddah. Nobody knows the half of what goes on. You work?'

'Yes,' she said. 'I'm a cartographer.'

'Oh well, you're redundant. They don't have maps.'

26

'They must have.'

'Too bloody secretive to have maps. Besides, the streets are never in the same place for more than a few weeks together.'

'They move the streets?'

'Certainly do. They're always building, you see, money no object, but they don't think ahead. They build a hospital and then decide to put a road through it. Fancy a new palace? Out with the bulldozer. A map would be out of date as soon as it was made. It would be waste paper the day it was printed.'

'But in a way it must be quite – exhilarating?'

He gave her a withering look. 'If you like that sort of thing.' He turned away, back to his companion. 'Have you got those end-of-year projections?' he asked. 'I really do wonder how Fairfax is doing in Kowloon, don't you? I don't believe they should ever have sent him. Trouble with Fairfax, he's got no credibility. They treat him like some bit of a kid.'

Frances closed her eyes again. Drifting, she caught bits of their conversation: jargon, catchphrases. At home, at her widowed mother's house in York, she had been reading books about her destination. Despite her scepticism, her better knowledge, their contrived images lingered in her mind: black tents at sunset, the call of the muezzin in clear desert air: the tang of cardamom, the burnish of sharp-snouted coffee-pots, the heat of the sand. 'We're building up the infrastructure,' said the man who despised Fairfax. Infrastructure was a word she had heard on Andrew's lips; he had grown fond of it. It seemed that when oil was discovered in the Eastern Province, Saudi Arabia had no infrastructure, but that it had one now: roads, schools, hospitals, factories, mines, market-gardens and chicken farms, airports and squash courts, telephones and filling stations, cold-stores and police stations, take-away food shops, and the ten-pin bowling facilities at the Albilad Hotel. All this she knew from her reading, because after the romantic travellers' tales came *Jeddah: A Businessman's Guide*. The black tents of the Bedu have been replaced by aluminium shacks. Air-conditioning is universal. Gazelles are hunted from the backs of pick-up trucks.

I must like it, she thought. I shall try to like it. When everyone is so negative about a place you begin to suspect it must have some virtues after all. 'No alcohol!' people say, as if you'd die without it. 'And women aren't allowed to drive? That's terrible.' There are lots of things more terrible, she thought, and even I have seen some of them. She dozed.

A touch on her arm woke her. It was the steward. 'We'll be beginning our descent in half an hour. I'm just doing a final drinks round. Another cognac?'

'Keep the young lady sober,' the businessman advised. 'She's got the customs to face, and it's her first time. They go through everything,' he told her. 'I hope you haven't got anything in your suitcase that you shouldn't have?'

'I haven't got a bottle of whisky or a shoulder of pork. What else will they be looking for?'

'Where do you buy your underwear?'

'What?'

'Marks & Spencer, you see, they call them Zionists. You have to cut the labels out. Didn't anybody tell you that? And they look at your books. This colleague of mine, when he was last in the Kingdom, he had his book of limericks confiscated. It had this drawing on the cover, a woman, you know.' He gestured in the air, describing half-circles. 'Naked, just a line-drawing. Chap said he hadn't noticed.'

'That seems unlikely,' she said. She added, to herself, 'a friend of yours'.

'It's all unlikely. Even when you've been coming in and out for years, you never know what they're going to be looking for. Our rep in Riyadh, he lives there, he should know. But then last year when he was coming back after his summer holidays they took away his Test Match videos. All his recorded highlights. Oh, they said he could have them back, when the customs had had a careful look. But he never went for them. He couldn't take the hassle.'

'Poor man.'

'You've not got any art books, have you? Rubens or anything? Because they can be very funny about art.'

'It's unIslamic,' Frances said, 'to worship the human form. It's idolatry.' The man stared at her.

'So I can't tempt you?' the steward asked. He peered into his empty ice-bucket. 'Gentlemen, don't leave any miniatures down the seat pockets, please, we don't want our ground-staff flogged.' He looked down at Frances. 'We're relinquishing this route next year,' he said. 'Give it to British Caledonian and welcome, that's what I say. No more to drink then?' He prepared to abandon her, move away. Sleeping executives stirred now, dribbling a little on to their airline blankets. There was a sound of subdued laughter; briefcases intruded into the aisles. The steward relented. He leaned over her seat. 'Listen, if anything goes wrong, if by some mischance hubby's not there, don't hang about, don't speak to anybody, get straight in our airline bus and come downtown with us to the Hyatt Regency. You check in, and I'll look after you, and he can come and find you in the morning.'

'Oh, I'm sure he'll be there,' she said. Or someone will. Jeff Pollard. At least he'd be a familiar face. 'I've got numbers to ring, in case anything goes wrong. And I could take a taxi.'

'You can't take a taxi. They won't carry you.'

She thought of that cheese, that people say French taxi-drivers won't let in their cabs. 'What, really not?'

'It's bad news, a man picking up a strange woman in a car. They can gaol you for it.'

'But he's a taxi-driver,' she said. 'That's his job, picking up strange people.'

'But you're a woman,' the steward said. 'You're a woman, aren't you? You're not a person any more.' Doggedly, courteously, as if their conversation had never occurred, he reached for a glass from his trolley: 'Would you like champagne?'

*

Soon, the crackle from the P/A system: Ladies and gentle-men, we are now beginning our descent to King Abdul Aziz International Airport. Those seated on the left-hand side of the aircraft will see below you the lights of Jeddah. Kindly fasten . . . kindly extinguish . . . (And to the right, blackness, tilting, and a glow of red, the slow fires that seem to ring cities at night.) We hope you have enjoyed, we hope to have the pleasure . . . we hope . . . we hope . . . and please to remain seated until the aircraft is stationary . . .

Half an hour later she is inside the terminal building. The date is 2 Muharram, by the Hijra calendar, and the evening temperature is 88°F; the year is 1405.

Muharram

———— ❧ ————

Ghazzah Street is situated to the east of Medina Road, behind the King's New Palace, and in the district of Al Aziziyya; it is a small street, which got its name quite recently when street names came into vogue, and a narrow street, made narrower by the big American cars, some of them falling to pieces, which its residents leave parked outside their apartment blocks. On one side is a stretch of waste ground, full of potholes; water collects in them when, three or four times a year, rain falls on the city. The residents complain about the mosquitoes which breed in the standing pools, but none of them can remember whether there was ever a building on the waste ground; no one has been in the area for more than a couple of years. Many of the tenants of Ghazzah Street still keep some of their possessions in cardboard boxes, or in shipper's crates bearing the names of the removal and transport companies of the subcontinent and the Near East. They are from Pakistan or Egypt, salesmen and clerical workers, or engaged in a mysterious line of work called Import–Export; or they are Palestinians perhaps, or they are picking up a family business that has been bombed out of Beirut.

The district is not opulent, not sleazy either; the small apartment blocks, two and three storeys high, are walled off from the street, so that you seldom catch sight of the residents, or know if there is anyone at home; women and babies are bundled from kerb to car, and sometimes schoolchildren, with grave dark faces, trail upstairs with their books in the late afternoon. No one ever stands and chats in Ghazzah Street. Neighbours know each other by sight, from glimpses on balconies and rooftops; the women speak by phone. There are a couple of offices, one of them a small forgotten offshoot of the Ministry of Pilgrimages, and one of them belonging to a firm which imports and distributes Scandinavian mineral water. Just around the corner on Al-Suror Street, there is a mosque, its dome illuminated at dusk with a green neon light; at the other end of the street, in the direction of the palace of Prince Abdullah bin Abdul Aziz, there is a small shop which sells computer supplies and spare parts.

At the moment Ghazzah Street is about a mile and a half from the Red Sea, but in this place land and sea are in flux, they are negotiable. So much land has been reclaimed, that villas built a few years ago with sea views now look out on the usual cityscape of blank white walls, moving traffic, building sites. On every vacant lot in time appears the jumble of brownish brick, the metal spines of scaffolding, the sheets of plate glass; then last of all the marble, the most popular facing material, held on to the plain walls behind it with some sort of adhesive. From a distance it lends a spurious air of antiquity to the scene. When the Jeddah earthquake comes – and it will come – all-seeing Allah will observe that the buildings are held together with glue; and he will peel the city apart like an onion.

The sea itself, sometimes cobalt in colour and sometimes turquoise, has a flat, domestic, well-used appearance. Small white-collared waves trip primly up to the precincts of the desalination plant, like a party of vicars on an industrial tour. The lights of the royal yacht wink in the dusty evenings; veiled ladies splash on the foreshore in the heat of the day. Benches, placed by the municipality, look out to sea. Around the bay sweeps an ambitious highway, designated The Corniche; now known as Al Kournaich, or the Cornish

Road. Public monuments line the sea-front, and crown the intersections of the endless, straight and eight-lane public highways; bizarre forms in twisted alloys, their planes glistening in the salt and smog air.

On Fridays, which are days for rest and prayer, families picnic around these monuments, black figures in a tundra of marble; stray cats breed on their slopes. The sun strikes from their metal spokes and fins; towering images of water-jugs, sea-horses, steel flowers; of a human hand, pointing to the sky. Vendors sell, from roadside vans, inflatable plastic camels in purple, orange and cerise.

If you walk, suitably dressed, along the Corniche, you can hear the sea-wind howl and sigh through the sewers beneath the pavements. It is an unceasing wail, modulated like the human voice, but trapped and far-away, like the mutinous cries of the damned. 'The people in hell remain alive,' says a Muslim commentator. 'They think, remember and quarrel; their skins are not burned, but cooked, and every time they are fully cooked, new skins are substituted for them to start the suffering afresh.' And if you pick your way, with muttered apologies, through the families ensconced on the ground, on the carpets they have unloaded from their cars, you will see the men and women sitting separately, one hunched group garbed in black and one in white, and the children playing under a servant's eye; the whole family turned to the sea, but the adults rapt, enthralled, by the American cartoons they are watching on their portable TV. A skin-diver, European, lobster-skinned, strikes out from an unfrequented part of the coastline for the coral reef.

Back on the road the teenaged children of the Arab families catcall and cruise, wrecking their Ferraris. Hot-rodding, the newspapers call it; the penalty is flogging. A single seabird hovers, etched sharp and white against the sky; and a solitary goat-faced Yemeni, his tartan skirts pulled up, putters on a clapped-out scooter in the direction of Obhur Creek. The horizon is a line of silver, and beyond it is the coast of the Sudan; enclosed within it is the smell of the city's effluent, more indecipherable, more complicated than you would think. At the weekend the children are given balloons, heart-shaped and helium-filled, which bob over the rubble and shale. On the paving stones at your feet are scrawled crude chalk drawings of female genitalia. Inland, wrecked cars line the desert roads, like skeletons from some public and exemplary punishment.

Whatever time you set out for Jeddah, you always seem to arrive in the small hours; so that the waste of pale marble which is the arrivals hall, the rude and silent customs men turning over your baggage, seem to be a kind of dream; so that from each side of the airport road dark and silent spaces stretch away, and then comes the town, the string of street-lights dazzling you, the white shapes of high buildings penning you in; you are delivered, to some villa or apartment block, you stumble into a bathroom and then into bed – and when you wake up, jerked out of a stuporous doze by the dawn prayer-call, the city has formed itself about you, highways, mosques, palaces and souks; grey-faced, staggering a little, you stumble into the rooms you are going to inhabit, draw back the curtain or blind and – with a faint smell of insecticide in your nostrils – confront the wall, the street, the tree with its roots in concrete and six months' accumulation of dun-coloured dust on its leaves; wake up, wake up, you have arrived. The first night has passed now, the severance is complete; the journey is a phantom, the real world recedes.

Andrew brought coffee. To her surprise, she felt chilly. He had always been bothered by the heat, and so it was his habit now to sleep with the air conditioners on, rattling and banging away all night. No wonder she hadn't slept properly. She had dreamt she was in a railway siding, with the endless shunting, and the scrape of metal wheels.

Andrew was already dressed, buttoning his white shirt, plucking a tie from inside the wardrobe door. His muddy

34

overalls and his safety helmet would be elsewhere, she supposed, although he had said in his letters that he would spend more time shuffling papers than he would at the site. 'Pity you couldn't come at a weekend,' he said. 'I feel bad about going off and leaving you to it.'

'What time is it?' She shivered.

'Six-thirty. Back at three. Sometimes I have a siesta and go into the office for the early evening, but I'll not do that today. We can go shopping. I'll show you round. Are you hungry?'

'No. Yes, a bit.'

'There's stuff in the fridge, you'll find it. Steak for dinner.'

So everything was ready for her, as he had said it would be. When she had blundered through the rooms, an hour ago, she saw pale airy spaces, a vast expanse of beige and freshly hoovered carpet. Pieces of furniture, new, smelling of plastic sheeting, stood grouped here and there; a dozen armchairs, a gleaming polished expanse of table-top, a white, antiseptic bathroom. Quite different from the old life: the donkey boiler at the back of the house, and the tin roof, and the sofas and beds which had gone from family to family.

'I may have been dreaming,' Andrew said, 'but did you go on a pre-dawn tour?'

'I'm sorry if I woke you.'

'The prayer call wakes me anyway. What do you think of the flat? There was a house, it was on a compound with some of the Ministry of Petroleum people, but Jeff lives there – you said you didn't want him for a neighbour. It's taken now anyway. You don't get a lot of choice, Turadup has to rent what it's told. It's a big source of income for Saudi families, letting houses to expats.'

'Who owns these flats?'

'I think it's the Deputy Minister's uncle.'

'Who paid for all the stuff? The new furniture?'

'The company. They've redecorated the whole place as well.'

'They're looking after us. It's not like Africa.'

'Well, in Africa nobody cared whether you came or went. If you found it too tough you just drifted off.'

'But here they care?'

'They try to keep you comfortable. The thing is it's not a very comfortable place. Still,' he said, recollecting himself, 'the money's the thing.'

Frances pushed back the sheets, swung her legs out of bed. 'One thing that seems rather odd ... last night when we arrived I saw those big front doors, I thought there'd be a shared hallway, but you brought me in through a side door, straight into our kitchen. I've found that side door, but where's our front door? How do I get into the hall?'

'You don't, at the moment. The front door's been blocked off. Pollard says there was this Arab couple living here before, quite well-off, the woman was related to our Minister, and they were staying here while they had a villa built, they were just married, you see. The husband was very strictly religious, and he had the doorway bricked up.'

'What, you mean he bricked her up inside it?'

'No. Twit.'

'I thought you meant like a nun in the Dark Ages. So she could pray all day.'

'They don't pray all day,' Andrew said, 'just the statutory five times, dawn, noon, mid-afternoon, sunset, and at night.' He was full of information; wide-awake, which she couldn't claim for herself. 'It's amazing, you know. Everything stops. The shops shut. People stop work. You're just stuck there.'

'This doorway, Andrew . . .'

'Yes, he bricked it up so that she couldn't go out into the hall, where she might run into one of the male neighbours, you see, or a tradesman. She could go out of the side door, in her veil of course, and just round the side of the building by the wall, and then her driver would pull into that little alleyway, and she'd step straight out of the side gate and into the car. And the cars have these curtains on the back windows, did you notice last night?'

'I didn't notice anything last night. You're not teasing me?'

36

'No, it's true. They have curtains, so once she's inside the car she can put her veil back.'

'How eminently sensible.' She looked down at her bare white knees, at her bare feet on the new beige carpet. Andrew had made love to her last night. She remembered nothing about it.

'It must be hot,' Andrew said, 'under those veils.' He put his empty coffee mug down on the dressing-table. 'Oh, there's yoghurt,' he said, 'if you feel like yoghurt for breakfast. There's cornflakes. Must go, I'm late.'

'Will you ring me?'

'No phone. Next week, *ins'allah*.' He paused in the doorway. 'I hate it when I hear myself say that, but everybody says it. If God wills this, and if God wills that. It seems so defeatist. I love you, Fran.'

'Yes.' She looked up to meet his eyes. What has God to do with the telephone company, she wondered. Andrew had gone. She heard a door slam and his key turn in the lock. For a second she was frozen with surprise. He had locked her in.

It's just habit, she said to herself; he'd been living here alone. Somewhere, lying around, there would be a bunch of keys for her own use. Not that she would be going out this morning. There didn't seem much to do in the flat, but she must unpack. On her first morning in her first house in Zambia, she had scrubbed a floor in the steamy heat. At eleven o'clock the neighbours came calling, to take her shopping list away with them and do it, and to issue dinner invitations, and ask if she wanted a kitten to keep snakes away; and then in the afternoon a procession of young men had come up the path, looking for work.

She sipped her coffee, listening to the distant hum of traffic. When she had finished it she sat for a long time, looking into the cup. In the end, with a small sigh, she put it down on the teak laminated bedside cabinet. Then she took a Kleenex from the box by the bed, and wiped up the ring it had made. She sat for a little longer, with the crumpled tissue in her hand. Later she would remember quite clearly these first few minutes alone on Ghazzah Street, these tired, half-automatic actions; how her first, her original response to Jeddah had been boredom, inertia, a disinclination to move from the bed or look out of the window to see what was going on outside. With hindsight she would think, if I had known then what I know now, I would have moved, I would have looked, I would have noticed everything and written it down; and my response would not have been boredom, but fear.

2

When Andrew Shore went to Jeddah he was thirty-three years old: a heavy, deliberate young man, bearded, with a professional expatriate's workaday suntan, and untidy clothes with many evident pockets; rather like the popular image of a war photographer. He had a flat blue eye, and a sceptical expression, and a capacity for sitting out any situation; this latter attribute had stood him in good stead in his professional life. In Africa it was always counter-productive to lose your temper. It made the local people laugh at you, and gave you high blood pressure. If you wanted to get anything done, the best way was to pretend that you were not interested in doing it at all; that you would, in fact, be happy to sit under this tree all day, and perhaps drink a can of beer. If you put pressure on people they cracked very quickly; then they pretended that what you were asking for was impossible, and that anyway there was no petrol, and that the labourers had injured their backs, and that they were urgently called away now because their grandmother had died in another town. It was better to leave people loopholes, and assume a studied casualness, and then, sometimes, things got done. Or not.

When he arrived in Jeddah, Eric Parsons said to him, 'We'll have to take you and introduce you to the Deputy Minister. It's only a formality.' When they arrived at the

Deputy Minister's office suite Andrew looked around and wondered why the Ministry thought it needed a new building; but he did not say anything, because the new building was his livelihood. They were shown in, and served mint tea, very sweet, in small glasses. The Deputy Minister had waved them each to a chair without looking at them, and now he continued not to look, but to turn over papers on his desk, and to talk on his special gold and onyx telephone; he conversed loudly in Arabic with men who came in and out.

'This is Mr Shore,' Parsons said after they had been there for some time unheeded. 'I told you about him, do you remember, he's going to be in charge of the new building. He's very anxious to set his targets and keep everything on schedule.'

The Deputy Minister did not reply, but picked up his Cartier pen and signed a few papers, with an air at once listless and grim. A Yemeni boy came in with a tray, and served cardamom coffee. Ten minutes passed; the coffee boy stood at the Deputy Minister's elbow, and when the Deputy Minister had taken three or four refills, he shook his cup to indicate that he wanted no more. The coffee boy collected his tray and went out, and the Deputy Minister reached for his telephone again, and grunted into it, then put it down and stared deliberately out of the window. One hand absently stroked his blotting pad, which was bound in dark green leather and embossed with the crossed scimitars and single palm tree of the House of Saud.

Then very slowly, his dark eyes, rather full like plums, but rather jaundiced like Victoria plums, travelled around the room, and came to rest for the briefest moment on the two men; and he nodded, almost imperceptibly. Parsons seemed to take this as some sort of signal. He rose, with a smooth air of accomplishment, and for just a second gripped Andrew Shore by the elbow; the bland smile he gave the Deputy Minister was quite at odds with the near-painful pressure of his finger and thumb. By the time they reached the office door the Deputy Minister was talking on the telephone again.

'Is that it?' Andrew said, in the corridor. Parsons did not reply; but persisted, to Andrew's annoyance, with his pseudo-mysterious smile. He was a company man, he knew the system and he played it; you would not find him muttering under his breath, or making V-signs outside closed office doors. They walked downstairs and out into the sun.

They were in the car-park, and it seemed that the Deputy Minister had made it before them; he must have come down in his private lift. As he strode across to his Daimler, his white *thobe* flapping about his legs, and his white *ghutra* fanning out around his head, a dozen people appeared as if from nowhere and mobbed him. They were identically dressed, except that some wore white headcloths, and others wore the red and white *ghutra* of tea-towel check. A stiff breeze got up, blowing in from the sea, and billowed out the men's *thobes*. With the thrusting arms, and the weaving bodies, it was soon impossible to distinguish the Deputy Minister from the mill of petitioners; and the whole resembled nothing so much as a basket of laundry animated by a poltergeist.

Andrew stopped to watch. 'What's happening?'

'They're just saying hello,' Parsons said. 'After all, he doesn't get to the Ministry very often, he's too busy for that.'

'Busy doing what?'

'Running his businesses.'

'It's not a full-time pursuit then, being a minister?'

'Oh my goodness, no. After all, he's not one of the royal family, you know. Why should he neglect his own business to run theirs?'

'You mean that the Kingdom is a family business?'

'If you like,' Parsons said. 'You could put it that way.' The Deputy Minister had almost reached his car now, but delayed further while the petitioners kissed him on the cheek. 'They're the Ministry's suppliers, I imagine.'

'They seem unnecessarily matey. For suppliers.'

'Most of them are probably his relatives as well. It's their tradition. Accessibility. You wouldn't want them walled off, would you, behind their civil service?'

Andrew looked sideways at Parsons, his expression incredulous. Parsons took his pipe out of the top pocket of his bush shirt and stuck it in his mouth. It seemed an odd time to choose; unless it was a tic, which expressed his real feelings, like the pinch on the elbow he had delivered earlier. 'I have to remark,' Andrew said, 'that he didn't seem very accessible to me.'

'There are different rules for us,' Parsons said, barely removing the pipe from his lips. 'Never forget, Andrew, that as individuals we are very unimportant in the Saudi scheme of things. We are only here on sufferance. They do need Western experts, but of course they are a very rich and proud people and it goes against the grain to admit that they need anyone.'

It had the air of a speech that had been made before. Andrew said, 'Do you mean that they are rich and proud, or are they just proud because they are rich?'

Parsons did not answer. Andrew was surprised at himself. It was more the question that his wife would have asked. The Deputy Minister had gained his Daimler now, and put the electric window down to converse further with his hangers-on. Andrew felt slightly nauseated from the cups of cardamom coffee which he had not known how to refuse. He felt exasperated by his inability to draw any proper human response from Parsons, anything that was not practised and emollient. 'Is Turadup very unimportant as well?' he asked.

Parsons took out his pipe again, and made the sort of movement with his mouth, a twitch of the lip, which in some Englishmen replaces a shrug. 'We have the contract for the building,' he said, 'and for the silos at the missile base, and for a few billion riyals' worth of work in Riyadh, but of course if they go off us they can always run us out of the place and hand out the work elsewhere. I mean they don't have the constraints, you see, that you find in the rest of the world. But then on the other hand the company has its

Saudi sponsor, and that sponsor gets his percentage, and is of course an even more highly placed gent than that gent you see over there; and think of the incidental profits we bring in, the rents and so on. I suppose you could say that as a company we are not entirely unimportant. But as individuals we are not expected to make our mark. The best we can do, as individuals, is to keep out of trouble.'

The Deputy Minister had put his window up now, and driven away. Almost as soon as the Daimler drew out of the gate a straggle of Saudi staff members emerged from the Ministry's main door and began to head for their cars; it was 1.30 already, and at 2.30 government offices shut down for the day.

'Ah, homeward bound,' Parsons said pleasantly, 'as we should be, I think, or at least, back to the old Portakabin, eh? I tell you what, Andrew, the best thing is, get into your own little routine. It isn't easy to get things done but I've found over the years that there's a certain satisfaction in achieving against the odds. Now of course you'll hear chaps like Pollard sounding off about the Saudis, that's their privilege, but what good does it do? You may as well learn to take the rough with the smooth.'

They had walked together to Eric Parsons's car. Parsons wound down the window for a moment, to let out the hot wet air trapped inside, and then wound it up again as the air-conditioner cut in. 'Bought a little Japanese motor, didn't you?' Parsons said. 'How's she running?'

'Fine,' Andrew said absently. 'Fine.'

He still felt sick. I was in that bloke's office for twenty minutes, he thought, and he didn't speak to me once.

Parsons said, 'You seem a steady type, Andrew, to me. You'll feel less strange when your wife comes out, there's nothing like family life to keep you going in this place. Keep your head down, you'll be all right.'

Later that night he tried to write to Frances. He struggled to get the words on to the page. He imagined her, in her red

42

dressing-gown perhaps, picking up the morning post in her mother's hall. He felt that he had not succeeded in describing the incident at the Ministry in any terms that would make sense to her. Was he sending her the right information at all? It was almost as if there was something desperately important that he should be telling her; and yet he had no idea what it was.

He had been carrying around, since they parted at Jan Smuts Airport, a small photograph of his wife. It was necessary to get a couple of dozen, passport size, for all the formalities that taking up residence in the Kingdom entailed, and he had clipped one off, and put it in his, wallet. He took it out and looked at it. Frances was thirty years old, perhaps looked and seemed younger, looked younger in this photograph: five feet tall, slight, neat. That is how I would describe her, he thought, how I suppose I have described her to Daphne Parsons, who asked in her condescending way, 'And what is your little wife like?' She had (but he did not go into such detail for Daphne) a freckled skin, and light brown hair, which formed a frizzy nimbus around her head, the result of an unfortunate perm; a small mouth, and light, curious eyes: of no particular colour, perhaps hazel. He had said to Mrs Parsons, 'Frances will be here soon, you can see for yourself.' Why should she think he would have a *little* wife?

Frances will be here soon, with her precise inquiries and her meticulous habits. She is the sort of person who rings dates on calendars, and does not trust to memory; who, when she writes a cheque, does a subtraction and writes a balance on the cheque stub. She knows where all their possessions are, everything that belongs to her and everything that belongs to him; she remembers people's birthdays, and retains telephone numbers in her head. She likes to make sense of the world by making lists, and writing things down. Perhaps, he thought, she will keep a diary. He picked up his pen to add another sentence, laboriously, to the letter: I am really missing you, Fran. He felt weak from missing her,

43

and ashamed of his weakness, so he took her photograph and laid it, face down, on the table.

The first thing I did was to go around the flat drawing back the curtains. This does not seem to me to be a particularly good way to start a diary, but it seems necessary to put down everything I did the first morning, so that I can be sure that I really did as little as I thought, and yet time did pass and I got through it. It reminded me of a particular day in Africa, when I was in our house alone, at home because I had been ill, and I was lying in bed. I'd had tick-bite fever but I was over it, still weak and full of aches and pains, and with no energy to do anything. The house was very quiet, because the maid was having her holidays and the dogs were asleep, and outside rain was falling steadily, that grey carpet of rain that used to come down sometimes for days on end. I remember that morning creeping by, in self-pity and looking at my watch every few minutes, and I couldn't imagine how time could move so slowly. Our bedroom was in semi-darkness, because I had wanted it that way when my head hurt so badly, and now although the pain had gone I didn't have the strength or initiative to get out of bed and let in what little light there was from outside. I felt utterly unreal on that day, and utterly alone, as if I were drifting on some tideless grey sea.

Feeling this on my first morning in Jeddah, I blamed fatigue, and the upset of flying, and self-pity again, because I wasn't entirely sure that I wanted to be here. But although flying does sap the energy it isn't as bad as tick-bite fever, and besides, years have passed since then, and I have taken myself more in hand. So this time I did go and open the curtains.

The curtains are the kind that look as if they are made out of knitted porridge. The carpet is beige and the wallpaper is beige and so is most of the furniture.

When I drew back the curtains I couldn't see out. There are blinds on the outside made of wooden slats, and hidden behind the curtains is a mechanism for raising them. In the living-room the blinds were not down, and when I drew back the curtains I realized that this was the view I had treated myself to on what Andrew called my pre-dawn tour. It was a wall.

I felt that I was getting frustrated now – first blinds, then wall. I walked around the flat and looked out of each window in turn: bedroom one, wall, bedroom two, wall, bedroom three, wall. And into the kitchen, but the kitchen doesn't have a window, though it does have the side door with a frosted glass panel. But that door was locked and I hadn't found any keys. I went into the bathroom, which has a small frosted window which slides. So I slid it. And there was the wall.

I suppose I hadn't realized last night that it ran right round the apartment block. But I don't think I'd expected a garden. There is one tree, the tree that I saw at dawn. It has a brown trunk and brown leaves.

I am keeping this diary so that I can write letters home. People expect you to have something exciting to tell them, though the truth is that once you have been in a place for a few weeks it is not exciting, or if it is, then it is not exciting in a way that the people at home understand or care for. By and large people at home are not interested in hearing about your experiences. They feel bound to put you in your place, as if by going away at all you were offering some sort of criticism of their own lives.

When I was back in England waiting for my visa, I went over to Scarborough to see my cousin, Clare. We used to get on pretty well before I went abroad. I took some photographs with me, of our house and garden in Botswana, which was probably a mistake and a boring thing to do, but it wasn't a bad enough thing to

45

account for those whiffs of hostility I kept getting from Clare. She said, I can't think what induces you to live in such places, I never would. And then she said, I suppose Andrew can't get a job at home? So I said, not at his new salary. I told her what it was, and that shut her up.

It doesn't matter, though, how uninterested people are, you still have to write them letters. And I have a feeling that very little will happen here. I couldn't, for instance, write much on The View From Our Front Window. Andrew says that your first impression of the Kingdom is that it is a stable and orderly place where the telephones work (when you can get one) and the household rubbish is collected every morning from your front gate. I know Clare will not want to read that. But I thought that if I write my diary every few days – I know I can't manage every day – then if anything happens at all, I can make more of it in my letters home.

This is a new departure for me. In Africa there was no need to keep a diary to convince yourself you had an interesting life. Things were always happening. The garden boy would get syphilis, for instance. Perhaps it is a relief not to have household help.

I found myself looking around the flat that first morning, thinking rather desperately, I wish this would get dirty, then I could clean it. Which is not at all my usual sort of wish.

I went into the kitchen and moved the food around in the fridge. I looked in the cupboards to see if I could make a list of what we needed, but we didn't seem to need anything. I went into an empty bedroom and moved a packing-case into it, so that it looked more occupied. But I did not feel at all in possession of the ground.

Then I unpacked my cases. The customs men had churned everything into a knot, and I found that one

46

of my shoes was missing. Only one, and there I was with the other shoe in my hand, new and unworn, and although I knew that my feelings were out of proportion I felt overwhelmed by a terrible sense of waste, and I thought damn them, damn those customs men, who do they think they are, and I said out loud, damn, damn, damn. Then I put most of my clothes in the washing-machine and ironed the rest, and hung them in the wardrobes, and it was still only half-past eleven.

I walked around the flat, thinking dire kinds of thoughts, such as, here I am, here I stay. I went into the bathroom and there, sitting in the washbasin, was the biggest cockroach I have ever seen. I looked at it for some time in a kind of admiring revulsion. Then the thought came to me that there were other people in the building, other lives going on around mine. I heard the distant ring of a telephone, and footsteps in the flat above. It seemed to wake me out of a dream. I can't go on like this, I thought, just wandering round aimlessly.

I went into the living-room. There aren't, as I'd thought earlier, a dozen armchairs, but there are eight, scattered here and there, and two long overstuffed oatmeal-coloured sofas. When there are so many choices there doesn't seem to be any reason for sitting in one chair and not another, so I stood there for a while thinking about it. Eventually I took the chair nearest the window, and sat in it rather stiffly, as though someone were watching me, and read the paperback I'd been reading on the flight. This made me feel as if in fact I hadn't arrived at all, as if I were still in transit, with my passport in my handbag, waiting for it all to begin.

After a few minutes I got up and put on the overhead light, and I thought, that will always be necessary, how depressing, because I hate the lights on during the day. It was very quiet. I heard the prayer call at noon. It seemed strange not to speak to another person all morning, and yet to know that people were there, in the flat next door, and up above my head, and in the street beyond the wall, and that there was a whole country out there which I had not yet seen.

At about two o'clock the cockroach entered the room. It strolled across the huge expanse of carpet and began to climb up one of the curtains. Somehow I was quite glad to see it.

On that first day, Andrew came home at half-past three. She followed him around the flat. 'Will it always be like this?' she asked.

Preoccupied, he dumped his briefcase on the table. 'I'm sorry I locked you in.'

'What about going out? How do I get around?'

'I'll have to talk to Jeff Pollard to see if the office can let you have a car to go shopping sometimes.'

'I'm not that fond of shopping, you know?' she said mildly. Andrew flipped the briefcase open and took a sheaf of papers out. He began to flick through them. 'Well, I don't know that besides shopping there's much else to do.'

'How do people get to see their friends?'

'I suppose they must come to some arrangement. Some of the women hire their own drivers. I don't think we can afford that.'

'Are there buses? Can I go on the bus?'

'There are buses.' He had found the piece of paper he wanted and was reading it. 'But I don't think it's advisable to take them.'

'What's wrong?' she said. 'What's the matter?'

'Oh, nothing. Just a bad day.'

'Can't you tell me?'

'No, I don't think I could begin to explain.' He tossed the papers back into his briefcase and snapped it shut. Need we sound so much like a husband and wife? she wondered. We

48

have never had this conversation before. It is as if it came from some central scripting unit.

Andrew crossed the room and threw himself into an armchair. She followed him. This big decision again; none of the chairs was so placed that they suited two people who wished to sit companionably, and talk to each other. It would seem unreasonably portentous to start moving the furniture now; although it was true that he had been in the house for ten minutes, and had not looked at her once, and this in itself seemed unreasonable. She chose a chair, rather at an angle from his own, and leaned back in it, trying consciously to relax; or at least to capture the appearance of it.

'I was tidying up,' she said, 'filing papers away. I couldn't find your passport.'

'It's in the safe at the office. Turadup keep it. I've got this identity document, it's called an *iqama*.' He produced it from his pocket and tossed it to her. 'I have to carry my driving licence too. If the police stop you and you haven't got your documents they take you off to gaol till it's sorted out. They're very keen on establishing who people are, you see, because of illegal immigrants. People come in at the end of the summer to do their pilgrimage to Mecca and then they try to get a job. I think there's some kind of black market in servants. They try to make a few bucks and get back to Kerala or wherever before the police catch up with them.'

'I can't think that the police would mistake you for somebody's illegal houseboy.'

'Well, what are you saying? That they should only stop people with certain colours of skin?'

'That would be the practical recommendation.'

'Oh, there's no colour prejudice in Saudi Arabia. At least, that's the theory. Somebody told me that when marriage settlements are negotiated the girl's skin is a major consideration. If the bloke's never seen her without her veil, I suppose he has to weigh up her brothers' pigmentation and take it on trust . . . What were we talking about?'

49

'Your passport. Can't you bring it home? You never know
. . . suppose something went wrong and we had to leave
suddenly?'

'Having a passport wouldn't be any use. You can't go out
of the country just like that. You have to apply for an exit
visa. You need signatures. An official stamp.' Andrew pushed
his *iqama* back into his pocket. He didn't mean to be parted
from it. 'If you want to leave you need permission from your
sponsor. My sponsor's His Royal Highness the Minister.
Your sponsor is me. If you wanted to go to another city
even, I'd have to give you a letter.'

'Would you? And that would be true if I were a Saudi
woman?'

'Oh yes. You can't just move around as you like.'

'It reminds me of something,' she said. 'The pass laws.'

'It's not that bad. A lot of countries have these rules. It's
just that we've spent most of our lives subject to a different
set. This isn't a free society. They haven't had any practice
at being free.'

'Freedom isn't a thing that needs practice,' she said. 'If
you have it, you know how to use it.'

'I don't know. Perhaps.' He sounded very tired. 'We're
not quarrelling, are we? I can't do anything about the
system, we'll have to make the best of it, and most of it
needn't bother us and is no concern of ours.' They sat in
silence for a moment. 'The first thing is to find out,' he said
at last, 'how to make daily life tolerable for you. I shall go
and see Pollard and insist that he gets on to the telephone
company. And we'll have to have that doorway unblocked,
so you can talk to the neighbours.'

'Do we need to have those blinds down?'

'We do at night. They're a security precaution. Against
burglars.'

'I didn't think there'd be burglars. I thought they cut
people's hands off.'

'They do. You get reports of it in the papers.'

'And isn't it a sufficient deterrent?'

'It can't be, can it? I have noticed that the papers don't carry reports of crimes, just reports of punishments. But if there are punishments, there must be crimes.'

He had been upset by something today, she saw, made angry, or very surprised. 'I'll make some tea, shall I?' she said. Because all I can do is be a good practical housewife, and offer a housewife's clichés. The fact is that he has come here and he knew it wouldn't be easy, he said that; and now he thinks that he has contracted for his problems, and deserves what he gets, and that he shouldn't be shocked, or baffled, or put into a rage.

'The truth is that you can't know if there are burglaries or not,' Andrew said. 'Except you hear that there are. You hear rumours.' He looked up. 'Everything is rumours. You can't ever, ever, find out what's going on in this bloody place.'

She got up. He followed her out to the kitchen. 'Frances,' he said, 'you must give it a chance. You'll make friends. People will start to call on you . . . people's wives. If there is anywhere you want to go I'll always take you.' She took a packet of milk out of the fridge. She waited. 'There's this man at the office,' he said, 'a kind of clerk, his name's Hasan. I thought he was mainly there for making the tea, and driving Daphne about, but it turns out that his speciality is bribing people. No wonder you can never find him when you want somebody to put the kettle on, he's out slipping baksheesh to some prince's factotum. He only bribes the lower officials, though, not the high-ups.'

'Who bribes the high-ups?'

'I don't know yet. Eric, maybe? They paid to get you your visa, and they paid to get me my driving licence, and you just go on paying out at every turn, you have to bribe people's clerks to get them even to pick up the telephone and speak to you. But it's a funny thing, because officially there is no bribery in the Kingdom of Saudi Arabia. And that again is a damn funny thing, because bribery in Saudi Arabia is a very serious crime, and people are charged with it and put in gaol and deported for it. Though of course it never happens, because it just doesn't exist.'

She took cups out of the cupboard. She was locating everything; this was home. 'Well, what did you expect?'

'I didn't know it would be quite like this. I didn't know there would be so many layers to the situation.' He paused. 'Do you think I'm naïve?'

'You are, a bit, if you need to ask the question. I expect you'll get used to it.'

'You'd think it would be a sort of abstract problem,' Andrew said, 'a matter of conscience. But then about once a day I realize what's happening in some particular situation, and I realize what I've let myself in for . . .' He put a hand to his ribs. 'It's like being kicked.'

Turadup, William and Schaper first came to Saudi Arabia in late 1974, a few months before King Faisal was shot by his nephew, when oil revenues were riding high, property prices in Riyadh had doubled in a month, and so urgent was the need to build that the Jeddah sky was black with helicopters ferrying bags of cement from the ships that packed the harbour. Since then they had expanded to Kuwait and the Emirates, been chucked out of Iran when the Shah fell, and accommodated themselves to Saudi labour law and the rise of Islamic architecture. They had a contract for a shopping mall in Riyadh, several schools in the Eastern Province, a military hospital, warehousing in Yanbu; there was the military project they did not talk about much, and there was the marble and gold-leaf ministerial HQ . . . Turadup and William are dead and forgotten now, but the son of Schaper is still around, and the company's recent success is due in no small part to his ready and willing adaptation to Middle Eastern business practices: tardiness, doublespeak, and graft.

Throughout the seventies, Schaper flew in and out, disbursing great wads of used notes. His briefcase became a legend, for what came out of it. Conscious of his role, he took

to clenching Havanas between his rubbery lips, and to wearing eccentric hats, as if he were a Texan. 'Buccaneering' was
a word he liked to hear applied to himself.

Turadup flew in teams of construction workers from
Britain, and housed them in temporary camps outside the
cities, giving them a makeshift supermarket selling fizzy
drinks, a mess serving American frozen beefburgers, a lecture
on sunstroke, an anti-tetanus shot, a dartboard, and three
leave tickets a year to see the families they had left behind.
The physical stress was crushing, their hours were ruinous,
their pay packets enormous. Off-duty hours they spent lying
on their beds, watching mosquitoes circling the cubicle
rooms; unused to letter-writing, they became like long-term
prisoners, subject to paranoia; to fears that were sometimes
not paranoid, but perfectly well-grounded, that their wives
were preparing to leave them for other men. When letters
reached them they were full of news about burst pipes and
minor car accidents, and vandalism on the housing estates
where they lived; and seemed to conceal much else, lying
between the blue-biro lines on the Basildon Bond Airmail.

They began to occupy themselves in brewing up liquor.
They wandered off towards the desert looking for a bit of
privacy, and caused search-parties. Their skins, after every
precaution, turned scarlet and blistered in the sun. Strange
rashes and chest complaints broke out. When they were
released for leave they sat at the back of the plane and got
sodden drunk within an hour of take-off; they squirted each
other with duty-free Nina Ricci, and laid hands on the stew-
ardesses, and threw their dinners about, and vomited on the
saris of dignified Indian ladies who were seated on their path
to the lavatories. At Heathrow they vanished, sucked into the
rain, an allowed-for percentage never to be seen again; this
was part of the company's calculations, for they were can-
non-fodder, quick and easy to recruit and cheap to replace.
Cheap, that is, by the standards of what Turadup was making
in those years; and cheap compared to what skilled men of
other nationalities might have taken as their due.

Then again, a certain number would be deported for misbehaviour, for offending against the tenets of Islam; run out of the country, sometimes flogged beforehand and sometimes not, or beaten on the streets by the 'religious police' for lighting up a cigarette during the Ramadhan fast. They were all informed of the risks upon arrival, and Turadup took no responsibility in such cases; they were adults after all, and they knew the rules. There came a point when these men became more trouble than they were worth, and so now only a few foremen and site managers were British. The labour was recruited from Korea, yellow, tractable men, reeling through a desert landscape: indentured coolies, expecting nothing.

On the other hand, Turadup had always prided itself on how it had treated its professional staff. Plush if prefabricated villas were erected, with fitted carpets and icy air-conditioning, and instant gardens of potted shrubs. School fees would be paid for the older children left behind, and there would be Yemeni drivers to run the wives about, and a swimming-pool for each compound (carefully fenced from local eyes) and perhaps a squash court. And perhaps a weekly film show, as TV in the Kingdom is in its infancy, and mainly confined to Tom and Jerry cartoons, and Prayer Call from Mecca, and expositions of the Holy Koran; and certainly, soft furnishings coordinated in person, down to the last fringed lampshade, by Daphne Parsons herself. Turadup picked up the medical bills, and gave its professionals and their families a splendid yearly bonus and ten weeks off every summer; so that they would say, 'We only have to last out till Ramadhan, and we don't come back till after Haj.' It was important that their lives should be made as smooth as possible, that they should not be ground down by the deprivations and the falsity of life in the Kingdom. They must be comforted and cossetted, because Turadup's professionals were responsible, discreet men, who could Deal With The Saudis; and they do not come ten-a-penny.

But by the time the Shores arrived in Jeddah the great days of Turadup were over. They had sold off their big housing compound and let some of their staff go. The price of oil was falling and the construction boom was finished. It was true that buildings were still going up all over the city, but every stage of a project needed an infusion of money, and often it was delayed, or doubtful, or didn't come at all. Eric Parsons got used to waiting on the Minister of Finance. He spent a lot of time in other people's offices, sipping cardamom coffee, waiting for people to get around to him. He had a sense, at times, of things eluding his grasp; of the good years slipping away.

Daphne Parsons would tell you, if asked, that the Jeddah social scene was not what it had been. The Saudis, of course, had never really mixed with the expatriates. That was as it should be; it avoided mutual embarrassment, and the thorny question of illicit liquor. The odd groveller would ask a Saudi to dinner, a colleague or a boss; but the man would turn up two hours late and without his wife (one should have known) and a place-setting would hastily be removed, and a man you had thought was a liberal, a modern Saudi, would sit glowering at the tense, sober company, as if expecting something.

What was it he expected? Was it a drink? Normally there would be home-made wine on the table. Tonight you've left it out, in deference to Islam – and because of the risk if your Saudi friend should later turn against you. He may drop a hint that he would like a little something; you produce it, but you're still afraid. Or he might not drop the hint, and let you suffer, on Perrier water, the drying up of the conversation and the covert glances at watches. And if you should so suffer, you will not know why; whether it is because he is really religious, or whether it is because he is as frightened as you; or whether it is simply that he has plenty of Glenfiddich at home.

Khawwadjihs, the Saudis call the white expatriates: light-haired ones. And nowadays the turnover in light-haired ones is so quick. Eighteen months is the average stay. There are people in Jeddah today, Mrs Parsons reflects, who didn't even know the Arnotts, who weren't here when Helen Smith died. People are scarcely around long enough to get involved in serious entertaining, or in the Hejaz Choral Society, or in running a Girl Guide troop. There are never enough helpers for the British Wives' annual bazaar at the Embassy, and the British Community Library staggers on with too few volunteers for weekend evenings. There is almost no one around, nowadays, who remembers what it was like before the giant shopping malls were built, when people had to shop for groceries in the souk. And Mrs Parsons does not know anyone who attended that fabled party in 1951, when young Prince Mishari, eighteenth surviving son of the great King Abdul Aziz, turned up in a drunken rage, sprayed all the guests with bullets, and murdered the British Consul.

Those were the days.

That evening Andrew drove her downtown. Her sense of unreality was intensified by the slow-moving traffic, bumper to bumper, by the blaring of horns in the semi-darkness; by the prayer call, broadcast through megaphones to the hot still air. Neon signs rotated and flashed against the sunset; on Medina Road the skyscrapers were hung with coloured lights, trembling against the encroaching night.

They executed a U-turn, inched through the traffic, and swerved into a great sweep of white buildings. They edged forward, jostling for a parking space; with no anger in his face, but with a kind of violent intent, Andrew put his fist on his horn. Cadillacs disgorged men in their *thobes* and *ghutras* and hand-made Italian sandals; women, veiled in black from head to foot, flitted between the cars.

Andrew took her hand briefly and squeezed it, standing close to her, as if shielding her with his solid body from view. 'I mustn't hold your hand,' he said, 'we mustn't touch in public. It causes offence.' They moved apart, and into the crowds.

Inside the supermarket, on the wall where the wire trolleys were parked, there was a notice which said

THIS SHOP CLOSES FOR PRAYER. BY ORDER OF THE COMMITTEE FOR THE PROMULGATION OF VIRTUE, AND THE ELIMINATION OF VICE.

'The religious police,' Andrew said. 'Vigilantes. You'll see them around. They carry sticks.'

'What do the secular police carry?'

'Guns.'

Frances took a trolley. She manoeuvred it to a gigantic freezer cabinet. Pale chilled veal from France and black-frozen American steaks swept before her for fifty feet. 'Do we need any of this?'

'Not really. I brought you to show you that you can get everything. Come and look at the fruit.'

There were things she had never seen before in her life; things grown for novelty, not for eating, bred for their jewel-like colours. 'They don't have seasons,' Andrew said. 'They fly this stuff in every morning.' She bought mangoes. She put them in a plastic bag and handed them to a Filipino man who stood behind a scale. He weighed them, and twisted the bag closed and handed it back to her, but he did not look her in the face. Andrew took the trolley from her. 'Don't think about the prices,' he advised. 'Or you'd never eat.'

In Botswana, in the last town where they had lived, the vegetable truck came twice a week. Carrots were a rarity, mushrooms were exotic. In the garden, baboons stripped the fig trees. Fallen oranges rolled through the grass; the gardener collected them up in baskets. There were tiny peaches, hard as wood, and the cloying scent of guavas in the crisp early mornings. Around her, women plucked tins from shelves; women trussed up in their modesty like funereal laundry, women with layers of thick black cloth where their faces should be. Only their hands reached out, sallow hands heavy with gold.

She caught up with Andrew, laying her hand on the handle of the trolley beside his, carefully not touching. 'Let me drive,' he said.

'I didn't know the veil was like this,' she whispered. 'I thought you would see their eyes. How do they breathe? Don't they feel stifled? Can they see where they're going?'

Andrew said, 'These are the liberated ones. They get to go shopping.'

They took their groceries to the car. 'We'll eat soon,' Andrew said. They wove themselves into the crowds; each brilliant window collected its admirers. The buildings here looked new, perhaps a month old, perhaps a week; perhaps they had sprung from the desert that morning, gleaming and stainless, and some old-style genie, almost redundant now, had caused to appear in them by an instant's magic all the luxury goods of the Western world. Cameras, television sets, Swiss watches, so crammed that they seemed to spill out on to the pavement; ancient silk carpets, and microwave ovens, and electric guitars. There was a furrier: fox, wild mink, sable. She wiped the sweat from her forehead. The smell of fried chicken mingled with the scent of Chanel and Armani. Between the Porsches, a fountain played in a marble basin. She stopped before a shoe shop; a window of tiny high-heeled sandals, green, lilac, red, gold. 'Why these?' she said. 'Westerners have more sober shoes.'

'I suppose that if you have to go out draped in black to your ankles, you want some way to express yourself.'

She followed Andrew. 'Can't they buy furs when they go abroad? They can't need them in this climate.'

'Money is a burden all the year round.'

They bought cassette tapes; cheap copies, pirated in Asia and imported by the shopful. All the latest stuff was on the shelves; rock music, and Vivaldi's Greatest Hits. She didn't buy the Vivaldi. She planned to fill the flat with noise. I am thirty years old, she thought, and I still buy this, whatever is current, whatever is loud. When they came out of the tape shop it was time for night prayers, and men were unrolling prayer carpets on the ground.

'There is no God but Allah, and Muhammed is his Prophet,' Andrew muttered. Grilles clashed down over the shop windows, doors were barred. In a space by the fountain – which now, unaccountably, had run dry – the worshippers jostled together in lines behind the imam, and then in time fell to their knees, and touched their foreheads to the ground, elevating their backsides. It was just as she had seen it in pictures; she was always surprised if anything was the same.

They stood watching, in the heat. Andrew looked as if he wished to speak; but perhaps he had no right to an opinion? She glanced at him sideways. 'Oh go on,' she muttered. 'Spit it out. I know you hate religion.'

'Oh, they must do as they like,' he said. 'It's not my business, is it? It's just the ablutions I mind. They have to wash before they pray, all sorts of inconvenient bits of themselves. When you go into the lavatories at the Ministry all the floor is flooded, and people are standing on one leg with their other foot in the handbasin. You can't . . . you want to laugh.' He took out his handkerchief from the pocket of his jeans and mopped his brow. 'We timed this trip badly. But people are always getting caught like this. There's only a couple of hours between sunset and night prayers.'

And then, she thought, eight hours till dawn. Her feet ached, still swollen perhaps from the flight. When prayers were over they went into a fast-food shop. Small Korean men in a uniform of check shirts and cowboy hats grilled hamburgers behind the counter, and stacked trays, and busily cleaned the tables. There was an all-male party of young Filipinos in one corner; and Saudi youths sprawled across the plastic benches, nourishing their puppy-fat and their incipient facial hair.

A sign said 'FAMILY ROOM', and an arrow pointed to a corner of the café marked off by a wooden lattice screen. Andrew steered her behind it. There were three tables, empty. They ate pizza and drank milk-shakes. Conversation between them died; but for a moment, over the comforting junk-food, she did feel real again, and uncalculating, whole, as though she were a child. But it is not really myself, she thought, as she pushed an olive around her plate, it is just an image I have been sold, in a film somewhere. A wide-eyed child of America; the innocent abroad.

The feeling did not last. They drove uptown, the roads packed and dangerous now that night prayers were over. 'At this hour,' Andrew said, 'Saudi men go out to visit their friends.'

'They drive like maniacs,' she said.

'Just think if they had alcohol.' His face was grim and set. He was almost used to it now, the six near-misses a day.

Each highway was straight; the same neon signs flashing between the streetlamps, Nissan, Sanyo, Mitsubishi. On the central reservation saplings wilted in the exhaust fumes. 'I don't know where we are,' she said.

'It takes weeks to learn your way around. It comes in time.' They turned off the main road. Now they were close to home, driving between apartment blocks. Subdued lights burned behind closed curtains. At just one first-floor window, at the corner of Ahmed Lari Street, the curtains were drawn back; on a balcony, brilliantly lit from the room behind, a small dark man in a singlet stooped over an ironing-board. Andrew slowed at the intersection; Frances looked up. The man swept a garment from the ironing-board, and held it aloft; it was a *thobe*, narrow, shirt-like, startling white against the shadows of the walls and the night sky. She imagined she could see the laundryman's face, creased with the weariness of long standing; as they turned the corner he laid the garment down again, and began to arrange its limbs.

They were back at Ghazzah Street. She got out of the car. The laundryman seemed to her as clear and sharp and meaningless as a figure in a dream; she knew she would never forget him. As the metal gate clanged shut, and Andrew turned to lock it, the dream closed in on her; they walked around the side of the building and he let them in through the kitchen door, into the dark cold silence of the apartment.

3

At last the doorway has been unblocked, and I feel that I am going to end this rather peculiar isolation in which I have been living. When I began this diary I described my first morning in the flat as if it were going to be exceptional. When Andrew locked me in, I thought, it doesn't matter, because I won't be going out today. As if not going out would be unusual. I didn't know that on that first day I was setting into a pattern, a routine, drifting around the flat alone, maybe reading for a bit, doing this and that, and daydreaming. I can see now that it will need a great effort not to let my whole life fall into this pattern.

Andrew thinks that perhaps after all we should have gone to live on a compound, where, he says, it is all bustle and sociability, and the wives run in and out of each other's houses the whole time. I'm not sure if I'd like that. I still think of myself as a working woman. I'm not used to coffee mornings. I think of myself in my office at Local Government and Lands. I was run off my feet, or at least I like to think so. Being here is a sort of convalescence. Or some form of sheltered accommodation. You think that after a dose of the English summer, after the hassle of getting out here, you will need a recovery period. You need peace and quiet. Then suddenly, you don't need it any more. Oh, but you have got it. It is like being under house arrest. Or a banned person.

After Andrew had spoken to Turadup, and they had spoken to the landlord, he sent some men around to unblock the doorway. Andrew had to stay at home for the event. It seems that workmen don't like to enter a house where there is a woman alone. In theory this is to protect me, but really it is to protect them from any accusation I might choose to level against them. From what I have seen so far it seems to me that the sexes here live in a state of deep mutual suspicion.

I did not mind the terrible mess the workmen left behind, because I am so interested at the prospect of meeting my neighbours. On the ground floor there is a Pakistani couple. Andrew has met them briefly and says they are very pleasant. They have a small child, but he is vague about age and sex. The man's name is Ashref Aziz Al Rahman, he is known as Raji, and he works for the Minister in some personal capacity. Andrew, who has become cynical in quite a short space of time, says that this means he organizes the importation of the Minister's personal crates of Scotch.

Then there are two flats on the floor above. The one directly over our head is empty. In the other flat there is a young Saudi couple, also with a baby I think. The man's name is Abdul Nasr, and Andrew says he is on the Ministry payroll, though not often seen there, and no one is sure what he does, if indeed he does anything, and this state of affairs is quite usual. I notice that this diary is full of 'Andrew says' but I have no other source of information yet. Every day he comes home with something else to tell me, usually something funny. Expatriates do have this habit of laughing at everything. I suppose it is the safest way of expressing dissent. Sometimes I think we should be more open-minded, and not think that we are the ones who are right, and that we should contrive to be more pious about other people's cultures. But after all, as Andrew says, we're not on Voluntary Service Overseas.

The company has given us a warning about our Arab neighbours. They say they are very religious, and like to keep to themselves, so we shouldn't make overtures to them, just be quiet neighbours and polite, and if we meet on the stairs – which I'm sure we will now the doorway is unblocked – we shouldn't strike up a conversation, but wait until we are spoken to, and meanwhile just nod and smile, but of course, if I am on my own and I meet the husband, better not smile too much. Eric Parsons came round one morning just to tell me this. I said, I know how to go on, in Africa I met the Queen. This is true, but the remark didn't go down well.

Jeff Pollard has been round as well. He came to show us how to make wine. We are going to begin on our social life, it seems, dinner parties and barbecues, and you must be able to give people something to drink. It is true that brewing liquor is illegal, but there seems to be a concept of some things being more illegal than others. So although it's very foolish to try to import proper stuff, you can make it in your home for your own consumption secure in the knowledge that the Saudi police do not enter private homes on a whim. They'll come if you attract attention to yourself – by, for instance, having a violent death on the premises – but if you manage to avoid that you'll probably get away with it.

Everybody knows it goes on. The shops sell grape juice, white and red, by the case. You pick up your sugar and your yeast and your plastic jerry cans and off you go, some kind friend like Pollard comes round to instruct you, you brew the stuff up in your bathroom, say, or wherever you have room, and just watch it for a day or two to make sure the yeast hasn't died, and then four or five weeks later you draw off some of the results and see if it's fit to drink. There are some people who go into it very seriously, of course, and strain it and clarify it and bottle it and declare vintages, and compete with each other in undercover competitions, but most people are content with something clean and drinkable, with no offensively large bits floating around in it.

You can brew beer, too, from the cans of non-alcoholic malt drinks that you find in the supermarkets. A few years ago these were banned for a time, because the religious authorities were afraid that the smell and taste of them might make the faithful imagine that they were the real thing – and that would be a sin. There's also a spirit called *siddiqui* which you can get expensively on the black market. It's just sugar and water distilled but when people try to make their own they usually blow their apartments up. And if you want it, and know who to ask, and are prepared to pay about ten times the UK price, you can always lay your hands on whisky or gin.

I am glad I have got that down. It will be sure to fascinate my cousin Clare, and she can tell it to her pitiful suburban neighbours when they have their Beaujolais Nouveau parties this year.

As Pollard says, you have to drink something. Here you are amongst all these people with whom you don't necessarily have anything in common, except that perhaps you work for the same outfit, and you're drifting through each other's lives, in transit, trying to make a go of your casual friendships so that even if you get bored you don't get lonely. But it's difficult to make conversation, difficult to keep each other entertained. The risk seems extraordinary – gaol, flogging, deportation (and who knows if this theory is true about how the police are supposed to behave) but I needed a drink really to get through the evening with Jeff – his silly sniggering jokes, and the way he seems to hate the Saudis and resent them because they have all the money and he (comparatively) hasn't. Andrew got quite angry when he had gone, and said, what's he complaining about, he's coining it, he's on the take;

what's he got to complain about, he's working the system to suit himself. Then Andrew said more thoughtfully, he probably hates himself for doing that, for what he has become. And we were very quiet, thinking, perhaps we shall become it?

We felt rather miserable, sitting in that impossible room with all the unused chairs, so we drank the bottle of Jeff's own wine that he had left behind for us, and next morning I was sick.

Now the prisoner is released. Frances could walk in the street; but to what purpose? You could not get anywhere. Only, after long hot miles, to Medina Road, where the traffic goes screaming by, out of town to the bypasses and motorways and on to the Holy City. Walking is pointless; but she can go out into the hall, where gritty dust blows continually under the big front door, and makes patterns on the mottled marble underfoot. She can go up to the flat roof, with her basket of washing, and hang it out, to bring it back an hour or two later, dry and stiff with heat, burnt-smelling, and covered in dust if the wind has veered round in the interim. There are washing lines for each of the flats, but she hasn't seen her neighbours use them. Perhaps they have more sense, or tumble-dryers.

She likes to be on the roof, and to look down on to the street, and on to the big secluded balconies of the two upper flats, and into the branches of the brown tree with its brown leaves. It is a secret view, a private perspective, and she reminds herself of some lonely woman, her own mother perhaps, peeping at the doings of the neighbours through a lace curtain. Not that she has learned much. The Saudi woman does not come out to take the sun and air; the doors to her balcony – a solid affair, like an extra room – remain firmly closed.

And the fourth flat is empty. Curious, that, because on her very first morning she had heard footsteps above her head. She remembers it – she remembers every detail of her first day – as the incident which jerked her out of her maudlin state, and made her know that there were people around her, and a new life to be lived. But Andrew says she must be mistaken.

From the roof of the apartment block there are long views over the dusty street; over the big turquoise rubbish skips that stand at each street corner, the property of Arabian Cleaning Enterprises; over the rows of parked cars. Fierce cats spit and howl and limp in the purlieus of the building, their fur torn into holes or worn away by skin diseases. As the first week of comparative liberty passes, the view comes to seem less edifying, the reasons for the climb fewer, and she begins to resent the two closed doors she passes on the way up, before she negotiates the final turn in the stairs and the short flight to the roof: Abdul Nasr's door, and the door of the fourth flat. And she begins to hate the stairs themselves, because they are made of that kind of marble patched with slabs of irregular rufus colour, flecked with black and a fatty cream, revoltingly edible, like some kind of Polish sausage. She avoids them. She phones up Eric Parsons and tells him that she is not happy and must have a tumble-dryer herself. A van arrives with one the following day. Nothing is too much trouble for Turadup.

So now she stays downstairs. From the living-room, a sliding door leads out on to the cracked pavement in the shadow of the wall. Beyond the wall, between the parked cars, boys play football in the street. Andrew is not happy about the sliding door. He no longer believes that the crime rate is low; he has heard some terrible stories. Someone he works with has advised him to block the track with a length of wood, so that it cannot be slid back from the outside, even if the handle is forced. He has done this.

If Frances is willing to prise out this piece of wood – not easy because he has made it fit so exactly – she can draw back the door and – careful to close it behind her, to keep the insects out and the cold air in – she can stand under the shabby tree, and the wall which is a foot higher than her

66

head. She can hear car engines revving up, and the children's shouts, and sometimes the soft thud of the football against the bricks. When she goes inside and shuts the door these sounds still come to her, muffled, very faint, as if they happened last year.

They have been out to dinner twice now, and to a party, and met a lot of people; they are becoming familiar with Jeddah cuisine, and with the strange but addictive taste of *siddiqui* and tonic. A telephone has been installed. The diary is kept less attentively, because her inner ear is attuned again to other people and the outside world. And yet, the first two weeks have changed her. Introspection has become her habit. There are things she was sure of, that she is not sure of now, and when her reverie is broken, and first unease and then fear become her habitual state of mind, she will have learned to distrust herself, to question her own perceptions, to be unsure – as she is unsure already – about the evidence of her own ears and the evidence of her own eyes.

Within a day or two the unblocking of the hallway brought Yasmin to the door, gesturing gracefully behind her; I am from Flat 2, I hope you will come and have a cup of tea with me. Frances followed her across the hall. She felt dull and badly dressed in her limp cotton skirt. Yasmin's glossy hair hung to her waist, and a gauzy veil floated about her shoulders. One slender arm from wrist to elbow was sheathed in gold bangles.

She closed the door of Flat 2, swept off the veil and handed it to her maid, who stood inside the doorway. 'Put on the kettle,' she said to the woman. The maid scuttled away; a short, dark, low-browed woman, with a faintly pugilistic air.

'She is from Sri Lanka,' Yasmin said. 'She is not much use, but thank goodness I have got her. Raji calls so many people for dinner every night that I have no time for the baby.'

'People don't seem to have much domestic help here. It surprises me.'

'In the grander households, of course, you will find it. But the Saudis are discouraging it now. They don't like the foreign influence. Of course, it is a good point, these young girls come to the Kingdom as housemaids, and then they cause trouble.'

'Do they?' Frances sat down, where she was bidden. 'What sort of trouble?'

'They get unhappy,' Yasmin said. 'Because they have left children behind them at home. Also the Saudi men, you know, they find that these girls are not very moral.' The maid came in; put down the tea-tray. Yasmin dismissed her with a nod. 'Then the poor things are trying to commit suicide. You would like some of this Crawford's shortbread?'

'Thank you,' Frances said. She took a piece. Yasmin gave her another composed smile; poured tea. 'How?' Frances said. 'How do they commit suicide?'

'They throw themselves from the balconies. Silly girls. But this one, I have got a reference for her. She is all right, I think.'

'What's her name?'

'It is Shams.'

Frances repeated it, tentatively. 'I can't quite get hold of it.'

'Shams,' Yasmin said. 'As in Champs Elysées.'

'Oh, I see.'

'Means sunny.' She tittered. 'I do not find her a little ray of sunshine about my house. But Raji was six months waiting for the work permit for her. He doesn't like to ask the Minister for favours. You are used to a servant, Frances?'

'I'm used to help. But it doesn't bother me, either way.'

Yasmin sighed. 'It is a problem,' she said.

In Yasmin's apartment, there was flowered wallpaper and patterned rugs, and little gilt tables with glass tops, and an enormous sideboard, crowned by family photographs. Yasmin with her new-born baby; earlier, Yasmin beneath a wedding veil of gold lace, her mouth painted emphatically red, and her delicate hand on the dark-suited arm of her plump husband. He looks older by some years; a handsome man, though, with a full expressive face, liquid eyes. Yasmin's own age is not easy to determine; she sits swinging one slippered foot, a long-nosed, spindly young woman, with a flawless ivory skin, a festinate way of speaking, and large eyes which are lustrous and intractable, like the eyes of a jibbing horse.

'So your husband's building is coming along?' she asked.

'I haven't been to see it yet.'

'Your husband is shy, I think. He runs away.'

'Really?'

Yasmin smiled. 'Samira would like to meet you.'

'The lady up above?'

'You will be surprised. She speaks good English.'

'I should like to meet some Saudi women.'

'She is very young. Nineteen. Some more tea?'

'Thank you.'

'You will see Selim, my son, when he wakes up just now. You are thinking of starting your family soon?'

This question. Oh dear. 'I've always worked,' Frances said.

'Jeddah is a good place for families.'

'Is it?'

'You have not been here long enough to see the advantages. You are still missing England, I expect. Your parents.' Yasmin's tone was encouraging. She proffered the biscuits again. 'Do take another one, Frances. You are so slim. You have seen this film, *Death of a Princess*?'

She did rush straight at things, Frances thought. Suicidal housemaids, decapitation. She put her shortbread down on her plate. 'I heard about it. But I didn't see it. I wasn't in England at the time.'

Relief showed on Yasmin's face. Is she the custodian of Saudi culture then? 'I remember the fuss it caused,' Frances said. 'Princess Misha, wasn't that her name? She was married, and she took off with another man. They caught her and she was executed.'

'This film has caused a lot of trouble between Saudi Arabia and Britain,' Yasmin said. 'They do not understand why it should be shown.'

'Oh,' Frances said, 'we are interested in other parts of the world. Foreign customs.'

Their eyes met. 'In any case, it is false,' Yasmin said firmly.

'False?'

'Oh yes. These things do not happen. Princess Misha, this girl, she was extremely spoiled, always wanting her own way.'

'So you think she deserved what she got?'

'You must try to understand a little the Saudi viewpoint.' She seemed to distance it from her own, by implication; and yet she seemed on edge. Her husband's position, Frances thought. 'She tried to go out of the country disguised as a man.'

'Did she really?'

'They caught her at the airport.'

'Obviously you see these things differently.'

'I am not a Saudi, of course. I am only giving . . . the Eastern viewpoint.'

'To me it seems incredible, to kill a woman for something like that.'

'But they did not, Frances. She is not dead. Her family have her in one of their houses.'

This is quite stupid, Frances thought. 'But she was executed, Yasmin. Her death was reported.'

Yasmin smiled knowingly, as if to say, how simple you are. 'Excuse me,' she said, 'but it is nonsense. The execution was made up by the filming people.'

Frances was silent. Then she said, 'Why should they do that?'

'It is their mentality,' Yasmin said. 'It is the mentality of the West, to discredit the Eastern people.'

It was now that Shams came in, with the baby in her arms; a little boy like a doll, half asleep, his head drooping on the servant's shoulder and his curved eyelashes resting on his cheeks. Frances stood up. She felt she was blushing, burning inwardly. Have I been rude to her? But what a topic! Why plunge straight into it like that?

Gratefully, she turned her flustered attention to the baby. 'He's beautiful, Yasmin.' The beetle-browed housemaid put the child in her arms. 'How old is he?'

'So you think he is cute?' Yasmin asked. She fluttered; her face yearned. The baby nuzzled his head into Frances's shoulder. She is so anxious, Frances thought, that I don't get the wrong impression. She knows we have prejudices. She wants me to hear her version, that's all.

'He walks a little,' Yasmin said. 'So active! Do you think he is forward?'

'Very forward.'

'Ah, what a lovely picture you make,' Yasmin said fondly. She spoke as if she had known her neighbour for half a lifetime. 'No, Selim, naughty.' She untangled the baby's fingers from Frances's hair. 'He is fascinated, your hair is so light, he just wants to grasp it.'

It was a leave-taking scene now. Yasmin touched Frances's elbow timidly. 'You will come again? Any morning.'

'Yes, of course. Or come to me.'

'If there is anything you need . . . or anything Raji can do for you. He knows this town so well.'

Yasmin took her to the door. Before she opened it she plucked the wisp of a veil from the hallstand and flicked it over her head. 'I will watch you across the hallway,' she said. Frances looked up into the stairwell. Those two closed doors at the top. She took her key out of the pocket of her skirt. Yasmin watched her until the door of Flat 1 clicked shut behind her; then gently drew herself inside, and closed her own door.

'No introductory moves,' Frances said. 'Just, when are you going to start your family, and then – wham – *Death of a*

71

Princess. How the West gets us wrong. I don't think I was super-tactful.'

'No,' Andrew said, 'I don't suppose you were.'

'Did you bring the *Saudi Gazette* home?'

'Yes, here it is.'

He had been kept late at the site, and she had been alone all afternoon. She followed him into the bedroom, the newspaper in her hand. He took off his shirt and dropped it on to the floor. She could see the muscles, knotted, at the back of his neck. He had just driven through the evening traffic; 'They are mad,' he breathed as he drove along, 'they are mad.' But he could see the day coming soon when he would be able to hold a normal conversation as he inched and swerved along. The drivers sit at traffic lights, reading magazines, their fists poised over their horns; when the lights change they bang down their fists together, the horns blare, and at the slightest sign of a delay, another lane will form; the cars roar forward, cutting each other out. Each intersection bears an accident that has just occurred.

'I have to take a shower,' Andrew said.

'I hope I didn't offend her. Yasmin.'

'I shouldn't worry.'

'Only she seemed so much on the defensive. As if I were bound to be building up some bad impressions.'

'You are, aren't you? You're not exactly seeing the country at its best.'

'No, but what do I do about it?'

'Frances, stop following me!' He turned on her, naked. 'I told you, I have to go and have a shower.'

She went back into the bedroom and threw herself on the bed. Her throat ached with resentment. Talk to me, please, when you come home. I can't live like this; this is not a natural sort of life. She heard the rushing and bubbling of water from next door; her eyes slid around to Andrew's shirt, lying on the floor.

She sighed, and rolled over; opened the newspaper, propping it against the pillows. The correspondence column was what she mostly liked. She located it, folding the paper over. Here's a letter from one Abdul Karim of Riyadh: *The Kingdom's social and cultural heritage does not allow women to mix with men either in life activities or in work. The right place for a woman is to look after her husband and children, prepare food, and manage the housework.* But foreigners were coming into the Kingdom, Karim alleged, and saying there was more to life than this. *When you work in another country, you should study its traditions and characteristics before you get in it.*

She folded up the paper and turned on her back again, letting Abdul Karim slide to the floor. I knew the facts, she thought, but I didn't know what impact they would make on me. I knew there were restrictions, but I didn't know what it would feel like to live under them. And now here is Yasmin, an intelligent woman, telling me that things are different here and I must swallow my objections.

Andrew was back. Holding a bath towel, he sat down on the edge of the bed. 'I'm sorry,' he said. 'Shouldn't have shouted. Just another bloody day. The Turadup people who are working at the missile base won't talk to me. They enjoy being secretive. You ask them a perfectly straightforward question about the best way to get something done, and they start tapping the side of their noses, you know what I mean? Americans run that base. They're even in uniform. It's no secret, but it is a secret. It's supposed to be missiles for local defence, but that's not what people say. They say it's a base for intercontinental missiles. And yet the Saudis loathe the Americans. Because they support Zionism. They've banned Ford cars. They've banned Coca-Cola. They'll just have weaponry, thank you.'

'And hamburgers and Cadillacs.' She reached for the newspaper. 'Have you seen the cartoon?' The President of the United States, a wizened mannikin in a Stars and Stripes waistcoat, balanced on the tip of a huge, hooked, dis-embodied nose. 'That's meant to be a Jew's nose, not an Arab's. You're supposed to understand that. It says in the letters column that you should study the customs of a country

73

before you get in it, but I think there's nothing like studying them when you're there. Much more enlightening.'

'Perhaps we shouldn't have come. If we are going to dislike all these things so much.'

'It's hard to take umbrage on a salary like yours.'

'I expect we'll survive it,' Andrew said. 'We'll have leave in the summer. We can start planning it.' He broke off. 'Oh, look at that cockroach. There were five in the shower when I got up this morning. There were three in there just now. Where the hell do they come from? Where's the spray?'

Swearing to himself, he padded out in his bare feet. Frances slid off the bed, rubbed her eyes, straightened the cover. She looked at Andrew's discarded shirt on the floor, picked it up, and dropped it in the basket.

Ten o'clock. Like someone testing the water, Frances stepped out through the glass sliding doors, and stood on the paving stones in the shadow of the wall. I'm going to come to grips with this place, she thought. The heat of the sun struck her lifted face. Satisfied, she turned, stepped inside again, and drew the door behind her.

Five minutes later she went out of the front door. She wore her baggiest smock, flat sandals. She held up a bunch of keys, peered at them in the light of the hallway. First the door of Flat 1. Then the main door. Then the iron gate. Perhaps I shall never get back in, she thought.

She was alone, out in the street. The stray cats fled away. A dark-faced boy in a car blew his horn at her. He cruised along the street. He put down his window. 'Madam, I love you,' he called. 'I want to fuck you.'

She walked on to the corner of the block. Every few yards it was necessary to step down from the eighteen-inch kerb and into the gutter; the municipality had planted saplings, etiolated and ill-doing plants inside concrete rectangles, and it did not seem to have occurred to anyone that the saplings would block the pavements, and that pavements are for walking on. But clearly they are not for walking on, she

74

thought. Men drive cars; women stay at home. Pavements are a buffer zone, to prevent the cars from running into the buildings.

By the time she reached the street corner she realized that it was far hotter than she had thought. The air felt wet, full of the clinging unsavoury fragrance of the sea. A trickle of sweat ran between her shoulder blades and down the backs of her legs. On her right stood a row of half-built shops, wires snaking from the brickwork. She stuck close to the wall; she had reached a main road. The dark fronds of shrubs spiked the air over the central reservation. A hot-dog van trundled past. A skip full of builder's rubble forced her into the road again. From out of the dazzling sunlight, moving slowly towards her, came two fellow pedestrians, two women in long zigzagged gowns, in African headcloths of vivid stripes; their blue-black flesh rolled towards her, and she saw their large spread feet, pale grey with dust, planted on the hot concrete. Smiling dazedly, hardly seeming to know that she was there, they parted to let her slip between them. Yasmin had told her of the West African hajjis, the pilgrims on their way to Mecca, who dropped their garments on to the shingle of the Corniche and ran naked into the waves. These women had stayed on, washed up in the city. They left behind them the scent of their passage; onions, the hot pepper smell of their skin and hair.

Frances turned back into the smaller streets, between apartment blocks, to cut back on herself. Over to her right, cranes and derricks split the sky. On her left a wall had been built, enclosing nothing; a gate gave access to nothing but a tract of muddy churned-up ground and some stagnant pools.

She stopped for a moment, unsure of where she was. Her sense of direction had almost never failed her. She steadied herself, her hand against a burning wall. Her own block of flats was ahead of her, seeming to shimmer a little in the heat; in the two first-floor apartments the wooden blinds were drawn down securely over the balcony windows, and the building had a desolate, uninhabited air.

A man in a Mercedes truck slowed to a crawl beside her. 'I give you lift, madam?' She ignored him. Quickened her step. 'Tell me where you want to go, madam. Just jump right in.' He leaned across, as if to open the near door. Frances turned and stared into his face; her own face bony, white, suffused with a narrow European rage. The man laughed. He waved a hand, dismissively, as if he were knocking off a fly, and drove away.

Inside the hallway, Yasmin stood by her front door. Her face was agitated. 'Frances, Frances, Shams was looking out and saw you just now in the street. Where have you been?'

'I went for a walk.'

'Come in, come in.' With a flapping motion of her arm, Yasmin drew her inside. Her bracelets clanked together. 'Sit, please sit. I will fetch you a cold drink.'

Frances perched on the edge of one of the heavy brocade armchairs. She felt dirty. She took a tissue from a box and wiped her hands. Yasmin hurried back with a little silver tray: a glass of Pepsi-Cola, a dish of ice, a saucer of sliced limes. She produced a spindle-legged table from its nest, placed the tray at Frances's elbow. She hovered above her, speaking not out of curiosity, but in proprietorial wrath. 'What made you do it?'

'I just wanted to see how I would get on.'

'But it is so hot, Frances. And men will shout at you from cars.'

'Yes. I know that now.'

'I could have told you and saved you the trouble. Frances, could not your husband's company give you a driver?'

'I think Mrs Parsons, the boss's wife, has got a monopoly on them.'

'I can get drivers. Raji's office will send a car, if I call up, but I don't like to ask too often.' She pressed her hands together. 'Just tell me where you want to go. I will arrange it. But don't be walking the streets.'

'It was only round the block,' Frances murmured.

'We can go to Al Mokhtar if you want anything for sewing. We can go to Happy Family Bakery. We can make an evening tour to the souk, Raji would be so happy. Just tell me where.'

'The trouble is, I don't know where. How can I find out about the city? How can I meet people? Can I learn Arabic?'

'I can teach you a few phrases. It is enough.'

'But what if I want to study it?'

'You can get a teacher. I have a private teacher, but it is for classical Arabic, it wouldn't interest you. Or perhaps, I don't know, maybe there is a class somewhere. Don't think about this now, Frances. You have to get your household in order. You will be meeting your husband's colleagues and entertaining them. You will be busy, I think.'

Yasmin leaned forward, and brushed the back of her sticky hand with a long, opalescent fingernail. 'Listen, Frances, I remember when I first got in Jeddah. I had come from Karachi, you see, where my family were all around me. I have been to Britain, fifteen months in St John's Wood, you know, when Raji was working over that side. I am a modern woman, Frances. I have the British passport. I have not lived my life behind the veil. It is hard, I know.' She paused, to let Frances feel her sympathy; took her hand. 'Soon you will meet the colleagues' wives,' she said persuasively. 'They will send their cars and carry you away to drink coffee every morning. Perhaps, who knows, you can have a baby soon. The Bakhsh hospital has very well-known and excellent maternity care.'

'Yes, who knows,' Frances said. She stood up.

Yasmin smiled, archly. 'So no more wandering the roads? Promise me?'

Frances fitted the key into her front-door lock. Again Yasmin stood at the door, watching her across the hall. The taste of the sweet drink lingered in her mouth. She did not feel that she had conquered the street; but she did not feel, either, that the street had conquered her.

Later that day she asked Andrew, 'Would you describe me as a timid person?'

'Quite the reverse.'

'Good,' she said. She had not told him about her trip out. She was not sure why she had not told him. She had not done anything wrong, so why was she keeping it from him? They had been married for almost five years, and in that time they had never had any secrets at all.

The following evening Raji rang the doorbell. 'I'm off downtown,' he said. 'What's it to be?'

Raji: silver wing tips of hair, a wide white boyish grin; a dark expensive Western suit, gold rings; comfortably plump, gently mocking. 'Well, Miss Frances? What is your desire right now? Box of Medina dates? Some nice sticky baklava? Large gin and tonic?'

'We've already made one major foray tonight,' Frances said. 'We've been to Safeway for the greengrocery.'

'Ah, a Safeway Superstore is streets ahead for iceberg lettuces. Say those who know.'

'It's such a major occupation, shopping.'

'We have to keep the womenfolk happy.' Raji spied Andrew, appearing behind her. 'Hello, old boy,' he said, his tone much more serious.

'How's tricks, Raji?'

Raji shook his head, smiling, and made a plummeting motion with one hand. 'Oil is down,' he said. 'So our Minister's temper not the best. We will be getting a cut in our funding for the department if this goes on, those fellows at the Ministry of Finance are so tight. They are having one mighty royal sheep-grab in Riyadh tonight, so that the Princes can talk it all over. That is how I come to be on the loose.' He turned to Frances. 'You've met Samira, from upstairs?'

'Not yet. Yasmin promised –'

'Me neither. I've seen her flitting shape, mark you. Yasmin chats with her every day, but I've never seen her face, you

78

know, which I find somewhat bizarre. Abdul Nasr keeps her locked up, the old devil.'

'That's not unusual, is it?'

'No, but that is one very religious man.' Raji slapped his palms together. 'Nothing, then, for you good people?' Producing his car keys, he made for the front door. 'I'll get Yasmin to call you for dinner one night,' he said over his shoulder.

Abdul Nasr was a young devil, in fact. Frances saw him striding down the stairs a couple of mornings later, about ten o'clock, when she was on her way out with a bag of rubbish. He was a lean young man, with a delicate bronze skin and a heavy black moustache. He nodded to her; did not look her in the face.

'Eyes like coals,' she said later to Andrew. 'Now I've seen them. I thought they were a fiction.'

FRANCES SHORE'S DIARY: *28 Muharram*

Wrote a batch of letters home today, Clare, my mother, Andrew's lot. He never writes to them, they wouldn't know if he was dead or alive. Strange to think that by the real calendar it's nearly November and that people in England are boosting up their heating bills and settling into their winter dourness. It seems no cooler here, though it should be. Whenever you mention the heat the old residents say, 'There's worse to come.' They enjoy telling you that.

When I look back on this diary it seems to be all about money. At least, it's always there between the lines. Some of the writers in the newspapers take the line that Saudi Arabia has been spoiled by its wealth, that before the oil there was a golden age when everyone lived in tents and was simple and religious and kind to old people. I am suspicious of this, but certainly greed is not attractive in anybody, is it? I'm waiting to see what our humble wealth will do to me, and if I shall

79

grow nastier and harsher in character, bank draft by bank draft. Andrew is quite right when he says that we must stay here and stick it out and make some money. We've spent our lives on living, not accumulating, and now it's time to start trying to do both, and to grow up, and be far-sighted, and not spend time agonizing over ideals we might once have possessed. In other words, we must try to have the same concerns as other people.

Safar

I

The man on the plane – Fairfax's colleague – had been
quite wrong. There was a map of Jeddah. Andrew brought
it home. 'Now I can begin to make sense of it,' Frances
said.

She spread out the map on the dining-room table. Five
minutes later she looked up, disappointed. 'It's useless. It's
too old. The shape of the coastline is different now. This
road appears to end in the sea. And look where they've put
Jeddah Shops. They're five blocks out.' She traced the length
of Medina Road. 'How old would you say these flats are?'

'Five years.'

'On this map we're a vacant lot.'

'Sorry,' Andrew said. 'Only trying to help. Thought bad
maps were better than no maps.'

'That's not so.' She picked up her pen and wrote on the
map 'CARTOGRAPHY BY KAFKA'. 'We don't exist,' she
said.

Pollard called her on the new telephone. 'Daphne Parsons
will come for you with a driver on Tuesday morning,' he
said, 'and take you to the souk.'

'Oh, will she?'

'Ten o'clock.'

'Well . . . thank you for arranging that for me.' Though I
could hardly claim, she thought, that I was doing something

else. Everyone knows what my life is like; I'm at their disposal.

'That's okay,' Pollard said. 'Any time. Tumble-drier all right?'

'Yes.'

'Happy with it?'

'Yes.'

There was a pause. He said, 'Is there anything else you want?'

'Yes, let me see . . . how about some flock wallpaper for the bathroom? And a half-tester bed?'

'Joking, are you?' Pollard said. She got rid of him. Only later she realized, with a kind of sick shame that she knew was unwarranted, that he might have been making her a sexual proposition.

She reported the conversation to Andrew; not to make trouble, but so that she could have his opinion. 'He asked me if there was anything else I wanted.'

'He probably meant a new ironing-board,' Andrew said.

'Do you think so?'

'You're fussy about ironing-boards, aren't you?'

She trawled her memory for instances. Perhaps she had expressed an occasional opinion about them, over the last week or two. Hausfrau's conversation, now. She felt that a change must be coming over her, but that Andrew took the change for granted.

'Yasmin said that she would teach me to do some of their cooking,' she said.

'Oh good. I like curries.'

From eleven each morning the smell of Yasmin's cooking hung over the flats. Shams was useless in the kitchen, she complained, and there was a dinner party most nights, and soon Raji's mother would be coming from Islamabad to stay for weeks and weeks, and she'd be asking all her Jeddah friends around. Yasmin stood in the kitchen, barefoot, chopping and frying, frying and chopping, dicing and stirring, her face shiny, the smell of ghee and herbs impregnating her clothes; tasting, muttering, licking her lips and frowning into the pans. Frances stood in the kitchen doorway, Selim straddling her hip. The air of formality between them had abated; the guest need no longer be entertained. One busy morning, when twenty people were expected, Frances washed the best dinner service, thin white china with the sheen of a pearl and a single chaste gold line, and then she polished the heavy crystal glasses that Shams was not allowed to touch, and set them out on the table, ready for the mineral water and orange juice they would contain that evening. 'I've got nothing like this,' she said.

Yasmin said, 'I'm sure you have very fine china, at your home in England. I'm sure you have beautiful things.'

'No, honestly. I haven't got anything.'

Yasmin looked up momentarily from the pan she was stirring, where something bubbled gently, something venomously red.

'Did you not have wedding presents, you and Andrew?'

'No, not to speak of. We didn't really have that kind of wedding. We just had a couple of witnesses down at the D C's office, and then we went for a drink. We got married in a bit of a hurry.'

Yasmin's wooden spoon hovered in the air for a moment. 'I see. Well, I didn't know that, Frances, you didn't tell me.' She looked at her appraisingly. 'Not to worry, I think most people have had some miscarriages.'

'Oh no . . . not that sort of hurry.'

'I thought you meant . . .' Yasmin broke off, and sighed. 'You see, because of living in England, I know how some young girls act. But not you, I felt sure.'

'I was in Africa when I got married. I just meant, it was informal.'

'A pity for you. It is a big day in a young girl's life.'

'I daresay. I wasn't a young girl exactly.'

'You had . . . men friends? Before?'

'One or two.'

Yasmin wished to know more. She took a cucumber and a

83

sharp knife and began to dice it very finely on to a wooden board. 'When I was in St John's Wood . . .' she said.

'Yes?'

'They were going to pass a law that all young girls in England must not go out at night, except with their fiancés.'

'Oh, but Yasmin, they couldn't. We could never have such a law.' Frances shifted Selim's weight to her other hip. 'You look hot,' she said crossly, 'shall I get you a drink out of the fridge?'

'I will have Fanta,' Yasmin said. 'Yes, because you see, most girls in the UK have lost their virginity by the age of twelve.'

'That's rubbish. Who told you that?'

'You only have to read the newspapers. Naturally Parliament is concerned.'

'But you must have got it wrong. We don't have those sort of laws. We don't have laws to make people moral. We don't think that's what law is for.'

'You should try to make people more moral,' Yasmin said. She pushed back a long strand of her black hair, and leaned over the pans again. 'The West is so decadent, and such behaviour makes people unhappy. In the long run. I am telling you.'

'England's not like that. Not really.'

'But I have seen it.'

'Then it must be a funny place, St John's Wood, that's all I can say.'

Yasmin never raised her voice, never insisted; just ploughed her lonely furrow. Almost every day she would unveil some new, astonishing viewpoint. Shams was on her knees in the hall, working on the carpets with a brush and pan, on red hand-knotted rugs whose seamless geometry recalled the unfathomable nature and eternal vigilance of Allah himself. The kitchen filled with steam.

When she was back in Flat 1 Frances found she could not follow Yasmin's recipes. 'Oh, you just take a handful of this,' Yasmin would say, 'and take some of that –'

84

'How much?'

'Oh, just what you think you need . . .'

And to Frances' objections, and queries, she would say, 'It comes with practice. All English food,' she would say, 'is boiled. That is why it has no taste.' She would tap her spoon against the side of the pan, and exhale with theatrical weariness, and hold out her hands so that Frances could pass her a towel to wipe them; the artistry was over, Shams would clear up the mess. 'I will send you some of this, later,' she would say. 'Shams will bring you a dish of it across.'

Frances got Andrew to take her uptown, to the lending library run by the British community. 'I want to borrow some cookery books,' she said, 'and get it all straight in my mind. Listen, Andrew, why doesn't Yasmin distinguish . . . why doesn't Yasmin distinguish . . . between private morality and public order?'

'Because Islam doesn't,' he said, his voice toneless, his eyes on the moving traffic. 'This country is governed by the Sharia law, which is Allah's own sentiments as revealed to the Prophet Muhammed. In Islam there are no private vices.'

'So there is no difference between sins and crimes.'

'Not that I can see.'

'So if you commit a crime –'

'You appear before a religious court. This is a theocracy. God rules, OK? Frances, shut up now, I'm driving.'

KEEP YOUR EYES ON THE ROAD AND AVOID DISTRACTION, a notice warned. The city passed: Shesh Mahal Restaurant, Electric Laundry, Wheels Balanced Here; a sculpture, twenty-five feet high, made of blue metal tubes like organ pipes. Small children swarmed loose in the speeding cars, scrambling over the seats, pulling at the drivers' *ghutras*, while the women in charge of them sat like black pillars, their hands in their laps; in any given year, how many of these little mites must crash howling through the windscreen to death or mutilation? 'Haven't they heard of seatbelts?' Frances inquired.

'Bit of a dodgy concept,' Andrew said. 'Allah has appointed a term to every life.'

'Who tells you this stuff?'

'Oh, guys at work.'

It was sunset; oily colours mingled in the sky. An aeroplane hung low over Prince Abdullah Street, unmoving, its roar drowned out by the usual noises of the city. On their left was a private villa built to resemble one of the minor Loire châteaux. On their right was a big expatriate housing compound, where the apartments looked like packing cases, stacked one on top of the other. YOU ARE FAST, said a sign, BUT DANGER IS FASTER. Another sculpture; a human fist.

At the British Community Library there were several excellent cookery books. They enrolled, and were given tickets. It all seemed so normal; there was a lady volunteer behind the desk, who wore a nice white blouse with a tie neck, and behaved as if she were in Tunbridge Wells. There was a notice-board, giving details of forthcoming concerts, and offering cars and hi-fi sets for sale. 'So many people are going home,' the nice lady said, 'you've come in at the end of things really. We've done seven years, it's passed in a flash. Well, yes, I'd say I've got a lot out of it really, I don't think it's right to moan all the time. We've learned scuba-diving, it's great fun, there are clubs if you're interested.' And 'Poor you,' she said, 'stuck in a block of flats without any European neighbours, no, I really don't envy you.'

It took them the best part of an hour to get home through the traffic. 'Do we need any shopping?' Andrew asked. 'Everywhere's open till ten o'clock.'

'No. I'm sick of shopping. Yasmin is sending us some food tonight. Would you like to be here for seven years?'

'No. But think of the money they must have stashed away.'

'Do you think they've suffered for it?'

'Not really. It depends what you want out of life. I can't think of anywhere better . . . for scuba diving.'

They pulled up in front of the flats. 'Well, there you are,' Andrew said. 'Dunroamin.'

'Yes, what a good name for it. Perhaps we could get one of those pokerwork signs made, and hang it on the gate.'

They went inside. 'I've got work,' Andrew said. He wandered off. Frances sat down at the desk in the living-room where she wrote her diary. She read the information sheet the library woman had given her, with its regulations and list of opening times. There was only one indication that life in Saudi had its tiny upsets. 'PLEASE,' begged the hand-out, 'make EVERY effort to return your books if you have to leave the Kingdom hurriedly and unexpectedly.'

The doorbell rang; there was Shams on the threshold, her face stretched in the grim ghost of a smile, an oval stainless-steel platter resting across her forearms. Legs and wings of chicken protruded from a great bed of rice. 'Thank you, Shams.'

Shams stepped back a pace. From beneath her arm, like a conjuror, she produced a length of black cloth. 'From Madam,' she said. 'For the souk. Tomorrow.'

Balancing the dish on one arm, Frances put out her other hand, hesitantly. 'A veil? She's telling me I need a veil?'

'For the head only,' Shams said, in her gloomy mutter. 'Leave open the face.'

'Damn right,' Frances said. She thrust the cloth back at Shams. Shams backed off another pace, and put her hands behind her back. The ghost of a smile had quite vanished. She rested her eyes on the dusty hall floor; thinking, perhaps, I shall have to clean this soon.

Frances closed the door on her. She carried the dish into the kitchen. Then she made for the bathroom, the cloth trailing from her hand. One edge of it had soaked up some of the fiery sauce which smothered the chicken. She turned on the bathroom light. On the floor, a party of ants, like pallbearers, were carrying a dead upturned cockroach. The cockroach influx had not been temporary; it was part of Jeddah life, she was told, a squalid corrective to luxury. She stepped over the funeral procession, which was making for the back of the bidet. Looking at herself in the mirror, she held up the material and draped it over her head. Outlined in black, she looked pale and tired. She pulled the folds down over her face. Now, together with the smell of pine disinfectant, she inhaled a faint odour of mothball. The outlines of the bathroom furniture were fuzzy; only the cold tiles under her hands told her that the world was solid and sharp.

She reached for the door handle, fumbled down the hall. 'Hi, Andrew. I'm a headless monster.'

Andrew had plans spread out all over the desk and the big table. He looked up. 'Where did you get that?'

'Yasmin sent it with the curry. She sent Shams to do the dirty work. She thinks I need it for the souk. She's propagandizing me. Trying to make me into a good Eastern wife.'

'Take it off. I don't like it.'

She spoke from beneath the layers. 'This morning she told me that the Saudis didn't mind seeing women's legs, it's their arms they mind. She said, since she is a Muslim, but she's not a Saudi, she doesn't feel she need cover her face, just her head, and her arms, and her legs. I can't work it out, can you?'

'Please take it off. It's sinister.'

She swept the veil off, and stood smiling at him. 'You've got something on your forehead,' he said, 'something red, what is it?'

It was very quiet in the flat; just the hum and rattle of the air-conditioners. She went back into the bathroom to wash away the red sauce. Perhaps Jeddah life is making me slightly deranged, she thought. It was strange how sound carried down the well at the centre of the building, echoing around the plumbing and the sanitary fittings of Dunroamin. Quite distinctly, she could hear, from the floor above, the sound of a woman sobbing.

Tuesday. Mrs Parsons's driver parked in Ghazzah Street

and blew his horn for Frances to come down. She picked up her bag from a chair in the hall, took the house keys in her hand. Andrew had locked her in again. You're always asleep when I leave, he said, or half-asleep, what else can I do? She turned the key to let herself out of the apartment – it was stiff, a poor fit – and found she had turned it the wrong way, and double-locked the door. She fumbled, felt her face flush, dropped the keys. How incompetent I am becoming, she thought, about even quite ordinary things.

She found the front-door key again, and again fitted it into the lock; she felt an irrational urge to hammer on the door, shout to whoever was listening, in the outside world, to come and spring her, get her out. The door opened. She stepped into the hall, closed the door, locked it behind her; double-locked it again, without meaning to. A long blast of the horn came from the street: Daphne and her driver, wondering where she was.

She looked over her shoulder, up the stairs. So far she had not even had a glimpse of Samira; though she had heard her, perhaps, last night. She glanced across at the closed front door of Flat 2. Was Yasmin standing behind it, her luminous long-tailed eye applied to the spy-hole? I shall get you one of those spy-holes, Andrew had said, and she had snapped at him, I'm not a child; if someone comes to the door I shall answer it, what do you think this is, Manhattan?

Now her sandals slapped against the hard marble floor. She wrenched open the heavy front door. It swung behind her on its stiff hinge, firmly ushering her out. Then the paving-stones, two paces, rank air, the gate in the wall; she drew back the metal bolts, swung it open, clattered it shut behind her. She chose another key. Wrong one. Another. Wrong one. She could feel the driver's eyes on her back, and a blush spreading upwards from her throat. When would she learn these keys? Locking in Yasmin, and Samira, and their children and maids; Parsons had told her to do it, told her she must remember, or her neighbours would be annoyed. Finally she dropped the bunch of keys into her handbag. Mrs Parsons was waiting in the back seat of her car, and she smiled as she leaned over and flicked the door handle for Frances to get in beside her.

'Always in the back when you're with a driver,' she said. 'Give the door a good slam, dear. I was just going to come after you. Weren't you ready?'

'Yes,' Frances said, 'I've been ready for an hour. But there are a lot of doors to lock and unlock.'

'Funny old block,' Mrs Parsons said. 'Very Saudi.' She leaned forward and said distinctly, 'Hasan, we want Queen's Building, you understand me, Queen's Building.'

'Yes, madam,' Hasan said.

'Because we don't want some other souk,' Mrs Parsons said, 'we want the main souk.' Her pale eyes slid to Frances. 'So how are you finding it?' she inquired.

Frances hesitated. Already she felt uncomfortable, her dress sticking to her under the arms. It would cool down towards Christmas, people said. She reached into her bag, checking that the keys were still there, not dropped in the gutter or down the car seat. She considered Mrs Parsons's question. 'It's . . . stultifying,' she said at last.

Mrs Parsons made no answer to this; or no immediate answer. Frances felt she knew her already, from a former phase of life: a sagging, soft-fleshed woman, with flushed weathered skin, a Home Counties voice. She wore a flowing kaftan with a batik pattern, and her freckled arms were encircled by heavy antique bracelets of traditional design; around her neck on a long chain she wore another beaten silver ornament, which bore an unfortunate resemblance to a gym-mistress's whistle. Her manner was benignly poisonous.

'I hope I'm properly dressed,' Frances said.

'You ought to get some kaftans really. Especially for the souk, you know, and for when you're out without your husband. The shop people won't serve you, if they don't think you're properly covered up.' Mrs Parsons looked her over. 'You don't want to be pestered, do you? You've got that fairish hair, you see, fair hair's always an attraction to them.'

'I thought I'd be all right if I covered my arms.'

'Well, of course, there aren't any hard and fast rules.' Mrs Parsons passed a hand over her own bare forearm. 'It isn't arms they mind, I understand, it's legs. Or if you want to just go out in your ordinary clothes, what you should do is get an *abaya*, you know, those black cloak things the Saudi ladies wear, and then you can just fling it on over everything.'

'Yes, but I'm not going to do that,' Frances said. She was silent for a moment. She had seen European women with the black wraps shrugged on for half-concealment; they trailed and flapped, and slid off the shoulders, like a student's or a barrister's gown; as they stood at the supermarket checkouts the women twitched at them whenever they had a hand free. These women looked absurd, she thought, as if they had stopped off for some groceries on their way to a degree ceremony. 'They're just dressing up,' she said. 'It's an affectation.'

'Oh, well,' Mrs Parsons said. 'They're only trying to keep out of trouble.'

'It's selling out.'

'You'll have to talk it over with your neighbours. Have you met your neighbours yet?'

'We've met the Pakistani couple, on the ground floor.'

'Yes, I thought old Raji's wife would be asking you over for a cup of tea.' She gave a little knowing laugh. 'Raji knows all the expats. Doesn't mix though. Oh no. Can't, in his position.'

'What exactly is his position?'

'He's very close to Amir, Eric tells me. That's the Minister, Amir. Does all his wheeling and dealing on the stockmarket. He's always jetting off to London or Tokyo. They have private fortunes, you know, these people, that they keep outside the Kingdom.' Again the laugh, without humour. 'Knows a lot, does old Raji. Met the Arab girl?'

'No.'

'I don't know her,' Mrs Parsons said, as if that settled the matter. 'I don't know her at all.'

They had left behind the narrow streets around Dunroamin; the driver put his foot down. They shot through a red light. 'Third one this morning,' Mrs Parsons muttered. 'Can't you slow down, Hasan?'

Frances looked out of the window. The sheer face of a twenty-storey bank building rose on their right. A National Guardsman in camouflage gear lounged in the gateway of a white-walled palace. He held a rifle; the wind, blowing in from the desert, whipped his red and white *ghutra* before his face. Mrs Parsons half-turned in her seat. 'Are you hoping to get a job?'

'I didn't think one could.'

'Oh, there are ways around it. There are sometimes office jobs. Secretarial work.'

'I'm not a secretary.'

'No, well, you seem a smart enough little girl, you'd pick it up. You can answer the telephone, I suppose?'

They screeched to a halt. Hasan had stabbed his foot on the brake; they were flung forward against the front seat. Mrs Parsons's bracelets clashed together loudly. 'Damn these women,' she said.

In front of them, a collection of black-veiled shapes had drifted into the road. They hovered for a moment, in the middle of the great highway, looking with their blind muffled faces into the car; then slowly, they began to bob across to the opposite kerb.

'There you are,' Mrs Parsons said sourly, as she rearranged herself in her seat and readjusted her jewellery. 'That's one of the few advantages of being female in this part of the world. They know that drivers will pull up for them.'

'Where are they going? Where have they come from?'

Mrs Parsons gestured around her. 'There are these little poor communities all along this road. It's surprising where

92

people live, in the middle of everything. They'll be Yemenis, or something, like Hasan there.'

Between the palaces of commerce, small lock-up shops flourished, little metal boxes, metal shacks, selling cheap clothing and flat bread. Even under the glacial slopes of the Hyatt Regency Hotel, men lounged in the greasy doorways of cheap cafés, their eyes on the moving traffic. Frances felt an impulse of frustration. She put her hand, momentarily, against the glass of the window. Mrs Parsons looked out at Jeddah, moving past them. 'It's called the Bride of the Red Sea,' she said. 'You'll find.'

A broken-down butcher's shop went by, the windows draped with grey intestines. A *thobe* maker displayed bale after bale of identical white cloth. Then Sleep-hi Mattresses, and Red Sea Video, and The Pearl of the Orient Cafeteria. 'Would the drivers stop for me?' Frances asked.

'I don't know. It might depend how you were dressed.'

These are such major preoccupations, Frances thought, nearly all-consuming preoccupations: the dress rules, the accident rate.

'Of course, they're not safety-conscious,' said Mrs Parsons. 'You know the worst thing? When there's an accident, no one wants to get involved, because of the police, and the blood-money system. If you stop you're a witness, and you might be held in gaol. And if you give somebody first-aid, you might be accused of making their injuries worse. Suppose you move someone, and they die? You might have to pay the blood-money yourself.'

'But that's ridiculous.'

'So the injured just lie there. If something else comes along and hits them – oh, my dear girl, don't look so alarmed. Everyone has accidents in Jeddah, but it's mainly just a shunt and a scrape for us expats. It's the Saudis that cause the havoc, all these twelve-year-olds in their sports cars, and all the Koreans and the Filipinos in those old wrecks they drive.'

'I wonder what the chances are, of getting out in one piece?'

'Oh, quite good, really. It's on the freeways that you have to watch yourself. It's not the roads in town that are dangerous. It's the roads out.'

Frances thought, I do not like the tenor of her conversation, I do not like the tone of it, and yet I should listen to what she says, because it is probably true. When she had first gone to Africa, she had expressed discomfiture, to an old resident, at the state of the servants' quarters of her bungalow. 'Wait till you see how they live in the villages,' the woman had said. Her tone had implied, they want nothing better. Frances hadn't liked her tone; but the woman had been right. Her houseboy had considered himself in luxurious circumstances, with his concrete-floored shower, and single whitewashed room. He put up pictures and curtains, and invited friends around. The burden of guilt had eased a little; had been easing, ever since.

'About this job,' she said. 'I thought women weren't allowed to have jobs that brought them into contact with men?'

'Not legally,' Daphne said. 'It's become more difficult now, but a little while ago you got a lot of British and American girls working in offices. The police would raid them every so often.'

'What, typist raids? Like drug raids?'

'The firm would just get a car to the back door and slip the girls out and they'd have to stay away for a few weeks. But then as I say, it's not so easy now, several companies got heavy fines, and nobody nowadays feels their position in the Kingdom is too secure.'

'What do they do now for typists?'

'Oh, they get Pakistanis in.' Mrs Parsons spoke as if she had said, they use robots, they've trained some apes. 'I could probably put out feelers,' she said. 'Eric knows a lot of people.'

Frances turned her face away, tilting up her chin a little. The shops crawled by: Prestige Autos, Modern Fashion, Elegant Man. Two elderly men in turbans sat on the sidewalk deep in conversation, crouched in the scant shade of a sapling, their flip-flops inches from the passing cars.

'There's not much to office work,' Mrs Parsons said. 'Did you work before?'

'I'm a cartographer.'

'How unusual.' Mrs Parsons thought for a moment. 'Nursery teachers are always in demand,' she said. 'You could have started a pre-school playgroup. Pity you weren't a nursery teacher.'

'I'm sure I would have been,' Frances said, 'if I'd thought of the advantages.'

Around the souk area the traffic slowed almost to a standstill. The driver put them down on the pavement outside a hotel. Mrs Parsons leaned through the window and spoke a few words of Arabic into the driver's face. 'An hour will be enough,' she said, over her shoulder to Frances. 'It's too hot for more than that.' She jerked her head back to Hasan, and as if doubting the power of her Arabic to do the job, she spat out the words 'One hour, one', and she jerked up a forefinger under Hasan's nose, as if she were an umpire giving him out.

Hasan drove away. Frances looked around her. 'Gabel Street,' Mrs Parsons said, indicating with her head that they should make a dive through the traffic and enter a narrow street on the far side. She took Frances by the elbow. With her free hand Frances wiped her hair from her forehead, feeling it sticky and damp. 'How do you find the heat?' Daphne inquired, above the rumble of the traffic.

'It's the humidity I mind. It's different from where we lived before.'

'We were in Zambia for a couple of years. Of course, it's not what I call Africa.'

'Oh no?' They teetered on the kerb.

'Now,' Daphne said. They began to thread their way through the crawling cars. 'When I was first married, we were in Nigeria.' Frances stepped on to a traffic island. She saw Mrs Parsons's face, blotched and mottled already by the

95

heat. 'We had a lovely life. A lovely home. We had four gardeners.'

'Really?' They sallied out again, into the traffic.

'Then we were in Malaya.' A long black Pontiac braked to let them pass. Frances inclined her head in thanks, but the sun struck across the windscreen, hiding the driver's face from view. They had reached the far side.

'And how many gardeners did you have in Malaya?' Frances asked.

Now it was for Mrs Parsons to dislike her tone. But her mind was elsewhere; she wanted to get into the goldsmiths. The souk, Frances saw, was modern and paved, with streetlighting and the same metal-box shops she had seen uptown. But above and beyond the souk were the houses of old Jeddah, with their leaning faded pastel walls, their crumbling harem grilles, the wood bleached out by sunlight and neglect to the colour of ashes.

'What's up there?' Frances said. Her spirits rose. All the time she had known that there was something more than she was seeing. 'Can we go up there and look?'

'I don't think Eric would like me to do that,' Mrs Parsons said with dignity. They plunged into Gabel Street.

2

FRANCES SHORE'S DIARY: 7 *Safar*

You should come at night to get the flavour of it, Mrs Parsons said, and this is what people do, apparently, they get up parties to go to the souk. I have to say that at 11 a.m., anyway, it's disappointing. Mainly there are just rows and rows of the little metal shops, selling perfectly ordinary things – tea-sets, and shock-absorbers, and lurid lengths of fabric with gold and silver threads running through. I did buy a set of orange non-stick saucepans, which seemed very cheap. I wondered if I should haggle over them, but Daphne said, no dear, just pay the price. I was relieved.

The goldsmiths are quite spectacular. The shops look so poverty-stricken and dreary, compared to the new places uptown, and it's hard to take in the value – thousands of riyals, millions of riyals – of what's in their windows. They go by weight here, they don't regard workmanship, and they certainly don't regard taste. Mrs Parsons walked into one of these shacks and peered around, nobody taking very much notice of her – as she said, they know that Europeans aren't going to buy, or not much more than a trinket, but if you shuffled in there in a veil they'd spring to attention all right. She said to the man behind the counter, what is today's price? Just as if she were after salad tomatoes. From some fold of her flowing garments she produced a pocket calculator, converted grams to ounces, then got him to weigh her a few bracelets. After she had done some more sums she said to him, thank you, *sucran*, and walked out. Then we went into a couple of shops selling Indian clothes, and she tossed the stock about a bit and said, trashy stuff. No one tried to sell us anything particularly, except that one shopkeeper pulled out a cardboard box from under a counter, which seemed to have in it the kind of dresses that get left behind at jumble sales. He held one or two up and said, viscose very smart, 100 per cent polyester, madam you love it. It was obvious we didn't, and he wasn't very interested anyway – his heart wasn't in it. Mrs Parsons told me not to smile at people too much, they might run away with the wrong idea. The souk smells quite a lot, and this seems an affectation in it. There are drains and street cleaners, so why should it smell?

After we had walked about aimlessly for half an hour, I noticed a few tables and chairs set out in front of a doorway, and just inside there was a very ancient decrepit man tending one of those rotating plastic bubbles of orange juice, the kind you get in British Home Stores cafeterias. Can we get a drink? I said.

Daphne said, I wonder, or is it men only? She said, it's not what you'd call a reliable café, I have got a drink here once or twice, but it depends if the religious police have been around lately. I said, what, you mean we can't sit down, because we're women, we can't have a drink? She looked around, and said better not risk it.

I was enraged, because I was so hot, and my non-stick pans were so heavy, and I was so tired of carrying them – perhaps I shouldn't have bought them, but every so often a woman must have a wild impulse, mustn't she? I said, my God, it's *exactly* like South Africa. Mrs Parsons smiled. She seemed pleased. Why, so it is, she said.

All the way home Mrs Parsons talked about something she called Entertaining. I gather that I am expected to give dinner parties. I am not quite sure how I am going to do this. In Africa people would come round and you would give them what you had by you, which was exactly what they had in their fridge at home. There was no place for one-upmanship, and spag. bog. was on the whole considered quite exotic. But I gather that spag. bog. will not do here.

Mrs Parsons goes to the British Wives' coffee morning at the Embassy on the first Monday of every month. They do handicrafts and good works and have lectures with slides about the wonders of the coral reef. She talked about this, and also about her Magimix, which she says is the Rolls-Royce of food-processors.

When I got home I took my box into the kitchen and unpacked it, and when I examined my pans closely and read the labels on the bottom, I found that they were not what I thought and not such a bargain after all, as the non-stick coating is made of something called Saudiflon. It was quite a blow. I lay on the bed for half an hour. I tried to compose some phrases about the souk which I could use in letters home. People talk so much about going to the souk that I feel I must be

missing something. Perhaps I am blinkered.
No doubt.

The architect who had designed the Ministry's new building had been given a commission to excel all the other strange and wonderful buildings of modern Jeddah. The building was to defy, for scale and cunning, the green giant of the Petroline building, and the Ministry of Labour's silver and chrome fantasy on Al Hamra Street. It was to exceed in strangeness, in denial of gravity, the flying tented roofs of the airport's Haj Terminal; it was to induce wonder and reverence, even greater awe than the pure white 3D triangle of the National Commercial Bank, which floats above Bagdadia lagoon.

The Ministerial HQ was to suggest to the beholder a miracle compound of all the elements, of earth, air, water and fire; as if to convey the mysterious grandeur of the Ministry's activities, the transcendent quality of its paper shuffling. It must be better than anything the West could do; but it must also be Islamic. Glorifying God was part of the brief.

In the architect's imagination, the Ministry's new building seemed lighter than the air around it; it was a shimmering iceberg, soaring above the hot pavements and the jungle of greenery that would root it to earth. At the time of Maghreb prayer, when the sun dipped into the ocean in a great flaring gaseous ball, its glass walls would melt and grow liquid. It would glow on the darkening skyline, a terror and a portent, a Koranic column of fire.

When this conception had to be put on paper, reduced to an artist's impression of colour and line, a more prosaic quality was sure to enter: still, the drawings in Andrew's paper folder were highly impressive. Tiny figures in *thobes* and *ghutras* rode the escalators, which looped smoothly behind the glass walls. Giant scarlet flowers bloomed in the foreground, a crystal fountain scored the summer air, and above all, a fluffy cloud sailed through a wash of cerulean blue.

When Frances went to see the building it was a humid, grey and overcast day. The air was laden with dust; it was a Friday, and the site was deserted. The project had reached that stage in the life of a building when it presents a picture less of construction than destruction; her first impression was of a bomb site. The brick looked raw; a confusion of pointless-looking wires snaked out of holes in walls. Some parts seemed almost finished; others were just foundations.

'You have to try to imagine what it will look like when we get the marble cladding,' Andrew said. 'It's supposed to be white, translucent, a sort of sheen, that's the idea, so that it looks less solid than it is. But I haven't seen the marble yet. I hope we don't end up with the kind that looks like old paint with brown cracks. The kind, you know, that they've got on the Bugshan Hospital.'

'Yes, I know.' Frances threaded her fingers into the mesh of the security fence. 'I may be wrong, but isn't there a lot more actual wall than in the artist's impression? It seemed to be made entirely of glass.'

'Mm.' Andrew frowned. 'There were certain im-practicalities in the basic design.' He cheered up. 'The mosque will be over there.'

'It's going to have its own mosque?'

'Oh yes. Every public building needs one. And there's going to be a heliport on top. At the centre will be a court-yard, with a fountain rising out of a base shaped like an incense burner. There are sixty-four fountains in Jeddah, and this will be the biggest. If you come here –'

Her loose sandals full of grit and dust, she skittered to-wards him over the clawed-up ground. He touched her shoulder lightly, turning her to see. 'If you look over there, that's going to be the Minister's private entrance.'

'Can't he go through an ordinary door?'

'No, he doesn't seem able to.'

'What about trees, are you having trees?'

'There are ten thousand flowering shrubs on order. They're going to be planted out along the street frontage, approximately where we're standing now. You don't know what a treat it is, to work without the penny-pinching you get everywhere else. This architect, he's an Egyptian, I did think at first that he'd got carried away, but they're prepared to back it, they'll put the resources in. You have this confidence, you see Fran, that when it's done it'll be absolutely right.'

'What about sculptures? Are you having sculptures?'

'Yes, there's a big one planned for the south side. It's a model of the solar system.'

'Working, is it?'

He squeezed her arm. 'It's going to be great. You'll see. The architects in Cairo have ordered this scale model, about table-top size – they're having it built specially in Los Angeles. I can't wait to have it, it should have been here before I came. Then, you see, I'll be able to get it over to people what it's going to look like.'

'I wish I could see it, when it comes. But I can't go to your office, can I?'

'I'll try to sneak you in, some weekend. During Friday prayers is the best time, when everybody's at the mosque.'

What a lot this building meant to him. She looked up into his face. 'It will be splendid. I'm sure.'

'Yes . . . but even so, I wish I'd been here a few years back, when it was really boom conditions. They're not building so much now, and not the space-age stuff, all those novel shapes. It's all so-called Islamic architecture now. There's no challenge in it, anybody can build some piffling little archways round a courtyard. Now this Egyptian, he's the right stuff; he's got all the little nods to the religious element, but he's got a sense of adventure as well.'

'Andrew –' she swivelled a glance over her shoulder, uneasy – 'there's a policeman across the road, he's staring at us.'

'Yes, better go, I suppose.' Andrew seemed unable to tear his eyes from the stacked-up pipes, the piles of builders' rubble.

'Do you know something, Fran – this will be the last of

the best. Now the oil price is coming down they won't build on this scale again. I should have come here years ago.'

He looked wistful as he said it, as if a golden age had passed. Construction sites were the pleasure gardens of his mind. As she picked her way over the ruts and gullies he put out a hand to help her, despite the policeman's presence. There was a great ditch between the site and the road. She teetered over it across a plank; Andrew followed.

FRANCES SHORE'S DIARY: *15 Safar*

The last of our air freight arrived today. There were things in the tea-chests I'd forgotten I'd packed. Those straw baskets we used to buy from boys on the streets, and those candlesticks from the pottery at Thamaga. And my soapstone tortoise, I'd missed him. I got him from a young boy who was selling them on the platform at Francistown station, when we were on our way to Victoria Falls. We went while the war was still on. The hotels were cheap. People on the sunset river cruise were getting shot out of the water.

Unpacking our stuff gave me a funny feeling. I was imagining myself when I packed the crates, thinking about the exciting future, which is now the dull present. I found places for the things around the flat. I imagined they'd make it seem more like home. But they didn't look right. They seemed to come from another life.

I have met a woman called Marion, who lives on Jeff Pollard's compound. She's the wife of one of the people at Mineral Resources, and they've got two little girls. They used to be in Zambia, so we have quite a lot to talk about, and I've found that I can actually walk round to her compound and get there before I expire from the heat or am accosted by kerb-crawlers more than a few times. There are twelve houses in the compound, which is where we would have been living if things had gone otherwise. I wonder what it would have been like to have Marion for a neighbour. But chance has made our life quite different.

The houses are all prefabs, quite big, but shabby. They were built to last five years, but they're now in their ninth. I'm sure that people at home think we lead glamorous lives here, bronzing ourselves by palm-fringed pools, and sipping 'illicit liquor', which always sounds more exciting than the normal kind, doesn't it? There are not quite so many cockroaches at Marion's place, but on the other hand their baths are held to the walls with sticky tape, and they have rats running about in their roofs.

Marion complains about the compound a lot, it's falling down and they can't get maintenance, etc., and they have distressing episodes with their drains, but she seems to be happy here in a way. She's been in Jeddah for two years and perhaps when we have been around that long I'll be used to it and see it in the same light. After all, she said yesterday, you can get anything you want in the shops. Now in Zambia there was no soap, we had no sugar for months, the eggs were always stale, we had to eat stringy chicken all the time and some weeks we had to live on spaghetti. So if somebody locked you in your local Sainsbury's, I asked her, would you be happy? She stared at me. She's an easy-going woman, too lethargic to be offended. It was meant to be a joke, but I think something is happening to my sense of humour.

The Brits here are all earning far more than they would anywhere else in the world. They talk about how their shares are doing, and about their next leave, which is usually going to be a round-the-world trip by air, taking in really boring places like Miami and Hong Kong, where they can spend their time in shopping malls, just in case they get homesick for Jeddah. Some people, though, are parsimonious. They stash away everything they can and treat their time here like a prison sentence, or a stint in an up-country field camp. They intend to stay on until they get a certain sum of money in the bank, but as they get towards their target, they decide they need more. They want to buy a house but house prices are rising so fast. They've put their children in boarding-school so that they could come abroad, but now the children are settled and it's unfair to take them away, so they've got to stay abroad to pay the fees. They've put Mother in a nursing-home because they weren't around to look after her and now she's got older and sicker and got ideas above her station. They always say, we'll just do another year. It's called the golden handcuffs.

No matter how much they complain about life here, they hate the thought of leaving. They see some gigantic insecurity staring them in the face, as if their lives would fall apart when they got their final exit visa, as if it would be instant ruin – as if it had to be straight from the Heathrow baggage hall and down to the DHSS. They just get too old to leave. They have to stay, if they're allowed – war, revolution, come what may. They don't know how to behave anywhere else.

The Americans are different. Usually they don't stay long. They don't know how to behave anywhere at all.

Marion's topic of conversation is her husband. Russel won't take her shopping. He doesn't think that's a man's job, bothering with groceries. His office sends her a car once a week, for a couple of hours, but she has to account for everything she spends, and he's not too keen on the idea of her shopping alone; she gets carried away, he says, and buys things like prawns. His idea is that they go out once a month and do everything, we've got a freezer, he says, so use it. But at the same time, he expects her to have everything on hand that he might want to eat. You're doing nothing else all day, he says, so why can't you organize the household? The other night he was going on, haven't we got any beetroot, why isn't there any beetroot?

Plus her Magimix has broken down.

When it gets a bit cooler, she says, we can sit outside and have coffee.

Men don't come very well out of this diary. On the other hand, women don't come very well out of it either. I said when I was writing before that the sexes live here in a state of deep mutual suspicion, but now I'm beginning to think it's more like a state of mutual terror. I wasn't sure before I came here if people were really executed for adultery. But since I've been here the *Saudi Gazette* has carried two or three reports of double executions. If you miss one, somebody will have cut it out, and will give you a photocopy. We're fascinated, we can't help it.

There was an execution in Mecca a little while ago. The woman of the house was having an affair with her driver. The husband got suspicious, and sacked him. The following night the woman let the driver into the house. Her husband was asleep. Her lover stabbed him to death. They put the body in a sack and tipped it down a well. Then they took off to Taif, posing as husband and wife. When they were caught they confessed. The man was publicly beheaded, for adultery and murder, and the woman was stoned to death for adultery.

I suppose there is no call to feel cultural superiority. The murder, anyway, is the same as crimes in the West. The punishment is not so different from what we have had until recently. But what chills my blood is the pious last paragraph that the newspaper tags on. 'While giving out details of the offence and punishment, the Interior Minister made it clear that the government would vigorously implement the Sharia laws to maintain the security of the land and to deter criminals . . . The executions were carried out after Friday prayers.'

I really must talk to Yasmin. When I read things like this it's beyond me how people like Marion can say, 'Oh, I don't mind it here really' – because you see, there are these nightmare occurrences. Probably I spend too much time on my own in the flat, reading the newspapers and trying to work things out. When Andrew came home yesterday he told me something very disturbing about the empty flat upstairs. I don't know if I should write it down. What if somebody gets hold of my diary, and reads it?

3

What she remembered now was the sound of sobbing she had heard, echoing through the bathroom pipes. She was not sure any longer which flat it had come from. Best to assume that it was Samira. Did people cry a lot, in arranged marriages? Marion's complaints nagged at her. People seemed to cry enough in the marriages they fixed up for themselves.

Perhaps Abdul Nasr had been exercising the right the Koran gave him to beat his wife. She saw him once more, mid-morning, striding out to his car. His sandals skidded over the marble, and the ends of his *ghutra* whiplashed out behind him. Yet Andrew said you never saw a Saudi in a hurry. She had time to notice only his frown, and the flash of his wristwatch. The contrast stuck in her mind – the clean Cartier lines, and the cloying odour of goatflesh which floated day after day down the stairs.

Frances had a headache. Perhaps, she thought, it was the effect of living with the air-conditioning; it couldn't be healthy, could it? Or perhaps it was the tension which was building up at the back of her neck.

She mentioned it to Andrew. 'What have you got to be tense about?' he asked. Then, 'Guess what, I've been paid. I'm going to the moneychanger's. Want to come?'

He would have to drive downtown to the bank first, and turn the Ministry's cheque into cash. Riyal notes are what work here – not personal cheques, not credit cards. He would extract a bundle of notes which would be their housekeeping money; and later they would subdivide it into smaller bundles, and stow it about the flat in cunning hiding-places.

Then he would need to take the cash that was left over, and exchange it for a sterling cheque. The moneychanger's sounded interesting: as if there might be a table in the open air, with people standing about in biblical attitudes. But it was just an ordinary office, in an ordinary street. She sat in the car, waiting for Andrew, watching the passers-by. Jeddah is a cosmopolitan city, it is said. All languages are heard, all colours of people mingle in the souks and squares. But they do not merge. Ghettos are formed, even on the pavement; garments are twitched aside. The stranger you see today will be stranger still tomorrow. People fall into their national stereotypes; you note the beef-red complexion, the kinked hair, the epicanthic fold.

She fiddled with the radio dial, trying to get some news from the World Service. It was the usual news when she found it, sliced through with a static crackle: bombs in Belfast, bombs in Beirut. But everything that concerned her seemed to be happening close to home. You see, she had said to Andrew, I was right; I did hear footsteps in the empty flat.

It was hot in the car; with the window open the dust blew in. A litter of ginger kittens ran like spiders up the side of a rubbish skip. Some larger cats, covered in scabs and scars, dragged a chicken carcass down the street. Old residents say that stray dogs used to be a menace, roaming in packs around the building sites. But they were rounded up by the municipality; and we hear no more of them.

Behind her sunglasses she could watch the Saudi men, and say to herself that if they returned her glance they would see a blank face, no expression, nothing more revealing than they would see if she were veiled. What an unflattering garment the *thobe* is, she thought. Before she came she imagined that they would wear flowing robes, not these stiff elongated white shirts. The late afternoon light shone through them. She saw spindly legs, and string vests.

But why should they dress like the cast of a nativity play, just to please her?

She looked at her watch. Go after him, why not? They have separate 'ladies' banks', but she has never heard of a ladies' moneychanger. Nobody seems to know exactly where women are allowed and where they are not. At least the South Africans put up notices: NIE BLANKES.

Once she was inside the moneychanger's, no one took the least notice of her. The place was crowded; she threaded her way through to Andrew and touched his arm. He jumped, and gave him a blank, dazed look, as if at first he hadn't recognized her. 'You're here,' he said.

It was down-at-heel: far from the pleasure-domes. As if this was where the serious business of the Kingdom was transacted, and comfort for once did not matter; the stuffing was coming out of the vinyl chairs. The customers shuffled from one disorderly queue to the next, thrusting banknotes at one grille, flourishing forms at the next; collecting signatures, amassing stamps, their eyes flickering constantly to the wall clock, to see if prayer time was imminent, and they were going to be locked in – locked in and left to mill and shout for thirty minutes, sweating, their clothes adhering to their backs and their earnings to their hands. Even the air-conditioning didn't seem to work properly. There were cheap carpet tiles on the floor, cigarette butts spilling out of ashtrays. Torn scraps of carbon paper lay where they fell.

The manager and his assistant sat behind their desks, in full view; the manager's desk had a black mirror surface on which the dust lay thick. His assistant's desk was metallic, less imposing, shorter by a foot and with fewer drawers; its dust lay even thicker. Sometimes the assistant, and after him the manager, would stretch out a careless hand, and sign with a flourish what the frantic queue pushed at them. But they seemed, on the whole, detached; like lords of the manor looking in at a villeins' feast. They grinned, talked on the telephone, scratched their chins. A contingent of Thai cleaning workers, still in their scarlet overalls, revolved from counter to counter in a fatigued minuet. An American, in a baseball cap and sneakers, waved his papers above his head; his eyes were bright, his belly swamped his belt. Three Brits, temporarily *hors de combat*, leaned against the wall. They were blue-chinned and balding, they sported sagging chain-store trousers, the polish had long worn from their shoes. They had an air of purposeful frailty, like Jarrow marchers. The hot burnt stench of money was in the air.

Andrew had no time to talk. He brushed her touch off his arm. Outside the traffic swarmed by, and the sun was setting over the sea. A little wooden cupboard disgorged yen, and thousands and thousands of Swiss francs. Two cheap suitcases stood casually under the stairs, as if for the use of more ambitious customers, and as Andrew, his face gleaming with aggression and sweat, signalled that they were finished, a rotund Arab descended the staircase, and picked them up; as he flexed his arms his cuff buttons strained, and his Rolex Oyster gleamed fatly. Outside, at the bottom of the steps, a vendor had spread out a tablecloth on the ground and was selling pocket calculators. Andrew took a deep breath of cooler air. The heat inside the office was increasing; the glass front doors were opaque with greasy smudges, the desperate palm prints of the patrons hurrying in.

'The pound's fallen,' Andrew said, as they climbed back into the car. 'Shall we go and get something for the headache?'

'Have you got one too?'

They were turning under the flyover by the Pepsi-Cola plant when the wail of the muezzin broke over the racetracks. The cars kept speeding; the Prophet said that travellers need not pray. 'Bugger,' Andrew said, hearing the prayer call. 'You always lose a half-hour somewhere.'

The night, now, in long purple swathes, in soft gradations of lemon and pink, hung over a vast car-park; a sky like ruffled silk. SANYO SANYO said a neon sign, beginning to wink. 'Why are Jeddah sunsets so beautiful?'

'It's all the dust in the air.'

'There's no wind today. It's not coming in from the desert.'

'No. It's from the cement works.'

'Andrew, what you told me . . . about the empty flat –'

He shifted uncomfortably in his seat. 'Don't go on about it, Fran.'

'I was wondering, how often . . .?'

'How should I know?' They sat in silence for a moment. The spaces around them began to fill up, as the end of prayers approached. Black shapes were disgorged from cars. Maids, and a few blonde nannies, clutched the hands of the small children. Little girls too young for the veil, with saucer eyes and beribboned topknots, wore sequined dresses with bouffant skirts, sewn over with scratchy lace. Charm bracelets clinked around their thin brown wrists; and sometimes a mother's *abaya* would drift a little, and you would see that she was draped and weighted with gold, with mayoral chains of it, from which hung gemstones the size and colour of boiled sweets.

'Just the average Saudi housewife, having a casual evening out,' Frances said. 'They look like . . . I can't think what they look like.'

'Prussian empresses . . . on coronation day.'

'The little girls look like a formation dancing team.'

'Women aren't allowed to dance.'

'I know, Yasmin told me that. Men dance. When they have a get-together.' She turned her head away, and caught sight of her face in the wing mirror; her obstinate mouth. 'Andrew, about the flat, the point is . . .'

'The one thing I have never understood,' Andrew said angrily, 'is this way you have, of suddenly developing concern about complete strangers.'

'Why? Don't you think I care about people, as a general rule?'

'I don't know. I don't know whether you do or not. But you're very down on people, aren't you? You take them apart.'

'Is that what I do?'

'You have your own ideas, about how people should live. And God help anybody who doesn't come up to your standards.'

'Oh well then, I'll stop.' She seemed spiritless, withdrawn; she licked her lips, dry from dust. 'I'll try just to have everyone else's ideas, shall I?'

'That might be better, for the while. And everybody's idea about the empty flat is that it's a bit of a joke. And none of our concern.'

'Okay,' she said meekly.

He squeezed her hand. 'Come on. Prayers must be over now.'

These monotonous marble halls again. The supermarkets are all well-stocked, but there is always some elusive item; this breeds the desire to go to more supermarkets. Shopping is the highest good in Saudi life. Every need and whim under one roof – Lebanese pastries, a Mont Blanc pen, a diamond snake with emerald eyes; a pound of pistachio nuts, two tickets to Bermuda, a nylon prayer rug with built-in compass. Perhaps some blueberry cheesecake ice-cream, and Louis Quinze *fauteuil*; a new Toyota, and a portrait of the King. The car-parks consume acres, the facades glitter like knives. Glass-fronted lifts whisk the shoppers from floor to floor; groves of dark green plants drip costly moisture, and dusky armies, with a slave-like motion, polish the marble at your feet.

They made for the pharmacy. There was a young Indian behind the counter. 'Could I have a bottle of paracetamol?' Frances said.

The man looked down at the glass-topped counter. He heard. His face, impassive, was dimly reflected; his black moustache, his melancholy eyes. 'Or aspirin? Something for a headache?'

She felt Andrew's presence behind her. The pharmacist looked up, over her left shoulder. 'Sir?' he said. 'Large bottle, sir, or small?'

They stood outside by a goldsmith's shop. 'Am I visible?' she asked.

'Perhaps too visible,' Andrew said. 'Shall we get some take-away pizza, and save you cooking?'

She seemed to have come to a dead halt – mulish, the bottle of pills in its blue plastic bag held between her hands.

'There's Marion,' Andrew said. 'Hi there, Marion.'

There was a small fountain, greenish water against mosaic tiles: THESE SEATS FOR FAMILY ONLY said a notice. Saudi youths occupied them, stick-thin, aquiline, blank-eyed, and watched Marion advance, puffing a little, pushing her shopping trolley, her thin Indian smock pulled tight across the bolster of her bosom.

'Hi,' Frances said. 'The man in the pharmacy's just ignored me. He gave me what I wanted but he pretended that Andrew had asked for it. As if I were a ventriloquist's doll.'

'Oh, well, yes.' Marion scraped her foot along the floor, as if in embarrassment; her baby-blue eyes were downcast. 'That's what they do.'

'They're afraid,' Andrew said. His voice seemed un-necessarily loud. 'They're afraid of looking at strange women. In case they're accused of something. Where's Russel?'

'He's at his field-camp. I'm with Jeff. He's buying a news-paper. Jeff's very good,' she said to Frances. Her soft, tone-less voice, if it had expression, would have been defensive. 'He takes me shopping. You know Russel never will.'

Frances too shuffled her feet; looked at her watch not too surreptitiously, to indicate, let's not wait around for Jeff.

'What have you been buying?' Marion asked.

'Headache pills.'

'Oh.' Marion sounded disappointed, as if she would have been just as happy to take part in someone else's spending. She indicated the pharmacy. 'Only they've got an offer on Chanel No. 5.'

They made for the nearest exit. The indoor streets were

kept icy cold; as they stepped outside, the door held open for them by an overalled Filipino, the hot air would drop over their heads like a blanket. A dozen TV sets, in the shop windows, showed Prince Sultan arriving at an airport; the screen flickered, the scene changed, and there Prince Abdullah was arriving at another. Between the bursts of commentary the national anthem played; it was a frisky, unmemorable tune. Before the Pierre Cardin boutique, turtles swam in gritty pools.

'Of course, you know what they do?' Andrew said.

'What who do?'

'The police – they seal this place off from time to time, wait until it's really crowded after night prayers, and then they block all the exits. They separate the men from the women and everybody has to show their identification. Then they match up the men with the women. And if the person you're shopping with isn't your wife or near relation – you're in trouble.'

They drove out of the car-park. 'What sort of trouble?'

'Deportation, for the expats. I don't know about the Saudis. Who knows what kind of trouble they have stored up for each other?'

It was slow to sink in. 'So Marion and Jeff...?'

'Are taking a risk.' He pulled up at a traffic light. 'But then, it's like drinking. Everybody does it. You have to take risks to live here at all.'

It often seemed to her now that it was only in the car they had their real conversations. She had become used to Andrew's profile, which gave so little away; to the interjection of a curse, as someone cut in on them; to conversations that died when his concentration switched elsewhere, as he executed a U-turn under one of the dark bridges. The simplest task – like posting a letter – seemed to mean an hour in a traffic jam; but what would she do if she were left at home? She had started reading novels, crime stories. Sometimes she was distracted when he came in, her eyes distant, her mind unravelling the complexities of the plot. What he was saying – about the building, about politics at the Turadup office – seemed to have nothing to do with her. She would rather have talked to Hercule Poirot, or Commander Adam Dalgleish.

'Look, Andrew,' she said, sitting up. 'Did you see that garden?'

He had turned off the main road, into a narrower, dimmer street; a gate stood open, a gate to a private villa, and for a second she glimpsed the house itself, ramshackle, with a tin roof. In front of the house there was a lawn; a moth-battered bulb, hanging from a wall on an iron bracket, cast a shivering light on to real grass. She wanted to catch at his arm and persuade him to turn the car around, so that she could see it again: a promise of greenness, turned to dappled monochrome by the onset of the night.

'Did you see? It must be the only lawn in Jeddah.'

'No, I missed it. I think the Embassies have lawns. You ought to go along to those wives' coffee mornings, if you're yearning for gardens.'

'Maybe. But they make you do handicrafts. You have to make Christmas crackers, for their bazaar.'

'And then there's that grass verge outside the airport, you know, where the Saudis go for picnics.'

'Yes, I remember it. They must spend millions of riyals on cultivating that grass verge. It gives a totally false impression of the country.'

They drove on in silence. She looked sideways at Andrew; a corner of the cheque he had got from the moneychanger protruded from the breast pocket of his shirt. He doesn't like anything here, she thought, he doesn't commend it, but he seems pleased with the way things are going. At the corner of Ahmed Lari Street she looked up automatically, to see if the laundryman was at work that night. But the curtains were drawn at the first-floor window, and the room behind was in darkness.

'Anyway,' Andrew said, as they pulled up outside Dunroamin, 'why don't you give it a go? Once you got down to it you'd probably be really good at making Christmas crackers.'

'I know,' she said. 'That's what I'm afraid of.'

Andrew let them in at the gate. He had an awesome proficiency with the locks and keys; she didn't go out enough to get the practice. Something scurried away, in the shadow of the wall.

'Was that a rat, do you think?' Andrew said. 'We have them on the site. We could put some poison down.' He unlocked the main door, with a scrape and a clank.

'The stray cats would eat it.'

'That would be no loss.'

The lights were on in the hall. There was a figure on the stairs, moving rapidly upwards; a woman, hunch-shouldered, her *abaya* flapping. She gathered up her skirt, taking the stairs two at a time, yet seeming to make no headway; a thin yellow calf trailed after her, a calloused heel in a flapping sandal. Andrew stopped in the open doorway, his arm stretched across it, as if to keep out the night. Frances ducked underneath. She put her own arm around him, her hand against his solid ribcage, and her head, as if she needed comfort, briefly against his shoulder. 'It's Abdul's maid,' she whispered. 'Come in. Close the door.'

It clanged behind them, and the woman stopped in her tracks, as if a pistol shot had been aimed at her back. She turned, for an instant, and showed a dark oval face, wet with tears, and a mouth stretched wide with panic or grief. Andrew called out after her. She vanished at the bend in the stairs. He stood with his lips pressed together then; to call out had been a natural reaction, which already he regretted.

'I don't know her name,' Frances said. 'I'm not even sure where she comes from. Yasmin thinks maybe Indonesia. She doesn't speak any English and only a few words of Arabic, so nobody knows much about her.'

'What do you think she's crying about?'

'I don't know.'

Andrew seemed upset. 'Let's have a drink,' he said, when they got inside the flat. 'The wine should be ready. I'll pour some off and see.'

He disappeared into the small second bathroom that they used for their home brewing. His voice carried to her in the kitchen, a muffled echo. 'It's a bit cloudy. But it's distinctly alcoholic.'

'Hush,' she said. If sound carried down from the bathrooms, sound must carry up. A few weeks earlier a warm odour of yeast had pervaded the flat; frowning, Yasmin had asked, 'What is that strange smell?'

Andrew met her in the hall, a brimming jug of red liquid in his hand. 'Get some glasses,' he said. 'I need this. Been a tough week. Do you know,' he followed her along the hall, 'it always says in the papers that foreign servants are an immoral influence.'

'Well, so they are. Yasmin says that the educated Saudi women are starting to want to go out to work, so the government's campaign against maids and nannies is a way of nipping that in the bud. Making sure they don't delegate stewing the goat.'

'But they used to have slaves,' Andrew said. 'They only abolished slavery in the sixties.'

'Yes, but I expect that was when they had to herd camels and make their own tents.'

'Yeah,' Andrew said. 'In the days when all the Arabs were happy and god-fearing, when every desert day was mini-paradise and there was no crime and no disease, before the wicked West came along and drilled for oil and gave them all that rotten rotten money.' He entered the living-room and threw himself into one of the many chairs. Even the experimental draught seemed to have gone to his head. He looked restless, reckless. A friend in Africa had once said, 'Whenever I see Andrew and he's had a drink, I can always tell. He reminds me of that expression, "a bull in a china shop".'

She handed him her glass.

The wine, poured out, was a soft raspberry red; a sediment was appearing at the bottom of the jug.

Yasmin said, 'You are looking pale.'

'Oh . . . I'm always pale.'

'Late nights?'

'Not really. We're usually in bed by eleven. Andrew gets up at six, he's out of the house by six-thirty.'

'Our guests don't disturb you, I hope? Leaving so late?' Yasmin sighed. It was becoming a habit with her. 'You think I'm a slave to the kitchen now, but wait till Raji's mother comes. Go through, Frances, sit down, I will make us some herb tea.'

Raji, like Abdul Nasr, never left for his office before mid-morning; but then he would work through the early evening, and entertain his guests into the small hours. Most of the guests were official ones, people to whom he was obliged; or people to whom he was extending patronage. Then there were nights when he would be entertained elsewhere: all-male occasions. 'We never sit down to dinner together,' Yasmin said. 'I envy you, Frances. Our life is not so simple.'

Frances trailed into the living-room and flopped into a brocade armchair. She knew that Yasmin did not envy her at all. She still felt weak and sick, the aftermath of their night's drinking. Andrew said that perhaps they would have to change their recipe. Maybe there were people around who brought a little more finesse to the business than Jeff Pollard.

'Yasmin,' she said, as her neighbour brought in the tray, 'I was reading this thing in the newspaper.'

'Oh yes?' Yasmin arranged the cups and saucers – a delicate clink of china, and the more decisive clink of her bracelets. Frances counted them: eight today. 'Frances, remind me, I have got for you a translation of the Holy Koran. Perhaps this will answer some of your questions. You must understand that the very language of the Holy

Koran is sacred, and so this Penguin Book is just a little lacking the nuances.'

'I'll bear that in mind.'

'Now,' she passed a cup, 'you wanted to ask me?'

'Well, I'm sorry to bring this up, I know it's only what ignorant Westerners are always asking, but —'

'Oh yes.' Yasmin nodded, almost brusque. 'I saw that dreadful case too. I thought it would be troubling you.'

'You're a mind reader.'

'Not really.' Yasmin smiled faintly. She too looked tired and pale. 'It's just that, as you say, all Westerners want to know the same thing. I remember even when I lived in St John's Wood, I was asked questions on this point.'

'You see, I've been trying not to be self-righteous about it, because we had capital punishment in England until quite recently.' Yasmin nodded. She raised her cup to her lips. 'But only for murder. The woman in Mecca wasn't accused of murder. Only of adultery.'

'Don't let the tea get cold,' Yasmin said. 'You see, Frances, although we may feel pity for someone, no one can reduce the punishments that Allah has laid down.'

'But if there was a case where no one was harmed, and there was no violence? Yasmin, surely these things must happen, sometimes, and people aren't found out?'

'I am sure they happen. When they come to light the punishment must be always the same, but it is much better if the need does not arise. The Prophet says that if you make some slip you should try to keep it secret, you see, so that it doesn't scandalize other people, and then you should try to do better in the future, and hope Allah will forgive you.'

'I see, so it's not a question of what you do, it's whether you're found out or not.'

'I think you are twisting my words just a little, Frances.'

'That's not real religion, is it? It's just law enforcement. Keeping people in a state of fear doesn't make them good people. You're just controlling their actions.'

'Surely controlling actions is enough,' Yasmin murmured.

'Who can look into the heart? Let me tell you, there are safeguards. There must be four male witnesses to the crime . . .'

'Male?'

'You cannot have the testimony of women, when it is a question of adultery.'

'Why not?'

'Think what women will do to each other! Think what they will say! Four witnesses, Frances, and they must have seen with their own eyes.'

'That can't happen very often.'

'This is what I am telling you.'

'And yet there are convictions?'

'There can be a confession, of course.'

'Ah, a confession.'

'It must be voluntary. The person must know what they are admitting. They must know the punishment.'

'Why should anyone confess then? Unless of course they were forced to?'

'You always think the worst, Frances.'

'It's a reasonable question.'

Yasmin dropped her eyes. 'Guilt. You know of guilt? Also, of course, if you take your punishment in this life you will not get it in the next.'

Frances took a sip of her herb tea. It had a bitter taste, which she couldn't place. 'What is it?'

'A family recipe.' Yasmin relaxed. 'My mother should be here to make it for you. My poor mother. She has been on one short visit since I was married, but she has the family, she is kept very much occupied. Raji's mother, of course, is a widow. He is always the favourite son.'

'I have the impression you don't get on.'

'In Pakistan it is unknown for the wife and the husband's mother to agree.' Yasmin made a minute rearrangement of the folds of her long skirt. 'Whatever I do for him can never be enough. And that is only the starting-point. That is the rule laid down before we begin.'

'You must stand up to her.'

Yasmin laughed shortly. 'I cannot. That is not our culture.'

'Why do you let your culture make you suffer? Can't you break out of it?'

'And besides, it is me, it is not just our culture, it is me, myself. Don't you see that? I am not married until twenty-nine, an old maid as you say. Oh, my family is good, the best – in origin we are Persian, Frances, did you know? But then again I am tall and have a long nose and have got myself over-educated. Let me tell you, the fight for Raji was long and expensive. And only then because his fiancée died . . . So you see, I am lucky to be a daughter-in-law at all.'

'I thought education was valued in Pakistan.'

'So it is, but then there are certain things which go along with education, as you know yourself, that if they reach the ears of young men make your value slip a little.'

'Like what?'

'Like asking questions,' Yasmin said. 'Like arguing. Like praying too much.'

'Do you pray too much?'

She shook her head, emphatically. 'No. It is just a perversion of the Prophet's real message to believe that women have a secondary kind of soul.' Frances put down her cup. 'Some more?' Yasmin said politely.

'No thanks.'

'It's nasty, but it's good for you. You will soon feel better.' She smiled.

In the hall, seeing her out, Yasmin picked up her *dupatta* and draped it over her head. 'My driver is coming,' she said. 'There is a big party tonight and I am going, so I must be taken to the bank to get my jewels out.'

'Oh, women will be there?'

'Yes. But of course we will have our own party. In our own room.'

Crossing the hall, Frances was angry with herself. Yasmin made her feel clumsy; yet she seemed to want to explain

things to her, and sometimes, in an obscure way, she seemed
to be asking for help. But what way could that be? Of course
she can't break out of her culture, Frances thought. No
more can I break out of mine. No more would I want to; no
more does she.

FRANCES SHORE'S DIARY: *24 Safar*

All right, so I will put down what Andrew told me
about the empty flat. I suppose I was being stupid and
paranoid last week. Who on earth would want to read
my diary?

Andrew was told by someone at Turadup that the
flat is kept empty for the use of the Deputy Minister's
brother. He is a married man, and meets a married
woman here. It seems it's a long-running affair.

Even Yasmin had to admit, it does go on. Even in
the Kingdom people aren't perfect. I don't suppose they
have much alternative to setting up an arrangement
like this. As Andrew says, they can't go to a hotel, can
they? I suppose they can meet each other outside the
Kingdom, but then even if they have their husband's
permission to go abroad, women here don't travel
without a retinue of relatives. Only it seems so risky.

I wonder if Yasmin knows? Or the people upstairs?
Is it just gossip at Turadup (because Turadup pays the
rent for the whole block) or is it gossip among the Saudi
men as well, down at the Ministry? Is it a thing that
happens so seldom that everybody's terrified? Or so
often that people just raise their eyebrows and giggle?

And where did they meet? How do a couple meet,
and strike up a relationship in the first place, if Saudi
social life is what people tell me? How do they get to
the stage of having an affair?

I asked Andrew all this and he said he didn't know.
He said that people at Turadup don't really talk about
it. You're told, but just so that you don't put your foot

in it. I said to him, is it true? He said, of course it's true, why would anybody want to make it up?

Then I wondered if my questions were naïve. You have to understand that there's a lot of hypocrisy, Andrew said. You mustn't believe the picture you get from the newspapers.

When Yasmin got home from the bank with her jewels she phoned me up. She quite often phones me, it's easier for her than getting dressed up to walk across the hall. She said there was something she'd forgotten to tell me. What is it? They don't actually stone the woman to death, she said. Not nowadays. They just throw a few stones, as a ritual, and then somebody shoots her.

This cheered me enormously. I had to bite my tongue to stop myself saying, oh well that's all right then, isn't it, very merciful. Yasmin probably wonders why I'm pursuing the topic with such energy. What if this couple made enemies? I try to imagine the four male witnesses, swaying about on ladders outside Dunroamin. But the blinds are always down in the empty flat. There's not even a chink you could peer through. You'd have to charge down the door. The more you think of it the more ludicrous it becomes.

But I wonder when they come here, at night or during the day? I wonder if they are in love? Perhaps one day I shall see a car draw up and the lady slip out, in her veil, and glide silently up the stairs. If I see her I shall press myself against the wall, as if I were a servant, and turn my face away. She has enough to worry her.

Rabi al-awal

❦

I

'Wait till the rain comes,' Samira said. 'Then you will see some shooting up. Even that old tree.'

At eleven in the morning, Samira's sitting-room had a twilit air; a heaviness in the atmosphere, a preponderance of fringes and beadings, gold tie-backs on the velvet curtains, and wallpaper of crimson flock. There was a scent of mothballs, spices, of lemon spray-polish, and the ineradicable smell of onions. A lamp in the shape of a clipper ship glowed dully on the sideboard. At one end, sofas were grouped about a glass coffee-table; at the other end, made insignificant by the dimensions of the room, stood a dining-table and twelve chairs in the ornate and gilded style known unkindly as Louis Farouk.

The large window, fronted by its balcony, looked on to the street; but the brown tree blocked the view, and made the room dark. Neither Yasmin nor Samira minded spending their days under artificial light, and it was often mid-morning before they would wind up the heavy slatted wooden blinds. And it was overcast today, the low sky seeming to press on the city's half-finished buildings. A chill damp blast from the air-conditioner stirred the pendant crystals of Samira's chandelier – which had been obtained, she said, as part of her marriage settlement, from Top Furniture of Palestine Road.

Frances shivered a little. 'Oh, you are becoming one of us,' Yasmin said. 'You feel the cold.'

Samira crossed the room and turned the air-conditioner to a lower setting. She asked, 'Would you like a shawl?'

'Thank you, I'm fine,' Frances said, with a formal courteous nod, and, vying with her in politeness, Samira said,

'It's no problem.'

'When will it rain?' Frances asked. 'It hasn't rained since I got here.'

'She misses her English weather,' Yasmin explained.

Samira looked doubtful. It seemed she would do everything she could to entertain her guest, but there were some things she could not guarantee. 'Oh, soon,' she said. And then, compelled to honesty, she added, 'There isn't any fixed season for it.'

'But when it does rain,' Yasmin said, 'I promise you it will rain hard.'

Frances sat on the edge of her armchair, her thin ankles wrapped tightly together, and even her voice sounding thin, constrained. It seemed impossible to relax; and the other two women looked wary, as if they thought a chance utterance might cause offence. Whereas really, Frances thought, it was much more likely that she would upset them. Every day she bridled at something, but she did not think of herself as the one offended. That was a step she had yet to take.

Samira went to the door, and spoke; and a moment later the maid hurried in, yellow face downcast, and handed Frances a shawl. 'There, much better,' Samira said, leaning forward to arrange it around Frances's shoulders. She gave her a brief, affectionate pat. Her child, Fat'ma, played on the floor with Selim. She was a sturdy infant, bigger than Selim though younger by some months; she wielded a plastic skittle which she used as a weapon, sometimes pounding the carpet, sometimes pounding the small curly-haired skull of Yasmin's child. Selim's cries of pain and protest were no more than squeaks, as if rigidly suppressed by a code of good manners. 'He must grow up hardy,' Yasmin said. 'He is a boy.'

'What's your maid's name?' Frances asked.

Samira told her. But she was no wiser. It sounded like 'Sarsaparilla'. But that was not possible. In answer to her questioning look, Samira merely shrugged. 'I did try to call her something simpler,' she said. 'But she won't answer to it.'

Sarsaparilla came in again, with a tray of coffee, and Samira stood up, took it from her, and put it on a side-table. Frances tried to catch the maid's eye; perhaps she might, just with a look, express her concern? But she failed. The girl slid out of the room, seeming to melt into the shadows of the heavy furniture, the gilt tassels, and out into the hallway with its bitter chemical tang of insecticides. 'Nescafé freeze-dried,' Samira said, with no little pride. 'Not Arabic coffee. No sugar?' She made a face. 'Frances, how can you?' She made another, more expressive face, for Yasmin's consumption.

Samira was a sallow, stockily built young woman, with a cascade of coarse dark hair that had something of an animal quality about it – as if it led a separate life from its owner, but on a lower plane. As she arranged the cups, it swung over her shoulder, crackling with static. She wore blue jeans, tight-fitting, very new and stiff, and a scarlet sweatshirt with a designer's monogram on the collar. On her left hand she wore a single carat solitaire diamond, in a surprisingly restrained setting; it blinked coldly in the grey light, like another eye.

'I was telling Frances,' Yasmin said, 'that your maid has left some children behind in Indonesia. That is why she goes about crying the whole time.'

'She's new, is she?' Frances asked.

Samira shrugged again. 'Not so new. I am training her. Not easy, as she doesn't speak any language. I just take her arm and I say, look you, do this. She is learning.'

'Well, she must speak some language,' Frances said.

'If she does nobody has found out what it is.'

'Does she come from Bandung?'

'No. Some country place.'

'She must have her own dialect.'

'Well, I don't know, I think she must,' Samira said. 'My friend has Indonesian maid, and she cannot speak to her.' She dropped three spoonfuls of brown sugar into her coffee, and stirred it thoughtfully. 'I expect maybe she is lonely.'

'Oh well,' Yasmin said. 'It is better if she doesn't have any contacts. At least she won't go bringing gangs of thieves to the house.'

'Are there gangs of thieves?' Frances said innocently. 'I didn't think there were any. It never mentions them in the newspapers.'

The two women exchanged a glance. It's funny, Frances thought, how two people think they can exchange glances without the third person noticing. 'It's not a problem,' Samira said. She sounded prim. But then she added, hotly, 'It is only in the West that they say, thieving Arabs. It is the Western media. Always they show us as thieving and ignorant and suffering from diseases.'

'Oh, I didn't mean . . .' Frances blushed faintly. 'Besides, they don't, you know. Not nowadays.'

'They are fair to the East?' Yasmin said. 'I don't think so.'

'But I'm sure people don't have those prejudices.'

'It is in the *Saudi Gazette*,' Samira insisted. 'Every day people are taken up in Marks & Spencer. They try to explain, no, no, I am not a thief, I am intending to pay for it, I am only taking it to that counter over there.' Her face lit, as she enacted the scene; her coffee cup trembled a little in its saucer. 'Perhaps they have never been in that country before. Perhaps their English is not so good. But no one listens to their pleas. They are thrown into gaol. And then they are asked huge sums of money, far more than what is the value of that original article.'

'That can't be right,' Frances said. She tried to keep her tone light. 'They couldn't arrest them, because you see, they'd have to be outside the shop –'

She stopped. Samira had set her jaw firmly. 'Many people who own shops in London,' she said, 'are Zionists.'

Frances nodded vaguely, not in assent, but because she was remembering what she had been told by the business-man on the plane. You have to cut the labels out of your underwear . . . too bloody secretive to have maps . . . nobody knows the half of what goes on. How long ago that seemed now; and yet this was only her third month on Ghazzah Street. Yasmin and Samira exchanged another glance, and this time, a slight smile.

'I have told Samira of your interest in the Sharia law. You must read the Holy Koran that I gave you. Then you will see how sensible it is.'

'I have been reading it,' Frances said.

'Of course, you do not get the full idea in translation.'

'You get enough.'

'And?' Samira said timidly. 'Yes?'

It was as if she had written it personally. Do be careful, Frances said to herself. Take care. 'It reminds me of the Bible.'

'Yes, quite so.' Yasmin leaned forward, took up the coffee-pot, and replenished her cup, as if she were at home. 'We have the Prophets, just the same, peace be upon them. We have Abraham. Moses. Adam and Eve. And Jesus.' She helped herself to sugar. 'We have Jesus.'

'It wasn't that so much,' Frances said. 'It was more the bits about gouging out people's eyes, and cutting off their hands and feet alternately, that sort of thing.' Her inner voice complained, this is not being careful.

'They give a what's the word,' said Samira, unexpectedly.

She looked up from where she was kneeling on the rug, prising her daughter's fingers from Selim's hair. The dark, frail little boy had his neck bent at a painful angle; he did not utter, and Yasmin regarded him, from her armchair, with a self-satisfied composure. 'An anaesthetic,' she supplied.

'Yes,' Samira said. 'That's it.'

'When they do an amputation,' Yasmin looked down at her own long hands, with their lacquered nails, 'there is a doctor in attendance. It doesn't go poisoned, they make sure of that. They don't let them bleed so much. Really, Frances, it isn't like you think.'

Frances felt a minute contraction in her throat, a tiny wash of nausea; as if something small had moved inside her, deep inside. They were quite new to her, these minute reactions between body and soul – the tension headaches, the tightness in the throat. Until now her body had been a quiet, efficient machine. She might say, 'It makes me sick, such a thing,' but until she came to Ghazzah Street, it had not really been true. She leaned forward, hiding her face, and put her coffee cup on the table.

'Some more?' Samira said. She gave a single, guttural yell, like a battle cry. It fetched Sarsaparilla. The maid stood in the doorway, her arms crossed over her bony chest. Frances kept her eyes on the floor. She examined the rug on which the children were playing. It was an antique rug, its chief colour a gentle, faded blue; it portrayed the Tree of Life, weighted with fruit.

'In America,' Yasmin said, when the tray had been taken away, 'every criminal hopes to be saved on the defence of insanity. If they are shoplifting, they just say Oh, I don't know what came over me. And if they have committed murder, they just say –'

'Oh, I don't know what came over me,' Samira put in helpfully. Yasmin nodded.

'They say, when I did this I was temporarily not in my right mind, but I am okay now, so you may let me go.'

'What do they say if –' Frances broke off.

'Yes? Go on?'

'No, it doesn't matter.'

'Do go on,' Yasmin invited. 'We are not offended.'

'But I'm afraid you are.'

'Oh no,' Samira said. 'We really are not, Frances. We like your questions.'

'How can we explain to you,' Yasmin said, 'if you don't ask?'

'Well, I just wondered, what you thought – I just wondered what you thought people in America say, when they have committed adultery?'

Yasmin and Samira smiled at each other. 'We don't know,' Samira said.

Yasmin said, 'Perhaps you are teasing us.'

'No, not really.' Sarsaparilla was back: another tray of coffee. She leaned over Frances, to lower the tray to the table, and almost brushed against her. The skin of her neck was creased and faded, like the skin of a much older woman. Samira spoke to her, a single word. The maid straightened up. And then she smiled; thinly, painfully, as if she had been told, very suddenly, to make herself pleasant. Frances caught the smell of her body, a thin odour, sharp and strange.

'I've been reading the religious column in the newspaper,' she said, as Samira leaned forward to refill her cup. 'Those questions and answers. Is it true that a man can divorce his wife by saying *I divorce you* three times?'

'That is a common misunderstanding,' Yasmin said gently.

'I thought it might be.'

'Really,' Samira said, 'he only has to say it once.'

There was a pause. 'Does this happen often?' Frances asked.

'Oh yes. But then very often they get remarried.'

'There is a waiting period,' Yasmin said. 'You must have read about this, yes? They wait three months, to see if the wife is pregnant, then if she is not, the divorce is valid, unless they decide they want to be married again, you see. They can go through this once, twice, three times, but then after the husband has got her divorced a third time, he can't marry her again.'

'Unless,' Samira said, 'she has been married to someone else in between.'

'Married to someone else, then divorced from someone else?'

'Yes, of course. Sometimes a man may fix for her to marry one of his friends, just in name only, then he can get her back.'

Frances sat, digesting this. 'There seems a great deal of — indecision,' she said. 'Who gets the children?'

'Oh, the father,' Samira said.

'And what if he doesn't want to marry her again, when the waiting period is over?'

'Then she must go back and live with her family.'

'And what if she wants to divorce him?'

'Well, that is possible,' Samira conceded.

'But,' Yasmin said with dignity, 'that is not what we do.'

Frances put down her coffee cup. There are a million questions, she thought. She looked at her watch. 'I'd better go,' she said. 'Thank you so much, Samira.'

'But no! Why do you have to go?'

'Well, I must . . . write a letter.'

'Frances keeps a diary,' Yasmin said teasingly.

'How do you know?'

'I have seen you put it away in a hurry. So it can only be a diary. Unless perhaps you have love letters?'

'I don't have love letters.'

'Perhaps you might,' Yasmin said. 'There are many bachelors in Jeddah. Also many Englishmen and Americans without their wife.'

'And,' Samira observed, 'you are quite pretty.'

'No, really.' Frances stood up. 'A diary, yes, but that's all.'

'Frances is in love with her husband,' Yasmin said. The two women laughed.

Samira took her to the door. Already a certain tension had left her face, the tension bred by talking to the outsider. She looked artless, very young. Once she had left, Frances knew, they would withdraw from the formal sitting-room, and into the smaller room, strewn with floor cushions, where Samira preferred to spend her mornings. She would gladly have joined them there; but she was a Westerner, and must sit on chairs.

'Will you come down to my flat?' she asked.

'Yes, I will come.'

'Your shawl –'

'No, keep it. Really you must. It suits you.'

'Oh, I can't.'

'It is my gift,' Samira said. She leaned forward and kissed Frances on the cheek.

Poor diary. If only it could have a change of scene! She is ashamed of its content, which she feels has become trivial and repetitious. She will write down her conversation with the women, knowing that upstairs, sprawled in comfort on the cushions, they are discussing her.

When she spent her first day alone in the flat, time moved in a slow, dreamlike way; now it moves at a normal speed. And yet she cannot think how she passes it. Reading; patrolling with the cockroach spray; cooking food for the freezer. Sometimes she walks to Marion's compound. The mornings have cooled slightly, and they sit outside the house. Marion sips Diet Pepsi; insects from miles around come specially to drown in her glass. Often the smell from the drains drives them indoors. And yet she is grateful for the outing. The compound has a small pool, fiercely chlorinated, and a few stunted trees. Perhaps, she thinks, when a house there comes free . . . But Marion says the compound families are always quarrelling.

Her letters home have already ceased to read like frontier dispatches, and now they are full of householder's complaints, and polite general inquiries: have you seen your sister lately, how is the cat? It is difficult to describe to people the kind of life they are living. And she does not describe their surroundings any more. She has almost ceased to notice them. If it were not for the empty flat, perhaps Frances would have stopped asking questions already. Curiosity is a transient phenomenon here. It is not that you learn everything; but you soon learn whatever you will be allowed to known. This is a private society, which does not publish its flaws, or disclose its reasoning, which replies to pressing inquirers with a floodtide of disinformation, and then reverts to its preferred silence. One door closes, and – while you are gathering your platitudes – another door slams shut.

2

FRANCES SHORE'S DIARY: *9 Rabi al-awal*

A few days ago I met Carla Zussman at the Sarawat supermarket. I last saw her in the audience at an amateur production of *The Crucible*, given in the Moth Hall, Gaborone. Hi there, Frances, she said. I asked, surprised to see me? Not really, she said. Still married? Yes, I said, and to the same man. You? Oh yes, she said, I'm here with Rickie, we're still a going concern.

So I persuaded Marion that we ought to take the bus and visit Carla. The buses are segregated, of course. Most of the bus is for men, but there is a small compartment at the back for women. There is a standard fare of one riyal, and a box to put it in, and this is why the women travel at the back, they can be trusted to pay up, whereas the men won't pay unless they're under the eye of the driver. We only had about ten minutes to wait, but we got very hot, even though the segregated bus shelter did shield us from the full glare of the sun. Bus shelters are a big advance here, they have only just got them, and they write about them in the newspapers as if they were moonshots or something. Although we were very respectably dressed, people still stared at us, and shouted from cars, so we were glad when the bus came.

We went along fairly confidently, being the only female passengers. I told Marion, just look out for the American Embassy compound, we can't miss it. As soon as we saw the Stars and Stripes fluttering between the construction sites, we leapt up and pressed the bell, but it didn't work. The front compartment was nearly empty too, so I banged on the glass panel, trying to attract the driver's attention, and shouted *Hinna! Hinna!* I was afraid to get involved in anything more complicated. But he didn't hear me. Two Yemenis in the front compartment turned round and looked at us. I pointed to the driver, but all they did was stare. I wouldn't have minded if they'd grinned, I wouldn't have minded if they'd laughed at us, because everybody laughs at them. I thought, somebody might as well have some pleasure out of this excursion. But they just went on staring. They didn't seem to have any initiative.

A few minutes later, Top Furniture went past, where Samira got her chandelier, and then we were on the Corniche. I persuaded Marion to get out, on the grounds that we knew where we were, and if we stayed on the bus any longer this might not be the case. There was hardly anyone around, just us, a few seagulls, and those strange non-human shapes, metal and stone objects on which the Mayor has spent so much – but it's his town. We sat down on one of the sculptures. It was white marble, and the sea was a hard blue, and I felt so good at being out of the house that I could have stayed there for ever. Marion got fretful, and the sun was burning. I would have liked to run down over the smooth brown rocks and into the waves. What a good thing I am not that sort of person. Another bus came along, and we got on it.

We thought, with luck, that we might find ourselves back near the Embassy, but we were not lucky that day, and Marion was getting more and more upset. The terminus is the place to be, I said, and then we can start again; but it would be too late to go to Carla's, the best we could do would be to get ourselves home. Think of it as an adventure, I said to Marion, but she said Russel wouldn't see it that way. Don't tell him, I said unfeelingly, and she looked at me in terror. I remembered the days, not very long ago, when I told Andrew everything too.

The bus got snarled up in the downtown traffic, and we ended up at the Queen's Building, near the souk. Shall we go and look around? I said; there are two of us after all. Marion said, a mother and daughter were raped in the souk, mind you they were wearing shorts, they were asking for it. They were Australians, she added. As if that made some sort of difference.

I lost my temper with her. I said, how can you repeat this sort of gossip? Who were these women? When did it happen? Who told you about it? I said, life is difficult enough in this town without believing everything you hear.

I imagined Carla waiting for us, with iced coffee, and something like banana bread, chocolate chip cookies perhaps, and maybe ringing up Dunroamin to see what had happened. I felt almost tearful. I wanted to prove to Marion that it was all right, that we could go out on our own without something terrible happening to us, and now just because we missed our bus stop all these fantasies about Australians were running around in her head. Even though I had lost my temper, I felt sorry for her, standing there in the street. It was past midday, and I could see her suffering, covered in a clammy sweat, and her ankles swelling before my eyes. I have to keep away from women like Marion. They may be company, but they're no good for me in the long run.

But then a day later, Marion turned up at Dunroamin. 'I had to come and talk to someone,' she said. She revolved slowly in the living-room, viewing the many chairs, a vacant and confused expression on her face. As soon as she had selected a chair, she began to cry, and mop up her tears with tissues which she tore angrily from a box on the coffee table. 'I'm so unhappy,' she said, 'he's just so mean, Fran, he's so mean. He says we're staying in Jeddah to see the next Five-Year Plan out, if they let him. That'll be 1990! I'll be forty! Can you imagine being forty in this place?'

Frances could not imagine being forty in any place at all. But she sat down to listen. 'I thought you liked it here?'

A medley of complaints burst out of Marion. She began to talk about sexual harassment, about the bottom-pinchers in the supermarkets, about the men who gave her trouble on the streets because of her blond hair. As she talked, her eyes began to shine, and a look of thrilled fear grew on her face. She must have learned that look in Africa; terrorists, rabies, armed robbers, are the subjects for morning sherry-parties. 'And besides,' she said, 'he says that when we finish here we're not going home to the UK. He says we're emigrating to Australia. He says Britain's finished. I don't think it's finished, do you, Frances?'

By the time Marion had got through her grievances a half-hour had gone by. Her little voice was a victim's voice, but her fingers, like a murderer's, shredded and twisted and tore. 'I don't know what I'd do without Jeff,' she said. 'He helps me out such a lot. He runs the girls to Brownies. He unblocked the lavatory for me last week. You know Russel, he won't do anything like that.'

Frances said, 'I can't stand Jeff.'

'Can't you?' Marion said wonderingly. 'Why ever not?'

Frances said, 'He's such a fascist, that's why.' She was ashamed of herself, but it was a way of bringing the conversation to an end.

She pitied Marion. Her thick pallid skin never coloured and never burned; between her large arms and legs, almost as an afterthought, was a thick-waisted child's body. Her clothes, even when designed to be voluminous, seemed ridiculously small and tight; she was prone to allergies and rashes, to swollen lips, swollen eyelids, conjunctivitis. Her husband was a bully, and her two daughters were petulant, demanding children, who had learned their mother's habit of sniffling when thwarted. Frances felt, and was ashamed of herself for feeling, that compared to Marion she was quite glamorous; and that she was witty, and lucky, and sane. But perhaps, she thought, Marion feels just the same about me.

Marion stood up, and a cascade of shredded Kleenex slid to the carpet. Her eyes were pinkish and her nose shone. 'But I've got it off my chest,' she said. They went out together to the gate. Marion glanced up at the building; Samira had her blinds down, and so of course did Flat 4. 'You know what goes on up there, don't you?' she asked, managing a miserable smile.

'Yes.'

'See much of your neighbours?'

'Quite a bit.'

'Don't tell anybody, will you?' Marion took a crumpled tissue out of her pocket and mopped her eyes again. 'Don't tell anybody what I've been saying about Russel. They don't like to know that people are unhappy. It could jeopardize his job.'

'Who doesn't like to know?'

'The Saudis,' she said. 'They like people to be, you know, just like robots.'

'Come to dinner,' Frances said. 'Will you? Wednesday week? Can you manage that?'

'I think so,' Marion said, sniffing.

Frances went indoors, out of the splashy yellow sunshine and into the cool and the dark. She thought, I wish I had a kinder heart.

When Andrew came home he was carrying two large plates covered by paper napkins. He said, 'Rickie Zussman stopped by the office.'

'I seem to hear his accents.'

'True,' Andrew said. 'I mean he dropped in. He called on me. I suppose I am getting a bit American. I've spent the morning talking to one of the Corps of Engineers people. You know, they run the missile base. Unofficially.'

'I thought you had nothing to do with the missile base.'

Frances lifted a corner of one of the napkins. 'Oh, it's Carla's banana bread.'

'And her pumpkin pie. No, I don't have anything to do with it really. I'm just being nosy.'

'I suppose she spent a day baking, and then when we didn't turn up she didn't know how to get rid of it. They're both on diets.'

'All the *khawwadjihs* are on diets,' Andrew complained. 'It must be next in popularity to snorkelling. Why do they do it? Some of them are quite scrawny.'

'It's guilt,' Frances said. She remembered Yasmin's sly question: you know of guilt? 'They feel bad because they're making so much money. They want to punish themselves a bit.'

'Do you think that's it?'

'Yes, it's like those people who go on fasts and give their lunch money to Oxfam. Religion without God.'

She took the plates from Andrew and carried them into the kitchen. He followed. 'I wonder if Carla would mind,' she said, removing the napkins, 'if I gave this stuff to Yasmin and Samira. Samira sent me some stuffed vine leaves yesterday. I'm in debt.'

'It would be a cross-cultural experience for them,' Andrew said. 'Are we always going to carry on this food-exchange?'

'Oh, it's a harmless hobby. Food's the only thing we can talk about without running into a lot of misunderstandings. By the way –'

'Put the kettle on, will you?' Andrew said.

'I was thinking about the empty flat. Is it supposed to be one woman the chap's seeing, or several?'

'Only one, I think.'

'Oh, this disgusting water,' Frances said. 'It's furring the kettle up. What I wondered is, why don't they just both get divorced. Divorce is easy here. So I'm told.'

'I don't know.' Andrew is baffled by how simple life sometimes seems to his wife. 'There could be all sorts of reasons. There might be family connections at stake.' Or what emotional complexities in the background, he thought: a devoted cuckold, a vulnerable wife. Might the Saudis have those emotions: or another set entirely? Frances seems to believe that nothing in the Kingdom can be taken for granted; that human nature, if indeed it exists anywhere, is not something that can be relied on here.

'They'd have to be very persuasive connections,' she said, 'for a couple to run this sort of risk. Come to that –' she reached down the teapot – 'only one of them would have to get divorced, the woman, because the man can have four wives, can't he?'

'They don't do that much nowadays. None of the Saudis I know at the Ministry has more than one wife. They leave that to the Bedu. They try to be modern.'

'Up to a point.'

'And besides, it's too expensive, getting married. The girls want a new house built for them, and all the furniture.'

'Yes, I know. They want chandeliers.'

'So now it's just like the rest of the world, what do you call it – serial polygamy.'

The water was boiling. 'Perhaps the woman upstairs has a possessive husband,' Frances said. 'Perhaps she doesn't think he'd play the game and say *I divorce you*.' She made the tea, picked up the tray, and headed for the living-room. 'Before we have the dinner party,' she said, 'we really must rearrange these chairs.'

Yasmin, after their conversation in Samira's flat, had been anxious to correct any wrong impression that Frances might have received. 'It seems to me,' Frances had said recklessly, 'that everybody could be good, if you could get a more or less instant divorce each time you saw someone you liked the look of – and then after a week or two you could get married again. On that principle, no one need ever commit adultery.'

She had thought, if I just give Yasmin a little push, I'll find out whether or not she's in the secret. But Yasmin seemed nettled. 'The Saudis do this,' she said. 'We wouldn't do this. In Pakistan a divorce is much rarer.'

'But the Saudis have lots. Why's that?'

Yasmin dropped her eyes. 'Because they are very passionate.'

'In the West we take marriage more seriously. We think if you don't like it you have to try to put it right. We promise it's for life.' She stopped, realizing how remote this was from her real experience; half Andrew's colleagues were on their second or third wife. 'Well, that's the theory,' she said.

Yasmin had sighed. She said, 'A realistic religion is best, isn't it?'

Just now, Andrew was not interested in talking about the empty flat. He flung himself into his chosen armchair and said, 'My model's not come yet. My model of the building, I mean. I'm worried about it. It's left LA. Jeff thinks the customs men might be holding it up. Searching it for drugs, or something.'

'Oh, surely not.'

'If it gets damaged I'll kill somebody.' Suddenly he was full of venom. 'Jeff's an idiot,' he said.

Andrew hugged his mug of tea, and lapsed into thought. He is losing faith in Turadup's bosses, in their technical competence. Not that they bother with him much. His building, the multimillion-riyal building, seems unimportant to them compared to the underground silo at the missile base. Whenever he wants something, Parsons and Pollard are having a high-level meeting; or say they are. People he doesn't know arrive at the airport, and occupy office space, and monopolize the telex machine; they break Turadup's photocopier, and expect him to mend it, as if he were a maintenance mechanic. Once he found that one of these strangers had taken over his Portakabin, and pushed all his drawings aside. 'You're not working on the silo, I gather?' this chap had asked him, and he had said, 'No, the building, I'm working on the building, and you are in my space.' He had been violently rude. Parsons, in his mild way, had upbraided him.

And anyway, he thought, sipping his tea, ignoring his

wife: isn't the whole project misconceived? Building an underground silo on limestone? It's permeable, it cracks, it's continually flooding. They should have put the missiles inland, on granite. The site's in the wrong place. It should be up on the escarpment, not down by the sea. But then, officially there are no missiles. There are no Americans. How can you point out the flaws in a project that doesn't exist?

And mixed up with his larger doubts (after all, Saudi defence strategy is not his affair) are the little things that niggle away. If he goes to the Ministry – the Ministry that wants the building so much – nobody seems prepared to deal with him. The fact is, they seem not to know who he is. Four or five men loll around in the Deputy Minister's anteroom, drink coffee and read the newspapers. They give him a blank stare, and return to their conversation.

When Jeff Pollard recruited him in Gaborone, he said that he would be a valued member of a team; but he doesn't feel like one. Parsons and Pollard don't know how to make someone feel valued. Havana-sucking half-wits, he thinks. Captain Hook and Smee had more notion of personnel management. Far more.

'Awful tea,' Frances said. 'Want another cup?'

He shook his head. 'I'm supposed to be getting this consultant out from London,' he said. 'Though when he's coming I don't know. Perhaps we can have him over to dinner when he does get here, keep him away from Parsons and Pollard. He's an expert on air-conditioning. His name's Fairfax.'

'Really?' Frances looked up. 'Who does he work for?'

He told her. 'I feel as if I know him,' she said. 'I came over on the plane with some of his colleagues. They talked shop the whole time. Poor Fairfax, I think they had a down on him, they weren't very complimentary.'

'Well, I hope he's some use. I spoke to him on the phone. He was going on about the Prophet's Mosque in Medina. Says they're doing it up and it's going to have the biggest central air-conditioning system in the world.'

'I suppose the Believers have to be kept cool.'

'I said to him, well, you can't go to Medina. Only Muslims can go to Mecca and Medina. He said, I really need the order, how can I convert? And then he started laughing like a maniac.'

'I'm sure that when he comes here he'll sober up.'

'Probably. You know what Rickie Zussman was telling me? He'd been to this management seminar, and they'd had a lecture from some Indian psychiatrist, a chap from Hyderabad. He was making a tour of the Middle East to research into the effects of stress on immigrant workers.'

'Strange,' Frances said, 'how Indians are immigrant workers, but we're professional expatriates.'

'He said all the Indians who work here are shot to pieces mentally. Totally paranoid. They come here and they're suddenly cut off from their families, they've got language problems, and they start to think everybody's out to get them. Our Indians are like that, at Turadup. They think all the other Indians are after their jobs. They think people are talking about them behind their backs. And they're always going up to Eric Parsons and asking him complicated questions about the labour law. They think he wants to cheat on the terms of their contract, do them out of their baggage allowances or something. They're obsessed with their baggage allowances.'

'I expect Europeans are the same, when they've been here for a while.'

'Yes, sure. This psychiatrist says so. He says there are phases. When you get here and everything's so strange, you feel isolated and got at – that's Phase One. But then you learn how to manage daily life, and for a while the place begins to seem normal, and you'll even defend the way things are done here, you'll start explaining to newcomers that it's all right really – that's Phase Two. You coast along, and then comes Phase Three, the second wave of paranoia. And this time around, it never goes.'

'So what do you do?'

'You leave, before you crack up.'

'But some of your lot at Turadup – they've been here a few years. They may not be up to much, but you can't say they've cracked up.'

'Oh, not in any obvious way. I don't mean they attack people, or scream and hammer the walls. They're just cracked up in small ways. You just listen to their conversation.' Andrew stared into the depth of his empty mug, as if he were reading the tea leaves. 'Parsons,' he said. 'You know that big flash car of his? It's got a tinted windscreen. It's tinted at the top, so you've got this arc of blue sky.'

'That's not insane, Andrew. It's just tacky.'

'It seems insane to me,' Andrew said. 'Nine days out of ten the sky is as blue as you could want. Unnaturally blue. But the real sky isn't good enough for these madmen.'

Frances was thoughtful. 'I wonder what phase we are in?'

'Getting into the second one, I suppose. Because we seem to be coping, don't we? There are days when I really feel the place is normal.'

Speak for yourself, Frances thinks. Dunroamin begins to feel a more and more problematical world. When she goes out into the hallway she is watchful; she listens; she casts a glance over her shoulder and up the stairs. If she hears a door open, her heart leaps. There is a feeling that something is going on, just outside her range of vision. If the time and the place came together, she would grasp it; she would know what it was.

'Perhaps the process can be accelerated,' she said to Andrew. 'Perhaps I've already reached the third stage.'

'Oh no,' Andrew said seriously. 'No, I wouldn't worry, Frances. This psychiatrist was talking about guest workers, expatriate labour. I don't think it applies to women at home.'

Letters home. Frances writes to her cousin Clare, and gives the letter to Andrew: 'Can you post this?'

Andrew's heart sinks. 'I'll be late then,' he says.

The post offices of Jeddah are breezeblock cubes, sited on vacant lots; they are difficult of access, and have eccentric opening hours. The people who man them seem to be chosen for their piety, because post offices are almost always closed for prayer. When at last the staff take down the grilles from the main door, and throw the office open, a long and cosmopolitan queue forms at once, and snakes outside the cube and into the dust by the roadside. The clerks deal with this queue at their own speed; they take time out to read the newspapers, *Okaz* and *Al-Madinah* and the *Saudi Gazette*: often perching cross-legged on the counters while they do so.

In the year 1403, a great innovation appeared in the Kingdom: post boxes. Mostly these too were situated on vacant lots, but a few were near the habitations of men, and friends could exchange news of them, and draw each other maps. At first it seemed that everyone would be saved a great deal of time and aggravation. But of course, to post letters in the post boxes, one needed stamps, so it was necessary to go to the post office anyway.

What happened next was a shortage of stamps. On the pavement outside the main post office, which in those days was situated near the Happy Family supermarket, a sort of sub-post-office system grew up; enterprising men sat on blankets, and sold stamps at black-market prices.

A little while after this, the main post office closed down. Overnight, it stood deserted, and for days no one knew where to find its successor. Post office boxes went missing, and clerks were out and about all over the city, looking for them.

O, Bride of the Red Sea! You give your suitors a hard time.

The post boxes, too, were a failure. They were seen every day to be stuffed with letters and small packages, with overflowing mail to Madras, to Salt Lake City, to Kuala Lumpur and to Leamington Spa; but was it fresh mail, or the same mail every day? A rumour got about that the boxes were never emptied; and the Europeans, at least, started their search for post offices again.

It was, of course, only a rumour. The *Arab News* says that the Kingdom has excellent postal services.

143

A week passed; and they were, as Yasmin put it, called for dinner. Yasmin had been cooking for three days; but when she opened the door to them she had banished the sweat and grease, the smell of spices that crept into her clothes and hair, and stood, smiling guardedly, in an embroidered *shalwar kameez*; she wore ruby studs in her ears, her lashes were heavily mascaraed, and her ivory skin seemed polished. 'Come in,' she said. 'Let me introduce you to our friends.'

She led them around the room. 'This is Shabana. This is her husband Mohammed, this is Mohammed's friend Farooq.' The men wore dark business suits; the women were dressed as Yasmin was, or else in their evening-party saris; one or two wore long velvet skirts, and high-necked blouses with frills. They smiled politely, and asked the routine questions: and how do you like Jeddah? And with the arrival of the Shores, the whole party, which had been conducted in Urdu, switched smoothly into English.

It was difficult. Shams, her eyes downcast, circulated with a tray: a choice of Pepsi, 7 Up, or a fizzy orange drink of a peculiar sickly sweetness. Shabana's dimpled paw hovered over the tray, her diamond rings glittering. She was a little doll of a woman, with faint dark down on her upper lip; her mouth was plump and cushioned, her manner confiding. 'And have you been to the carpet souk?' she asked. 'Are you wanting to collect some carpets?'

Raji appeared at Frances's side, and took her arm. 'If she wants carpets I will show her the best buys,' he said. 'Tell me, Frances, where do you want to go?'

Raji, that night, was ebullient, bouncing around from guest to guest. 'What I'd like to see,' Frances said, 'is this Tomb of Eve I've read about.'

'Ah,' Shabana said. 'I see you are becoming interested in some bits of Islam.'

'Yasmin has been explaining things to me. Is it really the tomb of Eve?'

'They say so. After Adam and Eve got reconciled with God, Eve died and was buried –'

'Downtown,' Raji said, smiling, 'behind a big wall. Near the Foreign Ministry, I think, isn't it?'

'Haven't you seen it?'

'I don't think it is widely publicized,' Raji said. 'It is not what the Saudis would make a tourist attraction. You must know, Frances, that here they are Sunni Muslims.' He sounded detached, almost cynical. 'They don't go for shrines and tombs and processions. They call these things superstition.'

'It is the Shia who go after such things,' Shabana said.

'You must ask Samira,' Raji said. 'Frances has a Saudi friend,' he explained. 'She will tell you that the Shia are so extreme. They are flagellants. Suicidals. Martyrs.' He touched his forehead delicately. 'They are all martyrs, you understand me, in the head.'

Shabana said, 'You must read the Holy Koran. Of course, in translation –'

'Yes, I know,' Frances said. 'I understand that without Arabic you can't really appreciate it. But you can look about you, and see its effects in the outside world.'

Raji laughed. 'You are often amusing yourself at our expense, Frances. You think I cannot tell when you are sarcastic. You do not think much of us, and who is to blame you.' An arm around her waist, he patted her, like a fond uncle. 'Come now, let's not be so solemn. You ought not to bother about such things as tombs. You must take your husband down to the gold souk, and make him buy you something nice.'

'Ah, have you heard?' Shabana turned aside and touched her husband's sleeve. 'Mohammed, will you tell about the latest goings-on at Jeddah International Market? Do please tell Raji.'

Mohammed obliged, clearing his throat, pushing toolarge spectacles back on his nose. 'The police are banning mirrors in the jewellers' shops. Or so they say. The Saudi women are down there provoking the shop assistants, getting them to fasten necklaces on them, while they look in the mirror.'

'That's right,' Shabana said, almost in a whisper. 'And they stretch out their hands, with their nails painted red, and let the men try bracelets on them.'

'Young women will find some way to flirt,' Raji said indulgently. 'It is the way of the world.'

Mohammed darted a look at Frances. 'Quite a hot-bed, they say, the Jeddah International Market. The story goes that the girls walk around looking in the shop windows, with a piece of paper hidden in their hand, and their telephone number on it. Well, you know how the young men hang around there. They just slip it to someone, and then they phone up.'

Shabana tittered. 'They have a relationship on the telephone.'

'It's rather sad,' Frances said. 'Don't you think?'

'Where's your sense of humour?' Raji demanded. 'We also enjoy laughing at the Saudis from time to time, you know. Oh, they know we do it. But then we are,' he said smoothly, 'only the hired help.'

'We are the hired help too,' Frances said. 'I was wondering, do you see much of Abdul Nasr? Our neighbour,' she explained to Shabana.

'I don't know him well,' Raji said. 'I don't have contact with him in my work. Of course, his family are not Saudi, you know. I think he was born here, but they come from Iran. So, he will never really get on.'

Yasmin approached, to urge them towards the table. 'Everything is ready, do please come and eat. You are talking of our neighbour?'

'We can hardly be on social terms,' Raji said. 'If we called them to dinner Samira would have to sit behind her veil. Thank God we don't all have to keep their rules, or there would be no parties like this one.'

'It seems a pity,' Frances said to Yasmin. 'When you two are such friends.'

146

Yasmin caught her eye. 'I don't know why you think it is a pity,' she said quietly. 'What ever would Raji and Samira find to talk about?' Then she smiled, and turned back to her guests.

The fruits of Yasmin's three days of labour were laid out as a buffet on the long table with its stiff white cloth. The party ate standing up, in a concentrated, voracious silence. Frances picked at the food, which was too spicy for her stomach, and turned it over with her fork. Andrew complimented Yasmin. He was enjoying himself. He could eat anything; it was one of his social assets. Raji alone talked between mouthfuls, holding forth on this and that. It seemed a pose, almost; look at me, he was saying, I am a worldly, charming man. If there had been a slight tension in the room – caused, Frances thought, by the European presence – it was now dissipating. But she looked across the table and saw Yasmin watching Raji, with an expression that was narrow and appraising. It was the face of a nun in a lingerie department: baffled, almost hungry, and yet full of a growing appreciation that things are worse than one had thought.

Samira came down. She rang the doorbell, and when Frances answered it – she had been busy in the kitchen – her neighbour was huddled into the doorframe, as if trying to efface her black shape into the texture of the wood. Inside the door, she unwound her head, revealing her perfect *maquillage*; her eyeshadow in three complementary shades, her shaped and frosted cheekbones, her precisely outlined and glossed-in lips. All this, Frances thought, for other women: and never, never for any men. Except your relations, of course. She held out an arm, and Samira's black silk *abaya* floated on to it; Frances laid it over the back of a chair. Samira wore her jeans again, and a silk shirt with a sequined butterfly embroidered across her large bosom. She had brought her little girl; the child had been dressed for an outing, in a frilly white dress with a

sash which made her appear as wide as she was high. Her
dark round face was truculent; she had a doll in one hand,
hanging by its blond hair, and with the other hand she
clutched and patted at her mother's unyielding denim
thighs.

'Oh, that woman of mine!' Samira said. She seated herself,
and threw her head back so that her long electric hair
crackled over Turadup's tasteful oatmeal cushions. 'That
ignorant woman! I have brought the kid down so that she
can get on with the sweeping.'

'Does she still cry so much?'

'All the time. Do you know, Frances, before we brought
Islam to those people they lived in the jungle and ate pigs.'
And now they are not grateful, her tone implied. 'They
coloured their body with pictures, what do you call it, tattoos.
Sometimes they ate each other.'

'Some coffee?'

'Yes, but don't set up that machine, just make it quickly
in the cup, it's all right.' Her exasperation, temporarily
quelled, broke out again. 'He says – Abdul says – I should
be glad that she doesn't speak Arabic. He says I don't want
her corrupting our children with foreign ways. By the by, I
am expecting again.'

'Are you?' Frances said. 'Congratulations. Are foreign
ways always corrupting?'

'You can't complain if we think so,' Samira said, with a
sigh. 'After all, we have seen so much of the youth going to
Europe and getting into bad ways with women and nightclubs. The newspapers are always ready to give them bad
publicity.'

'Have you been to Europe, yourself?'

'Yes, of course. We often go. Paris. Rome. Only,' she said
fretfully, 'Abdul never tells me his plans. He just says, come
on, we are travelling.'

Frances brought the coffee. Another illuminating
morning, she thought. She felt she was receiving a senti-
mental education; but that there was more to learn. The

148

child, with tiny strong fingers like pincers, was pulling out her doll's hair. Samira reached for the sugar bowl. Her mood of complaint had deepened.

'Abdul is never at home,' she said. 'He goes out in the evening on men's parties.'

'Did you know Abdul, before you were married?'

'No, it was arranged, of course.'

'So you didn't know what to expect?'

'Well, if he is a little kind . . . It is not good to have too many expectations.'

'Yes, people say that.' Frances raised her cup to her lips. 'But I didn't know expectations were wrong. I never thought of it that way.'

'Afterwards, after your marriage, then you get to know each other. We don't have many conflicts. Do you have many?'

'Oh, a few.'

'Because we don't talk all that much, you know. His life, my life – they are different. But that's natural, isn't it? Men and women, it has to be.'

'I don't know. You could get an education. Get a job. If you lived somewhere else, that is. In another country.'

'Oh, but,' Samira said. 'But. I have been to the Women's University, Frances.'

'I didn't know that.'

'I have studied French. English poetry, the works of Robert Burns. Anthropology – that is people's customs, you know. And biology.'

'Biology?'

'Helps one to run the home better. So you know how to take care of the children's health. And of course, Frances, we have women who work. There is the staff at the ladies' banks. And at some of the Ministries, they have women. They arrange it for them. They have a separate lift, and a floor by themselves.'

'But they must need to talk to the men sometimes. Consult them.'

'They can phone them up. And they have computers. They can send them a disk.'

'But what would happen . . . I mean, what would be so awful . . . if they did meet up?'

'Why, it would be like the West,' Samira said. 'There would be harassment. People would be all the time having love-affairs.'

How difficult it is, Frances thought, to fit it all together. Shabana told her that Adam and Eve were reconciled to God. The *Arab News*, which writes on these matters every Friday, says there is no original sin. People are naturally good, and they have free will, and Allah does not ask very much of them, certainly nothing unreasonable. The rules take account of human weaknesses; they are easy to keep. But the penal code does not reflect this optimism. Nor does the general tenor of society. It seems to expect depravity, the unreflective behaviour of animals; man and woman together, five minutes, clothes off, carnal knowledge; rape, mayhem, murder. Oh come, she says to herself: don't exaggerate. Drink your coffee. Be a good hostess and keep the conversation light. And she notices how Samira's careful orthodoxy cracks sometimes, as if by nature she were a wishful, rebellious girl; as if, by deduction, she had discovered there was something wrong in her life. Now she put down her coffee cup. 'Did you ever have an affair at your office?'

'Certainly not,' Frances said. 'It never crossed my mind.' She thought, no one ever asked me.

Samira looked sceptical, and perhaps disappointed. 'Also,' she went on, 'we need women to work as doctors. Many girls are attracted to this, thank God. Because some Saudi men would kill any male doctor who looked at their wife.'

'So what happened before any women doctors were trained? There must have been a time.'

'Oh yes,' Samira said. 'It is not so long ago that we got schools for girls, and even then many people didn't agree with it, there were riots, you know, lots of shooting. As for the lady doctors, I am mystified. I think we must have got them from Egypt.'

'And so what if you don't want to be a doctor, or work at the bank?'

'Home is best. You see, Frances, you women in the West, you think you are very free, but Islam has given us all the women's rights. They are guaranteed to us. We can have our own money. In the home we are the rulers. Men must provide for us, that is their duty.'

'But if you are divorced?'

'Then our fathers and brothers must look after us. They give us their protection. You women in the West are just exploited by men. They drive you out to work in offices and factories, and then when you come home you must cook for them and look after the children.'

'You think we should be happy to let men support us?'

'Yes, because that is their responsibility, and ours is to bring up the next generation. Frances,' she said seriously, 'you really must have some children. You will please Andrew. You cannot use contraception all your life.'

'Yes,' Frances said. 'I'm thinking about it.' The child, at her feet, was twisting off the doll's head. What had the *Arab News* said, only last week? *Every woman is a born mother.* 'And so what will you do with your education?' she asked. 'Your university education?'

'We have a saying,' Samira smiled. '"We will hang our certificates in the kitchen."'

She bent down, and pulled the doll from her daughter's grasp. She straightened its tortured limbs, and sat holding it by one leg, looking into its plastic face of pink and white. 'Tell me,' she said dreamily, 'have you ever met Princess Diana?'

'I'm afraid I haven't. I don't exactly move in those circles.'

'You don't know anyone in your royal family?'

'Ours is not as big as yours. They keep to themselves.'

'A pity. I would like to meet her. She is very beautiful, I think. Very fair.'

Diana looks out of all the magazines, peeping from under her fringe; blackish sapphires, like lacquered beetles, cling to her ears, and her coy expression is looped and scored with Arabic script. She is a heroine, a glamorous royal bride. Her décolletage, because it is a royal one, is somehow less indecent than others; the censor's felt-tip spares it.

'You know, with this one,' Samira gestured towards her child, 'I wanted to call her Diana. But Abdul Nasr does not agree. He says it is foreign custom.' Samira was suddenly indignant; her indignation broke down her English. 'Just when I wanted to have birthday party, he says that's foreign custom too. This time, if it is another girl ... though I hope,' she added hastily, 'it will be a boy ... I must get my choice over the name. I said to him, why not? My sister has got Diana, my cousin has got it, all these babies ... he says, this sounds uncanny to my ears.'

'So you settled for Fat'ma?'

'Well, it is just a starter name. It is just what you call the baby while you are thinking what to call her. So I said to him, for me it can stay at Fat'ma, what do I care?' She looked down at her daughter, with her corkscrew curls, her flat nose and round eyes. Her face was disgusted. She laughed a little. 'White nigger, isn't it? Must be from his family. Not mine.'

'Perhaps you should have a holiday in England,' Frances said. You could buy Fat'ma some dungarees, she thought, then she wouldn't look like a boxer in drag. 'Perhaps you might see Princess Diana.'

'Oh, but Frances, I have been in England. Did you not know? I have been there for six months.'

'I see. So that's how you learned such good English.'

'No, not really. That was at the university. Also, of course, the Berlitz tapes. When I am in England I don't really have much chance to learn.'

'Why was that?'

'Well, mainly of course I have to stay inside with my

brother-in-law's wife. One day we went to London. Harrods.'

'You weren't in London?'

'No, in Brighton. That is where my brother-in-law lives. He stays out of London because London is dangerous.'

'It corrupts him?' Frances suggested.

'No, not that. Dangerous for his life.' She stopped, and blushed. 'You know what it is,' she said hurriedly. All her transparency had darkened; she was thinking furiously. 'Well, you know, Frances, that where there are some Arabs together your police think they are bombing, or something. Really they are only going to their own clubs, reading the newspapers, so on. Discussing their home countries.'

'I don't think the police would shoot him, if they didn't like his social life.'

Though perhaps it is not only the police that worry him, Frances thought. Have we a political militant in the family? A terrorist? Surely not. We are just at cross-purposes.

'Anyway, he will be home soon, thank God,' Samira said piously. She tossed her denim legs over the arm of the chair, and looked as if she wanted a change of subject. It seemed dark, suddenly, inside the circle of chairs. But it was midday, a blazing sun outside, and perhaps Eric Parsons would be driving somewhere, across the city's harsh grid-plan, with this same sun a diffuse yellow flare in the artificial sky of his windscreen. And Andrew would be bending over a site plan, or stumping through the mud, the noonday heat on the exposed nape of his neck. Frances leaned across Samira, with a murmured apology, and switched on a small lamp with a pink shade. It cast a soft circle of light up on to the girl's face; her expression said, have I been simple-minded? Frances had already decided what to report to Andrew. Certificates in kitchens, yes. Terrorists in Brighton, no. You've got nothing to do, he would say; you sit around the house confabulating, making plots, and making your dull life brighter.

'But he is not so bad,' Samira said. 'I mean my husband.

Perhaps this time he will let me have my way on the name. After all, we do not have many conflicts really. Not like Yasmin and her husband.'

'Do they have many?'

Samira laughed. 'I hear her side of the story. She says he likes to enjoy himself too much, and this worries her. But I think when he wants her she is always praying.'

She wouldn't enlarge on it; swept up her child and her *abaya*, dressed herself for the journey up the stairs. 'Come and visit me soon,' she said. 'I want to know more about your life. Yasmin tells me you have married your husband very suddenly, when you are travelling in Africa. I think that's very romantic. I want to know about it.' She secured the child's wrist. They clung together, a diminishing female chain: mother, daughter, doll. At the door, Samira put out a hand from her wrappings, and touched Frances's cheek. 'Dear Frances,' she said. 'I am going to bring you a lipstick.'

Frances watched her go, and then, on an impulse, picked up her keys, closed her apartment door, and followed Samira up the stairs. Samira didn't hear her; she scuttled ahead, keeping close to the wall. She looked as if she had no right to be out. You could put a Western woman under all those layers, Frances thought, but she'd never achieve that apologetic gait. She'd never fool anyone; the way the Saudi woman walks is quite unique.

As Frances rounded the bend in the stairs she heard Samira's front door click shut. She stopped for a moment between the two closed doors, then mounted the half-flight, and unbolted the door that led on to the roof. At once the noon light leapt into the gap, and she stepped into a white-out, a featureless, silent glare. She craved just a moment's daylight, just a breath of air; but there was no wind, and a dizzying heat. And this, she thought, is winter. The walls and roofs of the apartment blocks around her shimmered, like towers of water. She saw the black outline of the waist-high wall which bounded the roof, and the abandoned cloth eslines scored against the air; stretched taut between their poles, they seemed to quiver and throb with some private energy, like telegraph wires.

FRANCES SHORE'S DIARY: 19 Rabi al-awal

Damn right Raji likes to have a good time. Last night
at about ten o'clock, when we were bringing in YET
ANOTHER load of shopping for the dinner party
(dear God I wish I had never started this) – we met Raji
in the hall. He came up behind us, and propped himself
against the wall, and began to talk about the stockmarket,
holding himself upright with one hand. He thinks he has
to make this conversation with Andrew. He thinks
Andrew is interested in stocks and bonds. Raji was drunk.

He reeled across the hall and rang his own doorbell.
We got ourselves inside. A few minutes later, when we
were putting the shopping away, we heard his engine
revving and his tyres squealing, and he was off again.

He must have been at the Minister's, Andrew said.
That's where they do the serious drinking in this town.
I suppose if he's stopped by the police, he's got
influence.

But what will Yasmin say, I wondered.

Yasmin rang the doorbell next day, at about twelve-thirty.
She had brought a bowl of clear chicken soup, from which
wafted a thin peppery aroma. It was a pretext. Usually she
sent Shams with the food.

'Here,' she said. 'You ought to eat at midday, Frances. I
know you are busy with your cooking so I brought you this.'

Yasmin's face looked bruised, bluish, as if she had not
slept. 'I can't stay,' she said. 'Raji says he ran into you last
night?'

'That's right,' Frances said.

Yasmin shifted her weight, from one slippered foot to the
other. 'He had been at His Highness's house. The Minister.'

155

'Yes. We thought so.'

There was a pause.

'He was kept so late, working. I think he was very tired when you saw him.'

'That must have been it,' Frances said.

Yasmin nodded. She withdrew, into the shadows of the hallway.

'He was not singing a little?' she asked tentatively.

'Not that we heard.'

'Oh good, good. I see you soon now. Don't work too hard.'

'I wouldn't worry,' Frances said. 'Lots of men sing when they're tired.'

She went back to cutting up the vegetables. How bored I am, she said to herself. Matchstick carrots, bitter thoughts: it's wonderful how travel narrows the mind.

Andrew said, 'Get one ahead?' He put down the glass he was polishing, and reached into the fridge for a carafe of white wine.

Holding her glass, Frances went to survey her table, laid for nine.

'I suppose you always get spare men in Jeddah,' Andrew said.

'I wouldn't call Pollard a spare man. I'd call him surplus.' She held her glass up to the light. 'At least it's clear. It's a bit sweet. I expect they'll drink it.'

'I think Eric and Daphne are homebrew snobs.'

'Don't make me nervous. I'm afraid it will poison someone.'

'They've all been here a long time. They've built up resistance.'

He followed her back to the kitchen. 'What do you think about Yasmin?' she said. 'Can she really not know that he drinks?'

'She must know.'

'Why pretend then? Why raise the topic?'

'That woman's conning you.'

She looked up at him, paring knife poised over slices of lemon. So Andrew didn't like Yasmin. But that seemed ridiculous. Yasmin was just a fact of her life, and touched only peripherally on Andrew's. Why should he like or dislike her?

'I don't really know what I mean,' he said, unhelpfully. 'But I've always had this feeling about her, that she's not what she seems.'

The guests were late. 'It shortens the agony,' Andrew said.

It was half-past eight when the Zussmans arrived. 'Road-block,' Rickie grunted, without preamble. He ran a hand through his shorn brown hair; he was a silent, observant, professorial man, with metal-rimmed glasses, a bleak, bony face; he dressed for dinner in bush-shirt and jeans. Carla wore her usual no-nonsense cotton kaftan, with a string of wooden beads as a concession to festivity. She was a tiny woman, with a strongly Jewish face; though if she had been Jewish, of course, she would not have been admitted to the Kingdom. I must ask her sometime, Frances thought.

'Do you have any beer?' Rickie said.

'We haven't got round to making beer yet.'

'Give you my recipe.' He accepted a glass of wine, and proffered something, diffidently. Andrew unwrapped, from the sports pages of the *Saudi Gazette*, a flat plain bottle. 'Half of Scotch,' Rickie said. 'That all right for you?'

Andrew was overwhelmed. 'It should improve the evening.'

'Put it away,' Rickie said. 'Carla and I can get this stuff any time. We get it through the Embassy. Anyway, we drink bourbon. Keep it for you and Frannie.'

'Okay. Won't waste it on Eric.' Andrew hurried off with it.

'Where was the roadblock?' Frances asked.

'Palestine Road.'

'What were they looking for?'

157

'Who can tell? Maybe just trouble.'

'And what did you do with the Scotch?'

'I put it,' Carla said, 'down the neck of my kaftan. They'd never dare.'

Jeff Pollard came next. 'Bloody boot search,' he said, in lieu of apology. 'Been to change my films.' He dumped his briefcase, with the video cassettes inside, by the front door. Film exchange was a shady business, dubiously legal, and gave the most innocent viewer a plain-paper-wrapper air. Jeff wore a tie, ancient and unsavoury. He looked uncomfortable.

'You shouldn't have bothered,' Frances said. 'To dress up.'

Then the Parsons; graciously resigned, Daphne saying, 'They weren't interested in the *khawwadjis*. They waved us through.' Then the Smallbones, who had only come around the corner, with Marion walking in the gutter, because the pavements were unsuitable for her high heels. Marion was wearing her *abaya*. She shrugged it off to reveal a strappy, backless dress, and a flamboyant pattern of scarlet mosquito bites sprayed across her tender pale shoulders. The party had begun.

Andrew had said once, when he was in a morose mood, that you should always expect the worst, so that if in the event you got something better, you'd be surprised. But why is it that if you expect the worst, and get the worst, you're still surprised? Frances wondered about it, idly. She noticed, in the dribble of garlic butter in which her prawns lay, a suspicious, unpleasant fleck of something black. Eric Parsons was talking about his iniquitous tax position, and Russel encouraged him, with grunts and nods. 'Of course I'm attracted to the Australian way of life,' Russel said. 'I'm thinking about Perth. But I suppose it's the same old story as everywhere else. The Communists have taken over.'

Rickie Zussman broke his silence, for the first time since the meal began. 'I don't know much about Western Australia,' he said. 'But I feel that must be a very mistaken notion.'

Frances began to collect the plates; Marion half rose from her chair, Frances said 'No, no,' but Marion followed her to the kitchen. 'Just stack up everything there,' Frances said. She turned her attention to the lemon sauce for the veal. Another floating speck; she tried to skim it off. Examined the carrots. Not good.

'What is it?' Marion asked, peering into the serving dishes.

'I'm afraid,' Frances said, 'the fucking Saudiflon is coming off the pans.'

Marion picked up a spoon and began to stab and scrape at the vegetables, her tongue between her teeth.

'You can't do that,' Frances said. 'We'll be here all night.'

'Slosh some more butter on. They'll never know.'

'That'll just make it float about on top.'

'Well, never mind,' Marion said. 'I'll bring the salad, shall I? I don't suppose Saudiflon tastes of anything. With luck they'll just think it's black pepper.'

When they got back to the dining-room Russel was smoking already. He offered a cigarette to Daphne. 'I don't mind women smoking,' he explained, 'but I don't like to see it in my wife.'

Marion sat down, without looking at him, and kicked off her shoes under the table. 'I'll find you an ashtray,' Frances said.

She disliked, in particular, the way the flesh welled over Russel's collar. She thought, you think you're such a phil-anthropist, don't you, to marry her and give her a couple of children; Mr Big-Heart. Carla Zussman, from the other end of the table, gave her a tight, compressed smile.

'Ah, Frances,' Eric Parsons said. 'If you've finished flitting about . . . I've heard of a job prospect. An old friend of mine is leaving the Kingdom, and his wife used to do a bit of filing for this firm . . . I've got her telephone number here.'

'I don't want to do filing,' Frances said, summoning a reserve of pleasantness. I must do better than this, she thought; after all, I invited them here.

'Oh, but it's an opportunity,' Daphne Parsons said. She tilted her head charmingly, and gave Frances her best poison-madonna smile; with her knife, she delicately scraped at the fragment of veal on her plate.

'It's not what I call an opportunity,' Frances said.

'You're not worried about the police, are you?'

'Not really, but then if you are going to do something illegal, it ought to be something a bit more exciting.'

'But what do you do all day? You don't see anyone, do you?'

'I see my neighbours.'

'Oh, you bother with Raji's wife.' Russel stubbed out his cigarette in the saucer she had found for him. 'Shouldn't be surprised if he doesn't try to put some sort of a deal your way, Andrew. Raji's a crook.'

Jeff said, with his mouth full, 'They're all crooks.' He reached for the carafe, and Andrew shifted in his chair, watchful host, ready to replenish it when there was a gap in the conversation. 'But then I'm a cynic,' Jeff said.

'Are you?' Frances asked him. 'Are you proud of that?'

'Yes . . . why not?'

'I think being a cynic only means you've had a lot of disappointments in your life. That's nothing to be proud of.'

There was a short pause. 'Very philosophical,' Russel said. 'Frances is a clever girl. She thinks she's above office work, Daphne.'

'I do, really,' Frances said.

'It's the best offer you'll get, I'm afraid,' Daphne said airily. 'You'll get awfully bored, as the months go by.'

'Yes, I know you mean for the best, but I'm just not cut out to be a filing clerk.'

Carla Zussman put down her fork. 'Honey,' she said firmly, 'if you don't want the job, you don't take it.'

The doorbell rang. Saved, Frances thought. 'I'll get it.' There's a limit to how rude you can be at your own dinner party, she thought; more's the pity.

Yasmin was giving a dinner party too, though for her it was more routine; Frances had made extra bowls of salad, and had taken one across the hall, and one upstairs to Samira. Sarsaparilla had opened the door, and a tear had run slowly down her cheek and dropped into the vinaigrette.

Now Yasmin had returned some dessert, a pale and creamy dish strewn with chopped nuts. Frances tasted it. Andrew came into the kitchen behind her. 'Are you going to give it to them? It looks a bit unappetizing.'

'It's nice.' She offered him some, on the tip of a spoon, but he backed off.

'Try and be nice yourself,' he said. 'What're those black spots that are in everything?'

'It came off the pans.'

'Oh, no . . . Did it? Why didn't you notice?'

'Because I'm incompetent,' she said calmly. She bent down to take a jug of cream from the fridge. 'I'd never make a filing clerk.'

As she returned to the dining-room she hugged herself, mentally, whispering consoling words. They've drunk their wine, haven't they, they've eaten their veal, or most of it. They haven't said, is this by any chance Saudiflon? They can't have seen it. Or politeness wouldn't constrain them. Politeness? Pollard? Russel Smallbone? They haven't really noticed the food, that's what it is. They're too busy boasting, about the vacations they're planning for next summer, about how their unit trusts have gone up. She resumed her seat. Only the Zussmans were not boasting. They had transferred their salad from their bowls to their plates, and they were cutting the lettuce up small, and eating every scrap, eating every leaf, with a concentrated energy; as if they had been told that some starving child in Africa would be glad of it. Rickie reached again for the salad bowl, the hairs on his arm

– he had rolled up his sleeves – a pale fuzzy crest in the candlelight.

'Have you heard what's going on at the Philippines Embassy?' Daphne said. 'It seems the place is full of maids who've run away from Saudi households. And the Embassy staff won't repatriate them until they come up with bribes. Apparently there are hundreds of them, camping out in the grounds.'

'How do you know?' Andrew said, interested. 'Has somebody seen them?'

'Well, I have it on good authority,' Mrs Parsons said. 'I was told by a committee member, at the British Wives.'

'Hundreds seems a lot,' Carla said. 'Still, you never know in this town.'

'And the Filipino nurses,' Marion said. 'Did you hear about the nurses, Fran?'

'I don't think I did.'

'I thought everybody knew.'

'She wouldn't hear it from her neighbours, would she?' Russel said. 'Have some sense, Marion.'

'There were two of them, and they were out with some Lebanese men. And the police stopped them, and wanted to see their documents. Well, of course, they weren't married, were they?'

'Get the story right, Marion,' Russel said. 'You may as well get it right, if you're going to tell it at all. These two couples were walking around Jeddah International Market. The police picked them up and put them in the back of a van.'

'I heard they let the men go,' Eric Parsons said. 'It was just the girls they took.'

'Well, you're right, you're right, but what actually happened, according to my source, was that they picked the two Lebanese up, but then they dumped them out somewhere –'

'Near the souk,' Daphne said.

'And then,' Russel resumed, 'the two girls were found

dead next day, in the car-park on the roof of Sarawat supermarket. They'd been raped, of course.'

A short pause. Frances scanned the table. The Zussmans had stopped eating at last. A particularly large speck of Saudiflon lay, like an exclamation mark, in the centre of Daphne's plate.

'That's funny,' Andrew said. 'I didn't think there was a car-park on the roof at Sarawat.'

'I heard,' Carla said, 'that it happened at Sarawat in Riyadh.'

'Oh well, I don't know,' Russel said. 'But I did definitely hear that they've got the five policemen involved.'

'Yes, I heard that,' Daphne said. 'And one of them was executed yesterday.'

'What about the mother and daughter in the souk?' Frances said. 'Those Australians. The rape. Did they execute anyone for that?'

'Let them go, as far as I heard,' Jeff said. 'The police wouldn't proceed. Women walking around the souk in shorts, they were asking for it, weren't they?'

'Well, right,' Russel said. 'Why can't they be careful? Marion's always careful. I mean you have to have rules, don't you? Otherwise you'd get women going down to the souk in bikinis.'

'I don't see why you would,' Frances said. 'You don't have dress rules in England, but you don't get people walking down Regent Street in bikinis.'

'It doesn't matter what they were wearing,' Carla Zussman said. 'They weren't asking for anything.' Andrew leaned towards her with the wine, and she covered her glass with her hand. 'Thanks, enough. I have to say, though, I've heard so many versions of that story, I don't know what to believe.'

'It scares me,' Marion said.

'Look,' Russel told her, 'you keep the rules, and you won't come to any harm in the Kingdom. Respect yourself, and you'll be respected, that's my view. You girls can say what you like, with your women's lib. nonsense, but as a family man I regard this place as a much better proposition for my wife and children than ever Africa was. You don't hear of armed robbery here, do you? No, because they know what they'd get.'

'Of course you don't hear of armed robbery,' Frances said. 'That doesn't mean it doesn't exist.'

'You hear,' Carla said, 'what they want you to hear. You think what they want you to think. Don't you know that yet, Russel?'

'Look,' Andrew said, 'more wine, anybody? Frances, I think we're ready for the pudding.'

They met up in the kitchen. 'I want some Perrier for Carla,' Andrew said. 'Listen, Frances, just cool it, will you? You shouldn't take Russel apart like that.'

'Carla was right.' She scraped vegetables into the bin. 'How can you know what goes on?' Bethinking herself, she took a can of insecticide from under the sink and sprayed the floor around the bin. 'You can't travel around inside the Kingdom. You can't go and see. You can't even go to the Philippines Embassy, I suppose, and count these hundreds of maids who are camping out.'

'You take a certain amount on trust,' Andrew said.

She rinsed her hands, and dried them. 'Here, carry this. I'll bring this pudding of Yasmin's. Somebody might want it.'

Andrew brought to the table a glazed tart of small, out-of-season strawberries, and a jug of thick yellow cream. 'Oh, how lovely,' Marion said, and yearning crossed her face. 'But I mustn't.'

'Marion has to watch her figure,' Russel explained.

'Don't we all!' said Daphne gaily. 'No, Frances dear, not for me. But it does look rather delicious, I must say.'

'Any black specs?' Jeff said, peering.

'Perhaps you'd like some of this?' Frances indicated Yasmin's dessert.

'What is it?' Rickie Zussman asked.

'I don't know, but I had a spoonful in the kitchen, it's nice. My neighbour sent it.'

'No thank you,' Rickie said. 'Carla and I never eat desserts,' he added politely. 'But I'm sure it tastes fine.'

Jeff picked up the serving spoon and dabbled it into the dish. A shred of coconut and a fleck of green pistachio floated to the surface, with the delicate scent of rosewater. 'Looks as if it's been regurgitated. Wouldn't touch Paki food at the best of times. Think I'll give it a miss.'

'Me too,' Russel said. 'You can give me some of the strawberry thing, if you will, my love. My goodness, Andrew, you do well for yourself. Married a good cook, eh?'

'As well as a philosopher.' Frances stood up. 'Excuse me.' As she turned away she caught her hip painfully on the corner of the table. Eric's wine spilled. 'I'll bring back a cloth,' she said, averting her face.

'That's all right,' Eric said absently, dabbing up the liquid with his white linen napkin. The red wine, which they had made with cherry juice, was dark and strong, and they had got through a number of bottles already.

In the kitchen, Frances heard Carla running down the hall towards her; heard the slap of Carla's feet, in her flat leather sandals. She turned to meet her, her face flushed, angry and defensive tears springing into her eyes.

'It's a failure,' she said. 'An utter mess.' She searched her pocket for a handkerchief, and Carla tore off a strip of kitchen roll and gave it to her. She blew her nose.

Carla's sparrow arms went around her neck. 'Nothing's a failure. What do you mean, failure? Your life doesn't ride on a Jeddah dinner party. Listen, they're here because you're obliged to them. That's all. You feed them and your obligation ends. If they want to squabble and tell scare stories, let them.'

'Oh, go back, Carla, would you?' Frances scrubbed the tears from her face, leaving it blotchy. 'Just keep the conversation going. If Pollard says anything else about my neighbour, just push a glass in his face, would you?'

'Yeah,' Carla said. Her quiff of tough dark hair seemed to bristle, like a terrier's. 'I'll scar him for life,' she said.

Frances made the coffee. When she took in the tray Russel had vacated his chair, and taken hers; he had got a piece of paper from somewhere, and was demonstrating to Jeff, by means of figures, that smart investors were moving into nickel. Having no choice, she sat down by Daphne, and began to set out the cups. Daphne leaned towards her. 'I hope you're not making a mistake about that job.'

'I don't think so. Coffee, everybody?'

'Carla and I usually drink herb tea,' Rickie offered.

'Pour the coffee,' Carla said.

'Okay,' Rickie said amiably. 'It was just information, you know, not a suggestion.'

'I'll pass these cups down, shall I?' Daphne resumed her confidential tone. 'Tell me, Frances, how long have you been married?'

'Five years.'

'That's nice.'

Frances felt a passion of enmity for the woman, a torrent of choked-off phrases, leaving a nasty taste in her mouth. Five years was nice, was it? What would fifteen years have been? Nicer still, or not nice at all? What would five months have been?

'So perhaps you're thinking of starting your family?'

'Not really.'

'You shouldn't leave it too late, you know.'

She felt Mrs Parsons looking her up and down: thinking, no doubt, perhaps she has a little problem. Maybe her natural tact, which she was always referring to, would forbid her to say more.

'I think you've forgotten the sugar, Frances dear.'

'Does anyone take sugar?'

'I do,' Russel said.

Andrew began to get up. 'I'll get it,' Frances said.

In the kitchen, she took the opportunity to rinse a few glasses. Soon be over, she told herself. A pity that it's taken a fortnight out of my life.

When she returned the topic of conversation had shifted.

'I see they've put a tank trap outside the American Embassy,' Jeff was saying.

'Perennially popular target, I should suppose,' Eric Parsons said.

'Who for?' She slid the sugar bowl down to Russel.

'Anybody, really. There are a lot of people who don't like the US influence here. Even people within the royal family.'

'The newspapers are always denouncing us,' Carla said. 'But it's only for show. They need our guns.'

'It keeps the fundamentalists happy,' Rickie said. 'All the – what do you call it. Rhetoric.'

'I wouldn't say it kept them happy,' Carla said. 'Not happy exactly. But you see, Frances, the Saudis are trying to keep the lid on things in this part of the world. They're rich, thank you. What do they want with the Islamic revolution? Though they have to pay lip-service.'

'So the Saudis give their money,' Rickie said. 'And other Arabs give their blood.'

'My neighbour told me – my Saudi neighbour, I mean – that when girls' schools were first opened, there were riots.'

'There were riots when TV was introduced,' Jeff said. 'The King's nephew was the ringleader. The security forces shot him dead.'

'They have a little go, every few years,' Mrs Parsons said. 'Some of them, they want the place to be like Iran.'

'They cut their *thobes* short, and grow their beards long,' Carla said. 'And then it's jihad, it's holy war. Martyrs. If you die in battle you go straight to heaven.'

'I didn't think that happened. Not here.'

'The place nearly fell apart in '79,' Parsons said. 'You must remember when those madmen took over the Grand Mosque in Mecca. God knows how many were killed. It was a full-scale military operation, winkling them out. They didn't want football, they said. They didn't want video games. They didn't want working women.'

'They didn't want the House of Saud,' Rickie said.

'That was it, really. They wanted to overthrow the royal

family. The same week, the Shia were rioting in the Eastern Province. Looting, burning buses. Funny thing was, at the time none of us knew what was going on. Total news blackout. But they were pretty close to the edge, if you ask me.'

'There are,' Rickie said, 'two distinct military bodies, the army and the National Guard. So if one decides to do its own thing, maybe the King can rely on the other. They're under the command of two different princes, of course.'

'The King doesn't trust his relatives?'

'Recent history,' Carla said, 'gives him no reason to.'

'I don't think I really knew this.'

'Nobody knows till they come here,' Daphne said.

Carla looked up. 'I should suppose the State Department knows. And the British Foreign Office. It's not that these things are secret. It's that we don't talk about them.'

'Why don't we?' Frances said. 'You mean really, it's not stable here, it's not safe? There are far worse things happening than people being raped in the souk?'

There was a silence. The guests looked down at their plates, as if slightly ashamed of themselves; as if they had egged someone on to tell a piece of scandal, and knew they had gone too far.

'Well, we know it won't last for ever, don't we?' Eric Parsons said at last; in his sane, reasonable, soothing tone, which Andrew had already learned to distrust. 'We're just here to do our jobs, make our pile, and get out. All we hope is that it will last our time.'

'I'll get some more coffee.' As she passed her husband, Frances rested her hand for a moment on his shoulder. She felt slightly queasy. As she left the room Jeff's voice floated after her.

'Of course, you know what the Al Saud do with their dissidents, don't you? Take them up in planes over the Empty Quarter, handcuff them, and drop them out without a parachute.'

'Yes, I heard that,' Carla was saying. 'But the handcuffs seem superfluous.'

This time it was Marion who followed her. She was clearly bored with the politics; she looked sleepy, and fractious, as if she were one of her own children. 'Lovely dinner, Fran,' she said. She stood by the sink, cooling her bare feet on the lino tiles, and picking at the strawberry tart, of which more than half remained.

'Here.' Frances cut her a slice. 'Eat it while he's not looking.'

'He does go on,' Marion said. 'About my weight. Have you got any cream left?' She licked her fingers. 'By the way, I meant to ask you, what are we going to do about Christmas?'

'Oh, not Christmas,' Frances groaned. 'What happens at Christmas? Are we allowed to have it?'

'The men get a day off. Unofficial, of course. We could get together at our compound and have Christmas dinner. You can come in the morning and help me cook. Carla and Rickie might like to come. It's always so sad at Christmas, when people haven't got children.'

'I'm sure we'll feel better for sharing yours.'

'Oh, I didn't mean you, Fran.' Marion's mouth was full of strawberries. 'I expect you'll have some, won't you? When you get round to it. Only Carla, she's so libby, know what I mean? It's probably cos she's not very attractive.'

'You ought to put something on those bites,' Frances said.

'Oh, do they show?' Marion sucked her spoon. She wasn't going to bother; she felt glamorous, anyway, and that was half the battle.

'So is it all right then? Will you come?'

'Will Jeff be there?'

'Oh, I always have Jeff, at Christmas.'

'Well, just promise me, will you, that if he starts talking about dirty Ay-rabs, and Pakis, and all that, you'll get up with me and walk out. Because I can't stand it.'

'He is a bit of a racialist,' Marion said fondly.

'Promise?'

'Okay,' Marion said vaguely. 'I'll take that coffee through, shall I?'

Andrew had managed to move them all from the table to the armchairs, which Frances had arranged earlier into a rough circle. The candles had burnt out. Jeff obtained from Andrew a private bottle of red wine, which he put on the floor by his chair. 'Not bad stuff this,' he said. 'You've got the knack.' Rickie Zussman occupied the end of a sofa, his face abstracted and his eyes on the far wall; his wife's hand rested loosely in his own. Neither of the Americans took further part in the conversation, but Eric and Jeff bored on for a while, about immigrants in the U K. 'Let's face it,' Jeff said. 'They've got different customs. They've got different values. They've got a different way of life.'

'Incidentally,' Russel said, 'do you ever catch a glimpse of the people in the empty flat?'

'The dark lady,' Daphne said.

Jeff chortled. 'Who knows what's under the veil?'

'No, we've never seen anybody,' Andrew said. 'Frances thought she heard footsteps once. But she wasn't sure.'

'The Deputy Minister's nephew, isn't it?' Marion said.

'Brother, I thought.' Andrew turned to Parsons. 'Eric, didn't you tell me his brother.'

'Did I? Must be then.'

'I thought it was the nephew,' Jeff said. 'Greasy character. Looks the type. You'd know him if you saw him, Andrew, he hangs around the Ministry.'

Andrew smiled. 'Don't think I would, you know, Jeff old boy. All these coloured chappies in white frocks look the same to me, don't you know? Teatowels on their heads. Filthy foreign food. Eat goats, you know. Dreadful types. All right with that bottle down there, are you? Get you another?'

Surely they would go home soon. Frances closed her eyes. She saw skeletons, neat, bleached, reticulated, on the vast desert floor. Andrew touched her. She jumped. 'I wasn't asleep,' she said.

'You were.'

It was two o'clock when everyone left. Andrew waved a

hand at them as he opened the gate, meaning hush, keep the
noise down. The roads were empty, the night air was mild.
They stood for a moment in the shadow of the wall, their
arms around each other, then re-entered Dunroamin,
locking the doors behind them. Inside, a procession of
cockroaches was wending its way along the hall towards the
kitchen bin. Andrew went for the spray. 'I'll sweep them up
in the morning,' he said; and then, violently, brought down
his foot on the largest of them, squashing it into the tiles.

'Oh, Christ,' Frances said. The mess was horrifying; quite
disproportionate. Blood, debris, detached legs. A slaughter-
house.

'The others will eat it,' Andrew said.

'I'll have to rinse all the plates off. There's ants, as well.'

Andrew took her shoulder, pulled her towards him, ran a
hand over her breast. 'Tomorrow,' he said. 'Come to bed.'

'You can't do it,' she said. 'You're too drunk.'

'I can try. Or do you hate all men tonight, is that it? I
don't think I'd blame you.'

Over his shoulder she saw the pans piled up in the sink,
the tray of sticky glasses, the saucer overflowing with Russel's
cigarette butts, and the stained napkins in a heap on the
draining-board. She laid her head against his chest. 'No,'
she said. 'You're all right.'

Rabi al-thani

Sometimes I wake up saying, I hope nobody crosses me today. Sometimes the air seems too thick to breathe.

Since the dinner party life has just gone on. I cook, and we shop. We sleep late at weekends, watch a film. When I am in a good mood I think of the money mounting up in the bank. Now the shops are full of 'seasonal trees'. The Embassies are holding carol services, which they call 'Family Welfare Meetings'. The word Christmas is not to be mentioned, but nobody can impede the progress of goodwill to all men.

Andrew accuses me of lacking tact. He says that it seems to him that I ask too many questions, and don't I remember that when we came to Dunroamin we were told to be careful? He says I shouldn't be allowed out into the hall without a UN peacekeeping force.

My neighbours say women are not veiled because they are despised, but because they are revered. It is out of self-respect that they cover their faces and bodies, and out of respect for them that men do not look. At first this is plausible – but it bothers me. Something is wrong. I know what it is. I just don't believe it.

Everything is fine, for about two weeks at a time. But then some word, some event, some trivial incident, will trigger off a screaming rage. I don't scream, of course, but sometimes I cry a little, in private, knowing that if

I could cry properly, yell and bawl and shed tears, I wouldn't wake up in the mornings with such a leaden weight inside my head. I would like to tear the roof off, and let some light into the flat. I would like to run down the street, hitting people. Run amok. I would like to stride up to the next veiled woman I see and tear the black cloth from her face, and rip it up before her eyes.

I know that would be wrong. But I would like to do it.

Andrew says the leaden feeling is sinus trouble. He says you get it from living with air-conditioning.

CONFIDENTIAL MEMORANDUM
FROM: Director, Turadup, William & Schaper, Kingdom of Saudi Arabia
TO: All expatriate staff
DATED: 2 Rabi al-thani/24 December
We have received extremely strong hints, from our valued and most reliable contacts, that the police will be out in force over the 'Festive Season', that breathalyser equipment has been issued and that random roadblocks and on-the-spot checks are to be expected. Everything indicates a blitz aimed at putting a damper on expatriate festivities therefore PLEASE remember that in the event of your being picked up under the influence there is very little that Turadup can do for you.

May I wish you all the compliments of the Season, and a happy and prosperous New Year . . .

When Frances went across the hall, and rang Yasmin's doorbell, a huge yellow sari opened the door; and Raji's mother looked down at her, in silence. She did not speak any English, or if she did, she didn't speak it now; and she folded her arms across her matron's bosom, seeming to squash it into overlapping layers and yellow folds. Her face was jowly, her eyes direct; her body was slow, deliberate, pachydermatous; soon she might bellow. There was a fringe of hair on her upper lip; and her arms were bare to the elbow, as if for combat.

'I'll call later,' Frances said.

But later there was a banging at the door, and Yasmin hurtled in, her pointed nose reddened at the tip, a square of lace handkerchief scrunched in her hand. 'Oh, she will kill me, she will kill me,' she said. 'She has called thirty people for dinner tomorrow night. She finds fault with everything, everything. She says Selim is stunted.'

'He looks all right to me,' Frances said.

'She says I am not feeding him. She is holding his nose and forcing things down his throat. Tell me, Frances, please find out from one of your friends – there must be some drug I can give him, to make him grow?'

'That doesn't sound a good idea.'

'She watches me every minute. And Shams is sulking because she is turned out of her room.'

'Where's she sleeping then?'

'Well of course, on the dining-room floor.'

'But your guests don't go till three, these mornings.'

Yasmin shrugged, crossly. 'It is me who is suffering, not Shams, I can tell you. Everything in my life is wrong for that woman. Everything I do.'

'How long's she staying?'

'How can I know? Raji says, it is my mother, as long as she likes. Really, Frances, she is blind to him. Blind to his faults –'

'Let's hope the singing doesn't keep her awake at night.'

Yasmin looked at her, directly, then brought her palms together, secreting the handkerchief between them. She dropped her eyes. 'I am interrupting you,' she said. 'I had forgotten it was Christmas Eve.'

'Send Shams across tomorrow night, and I'll give her some pudding for you.'

At the door, Yasmin said quietly, her eyes on the floor, 'Frances, I do not see why I should have to live with shame.'

*

174

'But they didn't, did they?' Jeff Pollard said. 'They couldn't, could they? Spoil our Christmas.'

It was the festive day now, 3 Rabi al-thani. Marion sat slumped at the other end of the table. 'I miss the Queen,' she said.

Carla looked up. 'I beg your pardon?'

'Her speech. She makes a speech.' Marion sighed heavily. 'Somebody ought to watch those kids in the pool.'

Somebody. But not me. Marion rubbed her forehead with a dazed, sweaty, gravy-stained hand. 'There's a huge lot of everything left.'

'Give it to the gatekeeper,' Russel said, lolling back in his chair. 'He can have his pals round.'

'Will he want cold sprouts?' Frances asked.

'He wants anything.'

'Onions and rice, that's what he eats,' Marion said. 'He's saving up to go back to India.'

It was four in the afternoon. The children had opened their presents, and were outside trying to drown each other. Christmas was the same everywhere, Marion thought. But hot, it was so hot here, and the drink was so poisonous and giddying. And she had worked so hard, what with this year's mysterious tinsel shortage, and the dearth of good potatoes for roasting. Dust lay already on the spines of the plastic tree; before I pack it away, she thought vaguely, I could just put it under the shower.

'At Ramadhan,' Jeff said, 'they make life a misery for us. They make sure we take account of *their* festivals.'

Frances said, hopelessly, 'It's their country.'

'I can't understand you,' Jeff said. He propped his elbow on the table, and fingered his Credit Suisse token; a purple streamer half-detached itself from the ceiling, and swung gently over his head. 'I can't make you out. First you attack these people, then you defend them.'

'Look, I don't have any theories. I just go issue by issue. I just speak as I find.'

'As long,' Jeff said, 'as you don't take them seriously. As

long as you remember that, basically, you're dealing with nignogs.'

Frances rose from her place, dabbing her mouth with her napkin and taking off her paper hat. 'Excuse me,' she said. She was not going to make a scene, but she meant to keep her promise. She dropped her napkin on her chair and looked across the table at Marion. Marion looked back at her, stupidly. Frances walked out of the room. She stood in the hall, trying not to listen to the conversation, and wondering if Marion would follow her. No one came; neither Marion to join her protest, nor Jeff to apologize, nor even her husband, to persuade her back to the table and give her a chance to state her objections.

After a few minutes, she realized that no one was ever going to come. They didn't know she had walked out in protest. They just thought she had gone to the lavatory. She went back in and sat down at the table, and put her paper hat back on.

Half an hour later, when the women were clearing up, the Parsons arrived. They were doing a round of the Turadup parties; they were anxious to assuage the uncaring impression of Eric's very necessary circular. So that he himself could drink, Eric had requisitioned Hasan for the day. 'Hello there, everybody, compliments of the season,' Eric called, walking in through the open door; his footprints left dust upon the carpet. Hasan sat outside, his car door wedged open, his sandalled feet in the dust; speaking a pidgin Arabic with the gatekeeper, and flicking his fingers at passing flies.

'Well?' Russel demanded. 'Been stopped, have you?'

'There was a roadblock on King Khalid Street.'

'Oh yes, Hasan get breathalysed?'

'Actually they were just asking for papers. Just took a look at us and waved us through.'

Russel grunted. 'Looking for somebody then, aren't they? Not interested in booze. I don't know why you're getting your knickers in a twist, Eric. Jesus, when I think back . . . those Wine Festivals we used to have, competitions, you know . . . had them at somebody's house, Andrew, every-thing done properly, evening dress . . . the Ambassador used to come. I remember the Arnotts showing up at one, when the Saudis let them out on bail.'

'Yes,' Eric Parsons said, a little more sharply than usual. 'But those days are over.'

Daphne spread herself on the sofa, gracious in her silk suit; she dissected a mince pie with a pastry fork, peering closely at every morsel she ate. 'Did you make these, Frances dear?' she inquired. To Marion, walking around with stacks of dirty plates, she said, 'Don't you have a dishwasher?'

The Shores walked home. It was the best time to be out: a sky of gold and dusty pink, blossoming lights in the evening streets, and the crackle of the mosque's loudspeakers, the muezzin's amplified wail. At weekends, cars jostle nose to tail on the Corniche, half the city turns out to see the sunset; which sometimes occurs with astonishing speed. Inland dark falls more quickly still, the sun dropping behind concrete towers. Night closes in on the city, as if night were its natural milieu.

'Do you remember the garden?' Frances said. Andrew walked along the pavement's high edge, as if to demonstrate that he was sober; she walked in the road, a foot below him, keeping close to his side. 'Do you remember, when we were shopping one night, I pointed it out to you?'

'Can't say I do. Where was that then?'

She thought about it. 'I'm not sure. I'd lost my bearings.'

'That's not like you.'

'It was a while ago.' They turned into Al-Suror Street. White figures, sharp in the gloom, hurried towards the mosque. 'But you must remember, there was a gate, and a light inside, and you could see a lawn. I've been wishing we could go past it again.'

'What for?'

'I'd just like to see it.'

He was prepared to gratify her; take her at once, if she liked. But 'Could be difficult to find,' he said. 'Haven't we passed it since?'

'We don't seem to have.'

'Perhaps we were going round a diversion, or something. Road works. Or maybe they've just changed the one-way system. They're always doing that.'

Inside the gate of the Ministry of Pilgrimages' office, a nightwatchman squatted in a kind of lean-to; lamplight splashed across his dhoti, and showed his downcast face, his hands hanging loose between his knees. Cats squalled, invisible, behind a wall.

'Don't you remember at all?' she asked.

He put a hand gently on her shoulder for a second as he stepped off the kerb. 'Why does it matter?'

'Oh, I've been thinking about that lawn. About what it might be like to have real grass, instead of Astroturf. When they plant flowers here they look like wax. The trees all seem to be dying. You really didn't see it? You don't remember me mentioning it?'

''Fraid not.' They were at Dunroamin now, outside the metal door in the wall; Andrew fumbled with his keys in the half-light. 'Seen any more rats lately?' he asked.

'No. I've heard them.'

'Damn.' Andrew dropped his keys on the step. He bent to retrieve them. She looked back over her shoulder, down the empty street. But it was not empty, because outside the computer-supplies shop, with its locked metal shutters, a man in a *thobe* stood in the shadow of the wall; he was looking away from her, his head turned towards the Medina road, and in his hand, butt downwards towards the pavement, he held a rifle.

'Andrew –'

Her voice died in her throat. She put out a hand, and softly touched his bent back. He straightened up, the keys jangling, and pushed one into the lock. There was a scrape

178

of metal. 'Must oil this,' he said. 'No use waiting for Raji to do it, might filthy up his best suit.' He pushed open the door, and stepped inside, behind the wall. She glanced back down the street. The man was still there, motionless. 'Come on,' Andrew said. She tore her eyes away, and stepped inside; he locked the gate behind her.

Next morning at eleven the doorbell rang. She expected Shams, with some of the leftovers from the dinner for thirty, but instead it was a male visitor – a scented little man, with a bristling, freshly trimmed beard, a *thobe*, and a briefcase. Under his *thobe* he had a tight little paunch, which seemed less a part of him than a prized possession; as his eyes passed over her, he patted it with his free hand. 'Hello, madam,' he said, and grinned broadly. 'I am the landlord. I come to introduce myself.'

'How do you do?' Frances said.

'Can I come in and look at my property?'

'Yes, if you like.'

He stepped in, put down his briefcase, and brought his hands together, with a little double clap. 'You have any complaints?' He spoke as if this were not possible; not even imaginable.

'There are rats,' Frances said.

'Outside?' said the landlord swiftly.

'Certainly, outside,' she admitted.

'But I am concern only with inside.'

'Yes, I see.'

'I may tour around?'

'Go ahead.' She sat down at the desk, to resume writing her diary; then got up as he left the room and wandered between the armchairs, restless, her arms folded protectively across her breasts.

When the landlord had toured around he came back to the sitting-room, with an expression of satisfaction. 'I compliment you,' he said. 'You keep it very nice. I am a lover of the British. What part you are from?'

'Yorkshire.'

'Yorkshire.' The landlord glowed, and kissed his bunched fingertips. 'I am knowing your Yorkshire. I am knowing that country so well. Windsor Castle, Tottenham Hotspur. William Wordsworth, the Bard of Avon. Your famous Langan's Brasserie.' His eyes slid over her again. 'Madam, how many children you have got?'

'I have four,' she said. 'All boys.'

'I congratulate you,' the landlord said, in simple pleasure. 'And yet you seem to be a girl of twenty-one, madam.' He took occasion to sidle up to her, and pat her waist. She moved away. 'You will be seeing more of me,' he promised.

'Don't forget your briefcase,' Frances said.

'That lady across, does she wear the veil?'

'Yes and no. She covers her head.'

'Ah,' said the landlord, with a pious look. 'Then I will not bother her. She will not open the door.'

Bother me, won't you, you fat little greasepot, Frances thought. She let him out and locked the door behind him. She hoped that he would hear the turn of the key.

FRANCES SHORE'S DIARY: *8 Rabi al-thani*

Yet another letter in the newspaper today, debating whether women are the source of evil and sin.

Yasmin says that the Bedu have hunting rifles, and sometimes bring them to town. I didn't tell her why I was asking.

Andrew's model arrived at last. It was detained by the customs men, and he and Jeff had to go up to the airport and collect it, taking Hasan with them in case anyone had to be bribed. They brought it back here, to my surprise, and put it down on the dining-room table. It was a perfect white palace sealed in a perspex box, like a spoiled child's toy. They looked like death. Jeff said, I shall have to go and borrow Russel's electric drill. I said, why, what are you going to do to it, isn't it right? Andrew said, The Ministry would go mad if they saw this.

And when I looked closely, I saw that the model-makers had peopled it, and that on its snaky glass escalators, and on its emerald plastic lawn, there were miniature women – pin-thin Californian executive women, in sharp suits, and flossy Californian secretary women, with mini-skirts, and tight sundresses showing off their glossy plastic shoulders and their half-bare plastic breasts.

Andrew stamped around saying, have we got a wire coathanger, have we got tweezers?

When Jeff brought back the drill they made a little hole in the back, and tied the tweezers to the coathanger, and pushed them through the hole. Then one by one, they got a grip on the plastic women, by their heads, and dragged them out, swearing, saying have they no bloody idea in Los Angeles? Well, there's my morning gone, Jeff said. I collected the little women in the palm of my hand. They were perfect, each one with the same doll's features, and crushed skull.

Jeff went back to the office then, but Andrew knelt down and looked at his model for a long time, his hands flat on the table and his chin resting on his hands, pretending to gaze up from street level. I said, to encourage him, it will be all right now, you can fill up the hole with glue. He said, the money is running out.

I was amazed. I thought that in the Kingdom I would never hear those words. It can't be running out.

He said, we are running out of money to pay the subcontractors, because the Saudi government has not paid us.

Why not?

Because oil has fallen, they're cutting back. It's hitting everybody, all the government departments. They're all fighting each other for cash.

But they must have vast reserves –

Of course, but Turadup K S A hasn't got vast

reserves. I may not get paid for another month.

But you will get paid?

Eventually. We are waiting for some money to be remitted from Riyadh.

He looked worried. Depressed. Said, I don't think somehow I will ever see the building finished. It is, he said, just like the rest of the world, you dream about something but they won't let you do it. I think I was dreaming about this building before I saw the architect's plan, before I'd ever heard of Turadup. But to them it's just another capital project.

I saw him gathering his wits, for months of silent effort. We'll just have to wait, he said, sit it out, but I really think, I really do think, that they've cheated me. The promises were false.

I put the Californians in my desk drawer. They looked carefree, even with their mutilations. Andrew will now start to think about the building day and night, and if there is anything else to be thought about, that will have to be done by me.

'I have to ask you something,' Frances said to Andrew. 'About the empty flat. Though I realize you may be bored with the topic.'

'I haven't found out anything new, if that's what you mean.'

'I was just thinking that an awful lot of people seem to know something about it. All the *khawwadjihs* have heard the rumour, even though they have different versions of it. And so, what they're doing, this couple, isn't it very risky?'

'Of course it is,' Andrew said. 'Presumably it's a risk they're prepared to take. You can't keep things quiet in this town.'

'Can't you? You see, he needn't use Dunroamin. Why does he? You said yourself that there were hundreds of villas empty in Jeddah, that there were whole apartment blocks to let.'

'I suppose that if you drove up to what is meant to be an empty block, or an empty house, and went into it, and if you did that a few times, people might notice and get suspicious.'

'That's true. So if he comes here, it would look as if he were visiting somebody.'

'Yes. Quite legit.'

'But what if our neighbours see him? Or see the woman? Are they in on it? Do they know?'

'Yasmin and Samira don't hang about on the stairs, do they, waiting to accost strangers?'

'But Raji? And Abdul Nasr?'

'Maybe they're in on it. This man is a VIP. They wouldn't cross him, would they?'

'But what about us?' Frances said. 'How can they rely on our discretion?'

'They probably think I'm too attached to my paycheck to rock the boat.'

'And the landlord – does he know?'

'I don't suppose there's a special adulterer's rent book.'

'But listen, Andrew, there is something wrong here – because if the *khawwadjihs* know about it, if they talk about it and speculate and make jokes, then the Saudis must know about it, too, mustn't they? So are you saying that there's a benign conspiracy, that everybody knows, but they turn a blind eye?'

'I don't know.' He was exasperated; she had known he would be, before too long. 'I don't see how you expect me to enter into the thought processes of a Saudi princeling having a bit on the side. What is it, Fran, have you finished your detective story? Do you want to go up to the library tonight?'

'Yes, we could do. I'm getting bored with them though. I'm never really happy with the motives. The books don't go into motives enough. It's all stuff about the footprints in the garden, and the calibre of the murder weapon, but you never find out what really interests you.'

'Maybe,' Andrew said tentatively, 'you shouldn't be so interested in the empty flat.'

'Sometimes I wonder if the whole thing hasn't been made up.'

'By whom?'

'Oh, by some bored expat. trying to brighten his life. After all, it's just the sort of thing we like to believe about the Saudis, that they're hypocrites, and that they do all this hole-in-corner stuff.'

'That would be boring for you, though. If none of it were true. I wonder if this chap up above has any idea how much time we spend discussing him?'

'I can't imagine.' She tried to imagine. She tried to picture the man, whom she knows that one day she must meet on the stairs – if the rumour is true at all. But she could only see a stiff white *thobe*, unoccupied, in two dimensions, like the one the laundryman held up to the streetlights and headlights of Al-Suror Street; she could only see a *ghutra* framing nothing, an emptiness where the face should be. His image wouldn't move, it wouldn't turn the key in the lock, it wouldn't climb the stairs; if I can't imagine it, she said, it can't happen. Surely nothing in Dunroamin can happen without my knowledge. 'Just suppose –' she said. But Andrew had lost interest in the conversation. She had taxed his patience; he had the building to think about, the great world outside the wall.

'I think,' he said, 'that you're on your own too much.'

She said, 'I like my own company.'

The weather had cooled down; not much, but enough. In the dead time between Christmas and New Year, Frances thought she might sunbathe on the roof. There were higher buildings around, but no one ever looked out of them; and she could hear cousin Clare's voice, speaking to her from the summer ahead, saying, why Frances, you're just as pale as when you went out there.

Hands flat on the warm parapet, she looked out over the city. Over on Medina Road an endless stream of traffic went by. There was distant snarling of engines, bestial but subdued, as if a hidden circus were in town. There was the usual dust haze, pierced by the bones of half-finished buildings, the scaffolding, derricks and cranes. In recent weeks there had been changes; earth-moving equipment had been trundling about the vacant lot on the other side of Ghazzah Street, and a deep ditch had been gouged by the side of the road; as she watched, a single dog, crouching, fled across the waste ground.

Frances crossed the roof to the back of the building, and looked down into the narrow streets behind Dunroamin. This was why, she remembered, she had liked the roof at first; this privileged and private view. It could have been another city; it was a domestic, small-scale scene, of back alleys and back yards, of side doors and washing lines. A coloured servant, her head wrapped in a scarlet cloth, turned a sharp angle of the next block; she had a bundle in her hand, something wrapped in newspaper, and she moved silently, with her flapping sandals, her dusty grey heels, towards the dustbin. The scholars have implored that the faithful should be careful how they wrap their rubbish; that they should not put their vegetable peelings into the *Saudi Gazette*, and throw them into the trash; that they should not tear up squares of *Al-Riyadh*, and hang them in a privy. For that newsprint may contain the sacred name of Allah.

Frances unfolded her canvas chair, sat down, rubbed suncream on her legs, opened her book. A fly circled her head; she flapped a hand at it. The traffic noise nagged at her. It was hotter than she thought, and windy; grit blew across the page. After five minutes, the print danced before her eyes. She stood up, and a pain lanced through her skull. She refolded her chair, tucked her book under her arm; went back down the stairs, stumbling a little, into cool silence.

In Flat 1 she lay on the sofa, her book splayed open on her ribcage; she held ice cubes, wrapped in one of Andrew's handkerchiefs, against her forehead. I shall go to the roof in the morning or the evening, she thought, for five minutes' spying, since that is my pleasure and my pleasures are now few; but to be on the roof in the heat of the day is a punishment, and I should have known better. Eyes closed, she imagined trees; the bark of silver birches, the dense black-green of pines, the scum of algae on English ponds. In July we will go home, she thought, for leave; into the needle-thin rain of the English summer, into dank unpromising Yorkshire mornings, and trees that are yellowing by September.

It was New Year's Eve. They were up at their usual time; Andrew took a shower, ate breakfast and left soon after seven to go to the site. These early starts gave her a sense of purpose, which she knew from experience would soon dissipate; there was no point, in the whole day, on which she could focus her energy. At eight o'clock she was already climbing the stairs to the roof; as if what was most necessary was to convince herself, by seeing the daylight, that another day had begun.

She opened the door at the top of the stairs, and came out into the early sunshine, shading her eyes. In the far corner of the roof she saw a thin veiled figure, wrapped in an *abaya*. Her pulse skipped. 'Yasmin?' she said. She approached, and saw the black shoulders stiffen with shock; then Yasmin turned, and pulled back the veil, her eyes wide, her expression guilty; she put a hand to her throat, a pantomime of consternation and fear.

Frances stopped a few paces from her. 'Did you think I was your mother-in-law?'

'I didn't expect anybody.' Although it was so early, Yasmin had made up her eyes, outlined their long shape in kohl, brushed in her lashes. But then, was she ever without her face? Was she ever without her careful, pre-judged moods? Their friend Samira spent her idle mornings in front of the TV set, watching Egyptian soap operas; the camera dwelled on the faces of suffering women, their painted faces larger than life, their emotions theatrical, rehearsed. Did Yasmin watch them too? Already her features were melting into the artful. 'I did not know you came up here, Frances.'

'I come for the fresh air.' Already by 8.30 a miasma rose from the pavements of Ghazzah Street; fried chicken, sewage, a cocktail of sweat and diesel fumes.

'I too. Just to get away.'

'And how is your mother-in-law?'

Yasmin made a graceful gesture. Everything she did, now, seemed staged; Frances had new eyes. 'Oh, you know . . .'

'I expect,' Frances said, 'that she is still asleep.' You are lying, she thought. You weren't taking the air. You were expecting somebody. Lover boy? So much falls into place. 'They have some conflicts.' Raji's worldly grin, his easy and flourishing career. Why Dunroamin? Because the lady has not far to go. Only a flight of stairs.

Inside she cried and protested: not you, oh not you oh not you.

There was a party that night. Frances slipped into her best white dress. She was losing weight, she noticed. She never thought of eating during the day, not until Andrew came home. She stood in the bathroom before the mirror, brushing her hair and fluffing it out, noticing that the little sun that it saw had streaked it, that it was a straw-like, irrecoverable mess. She took trouble over her make-up, but it seemed to lie on the surface of her skin, as if refusing its part in the charade.

In the car she was silent. 'Are you all right?' Andrew asked.

'I saw Yasmin on the roof this morning,' she said.

'I thought you had the roof to yourself.'

'So did I.'

He didn't say, she noticed, what on earth was Yasmin doing up there. He didn't express the least surprise. And already she was doubting herself. I cannot trust myself to make deductions, she thought; you cannot deduce anything from a flash of fear, sudden intuitions can be sudden errors. Something is wrong, but perhaps it is no particular thing; perhaps it is just the current of my life that has got diverted, that has washed me up in some shallows where I am alone with myself. Neon signs go by: Fun n'Food Garden Restaurant, Electric Laundry, Supermarket Singapore.

The party was held outdoors, and the ladies dabbed cologne on their legs, to keep the mosquitoes away. The hostess circulated with polystyrene cups of fruit punch, and the usual Jeddah party food on oval stainless-steel trays. Frances carried her cup to the light. Scraps of apple and banana floated on the surface of the liquid, each with their beading of grey bubbles. The drink smelled stale, nauseating. She clutched Andrew's arm, wanting him to talk to her. 'I have to go and circulate,' he said.

Something seemed lacking tonight, on the Jeddah party scene; it was a quiet, almost sober gathering. They were all partied to death; they had seen the same people, at one house or another, half a dozen times over the Christmas period, and now their store of small talk was running low, and no one was in the mood for party games, and conviviality must be ground out of them. The men stood in a knot, and spoke of the falling oil price. The women left the garden and huddled together in the kitchen, talking of teething, and microwave ovens, and displaying to each other the bits of gold they had got for presents. Frances hung about on the fringe of the group; turned shoulders seemed to exclude her. I try, don't I? she asked herself angrily. Always she tried to make polite conversation, to take an interest; but they seemed to know that her mind was elsewhere.

The conversation became more general at last, as the fruit punch and the *siddiqui* took its hold; the usual holiday chat. 'Did you hear about that girl from New Zealand who was sentenced to ninety lashes?' someone said. 'Twenty was for having drunk alcohol, and seventy was for being in a car with a man who wasn't her husband.'

'At the Smiths' party last year,' Marion said, 'we had this game. The men were all blindfolded, and the women stood on chairs, and the men had to come along and feel their legs and try to guess who was who. It was a laugh. You wouldn't play that, Frances, would you?'

Frances said, 'I'd rather die.'

'Frances is such a misery,' Marion said, *sotto voce*. 'She's not a bit broadminded. She bothers with those Saudi women in her flats.'

At eleven forty-five, party hats and streamers were distributed. There was a resurgence of merriment; everyone met up in the garden, breaking out of their huddles and cliques for a final assault on the festive spirit. They put on their hats, unfurled their streamers; a loose circle formed, and several people said that they could never remember the words of Auld Lang Syne. People asked what the time was; the minutes seemed to prolong themselves. Watches were consulted; women hauled at their husbands' shirtsleeves, and peered at the dials by the light of the coloured bulbs their host had strung on an outside wall. Conversation faltered and died, and the guests shifted from foot to foot, weariness crossing their faces; they did not seem to be waiting for midnight, but for a bus that was never going to come. Finally, at eleven fifty-seven, the New Year was declared, to trills of forced laughter, and the thin notes of penny whistles. They kissed each other, and stomped to and fro, singing raggedly. Clawing up the streamers from the ground, carrying dutifully into the kitchen plates of half-eaten food, they trooped inside, to dance to the Beach Boys and early Rolling Stones. By one o'clock the party was breaking up.

The Shores were amongst the first to leave. They drove home in a tired, companionable silence; as soon as they stepped out of their car, the traces of the holiday were wiped from their life; Frances scrubbed off her make-up. She went into the kitchen, and took out some damp towels from the washing-machine.

'I hope you haven't made any New Year Resolutions,' Andrew said, standing in the doorway.

'Why? Don't you want anything to change?'

'I want to keep us on an even keel.'

'Why pick on me?' she asked, shaking the towels out. 'What about your own resolutions?'

'With most people it wouldn't matter. They can make them in safety because they know they won't be kept. You can count on their futility.' He paused. 'But you're not like that.'

'What will happen to us next year?'

'I want to see the building through. You know that.'

'Nothing gives,' she said. She threw the towels on to a chair. A flood of words poured from her. 'There's no life in the land, it's just people, highways, endless straight roads and rubbish and dust, there's nothing to release you, there's nothing to set you free inside. You feel as if you're starving. No wonder they have such a bloody awful religion. No wonder that when they got rich and went to Europe all they could think of to do was to drink and take drugs and gamble, how would they know how to live their lives? They bought up beautiful houses and gutted them and filled them with nightclubs and Louis Farouk, they tore up gardens and made swimming-pools, all they want is white-skinned prostitutes and cocaine.'

'Oh, come on,' Andrew said. 'That's not entirely true.'

'It is entirely true,' she said, more quietly. 'But not the entire truth.'

'You say Jeff's a racist, but you're really just as bad.'

'I'm not a racist, Andrew, I'm a xenophobe. See – I've been going through the dictionary to find out what's wrong with me. There's England and France, and after that it's madness.'

He said, 'Do you want to go home?'

'No,' she said. 'It's too late for that.'

Andrew made love to her that night. As he entered her she felt as if she had plunged, suddenly and without hope, into a long dark tunnel; as if inch by inch, her body rigid, she fought towards her climax, while the walls of the tunnel fell in softly behind her, leaving her just one direction but no glimmer of an end. She felt herself sinking out of sight, her whole spirit toiling underground, darkness enfolding darkness; she was wiped out, she had forgotten her name. Andrew grunted, and lay on top of her with his whole weight. Suddenly she became conscious of the smell of soap on his skin, of a prickle of cramp in her legs; of the rattle and hum of the air-conditioner. She was back inside her own body. No subterranean toil for Andrew; it was as easy as crossing the road. Or, since this was Jeddah, easier.

When he released her she turned her face at once into the pillow. She would sleep. She would sleep soon. She would sleep in the next second. The rifleman, lurking on the sidewalk, was the last thing on her mind.

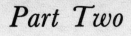

Part Two

Part Two

Jamadi al-awal

Anyone for Jeddah gin?

Take four large potatoes, four oranges, four lemons, four
grapefruit. Cut them up into small pieces. Put the pieces in a
plastic jerry can. Add five kilos of sugar. Top up with water.
Dissolve a tablespoonful of yeast; tip it in. Forget it for two
weeks.

Then pour the stuff out of the jerry can into saucepans.
Leave it till the sediment settles: two days. Pour it into
bottles – use a tea strainer, because there will still be large
bits of brownish fruit bobbing on the surface.

Tonic? Ice and lemon?

FRANCES SHORE'S DIARY: *1 Jamadi al-awal*

I really don't know how I went on before I had the
Saudi Gazette and the *Arab News* to tell me how to run
my married life. For a start I haven't been treating
Andrew right when he gets home from work. When he
says, 'What sort of day have you had, petal?' I say,
'Rotten. I have a headache, and the pipes have burst'
– or something to that effect. This is not the right way
to do it, because according to the *Arab News*, 'When he
enters his home it is his right to find complete relaxation
to regain his great powers and abilities in order to face
the next day.' If there are any problems I'm supposed
to have dealt with them myself, so that I can 'greet him
with a beautiful smile' – and if the problems have been

beyond my wits or capacity (and many problems must be beyond the capacity of the Saudi housewife) then I must wait for a suitable time, before raising them in the most tactful way. 'It's not reasonable, for example, to bring them up while eating. This might ruin the man's appetite and lead to an exchange of words between the two partners that could disturb the calm in their lives.'

Samira asks me probing questions about my past life. I don't know why I won't oblige her with tales of drunken parties and sexual perversion. Surely that's what she wants to hear. Or does she really care for me? In that case I could put her mind at rest, and tell her I was married a virgin. She would clasp my hands, and smile into my face, and her bracelets would jangle. The *Arab News* says, 'Love after marriage is the true, the long-lasting fond. Love before marriage is naïve, weak, and baseless.'

Since New Year there have not been many parties. All the people who saw too much of each other over the holiday are now staying at home, by unspoken agreement – as if they had called a truce. Andrew and I are alone most evenings, and meanwhile Yasmin's mother is still in residence across the hall, and the junketings get more strenuous week by week, and Yasmin gets more weak and tearful. In the mornings, if she can, she comes here for a cup of coffee, and for five minutes' refuge – and I commiserate with her. She does not mention our meeting on the roof. She says, And where have you and Andrew been? And I say, Oh, nowhere really.

I wish this man Fairfax would come. I'd like to spend an hour with someone from the real world.

Andrew and I talk a lot about our leave, about what we are going to do in the summer. July seems a long way off. I realize that we live in the future. That seems no healthier than living in the past.

Andrew's paycheck hasn't come yet. It's not just

Turadup. Other people are in the same position, all over town. Until now everyone was paid on time, by the Arabic calendar. So the men would look at the full moon, and say, in their romantic fashion, 'Ah, half-way to pay day.' But they don't say that any more.

We talk: about the building. Even when funds start to flow again, Andrew will have to cut corners, which is foreign to his nature. What can I say to him? There are other things I would like to talk about. How long are we going to stay here, and what kind of person will I have become before we leave? I might have become a Muslim. Or I might have joined one of those feminist groups which believes men should be kept in cages and periodically milked for their semen, so that it can be used for artificial insemination – there being no other use for them, and no other need, and they being the source of all misery and wars.

But when Andrew asked me if I wanted to go, I couldn't say yes. I know he would leave tomorrow, if he thought I were seriously unhappy. I'm not unhappy, not really. I just want to talk about the things that really bother me, but when I try to do that I get some sort of block, some sort of impediment in my throat. I think I am afraid that Andrew will laugh at me.

The *Saudi Gazette* says: 'Love may be a most important basis for marriage only in novels and poetry. In practical life, however, it does not provide a firm foundation for a happy married life. This is due to the fact that people change with the passage of time. It is well known in all societies that the overwhelming majority of marriage cases based on love do not last long.'

If we did leave here, where would we go? We don't belong anywhere, physically. If we didn't have each other we wouldn't belong anywhere emotionally. We sit in the evenings, looking at each other, and I feel that he wants something that I can't give him, and that I want something that he can't give me. A familiar problem in marriage, I suppose. I feel weak with need for him, mental need, physical need. Isn't it strange that no matter how many times you sleep together, you don't get any closer? I feel that perhaps by nature we are lonely people. Then I think, perhaps everyone is like this, and their need to be together is only just a bit stronger than their need to be apart. I agree that love doesn't guarantee anything. But with the odds stacked up as they are, love certainly doesn't do any harm.

One thing is clear, anyway. I cannot bring up the matter of the rifleman while Andrew is having his grilled sirloin and green salad. That would not be the time to do it. I cannot find a time to do it that would not upset our long-lasting fond.

January weather: overcast, windy, cool. A stack of concrete slabs has been moved on to the vacant lot, and some builders' vehicles; the Yemeni workmen have knocked together little shacks, which will keep the sun off them, when the sun comes back. But today the sky hangs low over Ghazzah Street, and the crane that bisects the view from the window seems very close to the ground. Every speck of grey dust is visible on the leaves of Dunroamin's single tree. Soon the King, the court, and the Muslim scholars will hold rain-prayers; but as they wish to reinforce faith, not to injure it, they will not ask for rain until the weather forecasters promise that it is in the offing. Meanwhile Dunroamin is quiet: the pipes gurgle, there is a crackle of voices from a radio, but there are no footsteps up above. Even the rats seem to have gone back into their holes. The branches of the tree toss soundlessly. A car engine splutters, out of sight. Inside the flat a dim silence reigns; but the doors rattle in the draught.

At a quarter to nine there was a battering at the door. It was the landlord, greasy and rotund as ever. Behind him stood a wan and gangling figure, unkempt, straggle-haired, knock-knees bare under a tunic and *dhoti*.

The landlord smiled at Frances. 'Madam,' he said, 'we are going to paint you. All buildings in Jeddah must be brilliant white. By Order. All unsightly wooden structures must be demolished.'

The bare-legged man rested his gaze on the lintel. He didn't acknowledge Frances, didn't seem to notice her presence at all. He looked, with his sepulchral features and his wrappings, like the subject of some dull religious painting, who is rising from the dead; and whose thoughts, understandably, are elsewhere.

'We haven't got any unsightly wooden structures,' Frances said. She felt unfriendly; blocked the doorway with her body.

The landlord stabbed his finger in the direction of the vacant lot. 'Unconformable to regulations,' he said. 'All these must go. Otherwise you will get the hajjis living in them. The pilgrims, if you understand me, madam. They come for their pilgrimages and try to stay. They will set up anywhere.'

'Really, will they?'

'These Third World persons are disease-bearing,' the landlord said. 'Have you not had the hajji flu, madam?'

'We weren't here at the pilgrimage season.'

'They have plagues,' the landlord said. 'Still, it is unlucky for them. Madam –' he paused, and smiled his bristling smile, seeming to remember why he had come; he pointed to the gangling man, drawing attention to him, as if he were an object in a picture book. 'Madam, this is an Egyptian. I want you to know this man.'

'Is he your foreman?'

'Boss-man, yes. I'm telling you so he don't alarm you, going up and down, up and down the stairs.'

'He don't alarm me,' Frances said. She felt an urge to stretch out her hand and give the Egyptian a little push, to see if he would keel over. Still he stared ahead of him; a film of sweat glistened on his face. 'Will he be going up and down for very many weeks?' she inquired.

'Finish next week,' the landlord said. 'I promise you.'

'*Ins'allah?*' Frances said.

'*Ins'allah.*'

Later that day the men began work. They wedged open the gate in the wall, and carried vats of white paint to various points about Dunroamin. They took great brushes, and sloshed about, accidentally painting the ground, and sometimes their feet. They broke off for noon prayers, and then brought ladders, and came at the upper storey; they splashed paint on to Samira's balcony, and splattered the leaves of the tree.

Frances watched from her window. Once she went out into the street, and watched from across the road, by the ditch. The landlord, bustling in and out, darted a look of horror at her short skirt and bare legs. He hesitated, and seemed about to cross the road and remonstrate with her; but she folded her arms, and gave him a hard look, and went back inside in her own good time.

The men carried some wooden boxes up the stairs; then they carried some wooden boxes down. Tools of their trade, perhaps; no doubt it was all part of the renovation work, of what Yasmin called The Beautification of Jeddah.

Early in the afternoon the landlord knocked at the door again.

'Hello, madam. We are going to varnish your blinds with shiny varnish. So when we are up to that, you must wind them down. You must keep them down for three days, to let the varnish dry.'

'But I'll be in the dark,' Frances complained. 'I won't be able to see out.'

'But it is for the good of my building!' the landlord said. He gave her what he took to be an appealing glance. 'Please give me the cooperation.'

'Okay,' Frances said. 'But I'm not putting them down

until you're ready to start work. So just give me the nod, will you?'

The landlord looked at her dubiously; uncertainly, he nodded.

'Yes,' she said. 'That's right.'

Frances understood that she must carry messages. It was her job to warn the other women of Dunroamin to stay indoors, because there were strange men at large. The landlord did her the courtesy of telling her what was happening, so that the far more important privacy of Muslim ladies would not be violated.

She rang Yasmin's doorbell. An eye appeared at the spyhole, and blinked, and vanished; it was Shams who opened the door. Yasmin emerged from one of the bedrooms; she looked cowed and miserable.

'Oh, Frances,' she said. 'I am missing talking to you.' Frances touched her shoulder. It was the most she could manage. If you want my sympathy, she thought, you must tell me what really ails you. To comfort you would be to embrace a time-bomb, and listen to the tick.

'We're being Beautified,' she said.

'Are we?' Yasmin managed a smile. But when she heard the extent of the work, she looked horrified. 'Selim,' she said, 'his chest is so delicate. The fumes, and the dust, and the noise . . . oh dear.'

'There will be people going up and down stairs. For a week.' Frances paused. She hoped it was a meaningful pause. 'You must take care.'

Yasmin nodded. Her eyes slid away. 'We must all take care,' she said.

Next day Frances went up to see Samira. The workmen stared at her rudely as she stepped over their planks and scaffolding. They were doing their best, she thought, to make sure that she felt in their way; they were doing their best to make it clear that she shouldn't be out. They were preparing to line the stairwell with patterned tiles; these, she supposed, must have been in the wooden boxes. The tiles were small, with a whirling pattern of black, white and red. Samira had taken a peep outside her front door. She sighed. 'I know what you will say, Frances. You will say, oh, Saudi taste!'

'Not at all,' Frances said politely. 'Though it's going to take them ages, and I think I preferred the plain white paint.'

When she came out of Samira's apartment, the men had stopped work. They must have gone to eat; it was quiet again, and fine plaster dust hung in the air. Across the landing the Egyptian stood at the door of the empty flat, fist raised as if to tap on it. She hurried across to him and touched his elbow. He sprang away from the contact. 'No one home,' she said. She smiled, and shook her head at him. 'No one lives there.'

The man glared at her; he put his hand to the spot she had touched, and held it, as if her fingers had burned him. 'No one home.' But still he glared.

Surely he understood a little English? Everyone did, especially Egyptians. She knew the Arabic for 'a house'. But not for 'an empty house'. Not for 'an illicit love-nest'. Not for 'push off if you know what's good for you'.

She cast a glance back at the closed door of Samira's apartment. Samira wouldn't come out to explain to him; and Sarsaparilla couldn't explain. Anyway, he understood her. She felt sure of that. It was just that she had upset him in some way. The glare, now, was positively threatening. 'Okay,' she said, in a pleasant firm tone. 'You knock all you like, sunshine. And if the man comes out and twists your balls off, don't say I didn't warn you.'

She went downstairs. A few tiles had been stuck on near the front door, and others on the top landing. When they met in the middle, the effect would be hellish. I mustn't come out here when I've been on the Jeddah gin, she thought. She stopped, in the dim light, to consider the pattern. Small faces: each tile with its splash of scarlet, its swirl of black. She felt as if she were being watched, by bloodied eyes; by the victims of some Koranic punishment.

And soon the men would start work again and the watchers would multiply.

Tarannum Siddiqi of Dhahran has written to the *Saudi Gazette*.

'I cannot imagine why some women are always moaning about male domination. Why can't they accept that the male has been created superior to the female? God has meant it to be this way. It is also referred to in the Koran in Surah "Al-Nisa", verse 34: "Men are in charge of women, because Allah has made one of them to excel the other."'

There is an item from Abu Dhabi, about a Filipino maid who has been put in gaol for setting fire to her employer's house and then trying to commit suicide. She says her employer attacked her with a knife, but her employer says her wounds are self-inflicted. Authorities in Sri Lanka have announced that maids who are going to work in the Gulf must undertake a martial arts course before proceeding to the region.

There has been a small earthquake in the Yemen. Russel and some of the other geologists are flying down there to see if they can find out why. But religious leaders say it was caused by Sin.

Andrew had decided to worry about her. Perhaps that was his New Year resolution.

'You don't get out much,' he said.

'No.'

'It's not healthy.'

'What do you think I should do? Go jogging?'

'Maybe you could make some arrangement to share a car. Just once or twice a week. Carla goes to a yoga class. Couldn't you do that?'

'Why?'

203

He couldn't think why.

'Stop nannying me,' she said. 'It's bad enough with Mrs Parsons.'

Mrs Parsons was worried about her too; or so she said. 'How do you feel now about getting a job?' she asked her, over the phone. 'Do you want Eric to put out feelers?'

She found it hard to be polite to Daphne. Hard to talk to her at all. Since Christmas her facility in making small talk seemed to have slipped away.

'I'm concerned about the kind of life you're leading,' Daphne said. 'If Turadup had a house free, Eric would move you. Perhaps he could rent you a house from somebody else. Terrex Mining must have houses coming free, because they're cutting back on their staff. They're out of town, up north, you go on the freeway. Shall I ask Eric?'

'You could do.'

'Leave it with me,' Daphne said.

The words come grudgingly out of Frances; she drags them out. It is as if, she thought, I am learning a foreign language, speaking it every day, and forgetting my own. But she has not learned Arabic; not more than a few words. Yasmin continues to insist that it is too difficult, that there is no need. It is as if she wishes, herself, to be the interpreter of the world. Samira says, 'Why do you need to learn Arabic? We are all speaking perfectly good English, aren't we?'

Andrew took her to the bookshop at the Caravan Shopping Centre. She bought a language tape, and a book to go with it, and during Jamadi al-awal she pored over this book, and set the careful slow voice of the language tutor echoing through Dunroamin. Good morning. Good morning, how are you? Well, praise be to God. Welcome! Will you drink coffee? How are your children? How is your wife? A footnote points out that customs vary widely within the Arab world; in some areas it would be considered insulting to ask after someone's wife. 'Families,' says the book, 'are safer, but not entirely without danger.'

The hero of her language book is a businessman, Mr Smith. Occasionally, in later lessons, he will express concern for the welfare of his wife and children, who are back in the USA. But mostly he leads a free, gay kind of life; the Arabic speakers he meets take a keen interest in all his doings. He goes to the souk to buy a carved chest; he travels a lot; he gets into endless wrangles about small change. It is a man's book; not for her. She would not need half these phrases. 'In a courtyard is a tree on which there are fruits whose colour is red. We sit in our garden. The weather is fine.'

Each guttural phrase, spoken aloud, was broken down for her on the page; but she didn't seem to make progress. Carla lent her another book. 'This is of cultural interest,' Carla said. Its title: *Courtesies in Saudi Arabia and the Gulf.* It is full of utterances, for greeting and parting; ceremonial utterances, from a gentle, ordered world.

Wednesday morning: she was returning from Marion's house. Marion seemed distracted these days; she was always smiling, at some privately gratifying thought. Frances had no idea what it might be. She wanted to take her by the arm, to shake her; to say to her, a man with a rifle is hanging about on Ghazzah Street.

A young man in a sports car slowed up beside her, and crawled along the kerb, his head stuck out of the window and the late January wind plucking at the ends of his check *ghutra.* 'You are my baby,' he called. 'You are my darling.' She supposed it was courtesy: of a kind.

As she let herself into Dunroamin she heard the noon prayer call. The varnishing had begun, and the smell crept under the doors and into the hall. The tiling was half-finished now; the malign pattern was growing.

In the hall, she heard a door open, up above. Not Samira's. She ran up to the bend in the stairs. Now the door slammed shut. Bare feet slapped on marble. Samira's maid had come out of the empty flat, and vanished, with a swirl of skirts, into her own.

*

So what now?

'I suppose Abdul Nasr has keys,' Andrew said. 'She must go in to – change the sheets, or something. Do the dusting. Even if you only use a place to go to bed in, it still gets dusty, doesn't it?'

'Then Samira knows,' Frances said.

'Obviously.'

'I thought Abdul Nasr was meant to be very religious. Super-puritanical.'

'That's what I was told. But you can't believe what you're told, can you?'

'Would you risk a maid knowing?'

'It's not much of a risk. You said yourself that they never let the girl out. You said she doesn't know Arabic, and that she speaks some peculiar dialect that no one understands.'

'That's true. They don't think of Sarsaparilla as a person. She's just labour.'

Andrew took her wrist. 'Frances,' he said, 'don't get involved.'

Andrew was not in a good mood. The cheque had come through at last, but Eric didn't know when he would be able to pay them again. Previously it had been such a consolation to unfile the bank statements, and see how the deposit account was building up. Andrew had been receiving brochures from a firm of London estate agents. They should buy a flat, he said, something to give them a base; something small, central, easy to let. 'We ought to have somewhere, you know. At our age. We can't keep drifting, can we, just crating things up and sending them from one country to the next, everything serviceable and disposable, no books, nothing of our own – living with other people's furniture?'

'It's not that bad, Andrew. We have our Saudiflon pans.'

'I'm going to organize it this summer,' he said. 'If they pay me, of course.'

'When are you expecting this man Fairfax?'

'Oh, quite soon. Next month maybe.'

*

Frances, taking out the rubbish, met the landlord on the stairs.

'You said one week,' she accused him. 'You've been here two already.'

The landlord seemed harassed. He didn't have time to chat. 'Please to stay indoors, out of noxious fumes,' he said crossly.

'When can I put my blinds up?'

'Wait a few days. If you put them up too early they will be stuck, and much good work will be undone.'

Frances said nothing. He made a little shooing motion at her. She leaned one hand against the wall, leisurely, insolent. He shrugged his shoulders and left by the front door. Frances looked after him. 'Hate the tiles,' she said softly. 'Saudi taste.'

Outside Yasmin's door, propped against the wall, was a wooden crate, in sections; it was stamped with the logo of the Hejaz Removals and Storage Co. 'Is this yours?' she asked Yasmin. 'Or does it belong to the landlord?'

'Mine,' Yasmin said. 'It is in your way?'

'No, not at all. I'm just being nosy. You're not moving, are you?'

'No. It is just for some things of Raji's.'

'Only I was sizing it up – when that crate's assembled you won't be able to get it through the internal doors.'

'Then he must pack it in the hall.'

'I just thought I'd warn you. How's mother-in-law?'

Yasmin drew her inside, dropped her voice. She seemed, as she so often did, on the point of tears. 'Her visit is so ill-timed,' she said.

'I suppose it is.'

'For Selim, I mean – this important stage in his development. Frances, have you asked your friends – are you sure there is not some drug I can give him to make him grow? It is not good for the child's psychology – she is holding his nose now, forcing him with orange juice.'

'Can't you talk to Raji? Can't he do anything?'

'Oh, he thinks she is always in the right. He is interfering with how I run the household. That is not what a man should do. Frances,' Yasmin moved closer, and touched her arm confidingly, 'we have had some dispute. Because I want to wear the veil. Completely, you understand, like the Saudi women do. Because I feel it is right. But Raji says, "We are modern." He has forbidden me. And I am so unhappy.'

Frances looked at her in disbelief. 'Have I got this right? You want to wear the veil?'

'Many Moslem women are doing this. In Pakistan. In Iran, which you know of. In Egypt even. Once they thought it was a great thing to get rid of the veil, but now they are not so sure. They see how men exploit them. They want to have their dignity back.'

'I'm the wrong person to talk to,' Frances said.

'I know you are. But to whom else can I talk? You are my friend.'

'What about Samira?'

'Oh, Samira – she has no deep thoughts. Getting jewellery is what she thinks about. Showing off her clothes, going to weddings. You are not like that. You are more like me.'

She savoured the compliment. It was difficult to meet her neighbour's eyes. 'Sometimes,' Yasmin said, 'it is my dearest wish to go away from these flats. I wish I could rewrite the past, but you cannot do that, can you?'

All this in whispers; a dark corner of the hallway, heads close together. Mother-in-law's voice rises from the bedroom, wheedling, insisting, threatening. 'What is it that you would like to change?'

Yasmin lifted her head, and in her luminous eyes there was an animal pain. She seemed about to speak, and to say – but then her expression clouded, she bit her lip, looked away. 'Perhaps it is you who should move away,' she said. 'There is a herb, it is called *mehti*. If you want to go away from where you are living, if you want a new home, this is the herb you plant. Shall I put some in a pot, Frances, and give it to you?'

*

208

Six months on Ghazzah Street, and spring was coming: bigger cockroaches, the smell of sewage. Hot weather would bring the strategies, the longueurs, of expatriate life: driver's hand jumping from hot metal, the drawn, shiny faces of the women, the apathy, the dust, the wilting of the intellect. All this is familiar; they have adapted without problems. But Andrew does not feel at ease. He feels that something more is required of them.

It seems that there are three cities: the fossil city, the epic city, the trivial city. Once Jeddah encompassed a square kilometre, enclosed within its coral walls; coral walls are grey and gritty, not what they sound. In the souk there are leaning buildings with latticed balconies, the wood rotting, the wood crumbling away: as even the glories of Islam may crumble into dust. This is the fossil city, dim, precarious, the lattices concealing other times, and dim, shadowy lives; you cannot escape the prison insignificance of your own nature.

The epic city throws flyovers into the sky and nets the desert with freeways. It grinds out statistics: biggest fountain in the world, second biggest fountain in the world, a mile of plate glass, a universe of marble. There are 10,000 post-office boxes, and 80,000 electric lamp-posts, and 2,664 hospital beds; there are 136,000 telephones. The weight of the city's daily garbage is 1,510 tons. There are eight million cultivated saplings, and all eight million are dying from their roots.

The trivial city runs between the giant roads and beneath bridges; black children kicking a football, a cart laden with water-melons, a shabby tree leaning over a wall. From the flyover near Sharia Siteen you can see this trivial city; as you roar above, imperilled and fast behind your windscreen, the alleys run far below, little one-storey buildings set at angles, humble mosques, decrepit air-conditioners leaning from walls, tiny windows open a crack to the odorous air; sagging balconies with ragged washing, the blink of truck lights, the slow progress of a water-seller's donkey between the shacks. There are figures in these streets, human figures, but they are not those seen elsewhere in the city. Distant, wide-shouldered, tapering towards the feet, they have the quality of those figures that architects use in their drawings; they are ghost-people, functions of scale. Far below you, the men seem to wear robes and turbans, and the black-veiled women seem to glide, singly and in pairs; no sound reaches you from their deep-below world.

But if you reach the end of the flyover, and turn back on yourself, this eerie scene is in fact the trivial city; the smell of stale cooking, vehicles nose-to-tail, and clever tunes played on car horns.

'Best price,' says the man in the carpet souk. 'I am giving you your first carpet very cheap, so that you will always buy from me.'

How many does he think we want? He looks homespun, shuffling in his slippers between the bales, but he was trading in Frankfurt last week, and the week before in New York, so he knows what the best price is. The shop is half-dark, and smells of must, and wool. On the shelves, battered coffee-pots jostle in sharp-snouted ranks, each one awaiting its buyer. On a display stand hang the beaded face-masks of forgotten women, their former owners emancipated, or deceased.

Carla held one up. 'Pretty,' she said.

Frances said, 'I'd rather buy a ball and chain.'

With a shrug, Carla put the mask down again.

It was the evening souk trip. Everybody does them. They had been planning it, the Shores and the Zussmans. The carpets are stacked around them, waist high; Rickie heaves over their corners, to show a little of the pattern of each. 'See that orange bit,' he says, pointing. 'That's aniline dye. That shows it's modern.' He flaps the stack down again. That is what Rickie knows about carpets; that is what everyone knows.

You hold something up, perhaps a silver box, perhaps a woven mat; the vendor names some exorbitant price. You smile in polite embarrassment. He says, 'What price you like?' Of course, this is a meaningless question. The only price you like is no price at all. But now it's no good putting it down again, no good acting diminished interest; in the vendor's mind, the only reason you do not buy is that the price has not been agreed. It's no good saying you asked out of curiosity. It's no use saying you've gone off it, or it's too big, or it's a nice design but the colour is all wrong. He will shame you into buying it, by insistently lowering his price. The only way to leave without it is to stop talking, turn your back, walk out of the shop; and even then he will follow you into the street, lowering his prices for the passers-by to hear.

And then the smell clings to your hair and clothes, that smell of lamp-oil, of mothballs, of the pilfered assets of the dead.

'Well, I guess it is a nice carpet,' Rickie said. He was trying to keep his spirits up. He unrolled it again, on Dunroamin's beige floor; it looked coarse now, and the dull colour of venous blood.

Lamplight: a bottle of the new batch of wine. Carla settled comfortably with a glass, her legs curled beneath her and her feet hidden in the folds of her kaftan. 'By the way, Frances,' she said, 'I hear the Jane Fonda workout's not the thing to do.'

'No?'

'No. Puts your back out.'

Rickie, squatting on the floor, toyed disconsolately with the rug's tatty fringe. Then he looked up, remembering something, animated. 'Hey, you guys, I saw this survey. I forgot to tell you.'

Nothing pleased Rickie like a survey. 'It was,' he said, 'about national attitudes to getting rich.'

'Oh yes?' Andrew poured himself another glass, and stretched out his legs.

'You know, British people are nothing like as interested in getting rich as the Americans or the Japanese.'

'They did a survey to establish that?' Frances said. 'I could have told them.'

'What about your friend Pollard?' Carla asked. 'I bet there's nothing he wouldn't do for a dollar.'

'There's nothing he hasn't done, for a riyal,' Andrew said. 'Perhaps he's the exception that proves the rule?'

'That's it, you see.' Rickie stabbed his forefinger at them. 'That's your typical British attitude. Forty-nine per cent of Brits surveyed believe that if you had zero to start with, but had gotten rich, then you must have something to hide.'

'In Pollard's case, 100 per cent of Brits believe it.'

'And also,' Rickie said, '26 per cent of Brits believe the rich exploit others, whereas in the USA 39 per cent believe the rich help others by creating jobs and prosperity.'

'It's amazing,' Frances said, 'how you keep all these statistics in your head.'

'Everybody's good for something,' Carla said. 'Rickie pretends to be some kind of *idiot savant*. He pretends it's all effortless, but really when he gets one of these crappy surveys he sits up all night memorizing it, just so as he can astound people.'

'It astounds me,' Frances said. 'Well, come on, Rickie, if the British aren't interested in getting rich, what are they interested in?'

'Oh, they say they're interested in living quiet lives. Eight per cent even say that they're interested in working on behalf of society. It's no wonder you people are in post-imperial decline, with a set of attitudes like that.'

'You've changed a lot,' Frances said. 'Since you were in Peace Corps.'

'Don't remind him,' Carla said. 'He hates to think of when he used to ride around Gaborone on a bicycle.'

'Come on then,' Andrew said. 'Let's have facts and figures, young man. Now what percentage of the Japanese –'

Frances's thoughts had been drifting all evening. 'Twelve per cent of Japanese –' Rickie was saying; but she was back with Yasmin, the badly lit hallway, her downcast face, the secrets on the tip of her tongue. Samira had laughed at Yasmin for being so pious. Was she really? Was it repentance? Was it hypocrisy? Hypocrisy is a science, here. The pure youth and chaste married men go to Bangkok, and bring back foul diseases. The Princes excoriate America, and beg it for missiles. And so is it possible that this moral city is just a network of pretences and counter-pretences? Is it possible that this holy city has the best liars in the world?

'Frances, are you listening?' Andrew said. 'When the rich were surveyed, 85 per cent of them thought they hadn't taken any particular risk to get their money.'

'Not like us,' she said. 'Andrew wants a flat in London, did he tell you? We have to stick it out here till we save up a healthy deposit.'

'The Brits think the rich are lazy,' Rickie said, 'and they think that they're ruthless and greedy. Sixty-two per cent think that they are snobbish.'

'You have to admit,' Andrew said, 'that unlimited cash doesn't seem to be good for people. I mean, if you judge by this place.'

'So what do you want, more than you want to be rich?'

'Peace,' Andrew said.

'Freedom,' Frances said.

'Yeah,' Rickie said. 'These are the abstractions the typical Brit goes for.'

'I'd settle for 50 per cent peace,' Andrew said. 'And say, 70 per cent freedom.'

'Freedom's indivisible,' Carla said. She leaned forward, holding out her glass for a refill. 'At least, that's what we were told in high school, but I've never known what it means.'

At 1 a.m. the Zussmans rolled up their carpet and departed. 'I'm tired,' Andrew said. He cleaned his teeth, dropped his clothes on the floor, fell into bed and into sleep. Within the space of five minutes she seemed to find herself alone, passed from polite chatter to restless isolation; she was wide awake, thoughts chasing each other like snapping dogs. She washed the glasses, went into the bathroom, and took a

Vitamin C tablet, as a precaution against a hangover. I will let myself out and go up on to the roof, she said; because every time I go up on to the roof, life gets more exciting.

She slipped the bunch of keys into her pocket, closing the front door quietly behind her; even the pressure of her finger on the hall light-switch was slow and easy, as if just a click could galvanize Dunroamin, make the hibernating monster mutter and stir.

The walls watched her, each separate tile with its own maleficent stare. She climbed the main stairs, climbed the half-flight, and opened the door to the roof. The air was cool. She took a deep breath. The whole city seemed to lie below her, as if she had climbed much farther than she thought; blank roads like distant snakes, and a million tiny lights. Somewhere, above the hazy emanations of light from factories and apartment blocks, there must be the stars. Samira had shown her a book, some ancient desert poet: 'The evening is a black bride, wearing silver necklaces.' But now what lights the night sky? An alien zodiac: SANYO SANYO SANYO. What sparkles over Arabia, silver and green, what leaches the darkness from the night? A sign blinks and flickers over the Mecca road, above the route to the Holy Places, over the path to the Ka'aba: 7 UP, 7 UP, 7 UP.

Frances stood for a while; then turned and went back down the stairs, on to the top landing. The workmen had nearly finished; there were a few planks of wood about, and empty paint tins. She stopped between the two closed doors; then moved towards the door of the empty flat, and put her ear to it.

Someone was in there. She could hear them speak; she could hear their movements. But not Yasmin, because Yasmin was entertaining: a buffet for twenty-five. She would have no chance to get away. Shams would not be asleep yet; she would be scrubbing pots in the kitchen, waiting for her billet on the dining-room floor. And mother-in-law, too, would not be asleep; she ranges through the world, seeking whom she may devour.

I am sorry for what I thought, she says to herself, making a mental apology to Yasmin; how could I think you would be so reckless? Someone is in there, but it is not you. But I must know. Who walks about in the dark?

She lifted her hand, as if to knock. Then let it fall by her side. Listened for a further moment, head inclined towards the door. Went downstairs. Let herself in, and shut and locked the door behind her. Double-locked the door, and slammed on the bolt. Once, she thought, this bunch of keys was a persecution, but now it is my friend. Her pulse, which had been racing, began to slow.

Jamadi al-thani

I wish I could tear the roof off and let some light into the flat. I thought it would be better when the blinds went up again, but it doesn't seem to have made much difference.

I have been reading in the *New Scientist* about a condition called Seasonal Affective Disorder. It is a more serious version of getting miserable during a long winter. It seems that human beings need sunlight, fluorescent tubes are not enough. Some people are more sensitive to the deprivation than others, and become severely depressed. Now that the cause of their disorder is known, they can be cured by getting up in the middle of the night, and sitting in front of special lamps, which have the properties of daylight.

There is a gland in the brain called the pineal gland, which is sensitive to light and dark. I wonder how sensitive it is? Sometimes it is called the Third Eye. A third eye is what I need, perhaps – one that would see more deeply than the other two.

One evening the wind changed. The moon hung huge and pallid in the sky, bisected by a lamp-post; a fuzzy globe of electric light encircled it, like another satellite. Towards morning there was a little rain. When Frances got up, drew back the curtains, wound up the blinds, she saw the leaves of the tree washed clean, saw for the first time their true, green colour.

Frances went up to the roof. It was 9 a.m.; the heat was building up, and there was a shimmer in the air. Traffic moved in the distance; the highways were thin bleached lines, and beyond them was another line, another highway, which was the sea. You could sense it this morning, and those few drops of rain bred hope; flowers might bloom out of concrete, trees shoulder through the dereliction. She looked down into her neighbours' courts and enclosures, at the broken line of roofs below her. Thirty feet down a striped cat lay, looking up; its eyes gazed into hers, offended. The cat should be above her, looking down; that was nature. Morning haze hung over the building sites, and gilded the scaffolding, like a veil over bones.

On the balcony of the empty flat there was a wooden crate. It was only by accident that she had spotted it; she had leaned over the branches of the parapet, to put her face into the tree, to catch the fugitive scent of leaves. She leaned farther, and there was the logo of the Hejaz Removals and Storage Company.

What she noticed, next, was the balcony floor, thinly veneered with mud. So when Sarsaparilla was cleaning, she didn't get round to the balcony; cement dust and sand had lain there for months, blown in through the leaves of the tree, and had stood, and thickened, and now formed a wet sticky deposit on the tiles. The balcony was not visible from the street; you could only see it by leaning over, by twisting your neck at an angle. That crate, she thought, must be classed as an unsightly wooden structure; and under the landlord's very nose. Even the most desperate hajji wouldn't live in it, though it was just big enough for a man, if he didn't mind doubling himself up, if he didn't mind some pain.

'It is just for some things of Raji's,' Yasmin had said. Someone has told me a lie, Frances thought. Or, what seems more likely now, someone has told me a series of lies.

Andrew came home. 'There's a crate on the roof,' she told him.

'What I mean is, there's a crate on the balcony of the empty flat.'

'Oh yes?'

'I think I've seen it before, that crate.'

Andrew was not attending. He was pulling documents out of his briefcase. 'Where's my pocket calculator?' he said.

'Is there a panic?'

'Only the annual panic. Or so Eric calls it. The end of the financial year's coming up.'

'Surely that was foreseeable.'

'Yes. Don't make sarcastic remarks, please. We're living on next year's expectations. Turadup's running out of everything. We're running out of building materials. If something breaks down I can't get it replaced. We've run out of photocopying paper, I'll have to go out tonight and buy a ream. God damn it, we've even run out of lavatory paper. We don't know what sort of money we're going to get in the new budget. Eric's gone to Riyadh. We might know something when he gets back.'

'What do you think this crate is?'

'Mm? I don't know. Maybe it's a chicken coop.'

FRANCES SHORE'S DIARY: *11 Jamadi al-thani*

. . . well, I don't know, but I don't think it is a chicken coop.

I was talking to Marion today. She says that Russel has had a bit of a setback in the Yemen. It seems that the geologists had gone along in their helicopter to the earthquake zone, and were putting their measuring instruments into the cracks, when two National Guardsmen arrived, in a truck with a machine-gun mounted on the back. Russel speaks some Arabic, but not enough to be persuasive, and although their papers were in order, and they had a permit from the government, that didn't help, because the National Guardsmen couldn't read. So they rounded up the whole party, and took them to the nearest gaol.

I have to say that Marion doesn't seem too bothered.

She says, oh, the Ministry will sort it out, when the telephone lines to Sana'a are working. I expect he'll be out in a day or two, she says. He'll be in a filthy temper when he gets back.

I cannot imagine what a Yemeni gaol might be like. But Marion seems to feel that Russel deserves all its amenities.

When Frances finished her diary, Andrew was still muttering and frowning over his papers. She got up, and wandered about the flat; she sorted some dirty clothes, and loaded the washing-machine and thought, go up to the roof. She measured the washing powder out and thought, go up to the roof. She turned the knobs to set the programme and thought, go up to the roof.

'I'm off now,' Andrew called. 'Do you want anything from the stationery shop?'

'Yes, I want another exercise book for my diary.' She slid down the hall, away from his voice, and locked herself in the bathroom. She didn't want him to see her plans written on her face.

'I'll have to be quick,' he said, from behind the closed door. 'I might just make it before they close for evening prayers.'

She heard the front door slam. She emerged. She waited; and when she had given him time to drive away, she let herself out of the apartment and began to climb the stairs.

There was someone on the top landing. She ran; two steps at a time, grabbing for the handrail at the top and swinging herself round on to the landing to confront, head on, Samira's maid. Sarsaparilla held in her hands a small covered dish, and a piece of flat Arab bread. She stepped back. Her face was stricken, and her hands closed like claws; and again Frances caught that strange thin smell from her skin, and as she caught it her mouth dried, and she also stepped back a pace, as if the air between them had become infected by consternation.

Then suddenly, the maid smiled. It was a terrible parody

of a smile, a rictus, in which she might have been rehearsed; she held out towards Frances the bowl, the piece of flat bread. 'For you from Madam,' she said. Her first words: high-pitched, quavering. Frances took the bread, took the bowl. Her hands shook. Sarsaparilla made a little gesture, gracious and rueful, to indicate that she had just that moment been on her way down. She kept her shoulder turned to the door of the empty flat; she kept her eyes averted from it.

Holding the food, Frances turned away. She could not bear the sight of the girl's panic. She went downstairs, much more slowly than she had come up. The maid remained, standing, looking after her. She will stay there for a decent length of time, Frances thought, and then she will go back into her own flat, and she will pretend that she has delivered the food, and whoever is in the empty flat will have to go without.

It was not that the food exchange had fallen into desuetude; but this little dish of lentils had not been meant as a gift. Neither had this piece of bread, which could be bought for a few hallalas on any street corner. She put the bowl down on the worktop in the kitchen, and thought, it is not just recently I have been told lies, I have been lied to all along, or rather I have been in error as to what I chose to believe. Is lentils the food of love? Will they wake, in their dangerous post-coital languor, these mystery lovers, this man with no face, this woman with no face, but whom I do not now think is Yasmin: will they wake up for a beggar's banquet? No, because there are no lovers. Someone is in the flat, but it is not who we think. I have swallowed down the rumour. It is a rumour that was tailor-made. It was tailor-made for Westerners, with their prurient minds; it was a rumour that we cherished, because it said everything about the Kingdom that we wished to believe.

She went into the hall again, and looked up the stairs. It was sunset, and she could hear the prayer call, and she wondered, casually, if Andrew had got to the shops in time. She thought of him driving away, fifteen minutes ago, by the clock; as if it were half a lifetime away, and in another country. She felt sick with knowledge.

She had taken the torch from the side of their bed. In Africa they had kept a pickaxe handle by their bed. Some people had kept guns.

It was still light enough, when she got to the roof, to survey the vacant lot. Holes had been dug; a few upright posts had been placed in the ground. No doubt that was progress. Cement bags blew across her path, and battered at the parapet.

She positioned herself carefully at the angle of the roof from which, yesterday, she had looked on to the balcony of the empty flat. The crate was still there. It was light enough to see; but she shone the torch anyway.

'I know it has moved,' she said.

Andrew said, 'It's dark.'

'It's dark now. An hour ago it wasn't. And I know it has moved because the corner of the crate has scraped a track through the mud.'

'Well, you say it's moved. You make it sound like a mystery. What you mean is, somebody's moved it.'

'How? By thought control?'

'No, just in the ordinary way.'

'To move the crate you'd have to step out on to the balcony. If you stepped out on to the balcony you'd leave your footprints in the mud. There are no footprints.'

'So it can't have moved.'

'Yes it can. If somebody is inside it.'

What am I saying? Again that inner protest, incredulity. The doorbell rings. They look at each other sharply. He does not offer. She does not want him to.

She opened the door herself. It was Sarsaparilla. She held a tray, covered with kitchen paper. Again she said, 'From Madam.'

'You're practising your English this evening,' Frances said. 'Come in.'

221

She held the door open. The maid did not move. Frances pointed to a spot on the floor of the hall, where she wished her to stand; and she kept pointing, as you might command an animal, a dog you were training; and after a moment Sarsaparilla stepped inside.

'Why were you going into Flat 4?' Frances said. 'Who's in there?' The woman shook her head, lost; and again that smell seeped out of her, out of her pores, out of her guts. 'Who are you feeding? Who are you hiding in there?'

The woman's eyes were blank. She withdrew them from Frances, and looked at the walls.

'Please tell me,' Frances said. 'If you can.'

But she had not understood. She had not understood anything. Only the parrot phrase: 'From madam.'

Frances took the tray from her. This, no doubt, was the evening's real food exchange. Frances dropped her head. She felt ashamed of herself. 'Okay,' she said. 'Go.'

Sarsaparilla moved towards the door. Then she stopped, and looked back imploringly at Frances. She raised her arm, and pushed back a fold of her *abaya*, above her elbow. She showed Frances the inner side of her arm; tattooed there, in blue ink, was the name ELIZABETH.

Andrew said, 'I have to work out how to pay our Indian labourers. I have to find the money from somewhere.' He was pacing the living-room, and what he was worrying about didn't concern her at all. 'I can't repatriate them,' he said, 'then bring them back when the next year's budget comes through. But if I keep them here I have to feed them. Eric doesn't seem to see that. I have to whistle up some funds from somewhere.'

Frances said, 'Come up to the roof with me.'

'No.'

'I want you to see.'

'I am not interested in any trouble.' He spoke in distinct, obstinate syllables. 'I am not interested in any trouble with our neighbours.'

'There won't be any. Just come with me.'

'You don't seem to have grasped, do you, even the fundamentals about living in this place?'

'Do you think I'm stupid?'

'No, I think you're overwrought.'

'But can you explain what I've seen?'

His look said, what you have seen is not reliable. It doesn't need explanation. It doesn't merit it. 'Perhaps,' he said, with a half-smile, 'the girlfriend has herself delivered. Perhaps it's some perversion they enjoy.'

'The maid has a name,' she said. She told him.

For a second he looked interested. He said, suddenly illuminating, 'That's a mission name. It must be. Do you remember, before we were married I had that housegirl called Matweshyego? And I couldn't get my tongue round it, so I just called her "you". And then when she was leaving, she suddenly upped and said, "I have a mission name, sir. It is Rosie."'

The recollection seemed to give him pleasure. Is he just an idiot, Frances thought, is he just an unfeeling brute, or am I failing to make myself clear? Something is wrong. I cannot give you chapter and verse, but something is horribly wrong. Those days with the blinds down, the noise, the footsteps, and everyone free to come and go, except the women trapped in Dunroamin, with the doors locked, in the dark. But what she said was, 'Yes, it must be a mission name.'

'Poor lass. It sounds as if she's been colonized before.'

'Andrew,' she asked, 'what does fear smell like? In my crime books it always says that fear has a smell.'

'People put a lot of stuff in books, don't they?' He considered, and said, 'Books are irresponsible. They give people ideas.'

The food that the maid had brought was a fish, baked whole. A crust of red spices lay on its hard blackish scales and spines, and it looked up at her with a small, dead, prehistoric eye.

*

Frances should go to Andrew and apologize. She should go to him and say, I should not entertain such ludicrous and fantastic thoughts. And then they can get on with their lives.

Next morning, early, she went up to the roof again. The crate had gone. The balcony had been swept clean.

'I see Ramadhan's begun,' Andrew said.

'I thought it was two months away.'

'Yes, but you know how back in the U K people complain that Christmas is getting earlier and earlier each year? It's just the same with Ramadhan. It's a time for an increase in holiness, you see. So all the *khawwadjihs* with their evil ways have to be given a bad time.'

The religious police, in fact, are out in force. It is the time of year when the vigilantes take up young men in the shopping centres, and shear off their hair if they deem it too long. One year, women considered to be flaunting their jewellery were stopped in the street, and had it confiscated. Their husbands had to go to the police station to reclaim it – a process which possibly was not made pleasant for them.

Western women, too, must be more cautious than usual. The religious police have cans of spray paint, with which they spray revealing garments, or exposed flesh – forearms for instance.

'This nurse, from the Bugshan hospital,' Marion said, on the phone. 'She was shopping at Sarawat. They sprayed her jeans with green paint.'

'I'd kill someone,' Frances said. She actually thinks it. If she were molested on the street, she would physically fight, she thinks, she could not contain her rage, she would spit and scratch and disable and mutilate, and be damned to the consequences, because if she did not the humiliation would kill her, it would eat away at her like a cancer until she died.

'Yes, she was furious,' Marion said. 'Because these jeans, they were a new pair, first time on.'

Russel had got out of gaol. 'He'll be home in a few days,' Marion said. 'Do you know what he says?' Her voice had the accents of satiated malice. 'He says that while he was locked up he lost half a stone. I said to him, well Russel, that won't do you any harm.'

Daphne Parsons phoned. 'Frances dear,' she said, 'do be careful when you go out.'

I can no longer be careful, Frances thought. Therefore perhaps I had better not go out.

'The police are getting very strict about dress rules. There was a nurse, from the Baksh hospital, she was shopping at the Sahari Centre. They sprayed her jeans with green paint.'

'I bet they were a new pair,' Frances said. 'First time on.'

'I shouldn't wonder,' Daphne said.

There are times when the effort of avoiding something is greater than the effort of doing it. There are times when omission becomes a tyranny of effort, when the task of diverting the mind becomes physically exhausting. Frances was involved, now, in not-thinking, in not-speculating, and the effort made her clench her jaw, made her shoulders stiffen, and made the muscles rigid at the back of her neck.

The crate couldn't fly down from the balcony. They can't have brought up a crane. It must be inside the flat. It can't go through the internal doors. It can't go through the front door. So it must be in the living-room above her head. Unless it has been taken apart again. And if it has, where are its contents?

Don't think like this. There is no reason to. Andrew says she has been obsessed with the empty flat ever since they moved in. It indicates some lack of balance in her nature.

Whenever she thinks about the crate, whenever she thinks about its contents, a single image comes to her mind: she remembers the laundryman, high on the balcony at the corner of Ahmed Lari Street; the night laundryman, holding up a *thobe* to the light, with its splayed white arms like a flattened corpse; and twisting it, and folding it, to be packed away.

In the toils of not-imagining, time drips by. It is like the early days on Ghazzah Street. But nevertheless time is passing. It is Tuesday, 21 Jamadi al-thani, 12 March in the real world: eleven o'clock in the morning. The doorbell rings. A little voice, pleasant but anxious, says: 'Do please let me in, Mrs Shore, before someone sees me.'

Her visitor was Shabana, Yasmin's friend, whom she had met at Raji's party. 'You do remember me,' Shabana said. 'I am so glad. I do hope I am not intruding on you.'

'I wasn't doing anything. Coffee?'

'That would be nice.'

'A car came for Yasmin. I think she's gone shopping.'

'Yes, I was hoping so. It is you I have come to see. And I would be so happy if you would not tell her I have been here.'

Frances went into the kitchen to make the coffee. Shabana did not follow her, as one of her own friends would have done; instead she took an armchair, and was sitting, her plump hands in her lap, when Frances returned. 'I am worried about Yasmin,' she said at once. 'She speaks of you as her friend, and that is why I thought we might talk.'

'I'm worried about her too.'

'I have known her for quite a while now. These days she seems, so . . . uncharacteristic . . . I don't know.'

'She's miserable. It's her mother-in-law. She came weeks ago and she doesn't show any signs of going.'

'This is part of it, no doubt.'

'She's run off her feet.' Frances found herself indignant. It is a false indignation, her heart warned her, grafted on to graver circumstances more deserving of it; but it seemed real, it sounded real, it was partly real. 'She's exhausted from pandering to that old woman's whims. She's worried about Selim. The mother-in-law, she's put it into her head that there's something wrong with him.'

'Yes, but you must understand,' Shabana said delicately, 'that we cannot interfere. This is the way things are. One day she will do it to her own daughter-in-law.'

Shabana spooned sugar into her coffee; she poured in cream. 'When I was first a bride,' she said, 'I cried every night for a month. Mohammed had been chosen for me, he was everything my family desired, but somehow, you know, I was romantic, and he is not a handsome man, he did not meet my expectations. My head was full of filmstars, you see. I thought he should bring me flowers and perfume, and talk to me,' she gave a little laugh, 'of love. When he did not, I thought he was a monster of cruelty and neglect. I complained to my mother about my unhappiness. But she said, When I was a bride, I cried every night for a year.'

That is an improving fable, Frances thought. 'And are you happy now?'

'Oh, I have accommodated. Yasmin, I think, was always more down to earth.'

'I don't think, though, that she is happy with Raji.'

'They seem at odds.' Shabana put down her cup, and sat twisting one of her heavy gold rings around her finger. 'Has she told you why?'

'My neighbour, Samira, says she prays too much. But I can hardly think that is the reason.'

'Has she spoken to you about the veil?'

'Yes. I'm afraid I wasn't very sympathetic.'

'The idea is repugnant to you.' Shabana sighed. 'Yes, I am glad we are having this talk. I shouldn't like you to make things worse for her, by lack of understanding.'

'You don't think, do you,' Frances said, 'you have never thought, have you . . . that Yasmin might be involved with another man?'

'God forbid!' Shabana said. 'You have no evidence of that, surely?'

'No. Only that one day she seemed to be waiting for someone . . . I did think it at one time. But I had no evidence. And I don't think it now. I imagine she was waiting for the person . . . for some other reason.'

'Her troubles are not of that nature, thank heaven.'

'Would it be the worst thing in the world?'

'You know the law here,' Shabana said drily. 'Westerners are always very well informed about it.'

'Okay,' Frances said. 'I'm sorry. It's a red herring.'

Politely, Shabana raised her eyebrows. 'A false clue,' Frances said. 'I thought she had a guilty secret, and we usually think those are to do with sex. But there are other kinds.'

She leaned forwards and refilled Shabana's cup. The movement seemed dreamlike, endlessly repeatable. She had done it for Yasmin, for Samira; six months of it. Pouring coffee, she thought, and passing it through the bars of our respective cages.

'I am not sure she has guilt,' Shabana said. 'It is rather the other way. You see, our religion is not a religion of excess, Mrs Shore . . . may I call you Frances? It is a religion for practical men and women. Muhammed, after all, was a soldier and a ruler, as well as a man of God. But in some cases, let us say, in Raji's case, one may become a little too practical. Raji is a businessman at heart. He flies here and he flies there. He spends time in London. He takes trips to New York. He prays and fasts, and Allah really hasn't asked us to do any more – but when he is not in the Kingdom, who knows? He is a sociable fellow. And the Minister, his boss, he is just another of the same type.'

'I gather from what Andrew says that the Minister isn't liked by everyone in the royal family.'

'That would be correct. He is a man who is fond of compromises. So is Raji, too. That is why Yasmin suspects he is not a very moral creature.'

Raji drinks and eyes up other women, Frances thought. Who am I to shop him to his wife's friend? Shabana, quite possibly, is Yasmin's spy.

The next moment she thought, that is ridiculous. I am far gone. I am paranoid. It has set in with me – Phase Three – just as the Indian psychiatrist said it would. She said, 'When I came here I had some talks with Yasmin about Islam. She was quite relaxed about it. I thought she was a liberal. But

228

she was only sugaring the pill for me. She is really a fundamentalist. Would that be the word?'

Shabana hesitated. She smoothed the black folds of her *abaya*, which she had laid over the arm of her chair. 'We must be clear,' she said. 'When we are talking about fundamentalism we are not talking about some sect within Islam, as you Christians, I know, have your different churches. It is true, of course, that there are differences between Muslims, throughout the world, but fundamentalism transcends these. You must think, Frances, what is the meaning of the word? We are thinking of what is basic, of what is the essence of Islam.'

'I understand what the word means.'

'Of course you do, I don't mean to patronize you. But it is not a question of choosing between doctrines, or feeling that one should have less of something, or more of something . . . It is a matter of being true to the essence. Things like the veil are only a symbol.'

'A symbol can be a very powerful thing.'

'That is quite true. And I said that it was a symbol, I did not say that it was a side issue. To Westerners the veil seems ridiculous, but we cannot just fall in with your prejudices. It is simply not possible for us to look at the Western world, to look at other religions, and say, yes please, we will have this from you, we will have this, but we don't want that. We cannot take your bits and pieces and fit them into Islam. You see, everything that you hold – what is it the Americans say? – that you hold self-evident . . . that democracy is good, that liberalism is good in itself . . . we have never taken these ideas as naturally true.'

'They're not part of your mental furniture.'

'Yes, that is right. You grow up with them, we do not. That is why it is so very difficult for people like me, who were educated in the West, and for people like Raji, leading his kind of life. Even those things that you are quite sure are virtues – let us say, tolerance – they are not necessarily virtues for us.'

'I understand that. I'm never sure myself if tolerance is a good thing. There are some things that are intolerable.'

'You think, no doubt, that you have seen some of them in the Kingdom.'

'I'm not one of those people who think that when you go to a foreign country you must leave your judgement at home.'

'And you would impose your judgement on us?'

'Probably. If I could.'

Shabana smiled slightly. 'It is people like you, Frances, who led the Crusades.'

'I'm sure you're right.'

'And you and Yasmin have an instinctive sympathy, I suspect.'

'That's why we've become friends.'

Watching her, Shabana played with her bracelets. She teased each one with her finger and thumb, pushing it a fraction of an inch along her arm, and letting it fall back, with a little clink of gold against gold. I hope, Frances thought, that the religious police don't spot you on your way home.

'But I am getting diverted,' Shabana said. 'Their marriage – Raji and Yasmin – was a very suitable one of course. He was a very good catch for her. But this is what may happen, in the very best arranged of marriages, that the two partners don't have this sympathy . . . they may seem to agree on most things, but they don't have just the same idea of how to manage life.'

'Andrew and I are like that.'

'You have found it?'

'Yes, we tackle things differently. He waits, and I act.'

'Then you may say he is at danger of being crushed by circumstances, but you, Frances, are at danger of collisions. If I may say . . . do be careful. This is not a good country for people who act.'

'Which sort of person are you?'

'Oh, I am your sort. That is why I came here today. I

thought, Yasmin is my friend, she is unhappy, I will talk with her other friend, and maybe between us we will explain the situation.'

'And do you think that we have?'

'I think we may have explained one or two other things.'

'There isn't much we can do to help.'

'I have thought of going to Raji, to ask him to accept that she may wear the veil, if that is what she feels she must do. But you see, Raji's Minister is one of the modern faction. He is a man of progress.'

'It would be a political embarrassment for Raji.'

'Certainly. You see, this is not a good time for the Saudis. They are not so rich as they were, and this causes squabbling. Some of the senior princes are in poor health, this is no secret. People are wondering, which way is the country going to go? Yasmin is not alone in her opinions. I think she may despise her husband, because, you are aware, all the Westerners know Raji. He has done deals with them. He is a kind of symbol in himself.'

'You think he has a lot of enemies?'

'Oh yes. Yes indeed.' Shabana gathered up her *abaya*. 'But now I must go. And I will give you my phone number. Then if you think that there is some crisis with them, if you hear quarrels, perhaps, then you may please telephone me.' She smiled brightly as she swathed herself in black. 'And I will try to do the marriage guidance, before it is too late.'

Frances got up. 'Here.' She proffered a pen. 'Write it in my book.'

Shabana did so. 'Do you know,' she said, 'what will do her good? If she can move from here. Get away from these walls and doors, and being shut up with other women. Our own culture does not demand that. She is always with the Arab girl, I think she is a bad influence. You know what is the life of the Arab girl, Frances. Not like you or I.'

'She said she might like to move.'

'Did she? Well, that is an advance. Perhaps there is hope then.' Shabana arranged a flimsy token veil over her hair. 'I know he has asked her many times to move to a nice villa in Al Hamra, that is more suitable for their station in life. But she would not. She has always said, No, I want to stay in these apartments.'

There was a time, Frances thought, when I didn't want to move. I would like to move, now. But the herb, *mehti*, has shrivelled in its pot. Andrew says she has over-watered it.

'Frances,' Shabana said, 'would you go out, please, and see if my driver is at the gate? That man has the bad habit of going shopping. And it is not the right thing to hang about on the street.'

She went out on to Ghazzah Street; the driver was waiting, his eyes closed, his window down, his radio playing. She returned, took Shabana through the hall, and let her out. 'I don't care for these tiles at all,' Shabana said. 'Saudi taste. Like eyes watching you. Thank you for the coffee.'

Each morning now the dawn prayer call wakes her from a doze. The morning sounds of the city – the early traffic, the first planes into the airport – remind her of a giant vacuum cleaner suddenly switched on. The weather is warming up, and the days seem long if you go without a siesta. But if she sleeps in the afternoon, she wakes up in the twilight with a start, her mouth full of saliva and a sick, sinking feeling in the pit of her stomach.

By nine in the evening she is wretchedly tired. She goes to bed, but can't sleep. Her body feels cramped, her hair irritates the skin of her neck, the pillow seems to have been filled with marbles. She dozes, dreams, wakes again, listening to the night sounds of the apartment, and perhaps for something more. 'If you think there is some crisis with them, if you hear quarrels . . .' After the dawn prayer call, she falls into a heavy sleep. Andrew gets up at six. He takes a shower, brings her coffee. It goes cold by her bedside. They hardly speak; she mutters something, incoherent fragments from a dream. He tiptoes out. Sometimes, absent-mindedly, he locks her into the apartment, as he did in the early days. It is as if she does not exist any more as definitely, as firmly as she used to. And it is true that she is going thin.

It is about nine o'clock when she surfaces. In a hot climate, this is late; the morning is half over. She feels guilty. People confuse early rising with moral worth; she is someone in whom this confusion is marked. She goes into the bathroom, and standing on the threshold, inspects the floor for cockroaches; then she inspects her own swollen face.

She feels shaky; each day a degree worse. She takes herself into the kitchen, washes Andrew's breakfast dishes, picks at something from the fridge – fruit, or a carton of yoghurt. She has no way of knowing what has happened in the three hours between six and nine, while she lay in that oblivious state, that trance-like, paralysing sleep. Anything might have happened, in other apartments, other rooms; but she has abdicated control. She feels that she once had a grip on the situation, but that now she has lost it.

On almost the last day of the month, Frances went to see the doctor. For the occasion, she borrowed Hasan and his car. She wondered at getting them so easily, for Daphne could seldom be parted from her transport. But when Hasan arrived, he put her in the picture. 'Garage this afternoon, Mrs Andrew.' He made alarming signs to indicate a fault in the steering; then added, as if it were a technical term, 'Is fucked-up.'

'Oh, Hasan, what have you done to it?' He was on his third clutch, Andrew had told her; there were dents in the sides, and hardly a week went by without a smashed indicator light and a fresh scrape. But if the office car died, would Eric find funds for another? 'Can it be fixed?' she asked him. 'I mean, is this car finished?'

Hasan regarded her irritably. He spoke the *lingua franca* of drivers, mechanics and maintenance men, left over from when Europeans did these jobs. 'Not *finished*, I told you. This car is just fucked-up, madam – not totally buggered.'

*

233

The doctor was an Englishman; he had a modern clinic near the Pepsi-Cola factory.

'We haven't met, Mrs Shore,' he said, rising from behind his desk and offering his hand.

'I've never been ill.'

The doctor had American colleagues; he had picked up their turn of phrase. 'How may I help you?' he said.

'My period is late.'

'How late?'

'I don't know.'

'Ah, you don't keep a diary.'

'Well, I do, but not that sort.'

'Anything else? A little nausea in the mornings?'

'Yes. As you mention it.'

He wanted details. Her gynaecological history. 'We'll do a little test,' he promised.

'But I don't think I can be pregnant,' she said. 'I'm losing weight.'

'Mrs Shore,' he asked her, 'are you under some sort of strain?'

Hasan dropped her off at the gate. It had been a futile excursion. The pregnancy test would prove negative, and the doctor would call her in, puzzle over her, order blood tests; in the end, no doubt, he would offer her a little bottle of tranquillizing pills. What is wrong with you, Mrs Shore? Doctor, I have a neurotic imagination.

Someone was in the hall, moving ahead of her – a veiled figure, going upstairs. I no longer believe in the veiled lady, she thought; I know she is a fiction, a lie. Has Samira a visitor? The figure moves, not at a visitor's pace, but head-long: not furtive, decisive: and the momentary glimpse she caught seemed to contradict some observation that she had once made. She heard the weighty, the unapologetic tread. She turned out the hall light.

It was true what the doctor said; she needed a holiday. She needed a little trip, an excursion, and she would take it

234

now; from the circumspect habits of a lifetime. She waited. She stood in shadow by her front door, the picture of patience; she stood listening to her own shallow breathing, her face tilted upwards to the stairwell.

Ten minutes passed. She heard the click of a front door: Flat 4. With the same hasty but deliberate tread, the figure came back down the stairs. Frances stepped forward, out of the shadow of the gleaming tiles with their multiple insect eyes. She blocked the foot of the stairs.

The visitor stopped dead. An outline of features beneath black cloth, no surprise discernible, no fear, no challenge, no expression at all. The visitor was tall; a strapping lass. Frances raised her hand. The visitor pulled back, but she had made contact. She tugged at the concealing *abaya*, felt it part, felt something cold, metallic, under her hand. She reached up, with her other hand, and clawed at the veil. But a veil is not something you can pull off. You can dream of doing it, but you cannot just accomplish it, because the black cloth is wound around the head. The head strains back; and then she is pushed away with all the visitor's ungirlish strength, sent flying against the wall. Her neck snaps backwards, her head hits the tiles, two long strides and the visitor has crossed the hall, and while she is recovering herself is already out of the front door, and out of the gate, and on to Ghazzah Street.

Frances stood up shakily. Surprisingly, she felt no pain; no evidence of the encounter, except the chilly bar of flesh in the palm of her hand, where she had touched the metal of the gun's barrel. She held her hand open for a moment, the fingers splayed to rid herself of the invisible stigmata. Cure this, doctor. Take my pain away.

Rajab

‚‚‚‚‚‚‚‚

I

The temperature had been moving upwards for a week; and
suddenly, the approaching summer moved into a new
dimension. All night, while they had been insensibly
dreaming together under a flowered sheet, the heat had
been abroad, gathering its forces in other rooms to hang in
dense clots from the walls; there was a white, scaly sky,
diseased and enfeebled by its own heat. Frances went about
her own house like a charwoman, lugging the vacuum
cleaner and the washing basket, her head bowed and her
hair pushed behind her ears. On Saturday the temperature
was 97°. Today it is 106°. In Riyadh it is 118°. Every day it
is rising. There is a leaden sky and a hot wind; the dust,
blowing continuously, lends a lunar aspect to the vacant
lots. You expect to see comets and portents, rabid alien life-
forms scuttling at your feet.

She was wrong to think that she was sick with knowledge.
While it is contained within her own head, and her own
body – the memory of that metal chill, of that dizzying reel
from the foot of the stairs – the knowledge can do no harm.
It is not the knowledge, but the potential of knowledge, that
makes her so dangerous. She is germinating a disaster; she
has a communicable disease.

Therefore she says nothing. Therefore she begins each
morning as if it were the first on Ghazzah Street. Therefore
she declines serious conversation. Listens without hearing.

Looks without seeing. Andrew had forgotten to get her a new exercise book for her diary; and she had not asked him again. Better not to write things down. Anyway, the diary's original purpose seems to have dissolved. She couldn't write to Clare, or to any of her correspondents, the sort of thing she had been putting in her diary recently. She imagined their replies, which seldom even acknowledged the content of her own letters: 'Well, I haven't much to tell you really. We haven't been doing much. The weather is still very cold . . .' No doubt they mislaid her letters, found them tiresome, put them in a drawer where they would not nag for replies.

Jeff Pollard, shopping at the Jeddah International Market, had his Credit Suisse token removed from his neck by a religious policeman. It was only a moderate amount of gold, in truth, but in this matter, as in others, there are different rules for men and women. He should have spent the money on a watch. He could have worn a Patek Philippe, and no one would have quarrelled. But in these stringent times it is not only the vigilantes who think it is in bad taste to wear your salary around your neck.

Russel has arrived back from the Yemen.

All over town people are purveying to each other rumours of sackings and redundancies. Wherever the expatriates get together they talk about their grievances, and about how badly the Saudis have treated them: fear and loathing at the St Patrick's Day barbecue.

It was getting too hot for the walk to Marion's house. But Marion didn't seem able to organize herself to come to Dunroamin. Marion's conversation had never been re-warding, but just to be at her house was a pleasure, to sit in a room with normal daylight, and to feel, for an hour, no curiosity and no threat.

The gateboy came out of his hut when Frances rang the bell, and let her into the compound. But Marion did not answer her doorbell. Frances peered through the front window. The living-room seemed strangely tidy. She went back to the gateboy, and pointed, inquiringly. He shook his head, and at the same time seemed consumed by some private joke.

So she set off home. There was a main road to negotiate, but it was mid-morning, fairly quiet, and she never had trouble crossing at the lights. A boy in a Mercedes pulled up, waved her in front of him. As she stepped out from the kerb, he revved his engine, the car sprang forward, and she had to leap from under its wheels. She heard the brakes applied; caught herself up, heart racing, and looked back at the driver of the car; understood that it had not been an accident. 'You are my darling, madam, you are my baby . . .' Saw on his face laughter and contempt.

When she got home she phoned Carla. 'Look,' Carla said, 'it's happened to me. Don't take everything so personally.'

'But why?' she insisted. She felt on the verge of tears. 'I just wanted to cross. I would have waited. I would have let him go by.'

Carla said tiredly, 'They don't want us on the streets. It's just a thing they do.'

'I went around to Marion's this morning,' she said to Andrew.

He looked at her in amazement. 'Didn't you know? Did nobody tell you? Russel's packed her off home. He's found out about her and Jeff.'

She stared at him, and a slow and unwelcome realization dawned on her face. 'Do you mean they've been having an affair?' She sat down, as people do, to take in the bad news. 'I didn't realize.'

Andrew looked at her in exasperation. 'Everybody else knew.'

'How long has it been going on?'

'Months.'

'I didn't know. I was always saying how foul he was.'

'Yes, I noticed, but I thought you knew about them and you were doing that anyway. I mean, I didn't think a consideration like that would hamper you.'

'But you never said anything! You never discussed it with me!'

'Why should I? It's no concern of mine.'

'And all the time you thought I knew about it . . . do you ever wonder, Andrew, whether you're missing things yourself?'

'I don't think I'm missing anything that matters.'

Frances crossed the room, and picked up the telephone receiver. She didn't dial; listened to the crackles and blips on the line. She handed him the receiver. 'Listen to that.'

He listened.

'When I rang Carla I got that. I rang Turadup –'

'What for?'

'What for doesn't matter. I'm explaining to you, it buzzes, it clicks – what do you think?'

'I think,' Andrew said, 'that what you have there is a typical Third World telephone.'

'It wasn't always like that. It's just started happening.'

'Oh, Frances.' He looked at her in disappointment. 'You're not going to be one of those people who believes that the phones are tapped?'

'Maybe they are.'

'Yes, maybe they are, there's a respectable body of opinion that says so. But the people who are always going on about it are the sort who –'

'Yes, I know. They're in Phase Three. They've cracked up. They have blue-tinted windscreens in their cars.'

'Even if they are tapped, what have we got to hide? We don't exchange brewing hints on the telephone.'

'That's not the point, is it?'

'To me, the point is that there are things that might be true . . . but you can't afford to believe them.' He struggled to explain it; as if she needed it explained. 'Because if you believe them you're really screwed up, you can't function. I have to function. I mean, I only want another year, but I have to stay here at any price.'

'What do you mean, at any price?'

But Andrew was thinking about the flat he was going to buy. A price, to him, was paid in money. To conversations like these, there are no sensible conclusions.

Earlier, she had talked to Eric Parsons. He had been jocular when he answered the phone to her, thinking it was social chit-chat. Daphne was out and about so much that her friends often left their messages with him. This was why Frances said, 'Eric, please don't talk to me as if I had asked to borrow the Magimix.'

'What is it then, my dear?'

Soon Eric was stupefied; hearing what he did not want to hear. And how can she put it delicately – I think that maybe upstairs there is an arms cache, a hideout, a torture chamber, a mortuary? That I have exhausted my imagination on what there may *not* be? 'I think,' she said, 'that there is a conspiracy, to which I have become a party, not a willing party . . .'

'But of course there is.' Eric cut in on her. He sounded angry. 'We shouldn't be talking about this over the phone. You know, you were told, about the empty flat. And you were told to be careful.'

'It isn't at all what you have been led to believe. Can I correct what I said? I don't think there is a conspiracy. I know.'

'Let me stop you there, Frances.' She heard heavy, exasperated breathing. 'Does Andrew know that you're speaking to me?'

'No.'

'No. I thought not. Do bear in mind, my love, that for anything you do in this place, your husband is responsible. I can understand it, of course – all you women together in the flats, you've got to know each other, that's nice, and you're sure to talk amongst yourselves. What do they say, women are the same the whole world over? But you see if you involve yourself – if you are thought, Frances, to be making a nuisance of yourself, to have come into possession of any information that you shouldn't have – then it will be Andrew who bears the brunt of any indiscretion.'

'But I think a crime has been committed.'

'Then do remember that the Saudi way with the witness of a crime is to hold the witness in gaol.' Eric's voice took on an official tone, a sort of stony rectitude. 'And if you persist in interfering, against all advice, then you have to take the consequences. The Embassy and the Foreign Office can do nothing for you. They will do nothing for you. There are trading agreements at stake, there are diplomatic agreements, and those agreements are far more important than you.'

There was a pause. She said, 'Won't you even listen to me?'

'No,' Eric said; pleasantly enough, courteously enough. 'I am first in the firing line, my dear, and there are some things I cannot afford to know. Once past a certain point, you see, you become an undesirable person, and then who knows what happens? Because there comes a certain point where they don't want you here, and if you see what I mean, they don't want you to leave either.'

'And have you ever known anyone who reached that point?'

'Oh no,' Eric said. 'I wouldn't know a person like that.'

Some days passed. She did not speak to Andrew, except about the trivial. She felt under threat; why should the threat extend to him? She said to herself, I will be careful from now on, and perhaps this will go no further. She did not believe this; either that she would be careful, or that there would be no repercussions. She had stepped into a parallel world whose existence she had suspected for so long, and she could not say, now, I lost my map, I did not mean to trespass, I will never do it again. Or, she could say it; it need not have any practical effect.

They were driving home; it was dark. Frances said, 'There it is.' It was the gates she recognized; and they were open.

The garden had gone. In its place was a white, foursquare, five-storey office block, with three steps up to a large front door; a door of wrought-iron curlicues, and chrome-tinted toughened glass. There was a plaque on the gate: Bohkari Establishment for Trade and Commerce.

Andrew slowed the car. He sounded puzzled. 'That building's always been there, Fran.'

'Nothing's always been there. Don't be silly.'

'Okay, let's say it's been there for months.'

'You must be wrong.'

'Look,' he said mildly, 'I have an eye for a building, right? What you see there may not be a distinguished example of modern architecture, but I'm not likely to mix it up with anything else. Do me a favour.'

She didn't answer; unclipped her seat-belt so that she could turn round properly, craning her neck.

'We can go back if you like. What's wrong?'

'I'll tell you what's wrong.' She felt enraged; why should he speak to her as if she were simple-minded? 'When I last saw that plot there was a garden there. They had a lawn. It was the only lawn I ever saw. I told you about it. Now there's a building. How can it have got there? How can it have got there without my noticing?'

'But we come this way twice a week.' His bewilderment was plain, she heard it in his voice. 'It didn't spring up overnight. They finished it before Christmas.'

'How could they? How could they?'

'I'll turn round, so that you can have another look. Do a U-ey, as Jeff puts it.'

'That's all right,' she said dully. 'You needn't.'

'I want you to be satisfied.'

He turned as soon as he could, drove slowly past the gates again. The garden had gone, and the ramshackle villa with its tin roof; the hanging lamp had gone, and the swaying light with its dappled flurry of moths' wings. 'Don't worry,' he said, 'there are places I passed in my first few weeks in Jeddah that I could swear I've never seen since, and yet they must be there, I know they must, it's just that you're coming at them from a different angle. And of course, you have to keep your eyes on the road.'

'I don't.'

'No, but you must have lost your bearings. This town changes fast.'

Who would have believed it? That they could put up a five-storey building, while your back was turned, while your attention was elsewhere? She has been looking at the external city; but the internal city is more important, the one that you construct inside your head. That is where the edifice of possibility grows, and grows without your knowledge; it is subject to no planner's control.

They pulled up outside Dunroamin. 'Fairfax is coming in a couple of days,' Andrew said. 'He really is, this time. I spoke to him on the phone. He's got his visa. I'm collecting him at the airport.' He got out, locked his door, opened the boot and pulled out a couple of the big brown bags which held their groceries. 'Can I ask him over for an evening?'

'Yes, of course.'

'Will it be all right? Only you seem so distracted, Fran.'

'I want to meet him. I've been looking forward to it.'

She picked up one of the bags herself, holding it in her arms like a heavy child. Andrew wedged a bag against the outside wall, propping it up with his knee while he fumbled for the right key; but she pushed the metal gate with her foot, and said, 'Look, it's open.'

'Shouldn't be,' Andrew said. 'We're supposed to keep the place secure.'

The front gate was ajar. 'Perhaps Raji is just dashing in and out,' she said.

Andrew let them into the flat. As soon as he opened the door, she knew that something was wrong. Andrew switched on the light. He stood, staring at the mess, and then lowered the bags of groceries carefully to the floor. 'We've been done over,' he said. 'Okay, let's not panic, leave everything just where it is and we'll have a look.'

They had been burgled before, in Africa; so often, so routinely, that Andrew was calm, summoning all the old feelings: a moderate, suitable annoyance, a measure of resignation, a calm, impervious front. But Frances felt that it was not something you got used to. She ran from room to room, sweeping each one with a glance. The wardrobe gaped open; some of their clothes had been dragged from the hangers, flung about the room. Drawers were pulled out. 'Our camera's gone,' she said.

'Let's check the cash, that's the first thing.'

They still had their housekeeping money. A bundle of it nested securely in its place underneath the dressing-table; it had not been a convenient arrangement, lifting the furniture around every few days, but it had served its purpose. 'I thought my African habits were over-cautious,' Andrew said. 'But seemingly not.' Casually, he heaved the dressing-table back into place. 'Found the rest?'

She had six five-hundred riyal notes, crisp new purple ones, inside the Holy Koran. 'Good girl,' Andrew said. 'Although you never know if thieves can read, do you?'

'Are we going to get the police?'

He looked around the living-room. It was obvious how the burglars had got in. They had come through the big window with its sliding panel; the length of wood that should have blocked the track lay on the carpet. It had been removed from the inside. 'You forgot to put it back,' Andrew said. He saw her face. 'I'm not blaming you. I know you want a breath of air sometimes. I can understand how it happened.'

'If I want air I go to the roof. I didn't take the wood out.'

'You must have. Who else could it have been?'

'No one.'

'But look.' He held it up. 'Here it is. It didn't jump out by itself.'

'I don't know how it happened.'

'The landlord's not been round again, has he?'

'Not while I've been here. I suppose he must have keys.'

'Who else has been in?'

'Only Yasmin. Oh, and Sarsaparilla. She brought a plate of something, I gave her something back.'

'Was she in here on her own?'

'Only for a minute.'

'It's just what they always say. Servants let thieves in. They take up with shady people on their day off, and there you are, they tell them your movements, they tell them the layout, and the next thing is you've been cleaned out.'

'But Sarsaparilla doesn't go anywhere. They don't let her out. She's too frightened to go out.'

'Okay then,' Andrew said, indifferently. 'If it wasn't her, it must have been Yasmin. One idea is considerably less ridiculous than the other, but take your pick.'

On the desk, papers had been scattered, letters had been ripped open. Andrew moved them around gingerly, with a fingertip. 'I reckon labourers must have done it, Yemenis or somebody. They think you stuff your letters home with banknotes for your old mother. Didn't take the video, did they?'

'They've taken the Thamaga candlesticks. Some food has gone, out of the fridge. Just eggs and things.'

'There you are then. Not a professional job, is it?'

She shook her head. 'It seems not. Unless it is in fact very professional. Professionals masquerading as blundering amateurs.'

'Still reading the detective books?' Andrew crossed the room, put his arms around her and pulled her gently towards him. He cradled her against his shoulder. She felt light and frail under his confident hands, just an assemblage of bones: and barely consoled. 'It's all right now, Fran. I don't think they've got anything that's worth much.' He held her tight, rocking her, solid and undisturbed; one of the sex war's élite corps, one of the shock troops home on a family visit. 'Listen, don't panic, Frances, it could have been much worse.' He was comforting her, for her own carelessness in having let the thieves in; the theory about the maid, which he had worked up so carefully, had been to allow her to save face.

'I wish you could believe me,' she said. 'But if you can't you can't. I'm just a woman after all, and unlikely to be able to keep track of my actions.'

She struggled free of him; went from room to room. She heard him pick up the phone, heard him speaking, calm and bluff and male; heard him give a little laugh. She went into the bedroom and sat down on the bed, fingering her mauled and despoiled summer frocks. They had rummaged through the drawer where she kept her make-up, looking for jewellery perhaps. Her soapstone tortoise had gone from the bedside table. What a stupid thing to take! How do burglars know, what sixth sense informs them, about the small, valueless things that you cannot bear to lose?

Andrew stood in the doorway. He had not taken offence, he understood her outburst; what's one little squawk, when the nest has been invaded? 'I've just talked to Eric,' he said. 'He says that unless we've lost something important, we shouldn't bother with the police. For a start we'd have to get all the booze out of the house. Then he says they sprinkle black fingerprint powder everywhere, and you can't get it off the carpets. I'd have to go down to the police station, and he says I might be there all night, we'd have to get Hasan over to interpret, there are endless forms to fill in, and they never catch anybody at the end of it all.'

'And if they did . . .'

'Yes, that's a thought. I wouldn't want that on my conscience. What about your clothes? Have they taken much?'

'Most things seem to be here. I can't be sure.'

'Shall we clean up then?'

She rose, tiredly. 'We may as well. Just let's get the stuff off the floor and back in the cupboards, and I'll do the rest tomorrow.' She thought, I wonder if they have taken my diary?

Andrew looked at her searchingly. A serious, responsible

expression took over his face; he frowned. 'You look pale,' he said.

'It was a shock.'

'You must put your feet up. I'll do the clearing up. I'll make you some tea.'

'What about that Scotch Rickie gave us?'

'Good idea. Where is it?'

'It's under the kitchen sink. With the cockroach spray and the bottles of bleach.'

Andrew grinned. 'That's a good place for it. Not even our thieves are interested in bottles of bleach. I'll pour you a large one, Watson.'

'Okay, Holmes,' she said.

She remained where she was, limp, dispirited, as if the strength had run out of her limbs. Andrew, she thought, his powers of recovery . . . he's a wonder. She should not resent it, should she? Then she heard his voice from the kitchen. 'Oh, you bastard,' he said.

She scrambled up, hurried after him. Andrew glowered over the remains of the bottle of Scotch; smashed, it lay on the draining-board.

'Oh well,' she said. 'At least somebody's had a good time tonight. If he drank it, of course. He might just have poured it away.'

She was not sure why the thought had occurred to her. They exchanged a glance; then Andrew turned quickly and made for the little bathroom where they kept their wine supplies. As soon as he opened the door a ripe heady odour from the upturned jerry cans rolled past them. Almost tangible, it billowed down the passageway, and washed through the flat. 'Keep back,' he said. 'There's glass all over the floor.'

There had been twenty-four bottles, in a cardboard box; even the box was ripped to shreds, and its remnants bobbed on the frothy tide from the jerry cans, a scum of yeast and water and half-fermented fruit. Standing behind Andrew, she touched his elbow. 'Imagine what it will do for the drains.'

But he was not going to laugh. 'I wouldn't have minded,'

247

Andrew said. 'If they'd drunk it. I wouldn't have minded.'

'I think,' Frances said, 'that we have been left a message.'

'Message? Rip off the *khawwadjis* and save them from sin, is that what you mean?'

'Something like that.'

'I don't think so,' Andrew said. 'I think that all they are interested in, from the Council of Ministers to the common thieves, is just making sure that we rue the day we ever saw this bloody place.'

She looked up into his face. 'I thought you said we had to stay at any price?'

'You don't need to tell me what I said. I said I'll see the project through. They said they wanted it done and I contracted to do it and I'm not going to be frightened off by the vagaries of my bloody imagination.' Andrew looked dangerous now – mutinous. She recognized his bull-in-china-shop face; as if he had been breathing in the alcohol, or had absorbed it through his skin. She felt afraid of him; of any impulses he might have. A few months ago, it might have made them laugh. She might have described them in her letters home, comically pitiable figures, wringing their hands in this pale pink yeasty sea. But now even above the stench of fermentation she smelled violence in the air, recognized the savage concentration with which the intruder had gone to work, smashing each bottle on the tiles, fragmenting it, and standing finally, one must suppose, with bleeding hands and feet, tidemarked with alcoholic foam.

Andrew laid his arm across her shoulders. 'You know those cages,' he said, 'in the terrorist trials in Italy, those glass cages they have for the defendants?'

'Yes, I've seen pictures of them.'

'No, you haven't. You can't take pictures of glass.'

'I've read about them.' Reports describe the cage; you believe that it is there; you see the prisoners, their foreheads laid against walls of air, their gestures cut short by invisible fetters.

'You have dozens of people crammed together month after

month in those cages,' Andrew said. 'The other year two terrorists had sex in the cage, and then nine months later when the trial was still going on the woman terrorist gave birth to twins.'

'Yes, I think I remember that.'

'I keep thinking about those terrorists, I suppose I must have a fellow-feeling with them. They have a kind of parody-life inside those glass cages, and I feel it's just like mine. And the months go by, and I feel I am being convicted of something.' He added calmly, 'And that is what I mean, before you ask me, about the vagaries of my bloody imagination.'

She slipped away from his grasp. 'I must clear up. I must clean up this mess.'

'I'll do it. You sit down.'

She went into the living-room, to the desk. Some of the drawers had been wrenched out. This had not alarmed them; they did not keep anything of importance there. 'They've stolen our postage stamps,' she called, and Andrew's voice came back, very practical now, very matter-of-fact:

'That's about par for the course.'

One of the drawers had been upended on the carpet. She picked her diary out of the mess. She flicked over the leaves. It was untorn, unmarked. There were no greasy fingerprints on its pages, no smudges that had not been there before. If I were to put my life under scrutiny, she thought, this is where I would start. But she had stopped keeping the diary. The pages had been filled, the space had run out, and now it seemed that events must cease to occur. Could she find anything if she had the policeman's aids, the magnifying glass, the test-tube, the graphite powder that marked the carpets? She had laid the book against her face, as if she might find a scent of something; alien sweat, nitroglycerine, the metal smell of blood.

Daphne telephoned next day, to commiserate. 'Still, you were wise not to involve the police,' she said. 'They make everything ten times worse. And, as Eric said, you might have ended up in custody yourself. That's the trouble with this place. Even if you aren't doing anything wrong, you always feel as if you are.'

Frances said, 'Can I borrow Hasan and the office car? The doctor rang me up, they want me to have some kind of tests.'

'I can recommend a gynaecologist,' Daphne said swiftly.

'I don't think that's what I need.'

'Oh, I see. Nothing wrong, Frances, is there?'

'Probably not.' She regretted beginning the conversation. 'Daphne, please don't tell everybody. Don't go spreading rumours that I'm ill.'

Daphne sounded startled. 'Of course not. I can assure you, my dear, that whatever you chose to confide in me would go no further.'

Liar, Frances thought. 'What about the car then?'

'There's a tiny problem – it's still at the garage, and when it comes back this man Fairfax is borrowing it. You'll have to get Andrew to take a couple of hours off during the day.'

'That doesn't sound a very good idea. About Fairfax, I mean. He'll get lost. He's never been here before. Someone should drive him around.'

'I'm not best pleased myself,' Daphne said, thinking of the batik workshop she would be forced to miss. 'But Eric says he simply hasn't the wherewithal to provide people with chauffeurs.'

'What's Hasan for?'

'My dear, would you like to be entrusted to Hasan on your first visit to the Kingdom? That man's only thought is to ditch you and sneak off to those smoking parlours they go to. Many's the time I've been stranded –' Daphne's voice ran on. Frances pictured her, teetering on the pavement outside the Pâtisserie Franco-Belge, a box of dissolving cream cakes balanced on her fingertips; helplessly scanning the traffic by the gold souk, while the morning sun burned, and her own ethnic trinkets seared her flesh. 'Fairfax,' Daphne said, 'will just have to shift for himself.'

*

Frances looked at her watch. Fairfax was due; dinner was cooking.

'I wonder what he will think of us?' Andrew said.

'Of you and me?'

'No, of the whole lot of us. The *khawwadjis*.'

'I imagine,' Francis said, 'that he'll think we're pathetic.'

As she set the table, she amplified the statement in her mind. The paychecks had not arrived yet. Full moon had come and gone. Alarm and despondency was the order of the day. 'If only they'd be straight with us,' people said. They began to talk about 'Saudi disinformation'. Companies were pulling out, writing off debts that they did not believe the government would repay. Now more than ever, the tone of expatriate conversation was callow, suspicious, a note of chronic complaint. Editorials appeared in the newspapers, alleging *khawwadji* mismanagement, corruption; issuing threats.

'Having money makes people bad enough,' Frances said. 'The threat of not having it seems to make them worse.'

'Don't be such a prig,' Andrew said. 'You are one of the people too.'

'I meant the Saudis. Although to be honest, the longer I am here, the more we seem to resemble them. We are both aspects of the same problem, I think.'

Everything in the flat – everything tangible – was dusted, sorted, put back to rights. So that they would have something to give Fairfax, they had borrowed some wine from Jeff Pollard. Jeff was in a bad mood over the loss of his mistress. Russel, he said, was persecuting him, and badmouthing him to the other compound dwellers, and fomenting quarrels around the swimming-pool. He would have to move out, he said, and hope that Terrex Mining would give him one of their houses. 'Take a case,' he said sulkily, when they called around for the wine. 'I won't be doing any entertaining.'

Fairfax was late. Frances turned the oven down, hoped for the best. She poured herself a glass of wine, and went to sit with Andrew. 'Do you think,' she said, 'that there is any chance of us going to live on the Terrex compound?'

'You want to follow Jeff about? It will start another rumour.'

'It's not that. But Daphne did say that she would inquire.'

'I'll talk to Eric. I could make out a case that you were especially miserable, after the burglary and everything.'

That burglar, she thought, may prove to be my friend. I shall pretend to a hopeless neurosis, about the sliding doors; I shall say I can't settle, I shall say I can't sleep at night; I will take all the burden of weakness on myself, the little woman: and in that way I will extricate us, I will get us out of here.

She got up to see to the food. It was nine o'clock. The gatebell rang. Soon she heard Andrew in the hall, saying, 'You made it,' Fairfax saying, 'Got hopelessly lost,' Andrew saying, 'I should have come for you.'

Fairfax stood in the doorway. He was young; he was a tall man, very tall and quite insubstantial. He had a transparent pallor, because he had come from England, and because he had come from England so recently, he had a transparent smile. Fairfax had dark red hair, unfashionably long, as fine as cobwebs, very straight: and guileless eyes. He wore a lightweight grey suit, the uniform of the travelling executive, and held something behind his back. He offered his other hand to Andrew. 'I know we've met five times today,' he said. 'But it's the local custom, isn't it?'

Andrew shook his hand. 'How do you do?'

'Worse,' Fairfax said. 'Much worse than when we parted at two o'clock. Since then I've suffered death by a thousand cuts. I shall become a cautionary tale in our company newsletter. He went out there to sell air-conditioning, and returned with scars on his soul.'

'Yes, I know,' Andrew said. 'You must have been taken to meet the Minister. Come in, you'll need a drink. This is Frances.'

Fairfax looked down at her. From behind his back he took a bouquet of white roses, and proffered it, diffidently.

Frances wiped her hands on her apron. 'Roses in Jeddah,' she said. 'Oh, Fairfax, these must have cost you the earth.'

Fairfax's eyes opened wide, as if he were reliving the purchase. 'I said to the man in the shop, surely you're joking? He wasn't. Never mind. Don't you ever bring her flowers?'

'Oh, Andrew can't afford to. He's saving up for a posh flat in London.'

'That's marvellous,' Fairfax said. 'Get somewhere nice, and then I'll come and stay with you when I'm down that way, I can't stand hotels.' He seemed sure of his welcome; but Frances puzzled him. He gazed down at her. 'I feel as if I know you from somewhere.'

Frances touched his elbow, drawing him into the room. 'Sit down, Fairfax.'

Andrew said, 'He's called Adam. You mustn't talk to him as if he were the butler.'

She was not surprised by his name. It seemed to suit him. Fairfax had an air of being impressed by the separate qualities of each moment, the air of one to whom the world was new, and unpredictable. He might be thirty perhaps, but it seemed that she had decided to think of the men around her as children; even though Eric said that they were accountable for her, and responsible for her thoughts.

'I shall still call you Fairfax,' she said. 'You see, although we don't know each other, I've been expecting you. Hasn't Andrew explained?'

'We've been too busy talking shop,' Andrew said.

'Well, explain now. Excuse me, I must put the flowers in water.'

She went into the kitchen. She stood by the fridge and smiled, doing nothing, letting a moment pass. When she came back Fairfax had folded his spectacular height into a chair. He looked avian, but not predatory, both vulnerable and sharp: the best kind of salesman.

'As we never have flowers,' she said, 'I haven't a vase. You must drink up the contents of this carafe between you, and then I can put the flowers in it. The rest of the wine can come straight from the bottles. You must watch the sediment, Fairfax. This wine was made by Jeff Pollard.'

'Oh, Jeff,' Fairfax said. 'What a man! Everybody's talking about some poor girl he had an affair with, aren't they? It's beyond imagination. At least, it's beyond mine. Do you know that poem? "Why have such scores of lovely gifted girls/ Married impossible men?" It's just the same with affairs, isn't it?'

'You shouldn't waste your sympathy on Marion Smallbone,' Andrew said. 'She wasn't lovely. Or gifted.'

'Oh, but comparatively,' Fairfax insisted; he sat forward in his chair, and locked his long fingers together. 'She must have been too good for Pollard. I've seen better things than Jeff in the Reptile House.'

'How does the rest of the poem go?' Frances said.

'Oh, it talks about idle men, illiterate men, dirty and sly, about men you have to make excuses for to casual passers-by. Intolerable men, full of self-pity. But then the man who wrote it, he wonders if they can really be so bad after all, whether he overvalues women.'

'Do you?'

'Yes.' Fairfax thought about it, seeming surprised. 'Perhaps I do.'

'You would never last the pace in Jeddah. This is no place for men who like women.'

'We're not all like the Saudis,' Andrew said.

'No, but you seem to collaborate with them.' She had not known she thought it, until she heard it pop out of her mouth. 'I had a letter from Marion, did you read it, Andrew? She's taken the children back to her mother, who is elderly and has a small flat in Nottingham. Russel's divorcing her, and she's going to live on social security. The origin of the romance,' she explained to Fairfax, 'was that he used to go round and unblock her lavatory. Oh well, I mustn't get bitter about it. There's probably no hope for people like that, separately or together. Do you know many poems, Fairfax?'

'I know a lot for an air-conditioning expert.'

'Why did you get lost? I sent you a map. Didn't Andrew give it to you?'

'Yes, but I'm afraid I just can't make any sense of this place. The traffic signs kept sending me places that I didn't want to go.'

'You ignore them,' Andrew said.

'Do you? Is that right?'

'I used to be good at maps,' Frances said. 'They were my living. I must be losing my touch.'

She went out, to bring the food to the table. The meat had dried out, and the vegetables were soggy, but Fairfax ate quite happily, his jacket slung over the back of his chair; he complimented her on her cooking. Andrew thought he was a groveller; you could see that by his expression. You could see that he wondered why a man who was in air-conditioning should have pretensions to charm. But Frances paid attention to her guest. In his presence she breathed more easily. The tension eased from her shoulders; Jeff's wine was sweet, syrupy, harmless, quite unlike his usual acid brew. It was soothing, like warm blackcurrant juice, and yet it had a certain potency; she felt languid, as if she would sleep well, and wake up somewhere better. She put her elbow on the table, and rested her cheek on her open hand. 'I've been waiting a long time to meet you.'

Fairfax looked modest about it, putting back a strand of his feather-like hair. 'People always say I'm a breath of fresh air. But that is our trade joke. We only have one. We are a sombre lot, in air-conditioning.'

Then Fairfax talked about his work; about the central air-conditioning plant for Andrew's building. A sort of ersatz reverence took him over, a weightless gravity; he looked like a schoolboy who had been given the task of imitating, in a pantomime, a governor of the Bank of England. Andrew was impressed, in spite of himself. He sat over the cheese and coffee, and pictured his building finished, its fountains of fire, its indoor forests deep and lush, its model of the solar system, its iceberg walls; he reached forward, his eyes blank and inward-looking, and refilled Fairfax's glass; he breathed the silent, circulating air that Fairfax would create – dust-free, perfumed, Alpine. Fairfax broke off. 'Are we boring you?' he said to Frances. 'We could talk about this in the morning.'

'That's all right.'

'I bet I know what they were saying, those blokes on the plane. Around our office I'm regarded as the resident imbecile.'

'I'm regarded as the errand boy,' Andrew said. He opened another bottle of wine. 'Ribena, Fairfax?' He said, 'This isn't like Jeff's wine. He must have stolen it from somebody.'

'Anyway, I'm only here at all because the chap who should have come is more incompetent still. He filled in the form for his visa, and where it said "RELIGION" he put "LATTER-DAY SAINT". The Saudis thought it was some kind of piss-take, I suppose. Now he'll never get in. You're supposed to put "CHRISTIAN", is that right?'

'Yes. They're not interested in any finer distinctions,' Andrew said. 'They ban atheists as well.'

'They told me all sorts of stories about this place before I came. "You'll like it, Fairfax," they said. "It's just like the *Arabian Nights*."'

'And now you're here?'

His smile died. He put down his glass, briefly. 'You must be mad to live here, Andrew. I haven't felt safe for a single minute.'

'The Saudis seem very tense just now. They're trying to keep out news from abroad. I bought a copy of *The Times* this morning, and when I held it up it had holes in it.'

'It was like a paper doily,' Frances said. 'What's bothering you, Fairfax? What's bothering you specifically?'

Fairfax ran a hand through his hair. 'I don't know . . . I keep accusing myself of racialism or something. I don't know what's worrying me, I suppose it isn't anything rational. The men on the streets, in those white *thobes* and head-dresses . . . I can't keep my eyes off them. They're like some obscene tribe of nuns. Like thuggish nuns.'

'Oh, you're like us,' Andrew said, 'you've got too much imagination. But we're on edge at the moment, it isn't always as bad as this. Or if it is . . . you get used to it.'

She took the coffee cups out to the kitchen. You never get used to it, she wanted to say, if you think you have got used to it that is the beginning of disaster; and she felt again, as she stacked the dishes, as she ran the tap, that cold bar of metal across her hand, and felt the Visitor's fist against her shoulder, fending her off, spinning her away from him. He could quite easily have knocked her unconscious, one blow would have done it; she had never been so conscious before of her physical frailty, it had never really mattered. Her flesh shrank when she thought of it – the Visitor's strength, and her own thin skin and snappable bones.

And here she is, getting a little dinner together, listening to men talk about thermostats. What else is there to be done? Dunroamin was very quiet; in four days she had not seen Yasmin or Samira, not even a glimpse. Until Fairfax came – if you did not count the phone call from Daphne – she had spoken to no one since the burglary. How could she begin, now, to unravel her thought processes for Andrew? How would she explain to him the hierarchy of suspicions, the discrete tiers of insight, the violent shock of fantasy confirmed? 'I watched it go up, the Visitor . . . I thought to myself, Saudi women don't move like that . . . then, no, I did not hide, I did not go inside and lock the door and double-lock the door, I waited for the Visitor, and I did a thing of unbelievable foolishness, of such horrible and frightening implications . . .' No, she can't tell him this.

Perhaps, she thought suddenly, I could tell Fairfax. Fairfax is not part of any of this. In three or four days' time he will take a plane, and disembark in London. Perhaps he could carry a message for me, like a message in a bottle, from me to the real world.

At once she discounted the idea. She pictured her guest's

face: dawning incomprehension. But while it lasted, the notion had offered a few seconds' hope; and that was not to be despised.

'And this is my wife,' Fairfax said. He passed the photograph to Frances, and she held it under the lamp. 'Judy is a giantess. Those are our three giant daughters, the eldest is five. Judy only married me so that she could wear high heels on her wedding day, instead of shuffling up the aisle in gym shoes with her knees bent.'

'Do you travel around much?'

'Oh yes. I go here and there. You see, the firm has moved to Cumbernauld, and we hardly sell much to the locals. I went to Kowloon. Of course, you know that.'

'Does Judy mind?'

'She always gets me back.' Fairfax's conversation had become a little rambling; a hiatus between each thought, and the odd line of poetry. So she was asking him short, simple questions. He drained his glass, and said, 'Strong stuff, this, Andrew. Not what I thought.'

Andrew had fallen asleep, sprawled on the sofa, his head flopped back against a cushion. Fairfax leaned across and touched his shoulder. 'Andrew, what shall I do, I'm drunk.'

Andrew sat upright, as if in slow motion, shaking his head. An hour or two seemed to pass. 'I think Jeff has conned us,' he said at last. 'His last batch of wine only made you throw up.' He surveyed Fairfax – whose grey eyes had developed a blazing concentration, though they were focused on nothing at all. 'I say,' Andrew said admiringly, 'you are drunk.' He seemed to pull his thoughts together. 'Fran, can you stagger into the kitchen and make us some black coffee?'

Frances stirred herself from the depth of her armchair. She did as he told her; and yet making for the kitchen she didn't stagger, but seemed to float. She felt warm, and pleased with everything she saw; she acted without planning to act, spoke without calculation. She drifted a hand to her eyes, as if to dispel a mist. What did Jeff put in his wine? There must be a secret.

Andrew was standing in the doorway. 'Fairfax must stay,' he said. 'He's not fit to drive.'

'Are you not fit to drive him?'

'Not remotely. And even if I were, I don't want to be stopped by the police with someone in that state in my passenger seat.'

She didn't comprehend. 'Why should the police stop you?' she asked gently.

'For any reason.'

'Oh, for any reason. Yes, I see. For just existing, you mean.'

She seemed to have lost direction. She had a jar of instant coffee in her hand, and seemed to have forgotten what she was doing with it. She looked at the cups and saucers as if she had never seen them before. 'Husband, please, can you take over?'

Andrew took the coffee jar from her limp hands. 'You don't usually get like this,' he said.

'I seem to be having an evening off from my life.'

'I thought for a little while that you were having an evening off from our marriage.'

'Oh, Andrew, are you jealous of Fairfax?'

'Yes,' Andrew said.

'But he's a joy. He's a delight.'

'For an air-conditioning expert.'

'Yes, for that.'

'Fairfax can sleep on the sofa,' he said. 'In fact, he is sleeping on the sofa already.' He didn't wait for his coffee. She heard him slam the bathroom door and run the taps. She took a cup of coffee into the living-room, tiptoeing.

He was right; Fairfax was asleep. He looked as if he had slipped, suddenly and silently, into another dimension; ten years had vanished, and his precision, his expertise; he looked vacant, vulnerable, as if all his life were to come. She put down the coffee cup on the floor, and went to find a blanket. When she came back Fairfax had not moved; she had never seen anyone sleep so profoundly, so totally. She covered him with the blanket. His body had a velvet, animal warmth, which perhaps it never possessed in Cumbernauld.

But the night would get colder. It was already two o'clock. She knelt by the sofa for a moment, her eyes closed, her forehead resting on the padded arm. A flurry of eidetic images rushed behind her eyelids: walls, staircases, open doors. 'In a courtyard is a tree on which there are fruits whose colour is red.' A grassy lawn, a sunny day, with a light breeze blowing; she cupped her hands, and the fruit fell into them. The image darkened; gave way to the meaningless flickers and streaks, the white noise of sleep, a static crackle from the universe of her neurones. She drifted for a second or two, in a starless waste. Then she woke, roused herself, and went slowly towards the bedroom, feeling her way with a hand on the wall, as if she had suddenly become blind.

2

Her own sleep was not total, not profound. She heard a noise, and thought it was the front door opening; knew it couldn't be, turned her face into the pillow, slept again. A slow cinema unrolled itself: her soapstone tortoise, grown to life-size, grown to giant-size, and set as a public monument before the oily sea. Herself a tiny figure squinting into the sun, at the stony reptile's feet; younger than her real self, years younger. And all her friends and family, all the people she had known, people she had not thought of in years, everyone gathering to be in the picture; then a shout, and a click, and the descent of darkness, a break in the film.

The shout had broken into her dreams. But it was further than her dreams, outside the purlieu of her imagination. It was not in her head, but in the room, in the passage, in the street. She sat up, scrabbled in the twisted sheets, fumbled for the alarm clock. Little green figures, glowing in a room still dark; it was only three o'clock. She thought she had slept for hours, but her head had hardly touched the pillow. She shuddered. She had become a connoisseur of insomnia, and three was the hour she could not love. The warm, healthy body runs at its lowest ebb then. Death certificates are prepared; night nurses usher the bereaved from public wards.

She leaned over her husband's naked body. His skin felt cool and damp. 'Get dressed. Something is wrong.' Her fingers skittered over the bedside table, where the soapstone tortoise used to bask and doze. She snapped on the bedside light, saw Andrew's eyelids flicker; he yawned.

'Funny,' he said sleepily. 'I heard a noise. Thought it was morning.'

'Get dressed.' She pulled a kaftan out of the wardrobe and dropped it over her head. She felt the burglar's fingers upon it, as she felt them on all her clothes. She shook: with the sudden cold, with fatigue, with an expectation of disaster. 'Did you remember to lock the front door?'

'No.' Andrew sat up. He stumbled out of bed. He reached for his jeans, started to pull them on, slow, fumbling, looking for his shoes. She was ready to go. But her nerve had failed. She was going to wait for him. 'No one could come in,' Andrew said. 'Unless they broke in.'

'They broke in before.'

Leaving the bedroom door open, she put on all the lights as she went: the passage, the empty bedroom. But there was no intruder. The living-room was empty. Fairfax's blanket, rucked up and cast aside, had slid to the floor. The front door was wide open.

Andrew stepped out into the hall. He turned on the lights to the stair well; then they saw Fairfax. He clutched the banister at the foot of the stairs; he looked upwards once, over his shoulder, and stumbled drunkenly towards them, half-crouching, in silence. He gripped the doorframe, sliding from it as though his hands were slippery; he took a step over the threshold, and huddled against the wall. Andrew

261

slammed the door. She took Fairfax's arm. His whole weight threatened to collapse on to her shoulders, and through the thin cotton she noticed how cold his clutching fingers were. Andrew draped Fairfax's other arm across his shoulder. Between them, they manoeuvred him into the flat, and let him slide on to the sofa. He seemed only semiconscious, stupefied, in shock. Frances took his face in her hands. 'What's happened to you? Fairfax, where did you go?'

'Nothing happened,' he said. His head dropped. She felt unable to support its weight; she could not get him to look at her, to focus his attention even for a second. 'Wanted air. Going to be sick.'

'That's quite obvious,' Andrew said.

'No, no,' Fairfax insisted. 'Was going to be sick. Went for a walk. Went for a bit of air. Couldn't get out of the main door. Went up to the roof.'

He was deathly white, his skin clammy; hardly able to sit upright. 'Did you meet someone?' Frances said.

'Who could he meet?' Andrew asked, yawning. 'Look, Fran, don't badger him, leave him alone. He just went walkabout, that's all. Let him go back to sleep, he'll sleep it off.'

'He's in a state of shock. Look, Andrew, look at him.'

'He's drunk, Fran. We should have been more careful, we've got used to this stuff, we don't realize . . .' As if to prove Andrew right, Fairfax slid down a little on to the sofa. His head dropped back, his eyelids fluttered and closed. 'He can't keep awake,' Andrew said. His own fright – and he had been frightened, by the open door – had turned to sleepy truculence. 'I have to be up at six, myself. I have to get into Turadup –'

'Oh, sod Turadup,' Frances said. 'Fairfax, wake up, tell us.' He did open his eyes, for an instant; he looked at her warily, directly. She saw pain and fear. But he said nothing.

'He's not really all that drunk,' she said. 'Not any more. He's just made a decision, I think.' She turned away, distraught. 'He's not going to tell us.'

'Do you want me to go up to the roof?' Andrew asked.

'No. No, please, I don't want you to do that.'

'Okay. So let's sort it out in the morning.'

'We ought to stay with him.'

'He isn't going anywhere.'

'But he looks so ill.'

Fairfax was sleeping properly now. He couldn't be pretending; the drink had struck him down. Again that peculiar emptiness invaded his face, as if whatever he lived through could be nullified, erased. Andrew said, more kindly, 'Frances, come to bed. Let's get a couple of hours' sleep. He's not going to tell us anything till the morning. If he did it wouldn't be coherent, would it?'

'No, I suppose not.' She tried to calm herself. 'Andrew,' – she took his outstretched hand – 'you know the burglary?'

'What now? Something else vanished?'

All week they had been missing things; small, inconsequential items. With each discovery the business looked more random, more purposeless.

'I meant to tell you, but I only just realized this morning. They took our photographs. All the photographs of Africa, those pictures from our wedding . . . they were in that big brown envelope in the desk drawer, I meant to get around to doing something with them . . . they've all gone.'

'For God's sake, why? That's just stupid.' Andrew was angry; but he recovered himself. He put an arm around her, helping her along towards the bedroom. 'It doesn't matter,' he said. 'But they're no use to anybody, are they? Why would they take those?'

'To upset us,' she said. 'To make us unhappy.'

She lay down on the bed still dressed, on top of the sheet, her legs bent awkwardly, too tired even to arrange her body into a more comfortable position. Her head ached, a throbbing pain. He was right, the photographs were of no value. And she should not think of them now.

But when she closed her eyes they flickered behind her closed lids, blurred coloured images, and she tried to fix them, before they slipped away: the only witness to their travels, the only testimony to their joint life. Andrew and Frances outside the DC's office, marriage certificate held out for the camera. Groups of friends at a restaurant table, the New Stanley Hotel, Nairobi, 1978. Andrew frowning into the sun, Cairo Airport, 1979. Frances in Bulawayo. Andrew in the Mall in Gaborone. Our house, our dogs, the man who did our garden: alive only in errant fallible memory, that private mirror, which distorts more and more as the years go by.

I must sleep, she thought. She allowed the muscles of her face to fall, relax. Nobody knows how they look when they are sleeping. Would her face take on that same defenceless emptiness? It might as well. For who was she, when she was unobserved? The loss of the photographs had achieved its object, it had disturbed and shaken her. She felt as if their past had been wiped out behind them.

The alarm rang as usual at six o'clock. She was awake at once. Andrew stirred. He groaned softly. 'Oh Christ, it isn't morning?' Barefoot in her creased kaftan, she went down the passage into the living-room.

Fairfax had gone. She pressed her lips together; her heart thudded painfully, and she put a hand to her ribs, and rubbed the spot where it beat – a vague, distracted gesture, as if she were offering consolation to someone else, to a frightened elderly woman.

And yet it seemed that he had made an orderly retreat. He had taken his jacket and tie, and picked up his car keys. His blanket lay draped over one arm of the sofa. She picked it up and folded it. Last night's cup of black coffee was on the floor where she had placed it, untouched. He might have stayed for breakfast, she thought. He might have told us what the fuss was about. Perhaps the night's events were illusory; perhaps, waking, he could not remember what had frightened him. It was a strangely lightless morning, the sun not visible or even in prospect: a hot morning, silent. Other cups of coffee, which she had poured for herself and Andrew,

264

lay in other rooms: waiting for her to collect them up and pour them away.

The building, at 8 a.m., seemed to have crept closer to the earth. There was no one on the roof, and nothing to see; but scraps of waste paper skittered across the parapet, borne on a low, keening wind. The air felt gritty, sulphurous; a soupy lemon-brown dust haze hung over Ghazzah Street and obscured the view below her. The vacant lot had now become a building site. She could make out the figures of the labourers, moving slowly, scarves bound across their noses and mouths. In that bruise-coloured light, hovering amongst the trenches and foundations, they looked like the natives of some razed city of the ancient world.

She went downstairs, and rang Yasmin's doorbell. I could have a pleasant chat, she thought; see how the land lies. But there was no answer. It was part of the unprecedented silence of the last few days. She stood waiting, rang again. Perhaps she was being watched through the spy-hole? But it had become second nature to think that.

Back in her own apartment, she picked up the phone. She thought of telephoning Yasmin, or Samira; if they were avoiding her, she would like to know why. But instead she rang the Sarabia Hotel. The desk clerk had a public voice, American sing-song, the common currency of airport check-in desks, car-hire agencies, fast-food joints: untrained to listen, but pitched to please.

'You don't have the room number, madam?' he said, slightly shocked. Reluctantly, he said, 'Just one moment.'

Fairfax might of course be sitting in a traffic jam somewhere. He might be at the Turadup office. He might be back in his room, catching up on his sleep. She wanted to speak to him. I should have persisted, last night, she thought. I should have dragged it out of him.

The clerk was back on the line: still more politely incredulous. 'You don't have the room number, madam?'

'No. But you have it. If you will take the trouble to look.'

A pause: then, 'I am trying for you.' Another pause, quite a short one this time. Then 'No answer.'

'Please let it ring.'

'No answer, madam.'

'Okay. Thanks. I'll try again later.'

'Okay, madam. Have a nice day.'

She rang Andrew, but he was at the site. She rang Eric Parsons, but the clerk who answered the phone said that he was at the Ministry. She asked if anyone knew where Fairfax was; but no one seemed able to help.

Around noon, Andrew called at the Turadup office to see if there was any mail. Hasan was manning the reception desk, overflowing a typist's chair, legs stretched out before him; he was turning over the pages of a book of Peanuts cartoons.

'Hello, Mr Andrew,' he said, getting up. 'You want to drink coffee?'

'No thanks, I'm in a rush.'

'No mail for you today, but one telephone message.' He pushed it to Andrew across the desk.

'I can't read this,' Andrew said. 'Who's it from?' He handed back the Arabic scrawl.

'Message from Mr Adam.'

'Good, I wondered where he'd got to.' Hasan said nothing. 'Come on then, what does it say? I'm only an ignorant *khawwaj*, Hasan.'

Hasan read it out, his voice expressionless. 'He says, I go up to your roof last night and saw two men with box and down the stairs carrying a person who is dead. I am advise you to leave that place.'

Andrew reached out and snatched back the piece of paper. He stared down at it, the loops and squiggles that defied comprehension. 'Did you take this message?'

'No, not me.'

'Who then?'

Hasan shrugged. He seemed to think it might be any passer-by.

266

'Well, it can't be the bloody tea-boy, Hasan, because he can't write, can he?'

'Perhaps,' Hasan said, 'he goes to school?'

'I want to know who took this message, and what time it came in.' Andrew slammed it down on the desk. 'I want to talk to whoever took this message, Hasan, and I want to talk to that person now.'

But even as he said this, even as he enacted the part of a furious man, a man horribly alarmed, he understood that he would never find out who had taken the message, or when. It was an unwanted message, as unwanted by him as by anyone else who received it; and just as suddenly he understood that the clerk had done him a favour, had offered him a warning.

'I think,' Hasan said, 'that it is a joke.' He spoke carefully, and his voice was full of foreboding. 'It is not a very funny joke, but best thing is that you know about it. You want to drink coffee now?'

'You took this message yourself,' Andrew said.

Calmly Hasan held out his hand for it, a creased yellow palm. He rested his eyes on Andrew's face; they seemed to express sympathy. 'Now I put it in the trash,' he said. 'You give it me, sir.'

Andrew glanced at it once more. Then he crumpled it up and dropped it into the clerk's open hand.

'You were having a party last night?' Hasan suggested.

'A party of sorts.'

'Too much mineral water,' Hasan said.

At half-past one Frances made herself some coffee. She sat down with her cassette tape and her phrase book. She felt she was making little progress with her Arabic; and perhaps she would not make any this morning either, but it seemed the best thing she could do was to pass the time, to pretend that nothing was wrong and this was her first morning on Ghazzah Street. She opened the book: Lesson Thirty.

Her businessman had worked through twenty-nine lessons. His passage had not been entirely smooth; at various times he had been owed money, he had fallen ill. He had experienced the usual exasperations and delays: 'The driver does not know this quarter. He is holding the map the wrong way up.' But on the whole his ventures had prospered: 'I have met all the representatives of all the companies. I have made an appointment with the secretary to the Minister. He will sign the contract tomorrow afternoon.'

And now it is time for him to leave; taking with him, presumably, the antique chest he bought in the souk, at the price of such linguistic turmoil. 'He prepares his luggage. He closes up the house. He takes a taxi to the airport.'

So Mr Smith is going home, she thinks. He will see his wife and children again, he will land on his native soil. It is all so simple for him. 'He gives his passport to the Security Services. He receives his stamp for exit. He gets on a bus with the other passengers. The bus takes them to the plane.'

Time dripped by. Frances sipped her coffee. She bent her head over her book. She did not switch the tape on; she felt too weak for any unnecessary effort. The wind tossed the leaves on Dunroamin's tree, turning up their pallid undersides; dust caked the windows, blown into patterns of mountain peaks, into a shifting geology that lived and died in seconds. Footsteps walked overhead.

Mr Smith has made it then. He is getting out for good. 'He has said a sorrowful goodbye to the new friends he has made. The passengers dismount the bus. His luggage has been carried to the plane. The passengers ascend the aircraft steps.'

And in a few moments he will be airborne. There is nothing to detain him. He has settled his affairs, he has honoured his commitments. No one wants to keep him here; no one would have a reason to. His passport has been stamped for him: EXIT VISA ONLY.

Now: she can try to persuade Andrew to break his contract. If she could convince him – about the rifleman, about the crate, about the visitor – if she could persuade him, they could go together, go now, go as soon as it could be arranged. I know, she will say, that I am not offering you a watertight case, a tidy plot, that there is much, almost everything really, still to learn; but let us go, Andrew, before we learn it. They cannot cut and run; they must go through the formalities, or they will not be allowed to leave. What they cannot do is go without attracting attention. You cannot slip out of the Kingdom. You go with permission, or not at all; your intentions must be advertised. Anyone who is interested can find out what you mean to do.

Or she can go alone. Pleading sickness, giving sickness as her excuse, she can apply for an exit visa, and see what happens; see if anyone cares enough to try to stop her. If she has the knowledge, she should bear the consequences of it; but the world does not work like that. Consequences are random here, no more discriminating than a burst of automatic fire; and yet they cut down the future. Consequences are what you get, not what you deserve.

And now the plane is taxiing down the runway. She enters into Mr Smith's feelings; he is happy and relieved. 'The passengers fasten their seatbelts. Their journey will last five hours.'

She heard Andrew's key in the door. Something was wrong; he never came home so early.

She threw the book aside and went to meet him. He stood in the doorway as Fairfax had done, a few hours earlier; his face was grey. 'Fairfax,' he said. 'Dead. There's been an accident.'

Hours passed. She made them some food: 'Because,' she said, 'we must eat something.' She was not sure which meal of the day it was supposed to be. It was almost dark; soon, perhaps, they would be calling evening prayers. Their mouths were dry; they pushed the food around their plates. Their eyes met, and she gathered the dishes towards her, and took them away into the kitchen without a word.

'What was he saying?' she asked: out loud for the third time. The conversation had a dazed, hypnotized quality, as if they were compelled to repeat the same formula again and again until it lost all meaning. 'What was he trying to say?' She looked up. 'Andrew, is there anything you are keeping from me?'

He shook his head slowly. He did not ask her the same question. He had not told her about the telephone message.

'Because you mustn't have any idea that you can spare me.'

'I can't spare you, Fran, or I would have spared you this.'

'Tell me everything again. Tell me where it happened.'

'It was on the ring road. It was between the Petrola plant and the airport. You must know it, you must remember, where you see the petrol storage tanks . . . the road crosses the wadi. There's an embankment, and it falls away ten or fifteen feet. The body was down there on the sand. The car had ploughed through the fence. It's only chicken wire. People have made holes in it, anyway, cutting through to get on to the freeway, trying to save a bit of time. It's a shocking stretch of road. Everybody says so. There's no central reservation. There aren't any lights . . .'

'But he didn't go at night, did he? Last night he was here, with us. What time was the body found?'

'I don't know, Fran. Nobody can get the story straight. I'm only telling you what the police told Eric Parsons, and God knows that was little enough. They reckon the car came off the road at speed, he was thrown out, his skull was fractured . . . I don't know. If there was another car involved they aren't prepared to say. It was just after one o'clock that Eric got a call.'

'So they're saying it happened sometime during the morning, in broad daylight? He lay there on the sand ten feet down from the road and died of a fractured skull and nobody helped him and nobody stopped?'

'They won't. They won't stop. You know that.'

'He must have been making for the airport. Mustn't he?'

'Eric wants to know why. He was supposed to be here for another three days.'

'So what did you tell Eric? Did you tell him about last night?'

Andrew shook his head. 'How could I? I can't make sense of what happened last night.'

'I don't know if it makes any better sense to you now. I mean I don't know whether . . . I'm not sure how to say this . . . whether you think that there is any chance at all that it wasn't an accident?'

For a while neither of them spoke. Then Frances said, 'No one saw him. We don't know what time he left here. I said that he was here with us last night, but he could have gone before dawn, for all we know. We don't know if he made it back to his hotel, do we? Someone could have stopped him as he left here, before he got around the corner.'

'Someone . . .' Andrew said. 'The elusive someone. Who are these people?'

People who lurk on the street corner with a rifle. People who walk overhead, who go up and down, veiled, armed. People who lay claim to packing cases. Who knows what people? Who presumes to inquire? It's their country, isn't it?

'They could have killed him,' she said, 'and dumped him from one car and run his own car off the road. It could have happened at any time. Think about it. No one saw him or heard from him after we went back to bed at four o'clock this morning.'

Andrew looked up at her, cornered, in pain. 'Actually they did. I mean, it can't be what you say, because he rang in to the office.'

'When? What time?'

'Sometime during the morning. Early, I think.'

'What did he say?'

'Oh, nothing really. It's not what he said. It's just the fact that he rang.'

'Who took the message? Can't you find out what he said?'

'Not really. It was very garbled.'

'Who did he speak to?'

'Just the tea-boy.'

*

271

Frances telephoned the Sarabia Hotel. It was the same desk clerk: or another with the same voice. 'What time did Mr Fairfax check out?' she asked.

The receiver was laid aside; she heard muttering in the background. The voice came back, wearily polite: 'One moment, madam.' A minute passed; he was back. 'Mr Fairfax did not check out, madam.'

'But what time did he leave?'

A pause. A muttered consultation. 'Madam, you are still there? We did not see him go. If you would like to give me the name of your company, we will send you on the bill.'

They sat opposite each other, in curiously formal poses, heads bowed, hands on their knees, observing another silence. Then Frances said, 'The car, you know . . . there's been a problem with the steering. I suppose that might have been it.'

'But you don't think so.'

'I don't think I shall ever believe that this was just pure chance.'

'He was frightened. We know that. I mean he was frightened before last night, maybe last night had nothing to do with it. He said himself, it wasn't rational. He'd decided to get out, he was making for the airport, he was driving at a fair speed –'

'Yes, I know. But what was he driving away from?'

The telephone startled them. Andrew had been about to speak; he broke off. 'Who will that be?' He reached for it. Her fists clenched in her lap. She tried to uncurl them. I have to be calm, she said to herself. I have to ask the right questions, very rigorous and unavoidable questions, before the answers slip away and vanish for ever. 'Oh, hello Eric,' Andrew said. He sounded calm. 'Yes, I have. Well, naturally she is.'

Eric spoke. Andrew listened. Andrew said, 'We feel that we are responsible for Fairfax. As much as anyone is.'

She got up, crossed the room and huddled at his side, listening in to the call. Eric said, '. . . some kind of certificate from the police, without which nothing. Unfortunately his passport seems to be missing –'

She took the phone from Andrew. 'Eric, listen to me. Where are Fairfax's things?'

Eric took a moment to understand this. It seemed, when he answered, that he had already taken on the accents of the police file, of the coroner's court. 'You mean his personal effects, Frances?'

'Yes, that's what I mean. Not just his passport, but his clothes, his suitcase, his toothbrush – do you see what I'm getting at, Eric?'

'I'm afraid I don't.'

'Were they with him in the car, or back at the hotel? The hotel says he never checked out.'

'You phoned them?'

'Yes, why not?'

'Because I don't want you to interfere, that's why not. Please give me Andrew.'

'No. Do listen please. We have to find out about his clothes.'

'Oh yes, I see . . . sorry, my dear, I didn't mean to snap at you. I suppose you think they ought to be returned to the widow. The Embassy has telephoned her, of course.' Eric sounded sorrowful now; he had convicted himself of insensitivity. Clearly he thought this concentration on the clothes, the suitcase, the personal effects, it was some feminine angle on mourning, some piece of etiquette he had forgotten. 'The fact is, Frances, we don't know. I mean, we presume they were in the car with him. That would seem to make sense. I know that he appears to have departed on impulse, but surely he'd stay to pack?'

'Then have the police recovered the stuff? From the roadside? Or from the car?'

'They haven't said.' Eric was bemused. 'They do deny all knowledge of the passport, but then they deny all knowledge of practically anything.'

'You'd better ask them.'

'But Frances, you've no idea, have you? You've no idea what I'm up against? Look, I have been dealing with these people for years. I have been dealing with these people since you were a little lamb in your school blazer. They don't tell you anything. That is their habit. That is their policy.'

'Have the police asked questions about the car? The steering?'

'Oh, look now.' Eric had forgotten his embarrassment; he was coldly hostile. 'Don't try to lay this at my door. The car had been fixed. I have the receipt, Frances, the receipt for the repairs. It's here in my petty-cash drawer. I have my hand on it now. I'll keep it for you, shall I? Andrew can drive you down. You can come in right now and inspect it.'

'For the record,' she said wearily, 'I don't think the faulty steering killed Fairfax. If I did, Eric, it would almost be a relief. That's not what I think. I can't prove what I think, but what would be the point? I tried to talk to you before, but you wouldn't listen. You're too thick to take in what I tell you, aren't you? You're too thick and too terrified.'

Andrew took the receiver out of her hand. She turned away, collapsed into her chair, not listening any more. Eric's voice ran on for a while. Then Andrew said, 'Okay. Yes, I think she'll insist on that. Call me when you find out where. Goodbye.'

He put the phone down. 'Well, I'll never work for Turadup again. After that outburst.'

'You do understand, don't you? We can't trace his movements, or know if he was taken away by force, unless we know whether he packed his things up. If he didn't – then it was sudden. Or he didn't even go back to the hotel. We do need to find them.'

Andrew sounded weary, resigned; much as Eric had, before she antagonized him. 'If you can take away a man, sweetie, you can take away his suitcase. If you can abduct a business-man, you can abduct his spare drip-dry suit.'

Frances didn't reply. She felt too tired to think about it any more. Life is not like detective stories. There is a wider scope for interpretation. The answers to all the questions that beset you are not in facts, which are the greatest illusion of all, but in your own heart, in your own habits, in your limitations, in your fear. She sees the vehicle spin out of control; she sees the panic-stricken driver. Then she sees, alternatively, the felon, the corpse, the car door swung open, the body slithering down the embankment: then she sees, in either case, the skid, the slide, the smashed bone, the spilled petrol, the sand, the sun, the sickening flux of human blood . . . the story is what you make it. In either case, the young man is dead.

She said to Andrew, 'I don't know, but I feel you are arguing against yourself.'

'Perhaps. Perhaps I am,' he said without emotion. 'You have always been better than me at getting hold of the unthinkable.'

'Can't we go now? Do we have to stay till July?'

He considered. 'I think it would be better to do everything calmly. Make our agreed exit. Don't you?'

Perhaps that was Fairfax's mistake. His exit had not been agreed. She remembered what Mrs Parsons had said, months ago, on their first trip to the souk: 'It isn't the roads in town that are dangerous, it's the roads out.'

Very soon Daphne Parsons was on the telephone. 'Imagine,' she said, 'what a peculiar thing to do, to take off like that! He planned to leave the car – my car – at the airport! Just dump it there! Of course, I did think when I met him, what a very strange young man. He did seem to be rather . . . erratic. Is that the word I want? Frances dear, you must be terribly upset. I know you had him over for supper, and you must feel that you got to know him a little. I hope it doesn't make your medical condition any worse?'

Then it was Rickie Zussman who called: with statistics. 'Carla said you sounded rattled when she spoke to you. She says you're trying to make something of it. Believe me, Frannie, this is just the way it goes. You shouldn't see any malfeasance here. One in six accidents in the Kingdom involve fatalities. Though Christ knows,' he added, 'I feel sorry for the guy.'

Then it was Eric again. 'Andrew thought you would want to see the body, Frances, and I don't suppose it is in my power to keep you away. Someone has to identify it, and we have been trying to find out where it was taken. We have been given various pieces of information, all of them inconsistent, and none of them necessarily accurate.'

'But someone must know.'

'I agree.'

'There is no chance, is there . . .' She could not continue.

'That it's some kind of mistake? I think that would be too much to hope for. But I know you don't believe what you're told, Frances. I know you won't take my word for anything.'

She checked the time. They arranged to meet; they would bring their own car, and Eric would collect Hasan, to interpret for them. It would be a long evening, Eric said, even if their first efforts were crowned with success.

She wandered about the flat, dazed, sticky; the air-conditioners did not seem to be working properly. She felt desperately hungry now, weak with hunger, and yet she felt that it would be almost indecent to sit down and eat. At some point she washed, and changed her clothes to go out.

After sunset prayers the young Saudi men go out to visit restaurants and meet up with their friends; they divert themselves at funfairs, which they call Luna Parks. Tonight the neon-lit spokes of the Great Wheels shone between the walls of the mosques. The city had taken on its nightmare life: a green moon, a vitiating heat.

They drove: the freeways, the highways, the roads off the map; the unknown quarters, the alien districts, streets and buildings they had never seen before. Eyes on the road, hour after hour, breathing in the dust and the diesel fumes, their clothes sticking to their flesh, their throats clogged with apprehension, and their minds still numb with shock. Be-

276

tween the concrete pillars of the flyovers, darkness blossomed into darkness, each man-made wilderness as empty of association as the surface of the moon. And their every second thought was of mortality; you could die here, your figure fleeing before the screaming cars, running till you dropped and expiring without a sound, like the sacrificial victims who are buried in bridges. Then you would haunt the freeways, your dead compass swinging, searching for home; until the city expanded, by its usual laws, and they built over your ghost.

Hasan argued with the porters at hospital gates. Eric Parsons stood by their car, in the evening's stupefying heat, and wrung his hands; she had never seen anyone do it before. 'I need papers,' he said. 'I need signatures. I need death certificates. I need copies for the airline. I need copies for the Embassy.' He spun slowly on his heel, beseeching. 'Tell the man, Hasan. Convey it to him somehow. Tell him I have it from the police that the body is here.'

'He says,' Hasan reported, 'not this hospital, Mr Eric.'

'Will nobody help us? Has nobody any sense? I have formalities to complete. Have you told him that?'

Now it was ten o'clock, and the evening lay behind them, an ordeal by which they would be marked. 'When I get out of here in July,' Andrew whispered to her, 'I'm not coming back.'

She looked sideways at him; thought of Mr Smith, of his confident approach to the security guards, his visas in his hand. 'Hush,' she said. She nodded towards Eric, who circled aimlessly in the dust, a few yards from their parked car. 'We'll talk about that tomorrow. Here comes Hasan again. He looks as if he has something to tell us.'

Andrew got out of the car. Hasan said, 'I think we have found the place. But we cannot go in.'

'Why not?'

'He says the man who has the key is praying.'

'What, at this time?'

'You must come tomorrow.'

'But we have been driving for hours,' Eric said. He seemed on the verge of weeping; all his experience had not prepared him for tonight. 'Tell him we have a lady with us. Tell him we must identify the body.'

'He says you cannot do it,' Hasan said. 'To identify, you need four Muslim men. Christian men will not do.'

'And Christian women?' Frances spoke from the passenger seat. Eric leaned down, to the open window. 'I suppose,' he said vengefully, 'that now you think he was murdered? I suppose you think this fiasco is part of some conspiracy?'

'No. I know a fiasco when I see one. I've been around the world enough.'

Eric wiped his hand across his forehead. 'It's always been the same, whenever an expat. has died. Whenever there has been even a suggestion of violence, they just close ranks. The one thing they don't like is people asking questions. The one thing they don't like is a body on their hands.' He took out his handkerchief, already soaked with sweat, and dabbed at his face. 'They always think we will blame them for something.'

Unwillingly, she felt sorry for him. He had issued all the right warnings, from the beginning, and she had not heeded him. Don't interfere, don't speculate; she had done everything he had warned her against. And now an example had been made; but not of her.

Andrew said, 'Just try again, Hasan. Tell them we don't believe the man is praying. Tell them we want to go into the mortuary. Tell them we don't want to identify, we just want to see. Okay?'

Hasan nodded. He trailed again across the hospital forecourt, and talked to the men behind the barrier. He was back within minutes, hitching at his clothing, patting at the little round skull cap he wore: his face impassive. 'It is true the man is not praying. They are saying that to make you go away.'

'Tell them we won't go,' Andrew said.

'They say we must go home again and wait until morning. Then they promise the man will come with the key.'

'*Ins'allah?*' Frances said.

'*Ins'allah,*' Hasan agreed.

'I don't believe this,' Andrew said.

But he got back into the car. You cannot really argue with hospital porters. They carry guns.

They said goodnight and began the long drive back across the city. The day's dust coated the rubbish skips, and the municipal greenery, with its raw sewage dressing, that wilted on the central reservations. It lay thick on the emerald plastic grass that the restaurants laid out before their doors, the emerald grass that their headlights turned to black.

'What were you going to say to me,' Frances asked, 'earlier this evening, before Eric called us the first time? I thought you were going to tell me something?'

Andrew looked at her warily, from the tail of his eye. Road signs swam through their headlights: Al Kournaich, Jeddah Central, Jeddah Islamic Port. STOP! YOU ARE FAST BUT DANGER IS FASTER! 'I love you,' he said. 'I don't want you to be frightened. I wish I had never brought you here.'

'That is not what you were going to say.' She turned her head and stared out of her window, into passing cars; re-alizing, from the response of their occupants, from the winks and nods and leers, that she must have developed the habit of keeping her gaze lowered, of censoring her vision. She said, 'Let's go to the hotel. We might find out something if we persist. Somebody must have seen him leave.'

Andrew did not reply; but he turned the car at the first opportunity. She looked at his face, for his expression of 'I shall have no peace till I do this'; but he was not wearing it.

In the foyer of the Sarabia Hotel, a fountain, impossibly blue, tinkled into a marble basin; tropical flowers, made of silk, bloomed in brass tubs. A waiter carried a tray: silver tray, crystal glasses, drinks the colour of crushed strawberries. The air was icy and the sweat dried on their skins.

The desk clerk was a small dark round-faced man of some

mongrel Near Eastern provenance. He gave them a respectful greeting; or he gave it to Andrew, averting his eyes from Frances with a lofty civility. She put her hands up, scooping her sticky hair from the back of her neck. The clerk's eyes flickered over her, like some mechanical scanner, noting the slight rise of her breasts, and she saw on his face for an instant a cruel suppressed avidity, a destructive infantine greed. She dropped her eyes.

Andrew put his hands on the reception desk. 'May I see the manager?'

She admired him: commanding size, cool voice, overbearing courtesy.

The clerk said, 'He is praying.'

'At this time?'

The clerk said, 'I regret.'

'Then I should like to see the under-manager.'

The clerk said, smiling, 'He is in Kuwait.'

Andrew drew back. He folded his arms. 'So who's running the hotel?'

'Perhaps I can help you?'

And Andrew said, with a fine show of racism, 'I doubt it, Ali.'

They looked around the lobby. Laundered *thobes* strolled to and fro, and smoked cigarettes; glass-fronted lifts carried the patrons to their suites, like prophets assumed to heaven. Frances said, 'Do you usually talk like that?'

Andrew said, 'I want to be Jeff Pollard when I grow up.'

The clerk fussed with some papers and forms; he seemed unwilling to leave them alone. 'You have some complaints?' he asked.

'You had a guest, a Mr Fairfax.'

The clerk looked interested. 'Excuse me,' he said, 'we have no guest of that name.'

'He isn't here now.'

'No. He has left.'

'He has a suitcase somewhere. Things that belong to him.'

'You have papers to collect them?'

280

'We are friends of his.' Andrew corrected himself: 'We were friends of his.'

'It is impossible,' the clerk said, 'because we have no guest of that name.'

Andrew ignored this. 'Did the police come and take his things away?'

The clerk shrugged. 'I did not see them, sir.'

'But if the police had been here you would have heard. You would know all about it.'

'Excuse me, sir, but I think there is a mistake. Perhaps your friend is at some other hotel?'

'No, my friend is dead.'

'Perhaps he is staying at the Nova Park?'

A voice called to them from across the foyer. 'Andrew! What are you doing in this neck of the woods?'

Andrew turned sharply. 'Raji, it's you. Come over here, would you?'

Raji slid across the tundra of polished marble, hands outstretched; the light from the chandeliers split and shattered in the diamond of his tie-pin. 'What, dining out?' he inquired. His eyes passed over her crumpled cotton smock, Andrew's bush shirt darkly patched with sweat. 'No, I see you are making some inquiry.'

'I want to get hold of the manager. It's about some things a friend of ours may have left behind.'

Raji took out his wallet. He opened it, and let his plump fingers hover; he selected a note, and handed it to the clerk as if it were a cloakroom ticket. He spoke; the clerk made a little gesture, as if to say 'Why did you not ask me before?' He vanished.

'I was trying to avoid that,' Andrew said. 'I was trying to employ terror. Here, Raji, let me reimburse you.'

'It is nothing,' Raji said. 'Put your money away. It helps, excuse me Frances, if you speak their bloody lingo.'

The manager soon appeared: could he be of any service? His English was impeccable, his moustache clipped, his nails finely manicured; he was the essence of Levantine courtesy, and he kept his eyes from the woman as if she wore an aura of barbed wire. Raji took charge. 'The name of your friend?' he asked. Andrew told him. Raji took the manager's arm and drew him aside.

They held some muttered conversation. A few moments passed. The manager darted a look over his shoulder; he shook his head.

Raji turned back to them. He looked worried. 'I understand it is a police matter.'

'Yes. There has been an accident.'

With a little bow in their general direction, the manager melted away.

'My friends,' Raji said, 'leave it alone. I advise you from a sincere heart. Once you are embroiled with those fellows then all sorts of misunderstanding may begin to occur.'

'Okay, Raji.' Andrew was downcast. 'Thanks. At least they don't deny all knowledge of him. Did he tell you, have the police been here, and taken his things away?'

'That is possible. But better if you do not press it.'

'We need to know,' Frances said.

Raji looked at her sorrowfully. 'My dear Frances, you need not think there is some conspiracy. Because people act as if they have something to hide does not mean that they really do. That is the first thing you must learn about living in the Kingdom. The puzzles are, how shall I put it, more apparent than real.'

'It's soothing to think so.'

Andrew said, 'I feel – Frances feels – that it must be possible to sort out what has really happened.'

'Oh, in a logical world,' Raji said. 'But the Kingdom is not a logical world, and besides' – he smiled – 'logic is not an ornament for young ladies.'

Frances walked away, and gazed into the fountain's basin, through the blue rippling water to the mosaic tiles. 'Are you meeting someone, Raji?' Andrew asked.

'Yes, I am here to take dinner with my dear friend Zulfikar, he is an old school pal of mine. We have a little notion

282

to open a restaurant of our own. Maybe a rather special one – sherry in your consommé, rum in your chocolate mousse, *vin* in your *coq* – oh, it must come to Jeddah. Don't you think?'

'It sounds a bit risky. Are you really going to try it?'

Raji showed his very white teeth. 'I am in the business of pushing out the frontiers of the possible. When we are open you will come as my guests, you will enjoy it. There is no profit without risk, you know. At least, that is what my friend and I were told, when we were at business school in Miami.'

They went back out to their car. Its trapped air was stifling; they moved into the stream of evening traffic. 'It will be cooler when we get going,' Andrew said. But they had hardly moved a hundred yards from the hotel entrance when a snarl-up and a traffic policeman brought them to a halt. 'We should have stayed and had a drink,' Andrew said. 'Lowered the tone a bit.'

The drivers around them put their fists on their car horns. Frances put her head out of the window to try to see the cause of the delay. A pick-up truck was slewed across the intersection ahead, one side bashed in; a curtained limousine disgorged a Saudi gentleman with a pointed, hennaed beard, and a long-suffering expression. Three young Filipino men in jeans and white tee-shirts stood mutely by the truck, and a traffic policeman, gun on hip, ripped their documents out of their hands.

'I hope they're carrying plenty of ready cash,' Andrew said. 'Or we'll be here all night.'

They were in a line-up of cars, five abreast; she turned her head, and said, 'Look, that's Abdul Nasr.'

Andrew looked. 'So it is. That's not his own car he's driving.'

'I haven't seen him for weeks.'

Andrew had returned his attention to the scene ahead; she returned hers to the next car, and their neighbour's bronze unyielding profile. Abdul Nasr took one hand from the wheel and fitted a cigarette between his lips. The man in the passenger seat leaned across and lit it for him. She caught a momentary glimpse of his face, and she knew him at once, even though she had seen him greasy and bareheaded, and he now wore an immaculate white *ghutra*. She remembered his lugubrious features, and the blank expression in his eyes when she had tried to deter him from knocking on the door of the empty flat. What was it the landlord had said? 'I want you to know this Egyptian.'

The back seat of the car also had an occupant; a woman, veiled, and so far shrunken into the dark velour upholstery that until she moved Frances had hardly registered her existence. As the Egyptian subsided into the passenger seat, hidden by Abdul Nasr, the woman hitched herself forward in the seat, as if to speak; she put a hand to her face, holding a square of something white, and for just a second, she raised her veil. How provident she was, on this stifling evening, thunder hanging in the air; Frances envied her for a moment, feeling the cold sting of the cologne tissue against burning skin. As the black cloth fell back into place, she recognized the woman; it was Yasmin.

She said nothing; she did not know what to say. Her mind revolved the possibilities. They drove; the policeman waved them on.

On Mecca Road, still miles from home, they were stopped at a roadblock; but their documents were not checked. Another policeman pressed his face to the windscreen, and then withdrew it. His colleagues flung up the boots of the cars ahead. 'What are they looking for?'

'Drugs,' Andrew said. 'Or weapons. Maybe a nice consignment of Kalashnikovs up from the Yemen?'

She said fearfully, 'Who wants them?'

'Me,' Andrew said. 'I could use some violence.'

They drove; behind them, the heart-churning cacophony of sirens, trailing across the bridges and the junctions and the highways in the sky.

*

When they got into the flat the phone was ringing. She picked it up. It was Eric. 'You finally made it home,' he said.

'Yes, we got stopped at a roadblock. The police are everywhere. It was like this at Christmas, remember?'

Eric grunted. 'More on that later. First of all, would you tell Andrew to get down to the site by seven o'clock tomorrow? Jeff says the Indians are having one of their mutinies. They've got a list of hard questions about their baggage allowances and they want to put them to a high authority.'

'I think Andrew hoped he might catch up on his sleep.'

'Look, we have a contract to fulfil. It won't help anybody if work comes to a halt.'

'Okay, I'll tell him.'

'I'm going to the airport first thing. I have to talk to the airline about sending the body home.'

'What body? We haven't got a body yet.'

'We'll find it. Meet me at the hospital at ten o'clock. Oh, and one more thing.' What she heard in Eric's voice, what she realized she had been hearing, was not his usual monotone urbanity, not even the night's deep fatigue: but a sort of numbness, like shell shock. 'There's a strong rumour that someone tried to kill your next-door neighbour a couple of hours ago. There's been a shooting at the Sarabia Hotel. So do me a favour. Keep your heads down. Just remember that whatever happens it's got nothing to do with you.'

3

Next morning dawn did not arrive. The dust, in a dirty brown cloud, blotted out the early sun; bowed figures, subfusc and gagged, groped their way down Ghazzah Street beyond the wall. 'I will be back soon,' Andrew promised her. 'I must drop by at the site and then I'll get hold of Eric and we'll go back to the hospital.' He kissed her. She huddled into the doorway. He coughed as he made his way to the car, the dust peppering his face.

At nine o'clock yesterday's wind began to blow, out of yesterday's yellow sky, and plastered the mountain ranges against the windows. It did not blow the dust away; there was an endless supply of it, a continent of dust. She looked out and watched it shifting, banking up. The street cats swarmed over the wall, looking for shelter, and dragged themselves before the glass. She watched them: scared cats, starving, alive with vermin, their faces battered, their broken limbs set crooked, their fur eaten away. She felt she could no longer live with doing nothing for these cats. Slow tears leaked out of her eyes.

When the telephone rang she almost did not answer it. But it might be Eric, with a message about the hospital; or Andrew, to say the Indians had delayed him. It was Daphne Parsons.

'Yes?' Frances said. 'What did you want?'

Daphne sounded hurt. 'Only to tell you the news. You've heard about Raji?' She didn't wait for an answer. 'I know Eric phoned you, but more's come out since then. Apparently he was having dinner at the Sarabia Hotel with some bigwig, a major in the security forces, and as they were leaving, as they were on the steps, somebody took a shot at him out of a car.'

'And?'

'They got the major. He was hit in the shoulder, he's going to be all right. Raji wasn't hurt, but I bet it shook him up a bit. Don't you know anything about it? I thought you would know. Shall I come over there?'

'How do you know they were aiming at Raji? Maybe it was this major they were after.' She put the question; it was idle, academic. Perhaps it was not the time for it, but she felt almost entertained.

'Well, I'm not entirely sure.' Daphne had taken offence. 'I'm only giving you the story as it was told to me. Perhaps there's more to it. Perhaps it's just the fact that Raji has so many enemies. It's what he stands for, isn't it?'

'And what do you think he stands for?'

286

'Oh,' Daphne said vaguely, 'progress, all that.'

There was a low, distant rumble of thunder, as she put the phone down on Daphne. Yesterday's newspaper had exhorted Muslims all over the Kingdom to join the *Isteska*, or rain prayer; the King himself recommended it. Soon those prayers will be answered. She let herself out and crossed the hall.

There was no answer when she rang Yasmin's doorbell, but then she had not expected it. She rang again; she put her finger on the buzzer and left it there. There seemed no occasion for politeness any more.

After a moment or two, Shams opened the door. Her head and shoulders were swathed in a dark cloth, and her face itself looked dark and strained. Unsmiling, she held the door open only so far as she needed; her eyes passed over Frances, and then she spoke. 'Gone away,' she said. 'Everybody gone. Finished.'

When the phone rang again it was Rickie Zussman. 'You heard about your neighbour? Jesus, Frannie, what a week for you! This guy they shot was some kind of arms dealer or something, he might have been from Iraq, and Raji was doing some go-between business. Or at least, they've found an arms cache somewhere, I don't know. They say this guy was shot in the stomach, that he's in intensive care. Raji was lucky, eh?'

And then Jeff Pollard: 'Did you hear about Raji? They say some pro-Iranian group took a shot at him while he was out with some business crony. They say they've been after him for months, waiting for an opportunity. Did you ever see anybody hanging around the flats? Anyway, they missed Raji and got the other guy. They say he was dead on arrival.'

In daylight, she could see that the hospital was some kind of government institution; a collection of long low huts, widely spaced, within a perimeter fence. The gateman raised the barrier for them, and they parked the car in a featureless compound, marked out by low concrete blocks. Eric was there already, sitting in his car, with Hasan in the passenger seat and his windows wound up tightly to keep out the dust. It swirled and hissed about his ankles as he got out to meet them, a nest of corroding serpents shaped by the hot wind.

He took her arm, oddly formal, hesitant. 'Frances? Did you sleep well?'

'I don't want to talk about Raji,' she said. 'Let's just do this first.'

'Well,' Eric said, 'there's no connection, is there? Yes, you're quite right, let's do this. But you know about the wife, don't you? Raji's wife? I'll tell you later.'

Andrew said, 'Did you go to the airport? How did you get on?'

'Oh, it will be okay, the airline will fix it,' Eric said vaguely. His eyes seemed unfocused. 'They've done it before. People have accidents. But do you know, Andrew,' he shook his head, 'I never thought I should land in the middle of a situation like this. When I have been so careful. When everyone has been so careful. When Turadup's reputation has always stood so high.'

'Fairfax was careless,' Frances said. 'Dying like that. He could jeopardize the contract, couldn't he?'

'Don't jump on me,' Eric said. He seemed almost cowed. The morning had changed him. 'I know you're not a fool, Frances. I never thought you were.' He took out his handkerchief, crisp and folded; dabbed at his lip, as if he might find blood there. 'I just thought that you were rather – pressed upon by your environment, if I can put it like that. I thought from the beginning that you were one of those people who should never have come here.'

'Yes, I know. You accused me of exercising my imagination, didn't you? Are you trying to tell me that I have been right about something?'

'Come on,' Andrew said. 'Let's not waste time.'

In the tiny office of the man in charge of the mortuary, there were four or five hangers-on whose function was uncertain; perhaps they were his cousins, or merely his cronies. Eric and Andrew seemed to take it for granted that these men should be there, leaning on the walls, reading the newspapers, smoking and chattering. They stood in the doorway, keeping Frances blocked from view with their shoulders, and waiting for some attention to come their way.

It was a while before the man in charge extricated himself, came out from behind his untidy desk, and held some conversation with Hasan. He was desultory, and scratched his head, and he seemed to say, though she could not follow any of his Arabic, that he did not know if what they wanted could be done. Then at last it seemed that Hasan uttered certain unspecified threats, which he indicated came from the *khawwadjis*, and which he only translated; and at this the little man, who was jaundiced and paunchy, became agitated, and gave vent to a stream of invective, and a series of operatic gestures; his cronies put down their newspapers, and stood up straighter around the walls, and looked vaguely interested and alert. Hasan said, 'He tells you this body cannot be released until he has the paperwork. He tells you he has been brought two bodies this morning and that is enough. But,' Hasan added surprisingly, 'he says he can do what you ask.'

They followed him out of his office, and through a corridor. Two hospital trolleys were parked at an angle, their wheels askew, and on them were bundled the two burdensome corpses to which the man had referred: white sheets covered them entirely, knotted casually above their heads. They turned into a long cold room that was itself like a corridor, with walls of steel, and a blue-burning striplight overhead. The man made a fussy gesture, to hurry them on; then briefly slid open the mortuary drawer, and showed them Fairfax's dead face. There was no error, no mistake in identity, and for all the inexpert eye could tell, he had died just as the police had given out. The head seemed twisted on the spinal column, the face was clamped, jaundiced, marked by a trickle of black blood; the expression was meaningless.

They went outside. A security guard with a rifle lounged against Eric's car, and as they came towards it he shifted unwillingly, his eyes moving above the bandana he wore. 'It is a quarantine hospital,' Hasan explained. 'That is why the guards. The man says he will fix up the body to send it to its home, he says he is the best for doing that in the whole of the Kingdom.'

'So that is what he was doing,' Frances said. 'Boasting.'

She thought of the two corpses in their knotted sheets. She had passed them with scarcely a look; they were not her affair. She felt cold, and strange, and speechless, and removed from what was happening about her. Once again Eric put his hand on her arm; perhaps he wondered if she might faint, or hoped she might, or do something else to discredit herself. But no, he was trying to get her attention; and she realized that he had been talking to Andrew, that he had begun some narration whose beginning she would never hear. '. . . with so much going on,' Eric said, 'we will never sort out the facts from the rumours, even if it were our affair, and I only tell you because you are the neighbours, you are in some sense caught up in it.'

'Is Yasmin dead?' she said.

Eric turned to her, surprised. 'Oh, no, thank God, nothing like that. Didn't you hear me, weren't you listening? She tried to leave the country. They stopped her at the airport. I was there this morning and I saw it with my own eyes, that's how I know, and Hasan here, he caught the drift . . . She had a ticket for Amman, but they think she was trying to pick up a connection from there to Tehran. The security men weren't happy, she – well, obviously she didn't have permission to travel from her husband. And the next thing was the police turned up, and took her away.'

'With your own eyes,' Frances said. 'You saw it with your own eyes. Some people's eyes are better than others, aren't they? They have higher status. They believe what they see.'

She leaned against their car, under the scrutiny of the armed guard, and she felt the slow heat move in the metal at her back, like a sulky fire. I shall never see Yasmin again, she thought. The woman's end was part of the woman's world; information was received at second hand, by courtesy, through the mouth of one of the city's male keepers. 'Did you know her?' she said. 'I mean, did you recognize her?'

'Yes. They pulled off her veil.'

'And then what happened?'

'They took her away.'

'I wish I had been there.' Frances raised a hand and pushed her hair from her forehead. 'I wish I had come with you to the airport. Then I would have seen it myself.'

'Don't you believe me?'

Andrew said softly, 'You have no choice.'

'What will happen to her?'

'God knows,' Eric said. 'Shouldn't think we ever will. People disappear in this place, don't they? I expect they'll want to keep her until they find out the ramifications of it. I shouldn't think her government will raise a fuss, if the Saudis tell them that she was mixed up in a plot to kill her husband.' He said, musingly, 'Daphne always said that they didn't get on. Seems a bit extreme, wouldn't you say? Most of Jeddah would be dead, wouldn't it, if we all went in for violence against our spouse?'

'I don't think you quite understand,' Frances said. 'It wasn't personal. Or not only a personal thing. It was a matter of ideals.'

'I don't see that.'

'He wasn't just a man, he wasn't just her husband. It was what he represented.'

Eric said, mystified, not hostile, 'Was it some feminist thing?'

'You might say that.'

'Or was it religious?'

'Partly.' She shifted away from the car and straightened up. She took a cotton scarf out of her pocket and slowly shook it out. 'My hair is full of dust, I should have done this before.' She folded the scarf into a triangle and flipped it over her head, knotting it firmly at the nape of her neck. Her eyes appeared larger, her features drawn. 'Who knows?' she said. 'Perhaps she just wanted to kill someone. Perhaps she just wanted to see them bleed.'

Eric looked down at her. 'Sorry,' he said. 'Sorry. I have to concede it's quite possible that there have been certain comings and goings at your place. But if the police should come bothering you, of course you know nothing.'

'Yes, I've grasped the point. I know the drill.' She thought, if I had been there, if I had gone to the airport with Eric, there would have been nothing I could have done for her. I could not have helped her. Now I have to think of my own life. What she had heard from Eric did not surprise her. The possibilities in the air of Dunroamin – those wraiths of violence and despair – had taken on flesh at last. She would never know more than she knew now; would never know, for instance, the name of the man who had been crated up alive. What had he done? What had he known? Someone – a torturer, perhaps – would find out the whole of it. But what's one body, more or less? Life is cheap enough. Islam hurries to inter the dead; but the story is not over. Allah has something reserved for corpses, whose nervous system, we must presume, remains intact; predicated on one's misdeeds in life, it is known to the writers of the religious columns as 'torment in the grave'.

Eric said, 'I think we'd better have you out of those flats today. It could be unpleasant. Go home and pack. You can stay with us tonight.'

Andrew took her arm, and led her to their car. Her face stung, her lips were raw; the sky had darkened over the huts behind them. Eric glanced up, apprehensive. 'Let's try to make it home before the rain,' he said.

But within minutes, the storm broke. The sky split open, and sickly lightning glimmered over the high-rise blocks; before they were uptown, the streets were a foot deep in water.

Andrew drove. 'Don't talk to me,' he said. 'If we have to stop we're finished, we'll never get started again.' The landscape emptied of moving life; cars, abandoned, were slewed across their path. The wind tore up saplings and the urban currents carried them along, as if they were making for the sea; the wind lifted the workmen's shelters from the building sites, and bore them away and smashed them to matchsticks against the habitations of the living. On Tahlia Street a billboard bearing the King's portrait had its centre punched out by the violence of the gale, leaving only the royal head-cloth and a fringe of beard to oversee the flooded highway. At the airport the lights went out. Planes overshot the runways.

They didn't leave Dunroamin that day. The roads were impassable; the city was not built for floods. They slept; falling on to their bed together, not touching, dropping through layers of fatigue into a willed annihilation; when they woke, groping in darkness, hungry, disorientated, the storm was over. Their throats ached; the air inside the flat was clammy and chilled.

'I want to phone Shabana,' she said. 'But I don't know her number. My address book is missing.'

'The burglars,' Andrew suggested.

'Probably.' They spoke grudgingly; simple words, simple thoughts. She did not know Shabana's full name. Her husband (she thought of everyone now in the past tense) had been called Mohammed. In a Muslim country, you cannot trace one unknown Mohammed. And besides, Jeddah has no telephone directory.

She telephoned Samira's flat, but there was no reply: number unobtainable.

The next morning the police came. She stood with her door open and watched them. If they had wanted secrecy, they should have come in the night. They ignored her. Perhaps they did not even notice that she was there; perhaps their religion had trained them so well.

They carried boxes down the stairs; they were the boxes that, some weeks before, the painters had carried up. But some evidence of the 'beautification' remained; the tiles looked down from the walls, each with its hostile eye and single scarlet tear.

At ten o'clock a limousine drew up outside the open gate, ploughing and splashing through Ghazzah Street's mud and standing pools. A Yemeni driver got out, a man she did not know.

The door opposite opened a crack, and Shams looked out, peeping up and down the hallway. She saw Frances, and drew back; and then after a few moments the door opened wider, and Raji came out, very pale, in his dark business suit, his features puffy. Frances thought, he is an old man. He was carrying an airline bag; he did not look at her, yet he spoke; his words quite casual, as if they had met just an hour before, but his tone empty and drugged. 'They say I should take a holiday, Frances. They say I should go out of the Kingdom. They tell me the airport is back to normal, except for the passengers stranded from yesterday.' He gave the ghost of a chuckle at the passengers' discomfiture; as if he were a man above the normal laws.

'Where are you going?' she asked him, from the doorway.

He did not reply, but marched out of the front door: out of her life. Shams followed him, her arms laden with baggage, darting a last look at Frances from under her beetle brows; and then finally came mother-in-law, vast, crumpled, yellow, her sari trailing in the thick wet dirt that had blown under the front door. She did not acknowledge Frances, but kept her eyes straight ahead; and in her arms, aged but still muscular arms, she held the child Selim. He slept against her shoulder, not caring where he was taken; and she carried him just as Frances, coming through the hall on the night of the burglary, had carried her bag of groceries.

Frances checked her watch. The police had gone, and in half an hour Andrew would be home. Their cases were in the hall; they were to go to Eric and Daphne. Though I hardly see why we should move out, she thought; it is all over now.

She went upstairs. There was an unaccustomed shaft of daylight on the landing; the front doors of the two upper flats were wide open, just as the police had left them. More than boxes had been taken away; and perhaps they had been in the night after all, while she and Andrew slept.

She went first into Abdul Nasr's flat. There was the familiar smell of goatflesh, of onions and herbs, of chemical air-freshener and baby powder, of the expensive scent that Samira wore; but the air-conditioners had been turned off, and this smell had now a thick and tangible quality, as if it were a tapestry with which the walls had been draped. The people had been removed: Samira with her snug denims and gracious manners, Abdul Nasr with his dictator's eyes, and the displaced servant, smelling of fear, holding up her tattooed arm. Fat'ma was gone; and the child Samira carried. The model ship sailed gaily on. The Tree of Life flourished on the fringed rug. Samira's chandelier, from Top Furniture of Palestine Road, reflected the clogged and still yellowish light. She walked through the bedrooms, the kitchen; a few pots and pans were left about, curiously dirty and cracked and old, like the kind of thing that slovenly people leave behind them when they move house.

She crossed the landing, letting the door swing shut behind her. It would lock itself; whoever had keys could unlock it again. She walked into the empty flat; who was to stop her? And there was little to see. She examined its tufted oatmeal carpet, its plain cream painted walls. It had been furnished by Turadup, she saw, for notional tenants; for lovers, gunmen, for all tastes and all requirements. Daphne must have chosen that pink lampshade, she thought; I recognize it. She recognized, too, the many armchairs, the tweed upholstery, the pale curtains with their open weave. There was nothing she did not recognize, for it might have been her own home: not a mirror image of it, but the thing itself.

When she emerged on to the landing and closed that door behind her, she was in near-darkness; it was just as it had always been. She went up the half-flight to the roof. She looked around her. What was it but an innocent square of asphalt, where washing lines hung, and litter accumulated, blown up by the recent high winds? The vacant lot was deserted; the workmen's huts had been carried away, and water filled the deep trench that the mechanical diggers had gouged out by the side of the road. It would be some days before the dislocated city recovered itself, and building work began again. The air, which had freshened after the storm, now had its familiar twice-breathed fetor.

She hung over the parapet, looking down on to the balcony of the empty flat. It was from this angle that she had seen the wooden crate, and she wondered again who its occupant had been; strange country, strange Kingdom, where unaccountable corpses can blight your daily life. Possibly she had passed, at the mortuary, so close that they might have touched. That is guesswork, she thought. There has been too much of that. She put her face into the branches of the tree, into the still sodden leaves; and she thought that it might have grown since she had looked at it last. All this time it had been as inert, as falsely promising, as a plastic tree. She feared that it might have been dying invisibly, from the inside out, from a helpless contagion: like a tree of knowledge. But the rain had come, and already, as Samira had forecast, it was putting out fresh green shoots.

She turned away, averting her face from the damage on Ghazzah Street. Scraping her sandalled feet through the mud, she went through the door from the roof to the stairs; she swung it closed behind her, and, from the inside, drew across the bolt.

Shaban

The new house is square and white. It has large rooms, full of sunlight, and plain stark white walls. When I came here the house had been empty for months, and on every surface clammy dirt lay thick.

We are outside the city now. Terrex has given us a house. This used to be a bustling compound, of a hundred units perhaps, but almost no one lives here any more. The cutbacks and the sackings have made it a ghost town, and since the storm weeds have pushed up through the cracks in the tennis court. But there is still a guard on the main gate. There are spaces between the houses; each one has its dusty plot. I never see my neighbours. I must have neighbours. They must be around somewhere.

The floor of the house is made of greyish vinyl tiles, of the sort I imagine might be used in a sanitarium. The main room has what estate agents call a double aspect, and four large windows; I have no curtains yet. From these windows you can see the plain slab walls of the neighbouring houses, their car-ports and empty rooms; and if you look above the line of their roofs and into the distance you can see the freeway, the Mecca–Medina road, with its flyover raised on concrete pillars, its regiment of sodium lamps arched like scimitars, and the silent toy cars creeping by to the city.

When we came here all the furniture was arranged around the outside of the room; as if some entertainment was to take place.

*

On the wall of the living-room there are two geckos. They are yellow-green, translucent, like jewels crawling on the white paint. One is slick and lithe; the other has a plump body and stubby legs. I spend a lot of time watching them, but I seldom see them move. I might go into the kitchen though, and when I come back, moments later, one of them has turned upside down. Are they male or female, I wonder? Do they know of each other's existence? Or does each of them think he is the only gecko in the world?

Every morning they are there: every evening.

Outside the main room of the house, there is a sort of patio, reached by sliding doors. I saw Andrew look at them with some suspicion, but it does not seem necessary to take any kind of security measure. We have put some folding chairs on the patio, and we could sit there, if the heat relented. Unobserved, quite private, we could sit and wait for the weeks to pass. Then it would be time to take our suitcases out. Then it would be time to ask for our exit visas. And then, if they are granted, it would be time to drive to the airport.

But all that seems very far ahead; the past seems very far behind. I have arranged the furniture; I have hung our clothes in the cupboards. I don't seem to make much impact on the dirt, but perhaps I am using the wrong cleaning materials. Perhaps one evening we should go to a super-market to get some more. Yet I feel reluctant to move off the compound. The hours go by here, each one the same. No one comes. The present moment draws itself out for ever. The harsh light never changes, until suddenly night falls.

There is a cane chair out on the patio, and I wonder, if I brought it in and put it in a corner of the kitchen, would it make the room look better? I draw back the sliding doors and step out, into the heat and light of the morning. There are a few trees up here, sustained by hard salty borehole water; their branches, no thicker than twigs, are bent by the currents of air that blow straight from the desert. Squinting into the sun, I can see the black spine of a stony hill, topped by a string of barbed wire. The sky is clear. It must be over 100° today. The glare bounces back at me from the walls of the car-port. I seem to flicker, I am whited-out. I pick up the chair, bounce it gently on the concrete to shake out the dust. I turn with it, and catch my reflection in the glass doors. My face is black, deeply shadowed, with empty eyes, and a pale ragged aureole encircles my head. I have become the negative of myself.

I go back into the house and put down the chair. I look out through the glass, on to the landscape, the distant prospect of travelling cars. Window one, the freeway: window two, the freeway. I turn away, cross the room to find a different view. Window three, the freeway: window four, the freeway.

READ MORE IN PENGUIN

In every corner of the world, on every subject under the sun, Penguin represents quality and variety – the very best in publishing today.

For complete information about books available from Penguin – including Puffins, Penguin Classics and Arkana – and how to order them, write to us at the appropriate address below. Please note that for copyright reasons the selection of books varies from country to country.

In the United Kingdom: Please write to *Dept. JC, Penguin Books Ltd, FREEPOST, West Drayton, Middlesex UB7 0BR*

If you have any difficulty in obtaining a title, please send your order with the correct money, plus ten per cent for postage and packaging, to *PO Box No. 11, West Drayton, Middlesex UB7 0BR*

In the United States: Please write to *Penguin USA Inc., 375 Hudson Street, New York, NY 10014*

In Canada: Please write to *Penguin Books Canada Ltd, 10 Alcorn Avenue, Suite 300, Toronto, Ontario M4V 3B2*

In Australia: Please write to *Penguin Books Australia Ltd, 487 Maroondah Highway, Ringwood, Victoria 3134*

In New Zealand: Please write to *Penguin Books (NZ) Ltd,182–190 Wairau Road, Private Bag, Takapuna, Auckland 9*

In India: Please write to *Penguin Books India Pvt Ltd, 706 Eros Apartments, 56 Nehru Place, New Delhi 110 019*

In the Netherlands: Please write to *Penguin Books Netherlands B.V., Keizersgracht 231 NL–1016 DV Amsterdam*

In Germany: Please write to *Penguin Books Deutschland GmbH, Friedrichstrasse 10–12, W–6000 Frankfurt/Main 1*

In Spain: Please write to *Penguin Books S. A., C. San Bernardo 117–6° E–28015 Madrid*

In Italy: Please write to *Penguin Italia s.r.l., Via Felice Casati 20, I–20124 Milano*

In France: Please write to *Penguin France S. A., 17 rue Lejeune, F–31000 Toulouse*

In Japan: Please write to *Penguin Books Japan, Ishikiribashi Building, 2–5–4, Suido, Tokyo 112*

In Greece: Please write to *Penguin Hellas Ltd, Dimocritou 3, GR–106 71 Athens*

In South Africa: Please write to *Longman Penguin Southern Africa (Pty) Ltd, Private Bag X08, Bertsham 2013*

FOR THE BEST IN PAPERBACKS, LOOK FOR THE 🐧

A CHOICE OF PENGUIN FICTION

The Captain and the Enemy Graham Greene

The Captain always maintained that he won Jim from his father at a game of backgammon…'It is good to find the best living writer … still in such first-rate form' – Francis King in the *Spectator*

The Book and the Brotherhood Iris Murdoch

'Why should we go on supporting a book which we detest?' Rose Curtland asks. 'The brotherhood of Western intellectuals versus the book of history,' Jenkin Riderhood suggests. 'A thoroughly gripping, stimulating and challenging fiction' – *The Times*

The King of the Fields Isaac Bashevis Singer

His profound and magical excursion into prehistory. '*The King of the Fields* reaps an abundant harvest … it has a deceptive biblical simplicity and carries the poetry of narrative to rare heights. At eighty-five, Isaac Bashevis Singer has lost none of his incomparable wonder-working power' – *Sunday Times*

The Enigma of Arrival V. S. Naipaul

'For sheer abundance of talent, there can hardly be a writer alive who surpasses V. S. Naipaul. Whatever we want in a novelist is to be found in his books' – Irving Howe in *The New York Times Book Review*

Lewis Percy Anita Brookner

'Anita Brookner shines again … [a] tender and cruel, funny and sad novel about an innocent idealist, whose gentle rearing by his widowed mother causes him to take too gallant a view of women' – *Daily Mail*. 'Vintage Brookner' – *The Times*

BY THE SAME AUTHOR

Every Day is Mother's Day

An outrageous story of lust, adultery, madness, death and the social services ...

Evelyn Axon and Muriel, her half-witted daughter, are a problem. Barricaded into their house filled with festering rubbish, unhealthy smells and their secrets, they baffle Isabel Field, the latest in a long line of social workers.

'A joy ... so assured, so finely bleak and funny' – Jill Tweedie

'Strange ... rather mad ... extremely funny ... she sometimes reminded me of the early Muriel Spark' – Auberon Waugh

'Hysterical, the dialogue is spot-on ... Muriel and her ma are cunning creations' – Margaret Forster

Vacant Possession

Muriel Axon is mad, bad and not at all harmless.

Muriel Axon is about to re-enter the lives of Colin Sidney – hapless husband, father and schoolmaster – and Isabel Field, now a practising neurotic. It has been ten years since we last encountered Muriel and there are still scores to be settled and truths to be faced. And, for Muriel, there is a certain amount of vengeance to be wreaked.

'The macabre and wonderfully funny plot has as many twists and turns as a well-made thriller' – *Standard*

'A major new talent' – *Daily Mail*

'Just lie back and laugh yourself silly: this is the best send up for a long, long time' – *New Statesman*

Fludd

'Set in the fictitious village of Fetherhoughton, buried in the northern moorland, Mantel's latest cleverly absorbing novel centres on the sheltered community's relationship with the Church, which "bears some but not much resemblance to the Roman Catholic Church in the real world"' – *Time Out*

'Then Fludd arrives. Fludd is a curate sent to assist Angwin – or is he? Loving beauty and language, sowing scandal and unrest in Fetherhoughton, might he not be the devil? *Fludd* is a quaint and lovely novel ... It doesn't only believe in miracles; it believes in happy endings' – *New Statesman and Society*

'The message of Hilary Mantel's excellent and ambitious novel is that the human form of this alchemy is perfectly possible; all one needs is love' – *Sunday Times*